The Evolution of Angels

The Evolution of Angels

Isobel Lynn

Paperback ISBN: 979-8-9885306-4-0

Ebook ISBN: 979-8-9885306-5-7

The evolution of life is driven by mutations. They're caused partly by natural radioactivity and cosmic rays. But *they're* both generated in the spectacular deaths of massive stars thousands of light-years distant.
—Carl Sagan and Ann Druyan, Cosmos

Chapter One

The demon king walked into a bar.

Ashmedai—eldest son of the watchers, lord of the ancient nephilim, and king of all demons—scowled at the state to which he'd apparently been reduced. He was the beginning of a bad joke or a sad, cautionary tale, the moral of which was clearly *don't abduct humans on a whim.* Humans needed to be cared for. Food, shelter, and intellectual stimulation all required money. And money, to the surprise of absolutely no one, did not grow on trees. Not that Ash was poor—far from it—but his fortune was limited, and now it seemed to be slipping through his fingers faster than he could tally it.

The hotel bar pretended class with mahogany veneer and gold paint. It wanted to be appreciated, but Ash would not give it the time of day. He resented being made to wait at the bar, of all places, for his order. Why not the restaurant or the hotel lobby?

"Hey, hun, you want to order a drink while you wait?"

Ash glanced up to see a woman leaning on the counter directly across from him. She looked to be in her fifties with a full figure and the most stunning silver streaks in her hair. He gave her his immediate attention, gracing her with his most winning smile. "Thank you, but I'm afraid I don't drink."

No matter how irritable Ash felt at any given time, he could always find his charm when confronted with a well-meaning woman. It had been a talent of his since he was a child, taught to him by his incomparable mother. Of course, his heart-shaped face, cupid's-bow mouth, and sharp, hooded eyes didn't hurt matters. His skin was dark with warm undertones, and his black hair shaved to the scalp. The demon king had been a desirable man while he was alive, and very little had changed now that he was dead. He was not ashamed to milk it either. He knew he looked particularly fine in a three-piece suit, so a three-piece suit was how he manifested. The look he went for on almost all occasions was that of a professional model dressed as a businessman who was quietly hiding billions in offshore accounts.

In reality, he was only hiding the world's last innocent man in his hotel room. And the last innocent man had to eat.

"Well, that's all right." The bartender smiled back at him. "How about I make you a virgin on the house?"

"Make me a virgin?" Ash blinked. He'd misunderstood, surely. Then again, he'd been bound in darkness for multiple millennia, and he hadn't spent any time in bars or brothels since his escape. Perhaps modern working women were more enigmatic than they'd been in ancient Mesopotamia. But what kind of offer was *how about I make you a virgin*? He squinted at the woman. "Forgive me, madam. Could you repeat that?"

She laughed quietly. She was amused but not unkind. "A virgin cocktail, hun. It means non-alcoholic. You look like you could use something to raise your spirits, that's all."

So she was only a bartender, after all. She was just too kind to let him brood alone. He tried not to let his disappointment show. He had a soft spot for sex workers, having grown up in the care of one, and he'd been homesick as of late. "Very well." He smiled warmly. "Make me this virgin cocktail, and my spirits will be raised."

She went to work mixing and muddling as she chatted away. "My daughter invented this one. I don't even know what to call it, but it's absolutely delicious. She's back in Kansas City going to school—majoring in architecture, you know—and her airhead mother went chasing her dreams and wound up tending bar in a hotel." She laughed. "Children, am I right? Always putting their parents to shame." She set the drink before Ash and dropped two tiny straws into it. "Give it a whirl."

The drink was sweet and sparkled nicely on his tongue. Ash was certain he tasted mango and coconut among other things, something tart, and just a touch of bitterness to balance out the sweet. "It's good," he said. "Why don't you name it after its inventor?"

The bartender's eyes turned to the ceiling as she considered it. "Samantha? Is that a good name for a drink?"

"Nope," someone else answered. "It's stupid."

In his periphery, Ash watched an inadequately groomed man approach, drop a plastic bag on the counter, and slap the bartender's ass. Ash might have stabbed the man's eyes out with the tiny straws in his drink, except his nametag boldly said *Manager* over the name *Jeff,* and Ash knew violence would only make trouble for the bartender.

"Get outta here, Tammy." Manager Jeff chuckled. "Nobody wants to stare at your wrinkled, old face all night." He turned to Ash and grinned like they were old friends. "Sorry about her, man. I've been looking for a younger one, but you know how it is. Nobody wants to work anymore. Anyway, I believe this is yours. Half sandwich with soup and a side of fries."

Ash took the bag of food and scowled. "I'd like to tip the bartender personally if I may."

For a moment, Manager Jeff looked confused. Then he shrugged, called the bartender over, and muttered, "Fucking weirdo," as he stomped back to the kitchen.

Ash dug out his wallet and began counting all the bills he had.

The bartender demurred. "Oh, this isn't necessary, sir. Really. I didn't mean to take up your time."

"The name's Ash," the demon king said, and he held out two hundred dollars, which was unfortunately all he had on him at the time. "And you're Tammy?"

"Tamera," the bartender corrected as she begrudgingly took the money. "He just calls me Tammy because he knows I don't like it. It's kind of a joke."

"He's kind of an ass, in my opinion." Ash reached into the pocket of his vest and pulled out a pair of round, gold-rimmed spectacles. "Tamera, will you take my hand?"

The bartender blushed and held out her hand. "For a tip like that, I guess, sure."

"This isn't service for pay." Ash balanced the spectacles on the bridge of his nose and squeezed Tamera's fingers. At her touch, he saw a child daydreaming in school, a teenager fumbling her first kiss, a woman giving birth to her first child, and a mother planting her first garden. Oh, but she was proud of her garden. Ash couldn't see everything—only those moments that made an enormous impact—and much of it was fuzzy around the edges. But a love of travel colored every image, and now Tamera sacrificed her freedom working for her daughter's tuition.

Ash folded his spectacles again and let go of the bartender's hand. "I need you to hear me, Tamera," he said. "I have a talent for spotting valuable things—that's how I came to be who I am—and you are valuable. Your manager would trade a ruby for resin because he's a fool."

"Oh, goodness, I don't think so." The bartender blushed again.

Ash frowned. "It's the truth. I've seen it. And you won't always need this job. Your daughter will graduate, and you'll have a garden again. I promise."

Tamera laughed to hide her shock. "What are you, some kind of psychic or something?"

"No." Ash pocketed his spectacles.

"Well . . ." She cleared her throat. "Um . . . Thanks for being so nice."

"I am most certainly the opposite of *nice.*" For one brief moment, Ash let the intimidating silhouette of his demonic wings blink into reality.

Tamera gasped and glanced around, but no one else had seen what she saw. "You . . . You're . . ."

"*Be not forgetful to entertain strangers, for thereby some have entertained angels unawares.*" Ash added to the scripture, "And demons, and kings. Your manager should be grateful to you. Right now, you're the only reason I haven't eaten him alive." The demon king stood and straightened his jacket. "Goodbye, Tamera. It was lovely chatting with you. Tell your daughter her drink was delicious." Then he picked up his takeout order and walked away.

The last innocent man in the world had piled all the hotel room's pillows behind him, and was now nestled comfortably at the head of his bed while he watched television. Before his abduction, he'd been Captain Jesús of *Papillon,* the fastest ship in the Black Armada. Now he was just hungry. Ash set his captive's dinner on the nightstand and sat down on the adjacent bed.

"Thanks." The captain tore into the takeout container like he hadn't already been fed three times that day. Ash watched him with what he told himself was mere intellectual curiosity. Before the captain had quite swallowed his first bite, he asked, "Hey, do demons ever eat?" Intellectual curiosity went both ways, apparently.

Taken aback and a little offended, Ash answered, "I can eat. My body is correctly fashioned." It wasn't entirely true, but Ash wasn't about to admit to the sad state of his feet. "I choose not to eat. It's a waste of time and resources, as far as I'm concerned."

"So, even if I offered you a fry, you wouldn't take it? Aren't 'cha missing out on a whole spectrum of experience?" Captain Jesús had a casual way of speaking, which Ash knew better than to chalk up to a lack of intelligence. He'd seen evidence of the man's intelligence for himself. "Do you like football at least? I can change the channel if you don't."

Ash cocked his head at the television screen. He hadn't really noticed the soccer game until now. "*Football,*" he mused. "Of course. I've been in America too long. I don't usually follow sports, Captain, but you're welcome to watch whatever makes you happy."

The last innocent man shrugged and turned up the volume. Ash couldn't help watching him instead of the screen. Captain Jesús was a slight man of medium height with thick, black hair and warm, hazel eyes—though some might have said his most defining features were the tattoos covering over ninety percent of his exposed flesh. It honestly didn't matter. The unfortunate truth was that he was the most beautiful creature Ashmedai had ever laid eyes on. The devastating reality was that, although Ash's spectacles had shown him an intimate future with the captain, the captain himself was still oblivious. To Jesús, the demon king was little more than a prison guard, and however painful it was, Ash was determined to keep it that way as long as he could. Years, if need be.

In his eons of existence, Ashmedai had never met another man like Jesús—a man who could be torn from his home and loved ones, and yet behave as though he were safe and content in the hands of his abductor. The captain trusted everyone implicitly, despite the betrayals he'd experienced in his life. And, dear god, had he been betrayed. Ash was certain he'd seen only a fraction of it through his spectacles. By rights, Jesús should have grown barbed and jaded years ago, but he hadn't. How? Ashmedai was determined to find out.

That was why he'd abducted Jesús, of course. It had nothing at all to do with visions of pushing his own well-manicured fingers through that tangle of black hair, of touching his lips to the tendons that frequently showed themselves in the captain's long neck. It wasn't in any way related to how his own body reacted to being so close to someone so unaccountably desirable.

In fact, from time to time, the desire got so bad Ash found himself needing to leave the room *for some air.* But he refused to give in to temptation. Of all those capable of corrupting the last innocent man's innocence, Ash knew the demon king probably topped the list.

"Anyway, you can have some if you wanna live a little," Jesús said. He tucked one foot under the opposite leg and popped several fries into his mouth, while Ash's mind went to all the wrong places. "You're the one who bought 'em, after all." Of course he meant the fries. Of course he did. Protecting the innocence of the last innocent man did not allow for offering to blow him in an overpriced hotel room.

Ashmedai had dealt with lust before—and admirably, if he did say so himself. King Solomon's guards had been more than a passing temptation. Their selection had not been accidental. So many were so beautifully put together that, to this day, Ash doubted Solomon himself was not tasting them in empty back-corridors on occasion. Ash, on the other hand, had taken pride in focusing on his studies and resisting them all. Well, most of them. There was one . . . Okay three, but the other two hardly counted.

The thing was, objectively, Captain Jesús was not remotely as tempting as Solomon's guards had been. He was just a wisp of a thing, really. Just a delicate bone structure, a pointed chin, sinewy arms, and svelte fingers that looked like they could work miracles given the right circumstances. His legs were long, and his feet—

Ash leapt up, horrified at the sight of his captive's bruised and swollen ankle. The cuff he'd fashioned to keep the man from bolting had not been kind. "Why didn't you tell me that was chafing?" He pointed a shaky, accusatory finger at the offending foot.

Jesús looked baffled. "Didn't think it would matter to you."

"What sort of monster do you take me for?" Ash snatched the plastic bag the takeout had come in and marched down the hall to the ice machine. He filled the bag with ice and tied it closed, all the while muttering about how inconvenient human fragility was. When he returned, he sat at the foot of Jesús' bed and began to unlock the shackle around his ankle. "You will not try to flee," Ash insisted. "If you do, I'll hunt you, and I will find you. I'll rip your head from your body and murder everyone who ever loved you." *Well done, demon king. Protecting innocence always involves detailed threats of graphic violence.*

But Jesús didn't seem at all worried. "I'm not gonna run," he said as a matter of fact. "Been looking forward to the freshwater showers, honestly." He grinned, and Ash had to look down in case his blush actually managed to burn through his complexion. He examined the injury more closely. There didn't appear to be any open sores, just some bruising and swelling on an otherwise perfect foot.

Ash stared a beat too long before he applied the bag of ice. Then he backed away like it was unexploded ordnance. "Keep that on it for a while."

Jesús nodded and picked up his to-go cup of lentil soup. Ideally, Ash would go out and get some air, but he'd just unshackled his captive and vigilance was necessary. So he paced the room instead, angry and looking for someone to blame. It was all that woman's fault in the end, wasn't it? Bryony—the little nothing-god who'd somehow managed to throw the demon king's life completely off its rails and send him into a self-destructive spiral that would leave even Samael appalled.

Clearly, pacing was getting him nowhere. To better occupy his mind, Ash opened his nightstand and took out the Bible he knew he would find there. The study of scripture had never failed him in the past. He reclined in his bed and began to flip through the onionskin pages. Peace at last. It was glorious, and it went on for a blissful twenty minutes or so. Ash was engrossed in his book, and Jesús was engrossed in his football, and neither one of them was engrossed in the other.

And then Jesús had to go and destroy the tranquility. "Do you always wear shoes to bed?" he asked . . . innocently.

Ash could feel himself blanch at the question. Of all things to notice. Of all things to ask! He kept his temper in check and answered, "Yes."

Jesús sucked his fingers clean and gulped down the water Ash had given him. "Why?" Innocence, it turned out, could be infuriating.

The truth was the demon king had never quite managed to manifest human feet. Everyone was terrible at something, and feet were Ashmedai's personal failing. He'd been called out for it more than once in his afterlife, but for some reason, the captain's casual question was far more mortifying. Ash deliberately kept his answer terse and vague. "I'm not human. My habits are not human. You'll have to get used to it."

Jesús shrugged. "Michael isn't entirely human, and he goes around barefoot all the time. Come to think of it, the only time I ever saw him in shoes was when he went ashore. Maybe he was trying to save the soles." He paused and then burst out laughing. "Pun unintended."

The captain's laugh drove a spike through Ash's bitterness. Sincere, warm, and god damned adorable was what it was, but it wasn't enough to challenge the demon king's resolve. "I am not Michael," he said. It came out sharper than he'd meant it, and he had to wonder why. Was this jealousy? He groaned. It probably was. Against all odds, Ash had managed to rein in his angelic nature over the years, but now . . . Now it seemed he envied the son of Samael, of all people, just because the bastard had normal feet and the last innocent man had seen them.

"It's okay if you're shy about it," Jesús said, and Ash had to actively prevent his jaw from dropping. How did the man read him so easily? "I used to be shy too. Life aboard with crew will hammer that out of ya real quick." He laughed again. "You don't have to take your shoes off if you don't want to, Your Majesty."

Oh. Damn. *Your Majesty* repeatedly coming out of that beautiful mouth was not going to make resisting temptation at all feasible. "You can call me Ash. Please . . . Please, just call me Ash." He stopped short of begging.

Jesús drew his feet in and readjusted the icepack. "Okay, Ash," he muttered, and Ashmedai pinched the bridge of his nose because it was no less enticing than *Your Majesty*. "Well, I suppose you should call me Chuy," said the world's last innocent man, "if we're gonna be friends."

Friends. Abruptly, Ash stood, took the uneaten food from his captive, turned off the television, and extinguished the lamp. "Go to sleep," he ordered. And because he couldn't resist—because it was a beautifully tailored jacket in a shop window, a mouthwatering cake at a wedding, the wine in the well—he sampled the name. "Chuy." As soon as Ash spoke it, he knew it had been a mistake. "I'm going to get some air," he announced to the darkened room. And he left his captive alone because staying would have been more dangerous.

Like the wine in the well, Ash knew he would taste that name again and again until he was drunk on it. It would weaken his resolve, his body, his mind, and leave him vulnerable to his enemies. In the end, of course, it would break him. He'd already seen it, but he couldn't seem to stop himself from indulging in his own destruction. In the hall, he took another sip. "Chuy." And another. "Chuy." And another . . .

Chapter Two

The nephilim were insatiable in all their appetites. By evening on the second day of her newly consummated relationship, Bryony had a full grasp of what that meant. As it happened, Michael had been a tower of strength during his life of celibacy. Naïvely, Bryony had taken pride in breaking through his wall. Now she understood the wall she'd recklessly demolished had been more of a dam. The torrent that followed threw her completely off balance. How was she supposed to prioritize anything else when her fiancé would spy her from the quarterdeck after taking his noon measurements and say, "Bryony, can you help with the adjustments?"

He did not need help with the adjustments. He'd been the Black Armada's navigator for at least fifteen years. No, what he wanted was to lead her to the captain's quarters, lift her into his arms, and devour her. She'd expected his passions to cool after the novelty of the first night, but they hadn't. And by the third day, he dropped all pretense. He would pass her on the deck, hold out his hand, and simply say, "Come."

Exhausted as she was, Bryony loved Michael's attention. His joy was infectious and his lovemaking downright addictive. Every night, she promised herself she would try to get some sleep, but every night, she saw the way he looked at her and caved. In vain, she tried to downplay her drowsiness. Her failure became disastrously apparent when her partner in the galley glanced over and said, "Darling, you look like you haven't slept in days."

The watcher Azazel was another of her shattered expectations. Had anyone told her a year ago that one of her dearest companions would be an angel, she would have laughed in their faces and then insisted it wasn't funny. But Azazel was one of the fallen, so Bryony told herself it didn't count.

The angel's excuse for following *her* around was more complicated. Every time she asked, he had a different answer. He enjoyed cooking, he said—true. He'd always wanted a life at sea—highly unlikely. He didn't have anywhere else to go—depressing but a probable lie. Bryony suspected the real reason Azza stayed was to keep a watchful eye on his new god. As far as she was concerned, it was a little too watchful.

"Is your betrothed wearing you out with his ardent affections?" He chuckled. "You can refuse him, you know. He won't know your preferred pace until you set it."

Bryony nearly cut off her finger instead of a carrot top, and there was no way she hadn't turned as red as the chili peppers she'd just finished seeding. "I thought we were being quiet. Sorry."

The angel laughed. She would never get used to how beautiful his laughter was. He could laugh at her to the end of the world, as far as she was concerned. "Heavens, darling, no one's heard you. You're mice, the both of you."

"Then how . . ." She cleared her throat. "How did you know?"

"Have you forgotten? My daughters were nephilim. I'm somewhat of an expert."

Azazel had gone green this week. His bobbed hair was a deep pine color, and his eye makeup was all the colors of oxidized brass. His lips were painted two different shades—kelp green on the top and metallic gold on the bottom. His long, earthy dress had the occasional splash of bright yellow among the darker browns and greens. Bryony thought he looked like a stage-musical version of the sea witch and wondered if it was intentional.

"So this is . . . normal for them?" she asked.

"Perfectly, yes. They're dealing with dual impulses, the poor petals."

Bryony went back to chopping carrots. "I don't know what that means."

"Hmm . . ." Azza tasted the sauce he was stirring, made a face, and added more cloves. "Well, angels lack a reproductive drive. What we have instead is an insatiable desire to serve and please whomever we love. That's why we make appealing partners in the first place. We become whatever our beloved needs us to be. We refuse them nothing. For example, let's say you and I were coupled." He grinned when she blushed. "Just as a hypothetical exercise. If you preferred a platonic relationship, that's what I would want too. If you preferred a same-sex relationship, my gender would change to suit you. If your deepest desire was to be a mother, I could not help but give a child to you."

Why on earth did he have to add that last example? "I don't want to be a mother," she reminded him.

"Which is lucky for your partner. He's half angel, so he has angelic impulses. Right now, he believes what you want is to be wanted, and so he wants you. But he's also half human, which means he has a human reproductive drive too. When his human and angelic natures agree in this way, what you wind up with is too many sleepless nights."

Embarrassing though it was, Bryony was grateful someone could explain these things to her. If it had to be anyone, she supposed Azza was ideal. He'd lived with her after all. And possessed her. And braided her hair. You couldn't get much closer than that. "What should I do?" she asked.

"It's quite simple, darling. Just let him know what you want. Redirect his angelic impulses until they balance out his human ones."

"So if I want just one good night's sleep?"

"Tell him. He'll long to give it to you, and your rest will satisfy a powerful need in him."

Okay, that was easier than she thought. Perhaps she'd worried for no reason. A partner like Michael could be perfectly compatible if she just communicated with him. It seemed so obvious, now that she thought about it. The same would be true of any relationship, wouldn't it? *Just talk to each other.* God she felt so stupid. She would have continued to berate herself for hours had Azza not abruptly murmured, "Are you hungry, darling?"

She was about to answer that she could eat but stopped short when she glanced up and saw his demeanor. His head was bowed and his eyes hidden, and she felt the nudge of his devotion hovering just outside her borders. He meant to ask if she needed worship. "No," she answered too quickly.

"Are you lying?"

Her shoulders tensed. Michael had been so distracted lately, so happy to be back and so madly in love, that he seemed to have forgotten all about worship. It was Azza who kept her sated now, and she didn't want to see Michael's face when he realized it. She dropped her knife and clenched her fists. "It feels like cheating."

"It isn't." Azza put the lid on the saucepot and turned to her. "You could tell him."

"I know!" She groaned. "And I mean to. It's just . . . every minute that goes by makes it so much harder to go through with it. Like, why did I keep it from him this long if there really isn't anything wrong with it?"

"Because you were afraid."

Bryony felt his hand on her shoulder and shrugged it off. She was desperate to trust him, but she feared part of her never would. Ashmedai had planted a seed of doubt, and as much as she wished it hadn't taken root, it seemed to have done just that. The watcher Azazel had a reputation as a seducer, Ash had told her. Bryony wanted to kick herself for listening to a rumor instead of trusting her own experience, but she tended toward doubt instinctively.

Azza sighed, dipped a ladle in the sauce he'd been making, and held it out to Bryony. "Taste it. Tell me what you think."

She took the ladle and let it cool a moment before she sipped it. "It's delicious! What is it? Is that chocolate?"

The angel grinned. "Yes. You have a good palate, little orb-weaver. But if it was so delicious, why did you take such a small taste?"

"Oh, because it was still hot." She was quick to placate him and slow to catch on to his meaning. "A little sip would be less likely to burn my tongue, that's all."

"I see." He took the ladle back and consumed the rest in one gulp. Bryony was certain he was just showing off until he came to his ultimate point. "Little sips feel safer, so let's just start with that. If you ever need a whole meal, tell me, and I'll give it to you gladly. In the meantime . . ." He nudged her with worship again. This time, it was far more subtle. "Little sips."

Bryony drew back but stopped herself. Everything Azza had just taught her about angelic impulses rang suddenly and undeniably true. "You need this, too, don't you?"

"Yes." Relief flooded his answer.

"Okay." She nodded. "Little sips." She would confess to Michael when the time was right, but for now, there was nothing wrong with helping a friend, as long as that's all it was.

"Thank you, kind god." Azza reached out and touched the back of her neck. She felt a quick rush of warmth, the briefest of highs, and she knew this could never really be just for his sake. Because his self-control was phenomenal, and deep down, Bryony wished he would lose it.

That night, when she emerged from her shower, Bryony patted her hair dry and said, "Michael, you know what would make me really happy? If you let me just fall asleep in your arms tonight."

Michael blinked at her from across the cabin. "Really?"

She nodded. "I love how safe you make me feel. I never sleep better than I do in your arms."

His smile broadened, and the change that came over him was not subtle. His muscles visibly relaxed, and his eyelids grew heavy. He yawned. "That sounds wonderful."

It had worked. Bryony could hardly believe how easy it was to just tell her fiancé the truth. There was no chance she'd take Azza's advice for granted again. She stepped into Michael's arms and kissed along his jaw. He warmed a little at her touch, but she felt no fire in him. They lay down together, and she curled up against him while he stroked her hair. Soon his hand went still, and she realized he'd already fallen asleep. He must have been exhausted too. She closed her eyes and quickly joined him. It was heaven, but it didn't last.

A full night's sleep would have been a miracle, but the deafening crack of lightning invaded Bryony's dreams. She and Michael were already falling by the time she woke. Michael shielded her with his body so she didn't go crashing into his work table. Then he grabbed a bolted-down table leg and braced for the ship to pitch in the opposite direction, but it never did. It felt like *Dragonfly* was surfing a colossal wave that came from the stern and tipped the whole vessel onto its bow.

Bryony screamed. And suddenly, the sea was still, as though it had heard her and responded. Her heart thundered, and the shock of adrenaline coursed through her body. "What was that?"

Michael panted. "I don't know. Rogue wave?"

Electricity lifted the fine hairs on her skin. Then Bryony heard the unbridled grief of the crew on watch, and everything began to make sense. "Oh, no. Michael, I think it's your father."

"Don't . . ." He shot to his feet but dropped down again, grunting and pressing the heel of his hand to his back. "Don't go out there."

But Bryony knew it was no use. "I have to. I'm probably the reason he's here."

"I don't care. He's my father. I'll deal with him." He stood and limped to the door. Bryony followed, folded her arms, and waited at the threshold. She knew what was bound to happen, but she also knew there was nothing she could say to stop Michael. No, he was determined, he was strong . . . and he was down. He'd looked up at the quarterdeck and fallen to his knees with his hands pressed to his face, just like everyone else.

Bryony took a deep breath and walked his path with her gaze locked on her feet. Halfway up the stairs, she lifted her chin, and it hit her—a wave of suffering so deep her knees buckled. But the little gothic healing god knew how to deal with this feeling. She knew how to savor and appreciate it like a fine wine. She breathed in the hopelessness, the emptiness, the too quiet house. She drew in the grief and wore it like armor. Shakily, she continued her slow march to the quarterdeck.

It felt like the world had been turned upside down. At the helm, Raeni clung to the wheel on her knees. Andrew, who'd been on watch with the commodore, was flat on the deck, his face pressed to the teak. Bryony heard the usually aloof deckhand whimper once before she had to focus all her energy on her extraordinarily troublesome, future father-in-law.

The Angel of Death stood perfectly still several feet from the top of the stairs. He looked like the inaccurate representation of angels Bryony used to find whenever she visited her neighborhood graveyard. But instead of crumbling stone, his robe, his skin, his hair and wings all appeared to be made of smooth, white marble. He still had an uncanny resemblance to Michael, and his eyes were still the deep, black voids she'd complained about the first time she'd seen him. She flushed at the memory and quickly cleared her throat. "Samael," she said, unable to disguise the tremor in her voice. "It's Bryony."

He nodded. "Ms. Moss." She'd forgotten just how soothing his voice was. It was irresistible and unsettling, like a cobra mesmerizing its prey. "I have come to discuss your progress."

"Prematurely," she muttered. It took most of her mental strength just to stay on her feet. She wasn't in the mood to plead her case.

"Am I to assume you have made no progress? All you have to do is conjure the archangel Michael and kill him. I've given you the means, and I know you have the ability."

"It's too soon!" she cried. "My conjuring partner is still exhausted from summoning *you*."

"Then get a new conjuring partner." His expression remained infuriatingly serene.

A new, hoarse voice joined the conversation. "How 'bout both of yuh get below so di rest of us can sail di damn ship." It was Raeni, still on her knees and weeping, but no less intimidating for that.

Bryony snapped to attention. "Yes, Commodore." Then she said, "Follow me," which seemed like the worst thing to say to the Angel of Death under any circumstances.

Partway down the stairs, she paused and glanced back to see that Samael hadn't moved at all. He stood perfectly still with his hand extended and his empty eyes staring straight ahead. Bryony could have slapped herself. She gritted her teeth and made her way back to the quarterdeck. "Sorry," she said, and she touched his hand in an offer to guide him. "I didn't realize you needed help."

He nodded once. "This is unfamiliar terrain," he explained. "I will learn it."

God she hoped he wouldn't visit often enough to keep that promise. Bryony shuddered as he slid his hand above her elbow and gripped her arm. "There are stairs," she warned. She guided him down to the main deck. He followed slowly, and Bryony marveled that the Angel of Death could still appear vulnerable with the entire crew of *Dragonfly* lying prone before him.

Michael knelt at the bottom of the stairway, his head bowed and his hands pressed over his eyes. "Father," he said in a cold greeting. "Don't hurt her."

Samael's mouth quirked into a wicked smile. "It was not on my agenda for today, son."

Michael did not smile back.

Bryony rolled her eyes. Every fresh minute she spent with the Angel of Death taught her something new about him. Apparently, he enjoyed teasing his son. She didn't know whether it was loveable or infuriating.

"Okay, we're coming to a door now." She stopped to gauge her situation and quickly discovered a problem. The traditional feathered wings crested up from the graveyard angel's shoulders. They made him taller and broader than he would have been otherwise. In this manifested body, there was no way he was going to fit through the door. "I think your wings are a problem." When she realized how her words could be misconstrued, she began a clumsy attempt to clarify. "I mean the ones you're wearing now won't fit through the door, not that I have a problem with your real wings. Your real wings are perfect—" She felt like a rambling fool and cut herself off, but she shouldn't have. *Perfectly fine* was what she'd been about to say. Now she'd given the most dangerous angel in the world an over-the-top compliment she didn't dare take back.

She had no excuse. Azza had warned her. Samael was sensitive about his extra limbs. Most seraphim had six wings, and he had twelve. As little as Bryony cared about the number of wings the monsters had, in the world of the seraphim, twelve was considered a deformity. Bryony started to fidget and turned to Azazel, who lay prone on the deck with everyone else. His shoulders shook with what Bryony first assumed was grief. But the longer she watched him, the more obvious it became that he was racked with maniacal laughter.

"*Perfect*," Samael said. So much for the vain hope that he hadn't really heard her. "Yet you insisted I appear *in fair and comely form, without noise or deformity.* And you insisted this after you had seen my seraphic body."

"You were too big!" she snapped and immediately regretted it. She softened her tone. "It was about size not appearance. You were going to sink the ship. You almost did it again tonight. Come to think of it, how did you find us so easily? No one conjured you."

"You are wearing my weapon," he answered matter-of-factly.

Bryony should have known. The ship had pitched stern over bow because she was sleeping in Michael's bunk when Samael rose up right beneath her. She was beginning to think she caused more problems for the Black Armada than any of the otherworldly beasts they fought.

The Angel of Death turned his face to the sky in mock consideration. "*Fair and comely*, you said. *Without noise* or *deformity*." He was not going to let it drop.

Bryony gritted her teeth and dug deep for her patience. "Those weren't my words, nor were they originally meant for you. It was just a stupid conjuration. I was only repeating what was fed to me." She glanced at Azazel and hoped she wasn't throwing him under the bus.

For a moment, the watcher found the strength to lift his head, and in the storm of grief around him, through all the wailing and gnashing of teeth, he mouthed the words, *Tell him.*

Unfortunately, Bryony knew exactly what he meant. He wanted her to tell Samael what she really thought of his appearance. She supposed she owed her longsuffering conjuration partner one indulgence, at least. She drew a deep breath and closed her eyes. "The truth is, when I first saw them, I thought your wings were beautiful—all twelve of them."

With that, the graveyard angel froze. He stopped speaking, breathing, or moving at all. When Bryony tried to urge him along, she found him as heavy and unresponsive as actual marble. Azza hadn't exaggerated when he'd suggested Samael couldn't take a sincere compliment. No matter how much he teased her over it, the moment Bryony gave in and confessed that she found him at all beautiful, Samael lost the ability to express himself entirely. Like Azza with mercy, the Angel of Death was overcome by appreciation.

Chapter Three

Azazel did not bother to hide his look of triumph. *Yes!* he mouthed through his tears and dropped his head back onto the deck. Slowly, the watcher's hand clenched and shifted until he was giving Bryony an unmistakable thumbs-up.

"For the love of god, they're no better than schoolchildren," she muttered as she tugged more ferociously on Samael's cold hand. "Come on!" She heaved. "The crew needs to move." She put her weight into it. "Come on, will you? Please, Sama!"

The statue drew in a sharp breath. "What did you call me?"

Shit. So she was doomed to put her foot in it repeatedly tonight. Well, this was what came of exhaustion, wasn't it? You did your job poorly when you didn't get enough sleep. And for now, it seemed, Bryony's job was placating monsters. "Sorry," she said. "Azza's got me in the habit of shortening names. I meant no disrespect."

Samael puffed out his chest, thought a moment, and said, "It is acceptable." When he breathed out again, his wings dropped from his back. Bryony jumped at the sound of them hitting the deck and crumbling to dust. Then he held out his hand as though nothing unusual had happened and waited for Bryony to take it.

Once inside the captain's quarters, Bryony lit the lamp and cleared her throat awkwardly. "So . . . these are the captain's quarters," she said. "Do you want me to describe them or something?"

"That would be the polite thing to do," he said.

The absurdity of being schooled on decorum by such a creature did not escape her, but Bryony swallowed her pride and did her best. "To your left is my bunk. It's in an alcove and pretty cozy, I think. In front of you is the stern of the ship with a row of windows and Michael's bunk. I don't think he believes in the concept of too many pillows. There's a desk to your right and a work table in the center. Would you like to sit down?"

"No, thank you." Samael lifted his chin and turned his head from side to side as though getting a feel for the space. Then he turned his unsettling attention back to Bryony and said, "Are you enjoying my son?"

"That's . . ." She coughed and was quietly grateful he could not see the shade her face had turned. "That's wildly inappropriate."

Samael blinked. "Is it?"

"Yes!"

"Oh." For a moment, she thought he actually had an ounce of shame, and then he said, "Well, are you?"

She decided to interpret it the most innocent way she could. "Fine. Yes, I'm enjoying him. He's good company, and I'm glad he exists. So, I guess, thank you for that." Perhaps he had meant it innocently after all. Maybe he was just socially awkward. Surely, the Angel of Death did not get invited to many parties, "Masque of the Red Death" notwithstanding. She chuckled.

But she should not have let her guard down, not when Samael was the other half of the conversation. He deadpanned, "Would you say he looks like me?"

For a moment, Bryony lost her composure. A wave of grief washed over her, and she had to brace herself against the table. She swallowed an oncoming wail and held back a flood of tears. She kept her body upright, though it would have been a great relief to just bow before the angel. His stubborn sense of humor had thrown her off, and now she had to find her footing again. "One . . . One moment," she said, her voice hoarse and pathetic.

Samael nodded and waited. He seemed used to the effect his poison had on others. It probably meant nothing to him, though to her, it was mortifying. She chided herself. She did not need the Angel of Death to like her. She just had to remember to breathe through the grief that poured from him like a thick fog. *Find the beauty in death. Find the beauty in decay. Dye it all black, and wear it to your favorite café.*

She straightened and regained her composure. "Your son looks like a seraph sometimes if that's what you mean."

"No." Samael pointed to his own face. "This is the body with which I sired him. Does he look like this?"

Bryony knew where the angel was taking this. The last thing she wanted to do was play along, but there was something sad about his never having known his child. Had he been human, she supposed, people would have told him repeatedly how much his son resembled him. But because he was blind, an angel, and an outcast, he never had the chance to know. "He has your mouth," she admitted. "And his hair curls the same way, although it's much darker."

Samael grinned, and Bryony drew back at the sight of Michael's broad smile on that merciless face. "The color, he gets from his mother," he said.

"Well, the rest of his complexion is very fair."

"That would be my contribution." The angel touched a finger to his marble cheek. "I am not good with color. I manifest it poorly, or so I've been told."

That the Angel of Death would acknowledge any kind of weakness in himself was a shock. Bryony cleared her throat and admitted the truth. "Then he looks a lot like you, I guess."

And Samael turned her confession against her with a look that could only accurately be described as devilish. "But is he *fair and comely*?"

Though she'd known it was coming, Bryony couldn't help sputtering in response to his taunt. *He's not a friend*, she reminded herself. *He's death.* Then she groaned when she thought of how inevitable it was that a personification of death would one day show up and mock her.

Samael chuckled at the sound of her discomfort, clearly pleased he was winning his game. "I will tell you a secret," he said out of absolutely nowhere. "It began in a garden."

Bryony snorted.

"Not *that* garden." The angel scowled. "It was a rose garden, north of here, and so vast one could easily lose oneself in it. After emigrating from India, Kavya found work tending the roses. One day, she noticed that someone had added a statue to her favorite corner of the garden. It was in terrible taste, of course, because the statue was an angel. And it had some ineffable quality, a malignance she couldn't quite name. None of the other gardeners wanted to get close to it. So Kavya's work grew lonelier by the day, and she developed the habit of singing to herself. Every time she dared to look at the angel, she felt the weight of overwhelming melancholy. Little did she know, it could have been worse—it could have been much, much worse—because the angel was real, and it held back its poison so it could stay and listen to her sing."

Bryony didn't even pretend the story wasn't about him. "Is that difficult to do, hold the poison back?"

Samael frowned. "Exceedingly. It feels like breathlessness. How long can you hold your breath?" Bryony didn't answer, and the graveyard angel continued his story, incorporating the analogy he'd just introduced. "Whenever the angel had to take a breath, Kavya fell to the ground. But all the time, she believed it was her own weakness that troubled her. All the time, she believed she was dying, and with no doctors to tell her otherwise, she had no reason to question it. One day, after falling, she reached out to the statue to pull herself to her feet. On a whim, she thanked it and squeezed its hand." Samael's own hand clenched at the memory. "And the statue squeezed back. Oh, how she screamed, but it was too late. The stone angel already loved her and had to offer her heart's desire to her. It thought, perhaps foolishly, that she would wish for it to become a man and live as her companion. Alas, Kavya did not love the statue in the garden, and her heart's desire was to have a child."

"Why do you speak about yourself that way?" Bryony asked.

Samael cocked his head. "What?"

"You keep calling yourself *it* as though you don't consider yourself an actual person." She folded her arms. "Why?"

Samael narrowed his empty eyes at her. "*I* gave her a son," he said defiantly. "And when she had her heart's desire, *I* gave her my absence, which she greatly wished for. I could not have known the boy would inherit my curse—none of my other children did—but the next time I met Kavya, she was not Kavya anymore. She had lost the ability to move and communicate. Now I know why. Infant nephilim, it seems, have trouble holding their breath."

The implication was clear, and Bryony shivered to hear it. "Are you saying Michael accidentally killed his own mother?"

Slowly, the graveyard angel nodded. "Though I dealt the lethal blow." He gestured to his weapon on Bryony's wrist. "She was already gone."

Bryony dug her fingernails into the underside of the table. It wasn't true. It couldn't be true, even though it made sense. Michael had explained resonance to her once he finally understood it. Apparently, a range of bonding activities could trigger it, like dancing and singing. All it took was synchronization, and Bryony could imagine a number of ways a mother might synchronize with her child.

"Now you know my secret, Ms. Moss." Samael smiled. "Now we're even."

She wrinkled her nose and took the bait. "Even?"

"Because I know your secret, it was only fair that you learn mine." Lightning quick, before she could take a breath to question him, he seized her by the upper arms. He slid one hand down to her left wrist and brushed his thumb over Azza's mark. "I wondered, when I first felt it, why Azazel had marked you. Then I smelled his worship on you, mingled with that of my son." He made a disgusted face. His thumb continued to trace the slightly raised lines on her wrist. It was a beautiful, copper tattoo, so intricate Bryony was stunned that Samael could recognize it as Azza's mark by touch alone. "But you've not told my son about your relationship with the watcher, have you? Because you know as well as I, he would not take it well. The things we keep from our loved ones to protect them, eh?" He spoke the last sentence as though it were a tedium shared between friends.

"You're lying." Bryony felt sick to her stomach. "You don't love him."

Samael dropped her hand and frowned. Now he was finished with his game. Now he would come to his point. "And *you* are lying about the exhaustion of your conjuring partner," he snapped, and she backed into the table. "You're protecting Azazel because he gives you what you need. You're afraid the archangel will consume him."

"That's not true!" Bryony shot back. "Azza *is* exhausted. And while you may be right that I'm putting off conjuring the archangel, you're one hundred percent wrong about why."

Samael spoke through his teeth. "Enlighten me."

There were, of course, innumerable reasons Bryony wanted to put off conjuring the archangel Michael, not the least of which was how much the very idea of him terrified her. She fished around for a reason Samael was likely to accept. "One of the armada's captains has been abducted. We have to rescue him first."

Samael closed his eyes and let out a sharp breath. "Fine," he grumbled. "I'll retrieve this captain for you. Who has taken him?"

It took Bryony several seconds to recover from her shock. Could it really be this easy? Were there some perks to having made a deal with the devil? She hesitated. This was either going to go incredibly well or very, very badly. "Um . . . Well, the demon king took him."

"Ashmedai." Samael nodded. "I am familiar with him."

Bryony gulped, afraid that if she so much as breathed in the wrong direction, she could destroy her precarious good fortune. "Apparently, Ashmedai has decided the captain is the only innocent man on earth, and he's determined to keep him under a bell jar—I guess—to protect his innocence."

"Then he'll not let this captain go so easily." Samael made a show of rubbing his chin. "Ashmedai is relentless, if nothing else. He will come for his prize again and again until its value is eliminated, which I'm certain I can accomplish with little effort."

Bryony was seconds away from telling him he was definitely calling the kettle black by using the word *relentless* to describe Ashmedai, when the full meaning behind his words hit her. "Wait a minute," she said, her eyes growing wider. "How do you plan to eliminate his value?"

Samael stared straight ahead and answered as though nothing could have been more obvious. "I will destroy his innocence."

"You will not destroy anything about him!" She was near shouting now.

"It shouldn't take much." The angel turned his face to the ceiling in thought. "Ashmedai measures by trust, if I recall. I simply have to break your captain's ability to trust, and he will be of no value to the demon king."

Samael was going to break Chuy, and Bryony couldn't stand the places her mind went to when she thought about how. Her first friend in the Black Armada—that sweet, kind man who trusted her and forgave her and comforted her after she'd hurt him—was now a target of the Angel of Death, and it was all Bryony's fault. She threw every ounce of courage she had into her protest. "You will not destroy his innocence. If you break him, I'll . . . I'll break our contract!"

"I don't think you will." The graveyard angel caught Bryony by the wrist, and this time, his hand felt like marble. "Because you know I can take everything from you, little god, my son included."

Bryony gasped. "No."

The Angel of Death dragged her to the cabin door like she was just a child having a tantrum. He took his time finding the doorknob while he held her wrist in a vice grip. "I will retrieve your captain and eliminate his value. Then you'll no longer be distracted from your task." He threw open the door and everyone on deck dropped to the planks.

Michael kneeled by the bulwarks and stared down at his hands.

"Where is my son?" Samael called out.

"I'm here." Michael answered automatically, and Bryony wished he wouldn't.

Samael dragged her across the deck while she struggled and tugged at her own wrist. It was no use. He may as well have been made of stone. She was beginning to see why Michael and Azza had reacted the way they did when she'd gone off script and summoned the Angel of Death. There was no bright side to having gained his attention. None. He stopped in front of Michael and held Bryony out like he was dropping a stray cat into the lap of someone who actually cared.

"I have returned your betrothed unharmed," he said, "though I'm not sure what it is you see in her. She's dishonest and deceitful. She has taken on a second congregant and failed to inform you. I can only imagine why."

"What?" Michael's voice cracked.

Samael bent down to speak candidly. "Another angel worships her. She doesn't need you anymore." Then he straightened up and struck the final blow. "Do what you will with the information, but I would rethink the nature of your relationship if I were you. She clearly cannot be trusted."

His true aim was clear. The Angel of Death was giving Bryony a taste of how easy it was to destroy trust. This was only a sample, she knew. He'd have to wreck more than one of Chuy's relationships to completely break his innocence. And whatever else he would do to achieve such a disgusting goal, she could not begin to imagine, nor did she want to.

Despite her ability to tolerate his poison, Bryony could no longer stand to look at Samael. As soon as he was gone, she leapt out of Michael's dead-weight arms and scrambled to the quarterdeck. "Raeni! Raeni!" Decorum be damned. This was an emergency. "We have to find Chuy! We have to find him now!"

"We already know where he is," Raeni answered, still clinging to the wheel, weak from the effects of the poison. Nevertheless, there was a calm in her that almost convinced Bryony everything was going to be all right. Almost. "Michael informed us that the demon had his hotel room booked for another week at least. Michael also informed us that the demon is habitually frugal and would not allow the room to go to waste. Tonight, we anchor and head ashore to bring our captain back."

"Thank god." Bryony was close to tears. "Thank god. We have to tell Ash to hide him better. We have to warn him. Samael is coming for Chuy."

CHAPTER FOUR

On rare occasions, Ashmedai wished his vision wasn't quite the miracle it was, and those occasions had recently multiplied. Among them, he could count every night since he abducted the captain of *Papillon*. Even in the dark with the curtains drawn, Ash could see him. He tried to focus on other things to no avail. Invariably, Chuy would stir in the corner of his eye, and it was as though a spotlight had been shined upon him.

Tonight, as a diversion, Ash decided to read the English Bible he'd pulled from his nightstand. He reclined against the headboard of his queen-sized bed with his feet up—shoes on, obviously—and he read in the dark. The only sounds he heard were the crinkling of onionskin pages, the distant rumble of city traffic, and the rhythmic breathing of the man in the bed next to his.

He reread the same passage five times before he finally took it in, while Chuy, in his sleep, kicked off the sheet that covered him. Ash groaned and keeled over. Why had he gone through with this ridiculous plan? Could it even be called a plan? It was more of an impulse, really. *Guard him. Protect him. Trust no one, especially not yourself.* Chuy took a deep breath, and Ash leapt out of bed as though the man had screamed at him. He snatched the rejected sheet off the floor and draped it gently over his captive's mostly naked body. For someone who could see so much of the future, Ash really ought to have allowed the captain to pack some things to wear.

By morning, Ash had given up altogether. He sat in bed beside an open and neglected Bible and imagined tracing the tip of his tongue over every line of ink on that sun-darkened skin. When Chuy began to wake, Ash hastily resumed reading.

The last innocent man opened one eye before the other and rolled onto his back. Then he peeked under his sheet, grumbled at his early morning erection, and fell back onto his pillows. He hadn't been lying about his lack of shyness.

Ash grinned at him. "The shower's free." It was a tease, a little flirtation. He meant to tempt Chuy to get up anyway. He couldn't believe he'd just up and said it. Luckily, his groggy captive didn't seem to notice the indiscretion, or maybe he just didn't care.

"Morning," Chuy mumbled, rubbing his eyes. He was not a morning person, which was something Ash had learned through his spectacles. Now he got to experience it in real time, and he loved it.

"Sleep well?" Ash's voice sounded downright cheery. Whatever this good mood was, he would have to nip it in the bud, and soon. He needed to be at least a little intimidating.

"Off and on," Chuy answered. "You?"

Ash felt his smile grow decidedly less sincere. "I no longer sleep, Captain. I'm no longer alive, if you recall."

"You're alive in all the ways that matter, right?" Chuy sat up. It took some effort to ignore the sight of him pulling one long arm behind his head in a luxurious stretch.

"When I'm exhausted, I can't sleep it away. My manifested flesh will simply dissolve. But I suppose . . ." Ash paused, realizing the implications behind the question. "For now, I'm alive in all the ways that matter."

"So what do you do with your nights then? Must be boring watching me sleep."

Boring was not the word Ash would have used to describe it. "Well, last night I spent reading about your namesake." He held up the Bible.

"Eh?" Chuy squinted at the book and grimaced. "Right. *Jesús* is just a family tradition. I really do prefer Chuy."

"Of course." Ash took one more sip of the wine in the well. "Chuy."

"Did you really spend all night reading the Bible?"

"The better part of it."

"You're kidding." Chuy laughed and shook his head. "My abuela would have loved you."

Ash's entire body involuntarily shivered at the word *abuela*. Family meant long-term. It meant a relationship that could last. The mere suggestion that Ash might one day be introduced to any of Chuy's family sent the blood to his cheeks. This was not good. Oh, this was most definitely the opposite of good. Abruptly, Ash stood. "I'm going to—"

"Get some air," Chuy finished for him. "I know, I know. Grab breakfast while you're down there?"

"Of course." Ash buttoned his jacket and walked out the door without looking back. Of course he would get breakfast. Of course he hadn't forgotten that the living needed to eat. That would have been ridiculous. That would have meant he was incurably distracted.

In the elevator, his thoughts drifted lazily to marriage, and he ground a knuckle into his thigh to redirect himself. This was all happening much faster than he'd predicted. How was he supposed to fight an oncoming train with only his wits and a head full of scripture? It was one thing to appreciate the attractiveness of a near stranger. It was quite another to fantasize about meeting his family. Such a powerful, physical craving for permanence meant it wasn't just his human nature lusting after his captive. It was his cherubic nature too. It was twofold desire. He was doomed.

He burst into the lobby and found the restaurant not yet open. A café then. There had to be one nearby. He marched toward the front doors. He was a man with purpose. He was a man in a suit. He was not a sad, lonely creature desperate to resist the only person in the world who could possibly make him happy . . . just for a little while.

"Mr. Daeva? Mr. Daeva!" Reception called to him and completely destroyed his momentum. "Sorry to catch you on your way out, Mr. Daeva," said the woman behind the desk. "We tried phoning your room, but no one picked up. You have a visitor. She says it's urgent."

Ash scanned the lobby and narrowed his eyes at the only person he recognized. He'd met her in battle several days ago on the deck of a black-sailed ship. She was most definitely trouble. Defending himself against this small, fleet-footed woman had been like fighting several men at once. "I'm here to deliver a message," she said. When he drew closer, her voice lowered to a near whisper. "On behalf of the armada."

Another glance around the lobby told Ash there was no one else here to ambush him. Either the Black Armada trusted this woman to take him on alone, or she really was just here to deliver a message. While the former wasn't entirely unthinkable, the latter was far more likely. "What's the message?" he said.

"I'm Dara." She held out her hand.

Ash just stared at it.

Dara rolled her eyes and dropped her hand. "Or we could *not* be civil. I suppose that's also an option." She was bold, and Ash thought what a shame it was that this woman was not on his side. She would have made an excellent warrior or guardian under the right circumstances. "I'll just assume you wish to be called *Mr. Daeva* then." She chuckled. "Subtle."

Ash was not amused. "It wasn't a planned pseudonym. I was pressed for time." Why he bothered to justify himself to an enemy, he could not have said. Some infuriating part of his brain suggested he cared what Chuy's people thought of him now, but he quickly shelved the idea. "I have many names and titles." He waved a dismissive hand. "The Aeshma Daeva is just one of them. Most people only recognize"—he cringed—"*Asmodeus*." The name always left a foul taste in his mouth.

"Well then, Asmodeus, I have a message for you." She had misunderstood monumentally.

"No, please. I . . ." Why did he care what this woman called him? He pinched the bridge of his nose. "Forget it. It doesn't matter. You're not getting your captain back. I thought I made myself clear. He belongs to me now. If you try to take him back, you won't live to regret it. He's under *my* protection."

To the demon king's utter shock, Dara gave him a curt nod. "Excellent. That's what we're counting on."

Ash had to stop and go back over her response a couple times before his mind would accept it. "I don't understand."

"The message I have for you is as follows." She cleared her throat and squared her shoulders. "Do not return the captain to the armada. Keep him safe. Hide him better." She glanced around the hotel and arched an eyebrow. "Much better."

"Why are you—"

She held up a finger to silence him. "I'm not finished. Don't let your guard down. Samael is coming for him."

"What!" Ash roared, and everyone in the lobby turned to stare at him. Who had done this? Why was Chuy even on the Angel of Death's radar? Before he could shout the oaths lining up at the back of his throat, Dara put her finger to her lips, and he bit his tongue.

"You're too conspicuous here," she whispered. "Look how easily we found you."

Ashmedai growled low. "I didn't consider you a threat."

Dara shrugged. "Maybe you should have. Anyway, what's done is done. It can't be taken back now. The only way is forward."

She wasn't wrong. Once Samael had a prize in his teeth, he never ever let go. "He'll have already commanded his host to search." *Damn it. Damn it.* Ash couldn't just fly away now. The skies weren't safe anymore. "I'll need a car," he muttered. "I know a place."

"Don't tell me where it is," Dara hissed. "Don't tell any of us. Protect him, Your Majesty. You're the only one who can."

"Yes." The use of his formal title cut to the core of him. It meant power. It meant responsibility, but just now, he felt too small to be king of anything.

He turned from Dara and walked back to his room. *Don't run,* he told himself. *Don't draw attention to yourself.* But he couldn't help his long strides, his frantic energy. He took the stairs this time because it would be faster than waiting on an elevator, and when he reached his room, he barged in without knocking. Both beds were empty.

Ash stopped breathing.

No.

When he heard the shower, he nearly collapsed with relief. He pounded on the bathroom door. "Get dressed. We're leaving."

The water shut off, and he heard Chuy's voice. "Why?"

"It doesn't matter why. We have to go. Now!" He put all the authority he could muster behind the command, but it didn't seem to have an effect. Chuy calmly exited the bathroom with dripping hair and a towel wrapped around his waist.

Ash stopped breathing again, but this time, it was for an entirely different reason. "Please," he begged. The sight of his captive's perfect bones shifting under that highly decorated skin forced him to sit.

"Whatever you say." Chuy shrugged and dropped his towel to dress. Ash stared down at his own lap. "Was planning to wash these today, though," Chuy complained, and Ash looked up just in time to see him tug his jeans over his hips.

"You can wash them later." While Chuy finished dressing, Ash called the front desk and demanded a cab. He insisted it pick them up around back. "Phone my room when it's here," he said. Then he called the nearest rental place and had them set aside their least conspicuous pickup truck.

"You gonna tell me what's going on?" Chuy asked, fully dressed now but still dripping wet.

Ash hesitated. He didn't want to frighten the captain, though that seemed all but impossible at this point, and Chuy deserved an explanation. "I've had word from the Black Armada," he began. Chuy's eyes lit up, and Ash tried not to take it personally. "The Angel of Death is on the hunt." Again, Ash hesitated. "For you."

The expression of hope that had just alighted on Chuy's beautiful face was replaced with one of absolute dread.

"Exactly," Ash replied to his unspoken words. He stood. "Come with me."

The deeper Ash drove into the old-growth forest, the more he resented the silence. The trees grew formidable and the sunlight scarce and dappled. The road gave way to gravel, then dirt, and eventually narrowed until it seemed more like a wide hiking trail than a road.

All the while, Chuy stared out the window with his chin on the heel of his hand, drumming his fingertips against his cheekbone. Finally, he said, "Why me, though?" to his own reflection. "Who am I to any of you? The demon king and the Angel of Death. What's so special about me? I mean aside from apparently being the world's only innocent man, which honestly makes no sense at all."

"It makes sense to me." Ash slowed the truck and took a corner far more cautiously than the corner deserved. He'd never been a reckless demon. Ashmedai lived a quiet life. He liked his daily routines, his study, his solitude. The last several weeks had been so atypical, he had to check regularly to make certain he wasn't seeing into someone else's life.

"But you saw my past," Chuy reminded him.

"Glimpses."

"You've gotta know I'm no innocent."

Ash shook his head and eased the truck back to speed. "If that's what you think, then you don't know what innocence is."

Chuy drew back from the window and stretched his arms behind his headrest. "Okay, I'll bite. What's innocence?"

"It isn't about lack of experience. It's how your experience changes you—or doesn't, in your case. Life doesn't tend to build faith in people. Life carves it out instead. You are, for lack of a better phrase, somehow left whole, still capable of real trust. You're like a child who follows anyone claiming to be sent by his parents, and this despite everything you've suffered."

Chuy gnawed his upper lip in thought.

Ash lowered his voice, only half sure he should admit what he was about to admit. "I know what your pendant means to you. I saw the moment you received it. I saw the man who gave it to you, and I saw when he wasn't there anymore. I saw betrayal and deception done to you over and over again, and yet . . . somehow, you still have faith."

"Wish you hadn't seen as much as you did." Chuy absentmind-edly clutched the pendant under his T-shirt.

"I am sorry for that." Ash felt a twinge of shame at his own little betrayal. "I'd take it back if I could." He let a few minutes of silence pass before he answered the other part of Chuy's question. "As for the Angel of Death's interest in you, you can probably blame the woman for that."

"*The woman?*" Chuy laughed. "You gonna narrow it down some for me?"

"Ms. Moss."

"Oh, Bryony!"

Ash gripped the steering wheel tighter. "She conjured Samael and likely brought you to his attention. She doesn't understand the fire she's playing with."

Chuy dropped his seatback to a horizontal position and crossed his arms behind his head. He was absurdly comfortable, considering his current predicament. "I'm sure she didn't mean anything by it. She was probably just trying to help."

Little by little, Ash increased their speed. His frustration was showing. "See, this is what I'm talking about. Your faith. That woman lied to you, manipulated you, and used you. Now she's sicced the Angel of Death on you, and you still believe in her. You still think she's a good person."

"Because she is." Chuy pulled his heels onto the seat. "She's just impulsive, that's all."

Ash breathed a deep, conflicted sigh. Innocence was both breathtaking and maddening. "I abducted you. I brought you to a hotel as my prisoner, and all you cared about was freshwater showers, whether demons eat and sleep, and whether I wanted to watch football with you. I'm currently driving you to a hunter's cabin in the middle of the forest, and look at you. I could do anything I wanted to you here. If you screamed, no one would come to your aid." He glanced at Chuy, searching for a modicum of concern. There was none. "You don't seem at all troubled. On the ship, I openly introduced myself as the Aeshma Daeva. I fought your people in demonic form. I have a reputation, and it isn't a good one. Why did you come with me?"

"Didn't have much of a choice." Chuy shrugged.

But Ash wasn't buying it. "There were two watchers, a Jötunn, and an entire fleet of people who would have fought for you had you asked. I didn't stand a chance against them."

"Maybe I didn't wanna make trouble for 'em."

"No, that isn't it."

Chuy chewed his thumbnail. "Maybe I decided you were a good person too."

Ash chuckled darkly. "I'm neither good nor a person, as you're well aware. I'm the ghost of an ancient nephil, a close relative of the angels you spent your entire life fighting against."

"Michael's related to an angel, and he's a good person."

"Exactly my point. You befriended the son of Samael, for god's sake!" Ash slapped the wheel for emphasis. "You're going to get yourself kil—" He caught himself and groaned. "Forgive me. I didn't mean to . . . What

I mean to say is you're a rare creature, whether you realize it or not. You're like the only living example of a long-extinct species. There's a reason men like you disappeared from the earth. I . . ." He massaged his brow. This was treacherous ground, but it needed to be said. "I can't let you go. I can't let anyone change you. Listen. From now on, I'll doubt on your behalf. I'll fight on your behalf. Just stay as you are, and let me worry about your survival." He turned the wheel, hand over hand, and pulled into a gravel drive. "We're here."

Chuy let his seatback return to its upright position and gazed out the windshield at the cabin. It was quite small, made entirely of cedar and oak. Ash had found it during one of his habitual wanderings and returned frequently enough to know it was abandoned. He often came here, not for the cabin itself, but for the solitude. It already felt strange to be here with another person.

Ash exited the truck and circled around to open the passenger door. Chuy sat rigid and wide-eyed. It seemed the seriousness of his situation was finally beginning to dawn on him. He pressed a palm to the pendant still tucked under his T-shirt, and Ash had to stifle an immediate pang of jealousy.

He cannot be yours, Ash reminded himself. *You're his protector not his lover. The most dangerous situation you could put him in would be a relationship with you.*

Ash offered his hand, but Chuy just stared at it. "Please," Ash begged. "Trust me. I won't betray you."

There was a moment, a breath during which Ash was certain, in his zeal to advise caution, he'd already cracked into that store of precious faith. He began to panic, but Chuy finally stepped from the truck, allowing a second of unneeded assistance from his captor. A second was all it took. A second would always be all it took. Ash felt those long fingers grip his hand, and he was undone. The callouses the captain had built up over years of handling line, scrubbing teak, and bracing himself through storms grazed Ash's skin. Somehow, he resisted the urge to run his thumb over the captain's scarred knuckles and trace the bones of his wrist. Somehow, he managed to let go, though the urge to hold on forever was staggering.

Chuy crossed his arms in front of the cabin and took in his surroundings. "Discreet. Why didn't you bring me here in the first place?"

"No electricity. No running water. No room service." Ash opened the front door with a sarcastic flourish. "But there's a well and pump out back and a wood-burning stove inside, so we should be fine until I come up with a better idea." The cabin had a single room with a brass-framed bed, a dusty sofa, and one small table. There were two oil lamps, kitchen utensils, a stock pot, and a cast iron pan. Tattered curtains were drawn over the cabin's only two windows, and a small pile of wood was neatly stacked beside the stove.

Chuy side-eyed the copper bathtub in the corner. "S'pose it's a good thing I'm not shy."

"Ah . . ." Ash blanched. He hadn't even considered privacy. But after Chuy's complaint that Ash had seen too much of his past, privacy seemed of the utmost importance. "I'll leave the cabin whenever you wish."

"Sure, if you think it'll help." Chuy laughed. "Should I wait outside while you change out of your suit?"

"What?" Ash glanced down at his own formal attire. These days, he rarely manifested anything other than a three-piece suit. He found it taxing to change his costume often. It reduced his body's longevity, so he only did it when the prevailing styles demanded change.

"Kind of conspicuous to wear a suit out hunting, don't ya think?"

"Fine." Ash shed his jacket and rolled up his shirtsleeves. His dress shoes, of course, would stay right where they were. "Better?"

Chuy snorted and shook his head. Then he glanced at the floor and blinked in disbelief. "Where'd your jacket go? I swear I saw you drop it, but it's just gone."

"I let it dissolve," Ash admitted. "It takes significant energy to manifest a garment not on my person. I'd rather save my strength for Samael's host." When Chuy's expression fell, Ash was quick to address it. "They won't come looking here any time soon. They know I prefer the comforts of the city."

"I guess you would." Chuy glanced around again. "Don't seem to be any books here—not even a Bible." He arched an eyebrow. "What'll you do with your nights now?"

Ash's heart quite literally came to a complete standstill. *Breathe,* he told himself. *Just breathe. He doesn't know what he's saying. The future you've seen can and will be delayed. You're still a stranger to him.* Regardless, Chuy wasn't wrong. Without any studies to occupy him, Ashmedai's long nights were certain to come to no good.

"I'm going to get some air," Ash muttered, and he was gone before Chuy could say a word in response.

Chapter Five

Bryony knew what the commodore had come to say before Raeni even opened her mouth. The Black Armada's now mediocre medic was no longer worth the risk. The most Bryony could do was some basic first aid, and she'd caused innumerable problems for the armada. She'd brought a shapeshifter aboard, stolen their chief navigator, endangered *Papillon*'s captain twice now, and become a magnet for the Angel of Death, who didn't seem capable of showing up without nearly capsizing the flagship.

"I'm thinking it's best if I leave." Bryony preempted what she already knew was coming.

Raeni folded her arms and cocked her head. She stood a full five inches taller than Bryony, with dark, cool-toned skin and long, braided hair. These days, the commodore rarely needed to say a word to Bryony, who was getting too good at predicting her own failure.

Bryony stared down at the commodore's tall, leather boots. "I'll pack my bags today."

Raeni breathed a deep sigh. "We've decided to wait out the rest of hurricane season here." It sounded like an afterthought, like salve on the wound. "So if you need us at all in the coming weeks, you'll know where to find us."

"Yes, Commodore." It was all Bryony could do not to burst into tears. She'd never been fired from a job before. Hell, she'd never even had a real one.

"Medic." Raeni laid a firm hand on Bryony's shoulder. "Don't take it personally. You brought back the Angel of Healing. You've done more to advance the agenda of the Black Armada than anyone here, and we're grateful—"

"But you have to think of the crew," Bryony finished for her.

Raeni nodded. "Their safety comes first." It was an odd thing to say for someone who ran one of the most brutal black-market operations in the world, in which crew only retired by being thrown overboard. The armada's secrets were precious. No one got out alive. Bryony thought she really ought to be grateful she and Michael were allowed to leave at all, but she couldn't help feeling the sting of rejection.

It didn't help that the captain's quarters were still heavy with the aura of Michael's ill mood. He sat at the edge of his bunk and sulked while Bryony packed. He hadn't said anything to her since his father had dropped her in his lap and casually dealt a crippling blow to their relationship. Or perhaps she had dealt it. She should take responsibility anyway. It had been her choice to keep the truth from Michael. If she'd just told him about Azazel right away, there might have been a moment of jealousy and a quick explanation on her part, but at least Michael would still feel he could trust her. Right now, he couldn't even look at her.

It wasn't until she began haphazardly emptying her drawers and stuffing everything into her duffle bag that he even bothered to address her. "What are you doing?" he muttered.

"What does it look like I'm doing?" She was not in the mood to deal with his seraphic side right now, but she supposed she was the one who'd brought it out in the first place. "I have to leave the armada."

"Why?"

She stuffed another drawer of clothes into her bag. "Because I'm a walking disaster, that's why. Lately, everything bad that's happened is my fault."

Michael softened a touch. "Everything good is your fault too."

"It doesn't matter." She shook her head. "It's safer if I go, so I'm going."

A silence followed, during which she could have sworn she saw Michael warring with himself. The human in him loved her, but the seraph was so angry, so utterly betrayed. Finally, the winner took the wheel. "Are you taking *him* with you?" It was the seraph.

She gave up packing and punched her duffle bag. "I hadn't planned to, but I'm guessing you don't want anything to do with me anymore, since I'm so deceitful and all. I can't believe you're taking your father's side over mine."

"Did he lie?" He was efficient and deadly with his arguments when he was truly angry. Bryony had learned this about him early on.

"No," she snapped. "But I only kept the truth from you because I knew how you'd react. You warned me about your nature in the beginning, so I—"

"Why do you need another worshiper?" He broke in as though he hadn't heard her at all. "You told me I was enough."

Was it possible to feel any worse than this? The hurt in his voice tore her to shreds. "You *are* enough." She sighed and forced herself to look at him. "You're more than enough."

He stood and bellowed, "Why then? Explain it to me because I want to understand. I need to understand." Then he quieted again, which only meant his anger had increased. "I want to believe you had no choice. Please, tell me you didn't allow this. Tell me he forced it on you, so I can go out there and rip him apart."

"Nothing was forced on me. It was a tactical decision. Please don't rip him apart." The threat of violence wasn't like Michael at all. He sounded like a stranger, and she had to remind herself it was the seraph in him that drove it. It all came down to fear. He'd bonded to her, probably more powerfully than any animal or human ever could, and the thought of losing her sent him into fits of irrational terror. She'd seen the seraph rear its head before, so it was no surprise to see it again now. What did surprise her was the baselessness of what brought it out. "I'm not going to leave you for an angel," she said.

"Then what do you call this?" He gestured to her bag. "It looks like leaving to me. So I'll ask again. Are you taking him with you?"

"If he wants to come, he can come." Bryony flinched at the sight of Samael's giant son clenching his fists, not because she feared he would hurt her, but because she hated having hurt him. She attempted to soothe him with the truth. "I assumed you'd be coming with me."

"Of course I'm coming with you—I love you!" His words did not match his tone at all. "You're never getting rid of me. I'll follow you for the rest of your life!"

"Good!" she shouted back. "That's exactly what I want!"

"Good!" He fumed and blushed, and his befuddlement was so adorable she didn't quite know what to do with it. For a moment, he wavered and lowered his voice. "I just . . . I never wanted to be part of a three-way relationship."

"It's not a three-way relationship."

"It is." Michael's cheeks darkened again. "He loves you. I'm not a fool, I can see as much. He loves you, and he worships you, and . . . And you don't need me anymore." He choked on his father's words.

Bryony quietly seethed, wishing Samael were here now so she could slap him. Angel of Death or not, how dare he use his own son as a pawn in his game? How dare he needlessly hurt someone so open and easy, and leave Bryony with no idea how to fix it? Nothing was worth hurting Michael like this. Why couldn't an immortal angel understand something as obvious as that? Bryony swallowed her rage and tried to speak in a measured voice. "Michael, I'm not with you because I need you. I already told you that."

"No." He countered quietly at first, though his words were dripping with sarcasm. "No, you're with me because I'm nice and I make you feel safe. I'm sure you'd never dream of leaving me for a watcher now that you've got a taste for angels." His voice rose. "Why on earth would you want a lover as perfect as Azazel when you have an absurd, lumbering giant to look forward to every night?"

Bryony closed her eyes and tried to compose herself. "You are neither of those things," she said, but she couldn't be sure he heard her. He seemed to be in his own bitter world.

"Why would you want an angel of legendary beauty and talent when you have a perfectly good carnival attraction on your arm? Such a shame to lose out on all that awkward attention. I'm sure you'd miss having to answer repeated questions about the size of my—"

"Stop!" Bryony shouted. Who even was he right now?

Tears welled in his eyes, but he didn't stop. It felt almost as though he couldn't stop, even if he wanted to. "Why would you want an immortal husband who'll be young and flawless forever, and has god knows how many years of experience in bed, when you could just keep your sad, aging fiancé who eats you out of house and home and has to blindfold you just to—"

"Michael!" That was quite enough. He could clearly insult himself forever, and Bryony was having trouble keeping up. She needed a moment to think of how to respond to his barrage of self-inflicted vitriol. But the look on his face, his whitened knuckles, and his shoulders drawn to his ears told her he wasn't ready to hear anything she had to say. He would only think she was placating him.

The truth was she loved Michael more than anyone else in the world. He was the most beautiful person she'd ever met, inside and out. He was graceful and strong, and she was ridiculously attracted to him. Even now, as he stood before her trembling with rage and fear, she wanted to climb him like a tree and kiss that pulsing vein in his neck until his skin warmed with need for her, until he took her to his bunk and made her world disappear in a haze of pleasure. She ached for him, but how could she convince him of that when he believed himself so fundamentally undesirable? All she could do was mutter, "You don't know anything."

When someone knocked on the door, Bryony automatically said, "Come in," before she realized it wasn't the best time for guests. Worse, when the door opened, it was none other than Azazel himself who stood in its frame. *Perfect.* Bryony groaned.

"Couldn't help but hear you, darlings." The watcher closed the door behind him and glided into the room. To Michael, he said, "I do appreciate the compliments, but I must say you were being a bit hard on yourself."

Michael stiffened and hissed, "Get out."

Azazel sat back comfortably against the table with a contented sigh. "I'm afraid that's not going to happen, petal. I've made a mess, it seems, and I intend to clean it up. No doubt you have questions, so ask."

Michael spun around and looked to Bryony. She shrugged and shook her head. "He's talking to you, Michael."

"Yes, Michael." Azza almost sang the name. "I intend to engage you specifically. You believe I've seduced your beloved. Not a completely unfounded concern—I'll give you that. You can't help imagining how far we must have taken things, but you're too afraid to ask her, so you've let your imagination run amok. Your thoughts have gone to the very worst places, and it will only escalate as the hours wear on. Soon, you'll be picturing our wedding, which will look nothing like the one I would have had, mind you, but it will torture you all the same."

Michael gaped at him, and Azza chuckled. "Now you're wondering how I know all your most intimate thoughts and shameful fantasies." He shrugged his elegant shoulders. "I can only say I've seen this sort of thing many times before. You're not unique. Right now, you need answers to quiet your pitiless imagination. But you're afraid if you ask your beloved outright, she'll leave you in a storm of righteous indignation, and she would be right to do so. You're afraid to accuse her, so accuse me. Ask, petal. I swear to answer every question honestly."

Michael glanced at Bryony, who nodded to encourage him. If Azza did manage to set this right, she would owe him even more than she already did. Michael turned back and hesitated. He pinched his lips between his teeth before the question finally burst out of him. "Did you sleep with her?"

Azza leaned back on his hands. "I do not sleep, so the direct answer to that question is no. However, I believe you mean to ask whether I've had sexual relations with the girl." He paused, and Bryony got the distinct impression he enjoyed the tension he created, just a touch. "The answer to that is also no."

Michael's shoulders visibly relaxed. He closed his eyes and breathed deep, readying himself for his next question. "Did you touch her?"

"Of course I touched her, but again, I don't believe that's what you really mean to ask."

"Fine," Michael grumbled. "Were you ever with her in a way that was . . . intimate?"

"Intimate to whom?"

"To her! To you! I don't care. Both." Michael was beginning to lose his usually boundless patience again, and Bryony couldn't blame him.

Azza finally answered. "To her, I don't think so. To me, absolutely."

Michael's shoulders rose again, and Bryony couldn't help the color that bloomed in her cheeks. When had they been intimate? Sure, they'd had a couple false starts, but nothing serious. She'd been much more intimate with near strangers than she was with Azza. She'd never even undressed around him. What had they done that meant so much more to him than it had to her? Michael ground his teeth in barely suppressed agony, and Bryony hated herself a little for failing to unmask Azazel sooner than she had.

"Did you kiss her?" Michael's deep voice cracked.

Azazel didn't hesitate this time. "Yes."

The whimper that escaped Michael's lips sent an empathetic pang through Bryony's heart. She hadn't really thought about how any of this looked from his perspective. This revelation felt almost as bad as the one in which he'd discovered she was both a liar and a god. Why he ever trusted her was beyond her.

"I was disguised as you, petal," Azza mercifully clarified. "She thought she was kissing you."

It was something, but clearly not enough. Michael asked his last question with the voice of a man who was already defeated. "Do you love her?"

The angel answered, "Yes."

Michael shuddered, dragged his feet across the cabin, and dropped onto the edge of his bunk. Then he doubled over and buried his face in his hands.

To Bryony's surprise, Azza followed and sat beside him. "You're treading on precarious ground," he said. "You've confused worship with sex. Are you aware of that?"

Almost imperceptibly, Michael nodded.

"Good. Awareness is the first step." Azza folded his hands in his lap before he continued, and Bryony was certain she saw a momentary hint of nervousness in him, a kind of stage fright that made her think he'd never really done this before. If that was true, he didn't let it creep into his voice. "Jealousy doesn't belong in worship. If you weren't confused, you'd be pleased your religion was growing. More congregants means a stronger god, a healthier god."

Michael nodded but didn't remove his head from his hands.

"You need to understand, I love her as my god. Because of what I am, worship comes naturally to me, certainly more naturally than it comes to you. I couldn't stop myself when she showed mercy. It was . . . so rare." His voice caught, and Bryony recalled how hard he'd wept when she'd told him he did not deserve to suffer, how he'd turned to glass and she'd thought he was dead. He cleared his throat and pressed on. "For some reason, you believe that means I want to take her to bed. It doesn't. I've not confused worship with sex the way you have." He paused. "The way your father has."

Michael's head shot up at that. He sat rigid and staring, and his hands gripped the edge of his mattress in a familiar gesture of deep conflict.

"Now you see how Samael has led you astray." Azazel smiled gently. "You managed it as well as you could, petal, but the two loves have blended in you. I can see that clear as day. You're on the brink of losing the battle. You're on the brink of losing your mind."

Bryony started to protest, but Azza held up a hand to quiet her. It wasn't possible, was it? Michael had promised he could fight it. He'd sworn he was not like his father, but could he have been wrong? It felt like he'd just been given a terminal diagnosis. *Azza's a surgeon,* she told herself, *carving a tumor from a dying heart. Let him work.*

"You need to disentangle your loves," Azazel said. "It won't be easy, but you haven't lost yet." His voice was kind and reassuring, and he reached up to squeeze Michael's shoulder. "I know you can do it."

Though Michael was several heads taller than the angel, he looked like a lost child when he glanced down and asked, "But how?"

"It's a practice," Azza said. "You'll learn it in time. I'll give you three tips to help you get started. First, keep in mind your god was worshiped before you came into her life. An entire community once loved her as I do. It should not be at all surprising when she begins to gather new congregants, and she will. Gods can't help it. Second, ease off worshipping her yourself. It isn't good for you. It only complicates matters. I'm not suggesting you stop completely. Just ease off, and should you ever decide to quit, remember that I can sustain her alone, and I will."

At that, Michael gripped the edge of his bunk so tight Bryony was surprised he didn't puncture the mattress.

It did not go unnoticed by the angel. "Remember to disentangle your loves. She doesn't need you in order to survive, and that's a good thing. You only want her to need you because you're afraid to lose her. Conquer your fear. Do not desire weakness in your beloved."

Michael's eyes flicked to Azza and back again in a subtle show of the anger he was fighting to suppress.

Azza just shook his head. "My third and final tip is this. If you ever find yourself losing the battle again, promise you'll come to me. I'll talk you through it. Don't try to fight it on your own." His voice softened. "I'll be here for you."

All Michael's anger seemed to melt away the instant he heard those five words. "Why?"

"Because I wasn't there for my daughters, and your father wasn't there for you." Azazel stood. On his feet, he could look Michael directly in the eyes. "We were both wrong, Samael and I, and I'm sorry for that. You deserved better. So did my girls. I'll never get another chance to be there for them. Some wrongs cannot be righted, but I'd like to atone at least." The angel reached out and cupped a hand to Michael's flushed cheek. "You're so young, petal. You're so young, and you're trying so hard to be good." His voice caught. "I won't let you down the way he did. Count on it."

On his way out the door, Azazel stooped to kiss Bryony's forehead and hugged her briefly to his chest. As he did, he murmured, "That one will love you to the end of time. You caught a treasure in your web, little orb-weaver. Don't ever let him go."

CHAPTER SIX

"What's that mean exactly, being king of the demons?" Chuy asked absently. Most of his attention was taken by the red-and-black checkerboard on the table in front of him.

"Very little, I'm afraid." Ash leaned back in his chair and watched the captain contemplate his next move. He enjoyed when Chuy was distracted and he didn't have to feign disinterest. He could stare at the bones of those nimble fingers with wild abandon. "It used to mean I was the oldest and wisest of my kind, although there's still some debate about that. These days, those who would be my subjects are either imprisoned or enslaved. Until they're freed again, my title is practically meaningless."

"You gonna try and free 'em one day?"

The question jarred the demon king because he hadn't even considered it, and he suddenly couldn't understand why. All those damned souls were his people. He'd grown up among many of them, hadn't he? He knew them by name, by face, by species. But when he'd finally broken out of his own prison, the first creature he'd sought to free was Azazel, a watcher. Perhaps the task of freeing the demons was so insurmountable, he hadn't considered it a possibility. But what kind of king was he if he didn't even try?

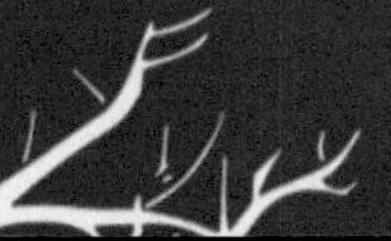

Chuy took his turn and leaned back with a satisfied grin. "If you ever do free 'em, I'll have to start calling you Moses."

Ash blanched at the suggestion. "I think not. Anyway, no more questions. You're taking the jackpot before the game is over."

The game had begun as an innocent way to pass the time, but Ash hadn't been able to resist making it into a wager. Chuy, having no belongings to gamble with, came up with the idea of playing for questions. The winner would be allowed to ask one question that the loser had no choice but to answer. Ash didn't hesitate to agree to it because he had no doubt about his ability to win. His unforeseen challenge became the erratic way Chuy played. No matter how good the demon king's strategy was, his opponent could not be predicted. It was infuriating, and Ash was already losing.

He blinked down at the board after Chuy finally moved. "Why the hell did you do that?"

Chuy shrugged. "Had a feeling it'd work out."

Impossible. The man was impossible. Ash cracked his knuckles and made what would turn out to be his last move.

Then Chuy won, knocked back his chair, and leapt to his feet. "Yes!" He punched the air in triumph. "Haha! Nuevo rey, nueva ley. Now you *have* to answer, demon."

Ash didn't like where this was headed. How could he have lost? It was unthinkable. Now he'd have to answer whatever question Chuy asked him. He'd lost a wager, and the demon king always, always anted up. It was compulsory. He braced himself for the worst.

Chuy could ask about his own future, his love life, or his death. He could ask to know the location of ancient treasures or the secret nature of the universe. Worst of all, he could ask how to pronounce the Ineffable Name—effectively the sonic key to the world of the angels—and Ash would have no choice but to teach it to him. If Chuy ever used that key to unlock the gates of heaven and enter the angels' realm, chances were, he would not survive it. Revealing the Ineffable Name had been the mistake that instigated the fall of the watchers, and

Ash had been quick to ridicule their chief captain, Shemjaza, for having made it. Now Ash was about to get his comeuppance. Over checkers. Love really did make a person incurably stupid.

But once again, Ashmedai failed to predict the captain's next move. Chuy took one long, deep breath and asked, "How come you never take your shoes off?"

Unbelievable. Ash had prepared himself for a difficult question with a sad or even dangerous answer. What he hadn't prepared himself for was an answer that would humiliate him. His eyes grew wide, and he gripped the edge of the table too tightly. As a reflex, he slid his feet back under his chair to hide them. "Ask something else."

Chuy crossed his arms and shook his head.

Ash stood, shaking. "Ask something else. Ask something else! *Ask something else!*" His demand dissolved into pleading. Even to him, his voice sounded pathetic, but he couldn't help himself. He didn't want to answer. He hated his feet. They were the only part of his mortal body he'd never managed to replicate. No matter what shape he took, they always looked like the feet of a giant rooster. They revealed him as some kind of absurd chimera rather than the well-dressed gentleman he worked so hard to epitomize.

For the briefest moment, Chuy actually recoiled from him, and Ash immediately regretted his outburst. He fell back into his chair, dropped his head in his hands, and muttered, "Forgive me."

From behind his hands, Ash heard Chuy sigh, no doubt summoning the courage he needed to stand his ground and demand an answer. Ash readied himself to be exposed, taunted, and disgraced. But again, he was wrong. What the captain had taken a moment to summon was mercy. "Something else, eh?" Chuy sat and lazily rocked his chair back on two legs. "Let's see . . . Hmm . . ."

Mercy. Ash stared, open-mouthed. No man would knowingly relinquish an ounce of control over the demon king, would he? It was reckless, inadvisable, unforgivably stupid. Only a fool would release a netted tiger, no matter how much the animal begged. But contrary to every expectation and lived experience Ash had, Chuy stood over the tiger in his net and gently untangled it. And all the beast could do in response was purr.

After a moment of thought, Chuy leaned on his elbow and rested his chin in the palm of his hand. "Okay. New question. What did you mean when you said I'd break your heart?"

Mercy aside, it seemed the captain was not going to let him off easy. At least this was the kind of difficult question Ash had prepared himself for. "Visions are not often clear. My sight works much like anyone else's, but with time instead of distance. The further from now the event is, the bigger it needs to be for me to see it clearly. If it's too close, I'll see only part of it, and maybe a hundred years down the road, I'll have enough perspective to see it for what it was. My own broken heart was . . . huge and close. I couldn't see all of it, just the break itself. But I saw it in *your* future, which means you have to be instrumental."

Chuy knit his brow and frowned. "You sure you have no idea how I do it? If you could tell me, I might be able to—ya know—not."

Ash shook his head with an involuntary smile. He'd answered the question as far as he was concerned. He didn't need to say more, but the earnest expression on Chuy's face was downright irresistible. Still, what could he say? To admit to the relationship itself would be a mistake. No matter how impossible it had proven in the past, Ash was determined to delay the future he'd seen. "I wish I knew how it happens," he said. "All it means is that you are, for some reason, important to me. You could be stolen, escape, or die. You could lose your innocence. You could kill me." *You could hate me and fall in love with someone else.*

"Kill you?" Chuy snorted. "Nah. I'm not the sort to go around killing people unless I'm afraid for my life, and you don't seem the sort to make me fear for my life." He shrugged. "Probably, it just means I die. Bound to happen sooner or later, right?"

Correct. Chuy was one hundred percent mortal, so the death of his body would mean the death of him. Ash couldn't bear to think of it, though he'd seen Chuy's absence looming like dark clouds on the horizon. One of the problems with seeing time all at once was the way the pain of life overshadowed the joy. People always talked about how the little joys in life made all the pain worth it. From Ash's perspective, that wasn't true at all. There was infinitely more suffering in the end, and Ash was sick of it.

Thankfully, Chuy seemed to have tired of the conversation. He stretched in his chair, and Ash had to look down at the checkerboard. The way those tattoos climbed the captain's arms and moved with his flesh sent shivers down Ashmedai's perfectly fabricated spine. *Beautiful, beautiful man.*

"Well, I hate to admit it," Chuy said. "But I've gotta eat. Is there food here?" He rose and began opening all the cupboards until he found one filled with cans of chili, corn, soup, and peas. There was nothing particularly seductive in anything he was doing. All the same, Ash found himself growing uncomfortably warm as he watched the captain squint at the labels on each can. "Hm." Chuy wrinkled his nose. "Not such a great selection." Ash let out the breath he'd been holding. This was getting ridiculous. Why was his desire so powerful? It shouldn't be this bad. Not unless—

Ash stood, his eyes wide. In the last twenty-four hours, three things had become painfully clear. First, despite his best efforts, he was falling in love. Second, his cherubic side desired to please the object of his affection. Third, what the object of his affection wanted right now, according to his own subconscious observations, was to be desired.

Oblivious to his host's new revelation, Chuy turned and nearly jumped out of his skin when he saw Ash's expression. "Uh . . ." He laughed nervously. "I'll need fire to cook."

Perfect. An excuse to get some air. "I'll collect more firewood." Ash was on his way out the door when an unwelcome thought occurred to him. He hadn't built a fire in the first place. It was evening, and it was autumn, and he hadn't even bothered to build a fire. He turned to his captive and noticed how the man held himself. His hands were on his elbows, his shoulders hunched. He was freezing. Ash marched over to him. "Why didn't you tell me you were cold?"

Chuy smiled and shrugged. "Oh, you know. Force of habit, I guess. Just soldier on, and things'll get better."

"I should have built a fire sooner." Ash narrowed his eyes. "You have to tell me these things. I don't get cold or hungry." He reached out to touch the gooseflesh on Chuy's arm but caught himself and withdrew. "I might have made you a coat at least," he murmured.

"You said it took a lot of energy to manifest clothes you aren't wearing."

"There's a difference between energy well spent and energy wasted." Ash swallowed hard. This was not going to be easy, in more ways than one. "Please, let me make you a coat," he said, sealing his own fate.

"Eh, why not?" Chuy spread his arms. "Sure, let's do it. Make me a coat, Your Majesty." He laughed, but Ash was far from laughing. *Your Majesty.*

"Hold still." Ash pressed the palm of his right hand to the captain's chest.

The beating of Chuy's heart quickened. "Uh . . . Will it hurt or anything?"

"It's a coat," Ash said. "It will feel like a coat." He was certain he'd assuaged Chuy's fears, but the heart under his palm kept up its accelerated pace. Ash stepped closer. Chuy's heart beat faster. And that's when the demon king knew, beyond a shadow of a doubt, the attraction was already mutual.

It was too soon. It was far too soon.

Ash closed his eyes and thought of wool, of woven strands and stitched seams. He thought of buttons and black dye and warmth. He dressed his captive in the best he could create, and all the while, the man's heart responded to his touch. When Ash opened his eyes again, Chuy was wearing a black wool coat that Ash was certain could not have looked better on anyone else's body.

Slowly, Ash pulled his hand away. It was like withdrawing from a house of cards after placing the final A-frame. "Now you can keep tabs on me," Ash said and immediately groaned at his own impulsivity. What was this? More flirtation? The hint of a promise? "What I mean to say is the coat will dissolve if I weaken or travel too far from you." No, that didn't make it any better.

"How far is too far?" Chuy's voice was low and nervous, and Ash wished he didn't know why.

"I'm not sure exactly. I've never tested it."

"Let's not start now."

"No. Let's not." Ashmedai did not step back when he could have. He waited, breathing in the scent of the captain, who smelled like the calm after a storm, like peace after violence, like the sea at night. He was everything Ash ever wanted. Life without him was as good as death.

Already . . .

Already . . .

I love you.

Ashmedai took another sip of the wine in the well.

CHAPTER SEVEN

Bryony had nowhere to go but home. She'd given it as much thought as she cared to, and this was the conclusion she'd come to. Anywhere public or densely populated would be too dangerous. Samael did not generally appear subtly or carefully, and he was bound to appear sooner or later. She was betting on sooner. If recent events were anything to go on, one virtue the Angel of Death most certainly lacked was patience.

Home was a blue, Victorian farmhouse with peeling paint and a thousand memories built up like dust on the furniture. Since her father's death, the land remained unworked and wild, except for a little grove of plum trees right beside the house. Bryony wasted no time in phoning Martha when she, Michael, and Azza arrived. She made a pretense of needing to get a message to Bill, but Martha—being Martha—took it as an invitation to come over. And Bill—being Loki—followed right behind her, invitation be damned.

That evening, the five of them fell into an easy, almost familial routine. Azazel and Martha worked together well. He was a warm, creative soul, and she a stalwart fortress of pragmatism. They prepared a meal together and exchanged near constant encouragement and flattery. It really was a wonder how quickly they seemed to bond. Loki was as bombastic and attention-seeking as ever, always prodding at Michael, who never did rise to the bait. And Bryony was happy to observe them all from the sidelines, feeling so content she almost forgot why they were there.

When thunder struck, Bryony covered her ears and screamed. Maybe at first she was startled, but when she realized what the sound meant, her scream became one of rage and frustration. Samael truly was going to ruin the rest of her life. He was going to appear in all her happiest moments and inject his misery into them. He would never let her forget she'd made the grave error of inviting him into her life, even after everyone—including him—had warned her not to. It took her a beat too long to stop screaming, and no doubt everyone already knew why. "Excuse me." She stood at last. "I believe someone is waiting for me."

Loki caught her arm. He'd heard the thunder before. He knew what it meant. "Don't you dare go out there alone," he said.

"She has to." Michael bowed his head. "She's the only one who can even look at him. The rest of us are useless."

"If that blind snake wants to speak to her, he can try and find her first."

"He already has," Michael said. "His weapon is a beacon for him. He'll always find her as long as she's wearing it." The defeat in his voice was unmistakable. Michael, the nearly eight-foot-tall, legendary godhunter of the Black Armada, couldn't even stand before his own father. It must have felt like the epitome of failure.

Bryony drew a deep breath, cloaked herself in melancholy, and headed for the back door. Martha squeezed her arm on her way out. "We'll be right here," she said, and Bryony almost lost her composure at that simple display of support. No matter how alone she felt in dealing with the Angel of Death, Bryony would know there were people waiting for her mere feet away. Friends. Family. Someone cared what happened to her, and that was all she needed.

The Angel of Death waited in her backyard. He manifested as a smaller version of the serpentine seraph that descended upon *Dragonfly* the day she'd met him. His twelve wings curled and uncurled as though each was a separate entity with a mind of its own. His many eye-shaped voids blinked in and out of existence like tiny black holes.

"I have come to discuss my progress," he said. His thunderous voice flooded and overwhelmed her. It was the roar of an angry sea in her ears. An unanticipated rush of fear pulsed through her. She had to remind herself that fear on its own was meaningless to keep from curling into a fetal ball on the ground.

"Please take your other form, Sama." She closed her eyes to him, hoping his abbreviated name would warm him to her again. "Please, this is too much." Then she remembered that he considered himself misshapen and ugly. "It's beautiful, but it's too much."

The world quieted at once, and Bryony was left standing with the wingless version of the graveyard angel. In the moonlight, he looked even more like white marble than he had before, though his skin, hair, and robe moved like he was a living, bleeding thing.

"I have come to discuss my progress," he repeated. Now his voice had that soft, mesmerizing tone she recognized as his. Briefly, she wished the death sword had remained a scythe. A staff to lean on would have been helpful for this occasion. She was too close to keeling over, not only from the proximity of death incarnate, but from the stress of knowing she was secretly working against him.

"Okay," was all the response she could manage. Best to keep her responses short anyway. Fewer chances to put her foot in it.

Samael either didn't notice or didn't care that she was scared beyond speech. Perhaps he was just used to it. "My host tracked Ashmedai to a hotel in the city." Bryony held her breath at the angel's well-timed pause. "He was gone by the time they arrived." She let it out again, but Samael wasn't finished. "He appears to have left earlier than his schedule dictated. He had paid for several more nights. Some of my host are of the opinion that the demon king was warned and fled."

Another pause. Bryony cleared her throat. "Oh, was he?"

She shrank back when the angel tilted his face down to her, certain her feigned ignorance was not remotely convincing. "Someone is working against you, Ms. Moss. I imagine that is why you have abandoned the armada."

How should she respond to that? Not at all, she decided. Let him come to whatever conclusions he was going to come to anyway.

He stood uncannily still in the moonlight. "I assure you, my host is still searching and will find your captain soon. Then I will eliminate his value so the demon king will no longer want him. I ask, in the meantime, that you find a new conjuring partner. Though there aren't many who can call up the archangel Michael, they do exist."

"Right." Bryony stared at the grass and dragged her toe along it to flatten it first in one direction and then in the other. "It isn't very sporting, though, is it? Conjuring him just to kill him. Shouldn't we maybe try to find him the regular way?"

To her utter shock and horror, the Angel of Death laughed at her. "This is not a game, Ms. Moss. Even if it were, do you think the archangel Michael would afford you the same courtesy? No, he would not. He killed millions with a thought, and he'd do it again if he felt threatened. One woman would not give him a moment's hesitation, especially not a woman who was in any way related to me." He nodded, and a wicked smile crossed his face. "Speaking of which, our business being concluded for today, I wish to be invited into your home."

"What?" Bryony practically shouted the question at him.

He turned his face to the sky in mock thought. "For tea," he concluded. "We are family, are we not? This is your home, I assume. Is it not?"

"Yes, it's my home, but—"

"Is my son inside?"

Relentless. The Angel of Death was relentless. And impatient, Bryony reminded herself. "Yes, he's inside, but he's not too happy with you right now. Are you sure you want to see him?"

"He is my son."

"Right." She rolled her eyes. Samael cared nothing for Michael. He wasn't here for tea or to visit his son. He was here to size Bryony up and intimidate her. She knew that much, but when he held out his hand, she had to take it. She guided him to her veranda. "There are four stairs here," she said.

"Up or down?"

That was information she hadn't thought to give. She blushed and then wondered why she was still worried about offending the beast who'd tried to destroy her relationship. "Up." She spoke loudly to give anyone who wanted to leave the chance to do so. "We'll enter the kitchen through the back door."

When she opened the door, she saw four figures fall to her kitchen floor. "Oh, for the love of god." She heaved an exhausted sigh. "I tried to warn you all."

"They didn't want you to deal with this alone." Michael spoke through unacknowledged tears. "Neither did I."

Samael recognized that exceptionally low voice at once. "Hello, son." Years of denying he even had a living son, and now he was going to hammer the point home every chance he got.

Michael responded with a terse greeting. "Father."

That seemed to satisfy the graveyard angel, who let go of Bryony's hand and stood proudly in the middle of her kitchen. The *Angel of Death* was in her kitchen. Had she not been so focused on resisting his poison, she might have hyperventilated at the thought. "Now I wish to be introduced to your friends," he said.

Bryony hesitated. Her world—her precious, little world—was being invaded by a monster. But what choice did she have? It was either placate the Angel of Death or insult him. Insulting him did not seem wise. "Well, um . . . Michael and Azazel you already know."

Samael bobbed his head in greeting. His performance of formal etiquette was unsettling. To Bryony, the occasion began to feel like the most awkward haunted dinner party anyone could ever dream of or imagine.

What exactly was Samael playing at? She didn't dare ask. "To your left is . . ." She mouthed a quick apology. How was one supposed to introduce one legendary creature to another? "Loki . . . the uh . . . the Norse trickster."

"*The* Loki?" Samael grinned. "I have certainly heard of you. What a surprise. It is a pleasure." He held out a hand in greeting, but Loki did not take it. The angel's hand hovered for several seconds before he casually withdrew it, as though such contempt for him was to be expected and did not bother him in the least. Bryony didn't buy the act. It had to bother him. No one was really an island. "Strange friends you have, Ms. Moss," Samael mused. "An escaped watcher and an exiled Jötunn. I wonder, will you invite them to your wedding?" He tapped his chin with a forefinger. "Will you invite me?"

Bryony coughed to hide her shock. "I . . . I think that might pose a few problems, don't you?" The Angel of Death frowned as though he'd actually expected an invitation. An image of walking down the aisle surrounded by a prostrate and wailing audience flashed through her imagination. God it would be terrible.

"Are you certain there would be a problem?" The corners of Samael's mouth twitched. "Even if I attended *in fair and comely form, without noise or—*"

"Okay!" Bryony cut him off. "That horse has been dead and buried for a week at least, and you just keep digging it up to beat it."

From her place on the floor, Martha stifled a laugh. Loki's eyes darted to her in horror.

"A woman." Samael turned vaguely in her direction. "I have not been introduced."

Loki growled, "Nor will you ever." The effort the Jötunn expended to push himself up with his shaking arms was downright impressive. "Stay away from her." He fell to the floor and pushed himself up again, determined. "Back off." His eyes flickered with orange light, but Bryony doubted there was much he could do. This was death, and no one escaped its influence, not even the immortals. It was a lesson Bryony had learned early on. As a force of nature, grief was nothing to trifle with.

Martha, on the other hand, seemed better able to deal with the poison in the room. Her eyes wept, but her body did not shudder. She wore a look of deep determination as she somehow found the strength to raise her arm and hold out her hand to the indomitable Angel of Death.

"Martha Cohen," she said. "Owner of Martha's Café." The steadiness of her voice was a shock to everyone in the room, Samael included. "It's a pleasure to meet you, sir." She kept her hand extended, waiting. Loki just stared at her, slack-jawed, as though he couldn't believe she even existed outside his nightmares.

For a moment, Bryony was conflicted. Loki glared at her from the floor, warning her to keep quiet, but Martha's look was just as stern. Between the two of them, Bryony was only a little surprised to discover it was Martha's disapproval she feared more.

"Martha is offering her hand," she said to Samael, and when he reached out, she helped guide him to where Martha waited.

The graveyard angel crouched to take the woman's hand. "I am Samael." He paused and apparently decided to echo Martha's introduction by including his own position. "Angel of Death."

Though Martha was on her knees, doubled over with her chin to her chest and her eyes staring at the black-and-white checkered floor, she still managed to shake that otherworldly hand. Bryony had never seen a braver person in her life.

Samael did not take it for granted either. "I appreciate the effort your introduction has cost you, Ms. Cohen. Civility is rare where I am concerned. I will not forget yours." Then he stood and turned back to Bryony. "Thank you for the introductions, Ms. Moss. Now I wish to be shown more of your home."

In a rare moment of agreement, Michael and Loki eyed one another, and both their looks plainly said, *What the hell does that creep think he's doing?*

The excuse to remove Samael from her companions' sight was not one Bryony was going to pass up. "Come with me then." She offered her arm and led the angel to her living room. She recalled how shocking it had been when Azazel first sat before her hearth, and she laughed at her younger, more naïve self. Azazel was a kitten in comparison. Her every nerve tingled with the instinct to run as she gently laid the angel's hand on the back of her couch. "This is the living room couch. To your left is a chair, and in front of us there's a hearth. Azza has built a fire and left all the windows open."

Samael nodded. "I feel it. He is a strange one."

"We all have our quirks." Bryony found it got easier to talk to the Angel of Death as she guided him further into the heart of her home, and she wasn't at all certain that was a good thing. When they came to the parlor, she showed him her father's old, upright piano.

To Bryony's shock, the angel took his time examining the instrument. He ran his fingers along the top, and she was suddenly aware she hadn't dusted in a while. He drew his palm over the decorative relief on the front, lifted the lid, and let his fingers slip silently over the keys. Then he depressed one. The instrument sang out, and Samael played another note, and another, and another, seemingly at random.

Bryony held her breath as he laid his hand over many keys at once and suddenly played them all. It was a cacophonous, dissonant sound. To her horror, he did it three more times. She could imagine Azza cringing in the kitchen. She hoped he wouldn't think it was her treating her piano like a child's toy, or he would never let her hear the end of it.

Samael lowered the lid. "It is a good piano," he concluded.

How he could tell just by smashing all the keys at once, Bryony had no idea. But the incident got her thinking about how close she had just come to losing her piano along with everything else in her house. "You kept your distance this time, didn't you? When you descended, you kept your distance to spare my house."

He blinked down at her. "I did."

"Thank you," she said and found she meant it. "May I show you one more thing?" He nodded, and she led him out the front door. "There are four steps down." She walked with him until they reached her little plum grove, and then she laid his palm against the trunk of a tree.

"These trees were my sanctuary when I was a girl. When they bloom, this becomes the most beautiful room in my home." She watched as he slowly paced the perimeter, found each tree and traced his fingers over their rough trunks. "I'd like to keep it, if I may," she said. "Can you remember where it is next time you visit?"

Partway around the grove, the angel froze and caught his breath. But why? What had she said that took him off guard? Was it the suggestion that he might return? But of course, he would have to come back to ensure she fulfilled her end of their contract. Perhaps it was her use of the word *visit*, as though she were inviting a social call. As soon as she considered the idea, she knew she'd hit upon the truth, and Samael as good as confirmed it when he turned to her and said, "Shall we sit down for tea now?"

Chapter Eight

With the Angel of Death comfortably settled on her couch, Bryony went to the kitchen to make his tea. By now, she was on autopilot. Everyone else, huddled around her kitchen table, leapt up as soon as they saw her.

"Is he gone?" Michael asked.

Still dazed, Bryony shook her head. "He . . . He wants tea."

Michael's expression twisted into one of such horror and disgust she scarcely recognized him. Loki predictably growled. Only Azza was of any help whatsoever. "Well, of course he does, darling," he said. "My goodness but we've been atrocious hosts, haven't we?" Good manners seemed to trump everything for the watcher. "Let me make it for you. Did he tell you what kind he wanted?"

"No," Bryony answered. "But . . . maybe we shouldn't caffeinate him."

Michael groaned. "It's a bit late to worry about exciting him, don't you think?"

Meanwhile, Azazel had already put the kettle on, and Martha began raiding the stash of loose-leaf tea she herself had supplied. "Something herbal then," she said. "You don't happen to know your father's flavor preferences, do you, Michael?"

Michael just gaped at her, unused to Martha's ability to adapt with aplomb to the world's most absurd and trying circumstances.

When it became apparent she'd be getting no input from her companions, Martha decided on her own. "Chamomile. He seems the type to like chamomile."

"And what type is that?" Loki asked, still horrified.

She shrugged. "The strong, silent type, I guess."

That seemed to break the tension for Azazel, who laughed heartily and put an arm around Martha's waist. "I love this woman. You know, I really think I do."

Bryony finally made her way back to her living room carrying two of her best teacups on saucers, and doing everything in her power to remain steady despite the oppressive presence of the seraph in her living room. She set her own cup on her coffee table. "I hope you like chamomile."

He held out his hand, and she brought the saucer to him. Then she sat in the chair beside the fire and picked up her own cup. Her hands trembled. She quickly took her cup off the saucer so the graveyard angel would not hear it rattling. For several agonizing minutes, they held their tea in silence. Neither one of them took a sip. Bryony assumed hers would be too hot, but she wasn't sure what Samael's reason for hesitation could be. Surely, he wasn't worried he would burn his tongue.

At last, he brought his cup to his lips and muttered into it. "Why do you call me beautiful?" His voice was so quiet and dreamlike that Bryony struggled to determine whether she heard or imagined it.

The Angel of Death sipped his tea, and Bryony felt she'd better answer him quickly so she did not appear to be lying. "Because it's true."

"It is not." He placed his cup in its saucer.

"Well," she said, "that's just your opinion."

"It is not." He lifted his cup again, and this time, he did not drink from it. If she didn't know any better, Bryony would have thought he was fidgeting. "Do you know how angels get their names, Ms. Moss?"

Bryony shrugged, quickly realized her mistake, and spoke her answer aloud. "Sort of. Not really."

"We're named for the essence we most closely resemble. My name means poison because that is what I most closely resemble. Do you think poison is beautiful?"

She wrinkled her nose. There were certainly poisons that could be considered beautiful—some were flowers, for example—but doubtless that was not the response the angel was looking for. "Fine," she conceded. "But you have another name, don't you? I mean who cares what the humans call you? What's your name in your own language?"

The angel chuckled, and the sound was so dark Bryony actually shivered despite being a bit too close to the fire. "You would not want to know it, Ms. Moss, even if you were willing to come close enough to receive it, but I will attempt to translate." He thought a moment. "Tell me, have you ever looked into the eyes of a corpse?"

The question jarred her, and not just because she hadn't expected it. Unbidden, the images of her postmortem mother, father, and little brother flashed before her eyes. They were always there, of course, quietly buried under everything else in her life. But now they'd been brought to the surface, and it was all she could do to keep from bursting into tears. She whispered her answer. "Yes."

Samael noted her discomfort and frowned. "The emptiness you see in that stare, the loss, the disgusting breakdown of something beautiful—that is the meaning of my name."

Bryony stiffened in her chair as righteous indignation flooded her and made her bold. "That's a terrible name!" She nearly shot to her feet in anger but managed to suppress the urge.

"Indeed." Samael took another sip of his tea and set his cup gracefully in its saucer. "But it is the essence of what I most closely resemble, is it not? I am like death, a perversion of life and a perversion of the seraphim."

"Well, I don't know anything about that," Bryony said dismissively. It only barely occurred to her that she was defending and comforting her enemy. She couldn't help herself. Wherever she found cruelty, it was her instinct to snuff it out. "I haven't met many seraphim, so I'm not sure what you're all supposed to look like. To me, you look—I don't know—like a lightning storm, or fireworks, or anything else brilliant and stunning and just *wow*, you know? There was a moment when I first saw you, for a split second, before I had to look away . . ." She shrugged. "You were beautiful. It's the truth. Anyway, names are just names. Mine means some plant, I guess. And my last name is also a plant if you think about it. If I let my names define me, I'm just foliage."

At that, Samael nearly choked on his tea. He coughed out a laugh and leaned back into the couch, and Bryony thought this was perhaps the first time she'd ever seen her future father-in-law begin to relax. When he recovered, he turned his face to the ceiling and mused, "I would have named you for your sanctuary."

Had Bryony been an angel, just then, she would have frozen completely. Her skin would have turned to some lifeless substance, and all the color would have drained from her hair and eyes. Impossibly, unthinkably, she was overwhelmed by the kindness behind those words—words from Samael no less—words from the Angel of Death. She stammered and failed to respond. How could one creature be simultaneously so cruel and so kind? He was an enigma. She much preferred dealing with Azazel, whose mood was even-keeled and warm, which reminded her. "Azza gave me a name in your language. It means something like finding home after it's been lost. I guess that's a little like a sanctuary, isn't it?"

Samael nodded. A long silence followed, in which the only sound Bryony heard was the ticking of her grandfather clock. She was beginning to feel utterly pedestrian beside this creature. Why had he wanted to have tea with her? What was he expecting to discuss? She couldn't bear the silence, so she clumsily broke it. "I thought the name you gave Michael was nice."

The angel tensed at the mention of his son. "It is a far better name than the one he gave himself. To this day, I do not understand why he chose it."

"I think . . ." She paused, unsure how much of Michael's motivation she should reveal. "I think he was angry when he chose it."

Samael scoffed. "In his anger, my son managed to saddle himself with a very poor name. The archangel Michael's name is a question, you see. *Who*, it asks, *is like God?* The answer is no one and nothing. In essence, my son has chosen a name that means nothing."

"But you gave him another name."

"Yes." Samael drank the last of his tea and held the cup and saucer in his lap. "He should learn to pronounce it." He let another minute of silence pass, during which he cocked his head and listened to the muffled sounds coming from the kitchen. "I enjoy your home, Ms. Moss. It is peaceful."

Oh please, don't ask to live here. Bryony thought he was perhaps the only person she would outright refuse at this point. Sharing a home with Samael might actually be worse than living in an empty one. *Remember what your mother taught you,* she reminded herself. *Wait for the curtain to fall before you drop your act.* "Then you must visit again, Sama. And please, if you don't mind, would you call me Bryony? It's strange to have family address me so formally."

At the word *family*, the angel's breath momentarily stopped, and Bryony was pleased to have gotten a little of her own back. Was she really keeping score? She supposed she was. So it was to be a war of sentimentality, was it?

"I will try to remember," Samael answered at last. He held out his cup, so she took it from him and set it beside her own on the coffee table. "I should take my leave, Bryony." She shivered and wondered if she hadn't made a mistake in asking that he use her given name. Well, it was too late now. The graveyard angel rose, and Bryony followed suit. "I will spare your guests another sight of me and exit through the front."

That stung because it was true. No one in the kitchen wanted to see him again. No matter how many times Bryony assured him he was beautiful, it would never outweigh the reactions he consistently got from everyone else in the world. She followed him to her front door, impressed at how quickly he seemed to have learned the layout of her living room and parlor. He paused with one hand on the doorframe and did not step out.

"Do you need help?" she asked.

"No."

Still he hovered like a ghost in her doorway, and Bryony got the distinct impression he didn't really want to go. "You could stay a bit longer," she mumbled and immediately regretted it.

Luckily, the Angel of Death refused her offer. "No, I could not. I've held back as much as I can, and I am tired."

"Held back?"

"The poison, Bryony." He stepped through the door. "Tell my son I wish he would learn to pronounce his name."

"I will," she said, following him out onto the veranda. "But he'll probably be rebellious about it."

Samael gripped the rail and carefully descended the stairs. "Then you should learn to pronounce yours."

"Could I?"

"Yes." He stepped onto the path and turned back to face her. "Ask Azazel to teach you. It may not be easy, but you are persistent and you will learn it. Then perhaps my son will be prompted to learn his own."

It was the closest Bryony had heard him come to real, spontaneous encouragement. He genuinely seemed to have warmed to her. She decided to take advantage of the moment and make a straightforward request. Maybe he would hear her this time. "Sama, can we call off the part where you destroy Chuy's value?"

Samael's answer was unfortunately firm. "No. It is a false value, and Ashmedai is obsessed with it. He will never leave your captain alone until that value is eliminated."

"False value?"

"Innocence is not a virtue," the angel said. "Scarcity does not make it so. Too much trust is dangerous. Take you, for example." Bryony stiffened at his turning the focus to her. "You are far from innocent. You do not trust me, nor should you. Yet still you treat me with courtesy. You're on your guard, but you are kind. That . . ." He paused and seemed to consider whether or not to complete his thought. "That is true virtue."

Was that a compliment? She shook off the haunted feeling his esteem inspired. "Please, there must be a way to make Chuy less interesting to the demon king without hurting him. I don't want him to get hurt. He's my friend."

Samael nodded. "I know, but it is impossible." Then he hesitated and bowed his head. "I wish it were not. I'm beginning to understand what my son has found in you, Bryony Moss. I will visit again soon."

Bryony watched the Angel of Death walk away and began to question everything. Had he really grown to like her? The idea was shocking, unthinkable, but she could imagine no other explanation for his behavior.

As soon as she set foot in her kitchen, her companions bombarded her with affectionate relief. Amidst all their warmth and camaraderie, she recalled the image of the graveyard angel walking alone into the night. She thought of his hesitancy to leave, and it suddenly occurred to her—the Angel of Death was eternally isolated. That had to be lonely. And Bryony, with a glow of hope, finally began to see the weakness in her adversary.

CHAPTER NINE

Chuy made himself breakfast wearing blue jeans and absolutely nothing else. His shirt and underwear soaked in a tub of dish soap and cold water while he heated a can of chili on the stove. Ashmedai sat at the table and wantonly stared at Chuy's back. His thoughts were flooded with memories of the future—memories of his own hands caressing that body, those bones, those beautiful tattoos. But the glint of gold that rested between Chuy's shoulder blades and followed the line of his spine caught Ash's eye again and again.

The cross pendant. Chuy had shifted it to his back to keep it out of the way while he cooked, and the damned thing was making Ash jealous. He hated to be jealous—it was such a vulgar emotion. But he'd only seen the moment Chuy was given that pendant because it was an important moment, and the man who had made the pendant was an enormous presence in Chuy's life. Ash saw the adoration with which Chuy looked at that man as though it were happening now, and he wanted Chuy to look at *him* that way instead. How distasteful. How sad. How childish.

Why did Chuy never remove that ridiculous pendant? Why was he still so focused on someone who was long dead and couldn't even manifest a body? Like a fool, Ash drew attention to his own weakness. "Why do you expend so much energy on the dead?"

Chuy turned and knit his brow. "Huh?"

"Your pendant." Ash tried not to let his envy surface, but his failure became more evident with every word he spoke. "You keep touching it. You never take it off."

"Oh." Chuy fingered the gold chain at his throat and spun the pendant around to his chest. The tenderness with which he handled the object made Ash want to grind it to dust. "Guess it just reminds me I was loved once."

You are loved now! Ash wanted to shout, but he couldn't. Instead, he said, "You'll be loved again one day."

Chuy laughed a good-natured laugh that was tinged with heartbreak. "Well, not if I'm spending the rest of my life in this cabin with you."

Ash flushed and bit his tongue, but god that thought was such bliss. "You won't spend the rest of your life here. This is just until Samael tires of his hunt."

"Will he, though?" Chuy looked doubtful. "Unless Daniel's a liar, the Angel of Death doesn't get tired of anything. Daniel says, once he's caught your scent, he won't let up 'til he has you in his teeth."

"He'll let up." Ash knew because he'd seen it. What he still didn't understand was why. Daniel was no liar. The Angel of Death was a veritable bloodhound. When Samael decided he wanted something, he would not stop until he got it. So why had Ashmedai seen a flash of not only blinding, but fading light in Chuy's future? For some unfathomable reason, death came close and then stepped back again.

Chuy cleared his throat in the awkward silence. "Well, in the meantime, at least we have coffee." He presented an enormous can of cheap grounds. "It's unopened, so I think it's still good. Do you want some?"

Ash shook his head. "Save the provisions for the one who needs them."

"I'm not gonna starve because I ran out of coffee." Chuy paused and appeared to consider the truth of his statement. "Probably. Anyway, I hate to eat alone. I won't force the canned food on ya, but sharing a cup would be nice."

Despite himself, Ash grinned. God help him, but any hint of domesticity was an irresistible temptation. "Go ahead then. Make me a cup."

Chuy smiled back, and his smile was like the sun in winter. Ash had already seen that smile a thousand times through his spectacles. It was always the same, no matter what it meant. It was overjoyed and heartbroken, familiar and new, holy and profane. It was the beginning and it was the end, but it was always, always beautiful.

"Also found some old newspapers in the closet," Chuy said. "Some of them have crosswords. Thought you might like something else to do besides babysitting me."

Something else to do? No, nothing was more important. But just now, for some reason, all Ash wanted to do was sip a cup of coffee and pore over a series of unchallenging clues like he wasn't being hunted by the literal Angel of Death. He realized, at once, that this desire came directly from Chuy. Right now, what Chuy needed was a quiet morning—something mundane to let him feel normal for a few minutes—and Ash was desperate to give it to him. "Do you have a pen?"

Chuy grinned. "Found a whole drawer full of 'em."

"Do any of them work?"

"A couple." Chuy sat down with the puzzle, a mug of coffee, and his skillet full of canned breakfast. It looked the opposite of appetizing.

"I'll go hunting today." Ash was almost certain he could get a rabbit at least, perhaps some fish from the nearby lake. "You'll have a fresh dinner tonight."

Chuy glanced up from the puzzle. "Can I talk ya out of it?"

"I . . . What?" Ash squinted at his captive.

"I'd rather not be left alone here. Especially with a bounty on my head, you know? I'll deal with a few more nights of chili and chicken soup. I draw the line at chowder, though."

Ash laughed under his breath. Then he thought about what Chuy was telling him and frowned. There was so much more to it than dinner. Ash had seen it for himself, hadn't he? Little glimpses here and there of compromises, sacrifices, all made in the interest of staving off one curse—loneliness. "You don't do well in isolation, do you? Hiding out here is going to be hard on you."

"Not if you're here." Chuy patted the table beside him. "Come on. Let's beat this probably awful puzzle."

Ash moved his chair beside Chuy's, but before he sat, he retrieved the coat he'd made from the bedpost. "Wear this." He offered it like an enormous house cat offering a dead rat to its most beloved person.

Chuy hardly noticed. He bit his thumb at the crossword puzzle and mumbled, "Not cold."

But it wasn't about the cold. Ash couldn't stand seeing that pendant nestled against Chuy's smooth, decorated chest. It meant someone else had been where he wanted to be. Someone else had desired the last innocent man and then had just taken him, as though the very act didn't jeopardize the quality to which they were undoubtedly drawn in the first place. "Just take it."

Chuy shrugged and accepted the coat, but to Ash's supreme disappointment—and involuntary pleasure—he did not zip it up. He just sat back down, his bare chest and that damned pendant peeking out from behind the wool. "Okay," Chuy said. "First clue, one across."

The crossword puzzle did not take a fraction of Ashmedai's thoughts from his present predicament. He quickly rattled off answers as Chuy read the clues to him. Nothing could be as challenging as just sitting beside this man, watching that glint of gold swing in and out of his open coat. Chuy filled in squares with an old ballpoint pen that needed to be continually scribbled along the margins to get the ink flowing again. Frequently, his elbow would brush Ash's forearm, and Ash responded by bouncing one leg under the table.

"*Eden*," Ash announced impatiently. "Five down is *Eden*."

Chuy rolled the end of the pen between his teeth. "Puzzles aren't gonna last at this rate. Are you this good at sudoku too? We'll run out in a week. Couldn't you just . . . pretend not to know a few answers? I mean make 'em easy ones so I have a chance to feel smart."

No, Ash could not pretend anything at the moment. Clearly. His own warring drives were setting his heel to bouncing so aggressively that his entire body trembled with the motion. Half of him needed to make this moment normal, peaceful, everything Chuy wanted it to be. The other half needed to pin the captain to the table and promise him the greatest pleasure he could ever hope to experience in his short lifetime. Unfortunately, Chuy must have felt the heat rolling off the demon king because his longing for peace receded and revealed a trace of desire that too closely matched Ash's own. It was only a trace, but that's all it took to tip the scales.

It was too late. There was no getting out of this situation without shining a light on everything wrong about it. Ash imagined this scene playing out every day over the next fifty years—sitting at a table, sipping coffee, completing an old crossword puzzle—and it was heaven. His imagination was so vivid, he had a hard time distinguishing it from his memories of Chuy's future. He saw those beautiful tattoos begin to age, the inevitable slowing of the captain's sharp mind, and the growing thickness of his glasses. He saw promises kept and arguments lost and a thousand familiar kisses. Or was it one kiss? One repeated over the years, a copy of a copy of a copy, until it was unrecognizable and new again.

Ash hadn't been this out of control since before he died. This was a *manifested* body, for god's sake. He'd built the damn thing himself, and now he couldn't even keep it in check. He actually had to adjust himself under the table like an overexcited teenager and hope he'd been discreet enough. It was all he could do to keep from leaping out of his chair when Chuy finally laid a hand on his arm. "Hey, if this is boring you, we don't have to finish. You could've just told me you didn't like crosswords."

Like a petulant child, Ash snatched his arm away and stood. "It's not boring me. I just . . . can't do this right now."

Chuy groaned and waved a hand. "Go get some air."

There was something so unsatisfactory about being predictable, but what choice did Ash have? It was either leave or admit defeat and his own formidable feelings. He stared down at the captain, who met his gaze defiantly. Wide, warm eyes looked up at him. Dark hair reflected the morning light like onyx and hid a trail of interlaced tattoos that climbed the back of that long, exquisite neck.

God help him, Ash actually considered giving up and confessing everything right there. The disappointment in the captain's face was evident, and Ashmedai hated the sight of it. There was anxiety there too—a rising dread that Ash now knew to be his captive's deep-seated fear of abandonment. "I won't leave you alone," Ash said in a hasty attempt to reassure him. "I swear." He picked up a bucket next to the bath and headed for the back door. "I'll just pump more water so you can finish your laundry, all right? If you need me, I'll be right outside."

It sounded like placation because it was. Chuy would have been right to scoff at it, but he didn't. He just resumed working on the puzzle, gently holding the pen between his teeth.

The outdoors offered little in the way of relief. Ash pumped water without a thought in his head that didn't include an image of Chuy—the pen between his teeth, his brow knit in concentration, the way the bones in his hands moved like the long levers of an exposed piano. Ash was just beginning to wish he had a second bucket to fill when all the molecules that made up his carefully crafted body began to loosen. The spaces between them grew. He became weak and empty and cold.

No.

He knew what this meant, and it wasn't anything good. It was quite bad, in fact—the very worst thing he could imagine right now. He stumbled over the bucket and made his way back to the cabin. He leaned on the doorframe and fought to hold himself together long enough to speak.

"Chuy," he said, desperate and panting. "There's been a conjuration. I've been summoned."

"What?" Chuy dropped his pen and stood. "How do we stop it?"

"We can't. I can't. I'm sorry. I didn't think . . . I didn't know this would happen." Ash wanted to step closer, but he was afraid to let go of the doorframe lest his entire body immediately fall to dust. "I'll come back as soon as I can. I swear it. I'll murder the man who conjured me and make my way back to you." He spoke the words before he heard the song that called him away. The voice was feminine. Ash thought of Bryony and Azazel and immediately began composing all the indelicate things he would say to them as soon as he arrived in their circle.

"Fight it." Chuy's voice was desperate. There was real terror on that sweet face. "What's happening? Why can I see through you? Please don't go!"

Ash called back. "I cannot refuse a summons. Forgive me—it's impossible. Damn it!" His body was splitting apart now, fading into the atmosphere. "I *will* come back. Stay here. Stay hidden. Stay safe." But Ash couldn't be sure Chuy heard any of it. He was already stretched between worlds, pulled like silk through a keyhole into the realm of the angels and back out the other side.

Somewhere new.

Somewhere strange.

Ashmedai looked down to see four young faces staring up at him.

Chapter Ten

Bryony sat in her kitchen, sipped a cup of coffee—into which she'd snuck a drop or two of whisky—and waited for Azza to finish steeping his tea. The angel's new look included dark blue hair with orange and yellow eddies around his eyes. He looked like the fashion world's version of Van Gogh's "The Starry Night" with his shadowy tunic cinched at the waist, black trousers, and unaccountably gold shoes. Bryony couldn't stop staring at him.

He sat down across from her with his teacup, a saucer, and one cube of sugar, which he delicately dropped into his cup. Then he propped his elbows on the table, laced his fingers together, and rested his chin on the bridge he'd created. "So," he said. "May I begin by asking why you have a sudden interest in learning to pronounce the name I gave you?"

"Oh, you know." Bryony did her best to look nonchalant. "Just curious.

"Mm-hmm." The angel's barely suppressed smile told her he wasn't buying a word of it.

Lying was never going to be easy with him, was it? "Okay, fine. Samael asked me to learn the pronunciation of my angelic name because Michael will absolutely refuse to learn the pronunciation of his without some provocation. Also, I want to learn my name because I like it."

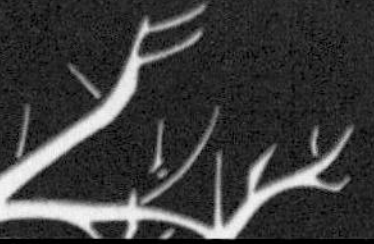

"Don't you just!" Azza beamed from across the table. "I knew you would. I told myself, 'She's going to be absolutely mad about this name, Azza.' Tell me, do you plan to introduce yourself to many of my kind?"

"What's your *kind*—angels, ishim, watchers?"

"All of the above. Although I do believe there's only one unbound watcher other than myself." He leaned in further and grinned. "Will you introduce yourself to Daniel?"

She narrowed her eyes. "Should I? Why is this conversation making you look like a fox in a henhouse?"

Azza burst out laughing and leaned back in his chair. "I just find it cute."

"Find what cute?"

"How naïve you are, sweet god." He sighed, and his face grew suddenly serious. "It'll be prudent for me to admit something to you now rather than later. I imagine my confession will not please you much, but I do hope you'll understand."

Bryony clutched her mug perhaps a little too tightly. "Understand what exactly?"

He hesitated a moment but quickly resigned himself to the inevitable. "Introductions are not an everyday courtesy in our world. Individuality, as you know, is discouraged. Divergence is punished. Only those closest to an angel know the depths of who they are on a personal level. That's why it feels like a kiss, you see? To us, introductions are . . . extraordinarily intimate."

"Excuse me? How intimate exactly?" Bryony heard her own voice rise in pitch.

Azza rocked his head from side to side and hummed as he deliberated. "How to put it. Well, I could show you."

"I'd really rather you didn't, and I'm certain Michael would agree."

The angel chuckled. "Poor petal. He's fighting his inherited jealousy so valiantly. I'm proud of him—going to the shops on his own, leaving the two of us alone. He really, really shouldn't have."

Oh, Michael was definitely not going to be fine with this. "Are you trying to prove Ashmedai right? I was under the impression he was spreading false rumors when he called you a seducer."

Azza sipped his tea innocently. "*Rumors*, yes. *False*, not so much." He held up a hand before she could find the words to hurl at him. "Fear not, darling—I'm only teasing. I've been hesitant to reveal the weight behind our little moments because I didn't want you to misunderstand. I knew they wouldn't mean as much to you as they did to me. I'm only sharing this now because, if you intend to start introducing yourself to angels, you might find yourself at the receiving end of uninvited devotion." He tapped a finger to his chin. "Well, not entirely uninvited from their perspective. Or they could take offense, depending on the angel. Daniel will know better—he's familiar with mankind's cultural peculiarities. Non-watchers, on the other hand, may be a bit on the sticky side of things. Raphael, as always, is a wild card."

Bryony frowned. Just what had Samael gotten her into now? Nothing she agreed to do for him was ever straightforward, was it? "I suppose learning my name will require further intimacy?"

"I do apologize." Azazel gave her a sympathetic look. "It's not quite sex if that helps."

She grimaced.

He held up a finger. "More like a French kiss."

She groaned.

Azza chuckled. "Perhaps some heavy petting."

"I really need something to throw at you other than my coffee."

"I'm kidding, darling!" He burst out laughing again. "It's just so wonderful to make you blush without a brush." He mimed applying rouge to his cheeks. "It might help to recall that you witnessed this kind of intimacy shared between father and son. It's one of the deepest levels of intimacy we have, but it isn't sex. Angels don't have an equivalent for sex. That was why the watchers were considered aberrant. Do you understand?"

She wrinkled her nose and nodded.

"Good."

"You'd better be telling the truth about this," she grumbled, "or you'll be making your god very angry." The nature of their awkward, hierarchical relationship had to be good for something, even if it was only idle threats.

"I swear it." He crossed his heart. "What I mean to say is . . . maybe avoid introducing yourself to the archangel Michael when you meet him. I do believe he would have a proverbial aneurysm right after running you through for taking liberties with his person."

Azza stood and brought his chair closer to Bryony. This was not going to be as easy as it was before, now that she knew what it really meant. She drummed her fingers on the table, as nervous as she'd be if she were getting a tooth pulled.

"Don't look so frightened, darling. We've done this before."

"I know, I know."

He took her hand and kissed it. "Some humans are so afraid of love, as much as they seem to need it. It has always fascinated me." He straightened his shoulders and leaned toward her. "Now, when I give you your name, try to hold on to it. Keep the feeling, even after the image your mind calls up to match it fades. Think of this as the memorization of a new word. I'm going to pronounce it for you, and I want you to say it over and over again in your head until you know it by heart."

She nodded.

He placed one hand on either side of her head, his thumbs just brushing her cheeks. Then he barely touched his lips to hers and breathed out. The scent of his cinnamon tea followed, along with the powerful feeling of finding home. This time, the memory that came with it was of a carnival Bryony had gone to with her parents, years before her brother was born. She'd gotten separated from them and wound up wandering behind the tents, back where ticket holders were not supposed to go. All the lights were strung out front, so Bryony had walked a path darkened by long shadows as carnival staff shouted at her to leave the area. She'd cried, and her tears made all the unfamiliar figures blur together. Then, suddenly, her mother's arms were around her. And she was warm, and she was safe, and she was home.

After Azza withdrew, Bryony kept her eyes closed and clung to the feeling he'd given her. She repeated it in her head over and over again. *How does it feel to find home? Like this. Like this. Like this.* Then she opened her eyes.

"Have you got it?" Azza asked.

"I think so."

"Try to give it back to me." He leaned in again.

Bryony tried to mimic him, placing a hand on either side of his head. She brought her mouth to his, got within an inch, and burst out laughing. "I'm sorry!" She cackled. "It's just so weird."

He leaned back and crossed his arms. "What did you feel when you touched me just now?"

"Awkward," she admitted. "Sorry. It's . . . not something I'm used to doing."

"You should feel closeness, affection. In short, you should feel love. If you don't, it will be impossible to share your name."

It felt just like she'd rejected him. She cringed. Azazel loved her enough to introduce himself to her, but she couldn't respond the same way. "But I do love you. I do. You're like family to me now."

"Thank you for saying so." He smiled.

"It's true! I just can't think of it when I'm mirroring your face like that. It feels too weird, like some kind of theater exercise or something."

Azazel took another sip of tea and thought. When he set his cup down again, his expression took on that same mischievous look that had worried her before. "Then it will have to be a kiss," he concluded. "It should feel like a kiss, and for you, I suppose that means it needs to actually be one."

She gaped at him. "Oh, I don't think so."

"Remember that moment between Samael and his son."

She nodded. It had been a strange moment of closeness, a gesture that wanted forgiveness and understanding, but demanded no love in return. Azza was right. It wasn't the same kind of intimacy she was thinking of.

"It's a cultural difference, darling, but I understand why you're uneasy. Just imagine you're bestowing a blessing upon a congregant. Above all, you must send your name with love. Shall I pronounce it for you again or can you call it up on your own?"

Damn. She'd forgotten already. Sure, she could recall the memories the feeling evoked, but the feeling itself had faded. It was like calling to mind a favorite meal but repeatedly failing to reproduce the flavor. "One more time," she said.

He repeated the gesture, and the air was filled with the scent of cinnamon and the feeling of finding home. Bryony memorized the feeling. It was a soaring kind of relief, like the first expansion of the chest after a long constriction, a great happiness tinged with the memory of fear and despair. Before she could forget it again, Bryony leaned in and kissed him.

The kiss was soft and sweet. The angel's lips felt incredibly human. He wrapped his fingers around her wrist, and his chair creaked as he leaned closer. She recalled the way he treasured her forgiveness, the prayers he sent her, the meals he made, the warmth he brought to her home. She never felt unsafe in his presence. Never. She opened her mouth and sent him the feeling that was her name. And she sent it with all the love she had for him.

His hand tightened around her wrist when her breath entered his lungs, and then it was done. She stood and felt heat creep into her cheeks. "Did I say it right?"

Azza kept his eyes closed. "Yes," he breathed. "You pronounced it well, though there was a slight accent." He grinned, but when he finally opened his eyes again, all the playfulness had gone from his expression. "You sent more than your name, darling. I thought you should know."

"I did?"

He stood and pulled her into his arms. A heartbeat sounded in his chest, and she knew it was there for her sake. "Thank you," he whispered, "for loving me that much."

Chapter Eleven

Four young faces looked up at the demon king and screamed. Four young bodies sitting cross-legged on the floor kicked backward to get away from him. They were in unison, these children—these teenaged girls. Their movements matched like a choreographed dance depicting abject terror, but their net was more than solid. Ashmedai could not begin to break out of the circle they'd built. He roared as loudly and ferociously as he could. They should be terrified, these amateur conjurors. They should be pissing themselves in fear. He was angry, and he had every intention of taking it out on the four witless brats.

One blonde girl found her voice. "Ohmygod ohmygod ohmygod! It worked! Did you actually think it would work? Beth! You have to tell him what to do now. Remember?"

Beth, it turned out, was the little redhead in the middle who'd been reading aloud from some enormous tome. She glanced up in horror and desperately searched for her tongue. When she found it, she was even more infuriating than her companions. "Be quiet!" she shouted at the demon king. "I command you."

Ash's mouth snapped shut.

The girls all murmured together. "It worked."

"It's working."

"Oh my god, she's doing it."

Ashmedai scowled down at them. This was a slumber party. He'd been conjured for a fucking slumber party. He'd been dragged from the man he loved, forced to leave his treasure to the tender mercies of the Angel of Death, all so he could become a lazy-morning parlor trick for a "coven" of sixteen-year-old girls. If they'd been men, Ash would have enjoyed killing them.

The one called Beth crawled forward on her knees and sat closer to the edge of the circle. Her hair was cut short, and she wore round glasses and plaid pajamas. She was the only one wearing actual pajamas. The rest were in activewear. Beth cleared her throat and glanced down at the pages of her book. "Are you Asmodeus, king of the demons?"

Ash growled at her.

She straightened her glasses and tried again. "Are you Asmodeus, king of the demons?"

Ash pointed to his own mouth and shrugged.

"Oh." She sat up a little straighter. "I get it. Um . . . you can speak now. You have my permission to speak."

Ash closed his eyes and prayed for patience. "I am the demon king. My name is Ashmedai. You may call me *Your Majesty* should you wish to address me before you die." There. Scaring a little respect into them would go a long way.

The other girls gathered closer and whispered among themselves. He heard, *Don't let him scare you . . . trapped in the circle . . . can't do anything . . .*

Patience was not forthcoming. "You will release me this instant or I'll grind your bones to dust and feed them to your unwitting parents, you revolting little shits!"

One of the girls leaned close to Beth and started pointing out passages in the book. "It says, *Be on your guard. The king of demons will say anything to convince you to release him. He will threaten and deceive you.*"

Ash decided, then and there, that the author of this mysterious book would wake to find themselves at the pointy ends of his sharpest talons, just as soon as he could figure out who the author was.

The girls went on without any concern for their own health or safety. "It says you have to make a deal with him. Ask for something in exchange for his freedom."

Beth's mouth went crooked in thought. "But I don't know what to ask for."

One of the other girls snorted. "Ask him for a date. He's pretty hot, right? I didn't think he'd be so handsome."

Another chimed in. "Yeah, Beth, ask him for a date. It's probably the only way you'll get one anyway." Everyone laughed, and Beth was expected to join in, so she did halfheartedly.

Ash dug in his pocket and withdrew his spectacles to get a better sense of what he was dealing with. As soon as he had them on his nose, he saw flashes of the girls' histories—just a moment here, a deep scar there, a lingering feeling or two—but it was enough to tell him a few things about them. He folded his spectacles and put them away. Two of the girls had been recently assaulted, one by a family member, which made him less inclined to punish them for their insolence. Another had so much pressure to perform in school, she could hardly focus on anything else. Last night's party must have been a rare treat.

Beth, on the other hand, was a wallflower. She believed herself of little value and even less beauty, and she'd resigned herself to a loveless future. God he hated to pull out seduction for a predicament like this. But he'd already been away too long, and it would undoubtedly take him far longer to get back. He'd be a fool to fly. Samael's host was surely watching the skies. Ash would have to drive. It could take days. "Where am I?" he demanded without thinking.

Beth looked up from her book. "Oh . . . Um, this is Portland."

Ash glared at her. "Which Portland?"

"Oregon."

Two things made Ash instantly more optimistic about his situation. The first was that he was within a day's drive of the hunting cabin. It would take hours, but there was a chance he could get back by nightfall. Secondly, Beth seemed more malleable than her companions, and Ash was growing more confident in his ability to manipulate her.

He squatted down to her level and looked her in the eye with as much smolder as he could manage. "Elizabeth." He used her full name to thrill her, and it clearly worked. The girl's cheeks were pink as peonies. "I'm so glad to have been conjured by a sorceress as kind and beautiful as you. I wish to break free of this circle. I know your book tells you not to release me, but I also know your heart disagrees. Listen to your heart, Elizabeth. Do I look like someone who would hurt you?" The other three girls barely suppressed their hysterical laughter. Damn them to hell, anyway. "Elizabeth. If you release me, I'll grant your deepest wish without your having to demand it, and I'll be in your debt. Isn't it better to have the demon king in your debt than to have him seek vengeance upon you once he's free?"

"Don't listen to him," the blonde girl warned. "He'll try anything, remember? He'll trick you."

"Oh, for crying out . . ." Ash stood and threw out his hands. "I am not trying to trick you!"

"But that's exactly what you'd say if you were," said the shrewd blonde.

"Look. I'll pay you." Ash pulled out his wallet, and then remembered that the money inside it was not manifested and therefore had not come with him into the circle. "Damn it!" He threw his wallet down and breathed deep to control his temper. Time to try another angle. "Listen, girls. You've had your fun, and I hope I've been entertaining for you. But I'm in a bit of a rush here. When you called to me, I was making my escape from the Angel of Death, who is right on my heels, I assure you. If you don't release me, he'll follow, and he won't worry about collateral damage when he finds me." A half-truth, but still.

They all blinked up at him.

"You're the collateral damage," Ash clarified. "I've been dead for ages, and you're seconds away from joining me, only you won't have the benefit of an afterlife. You'll be dust. Gone. Do you get it? You're playing with forces you can't begin to understand."

The two dark-haired girls leaned their heads together. "He's not as impressive as I thought he'd be," one whispered.

"Still a hottie, though."

The first one giggled. "We should make him stay the whole weekend."

"No!" Ash screamed at them. Then he clenched his teeth and calmly repeated, "No. Don't keep me here. I'm begging you." Children. He'd been reduced to begging from children. They were laughing, conspiring, gossiping like he wasn't even there. To them, he was some kind of illusion, a hologram they'd grown tired of watching. Only Beth still stared up at him, and he returned her gaze with a frown that was meant to be imposing but must have looked pathetic.

She whispered to him, "If I . . . If I let you go, you won't hurt me?"

Her mannerisms reminded Ashmedai of someone he'd long forgotten—one of King Solomon's concubines, an unwilling one if the way she carried herself was any indication. She'd believed herself a woman of little to no value, a boring girl with no standout feature for men to write poetry about. She wasn't entirely wrong. Solomon himself seemed to forget she existed for months on end. Ash had found her fascinating. Being half cherub, he had an easier time understanding the social constructs of elephants than those of men. And as much as he enjoyed their company, to him, most women were the same. He marveled at the internal hierarchies they formed using criteria he couldn't begin to comprehend. It all seemed to revolve around men—whether men found them desirable or would take them to wife—especially in those days.

So, as soon as he'd taken the place of King Solomon, Ash got to work experimentally rearranging the hierarchy of the king's women, and he did it by giving the most attention to the little concubine at the bottom of the food chain. Despite his efforts to remain an impartial observer, over the years, the girl became a true friend. She was the one who convinced the others to accept him when they discovered he was a counterfeit. She was the one who always rose up and defended him. She had been the bravest of the bunch.

And Beth was at the bottom of this food chain.

The demon king crouched again. He spared a quick glance for the other girls, who were busy plotting what they would demand of him. When he was sure no one else was watching, he reached out. "Elizabeth, take my hand."

Beth shook her head vigorously.

He held his hand out further. "I still won't be able to leave the circle. I just want you to know I'm real."

Tentatively, she reached out to him, flinching when they came within inches of touching. She glanced to her friends, but none of them looked her way, so she let her fingers drop into the demon king's hand. Her eyes grew wide. "You're solid . . . and warm."

"Yes. I'm just as real as you are." He closed his fingers gently over hers. "And right now, I'm just as frightened as you are. You think you've caught a vicious beast in your trap, and you don't feel like you can safely let me go. I won't say I'm not dangerous, but right now, I'm as afraid of you as you are of me. Do you understand? I need . . . I need to get out of this trap." He choked before he realized he was allowing his actual feelings to worm their way into his voice. "I lied before. The Angel of Death is not hunting for me. He's hunting for the man I love. I have to get back to him. I have to protect him."

"Oh!" Beth clapped a hand over her mouth and then whispered, "You like men?"

Lord help him, this might actually work. She was seeing him as a person. "Yes. Please don't tell the others. I don't think they'd understand."

She leaned in. "What's his name?"

Ash didn't hesitate. "Jesús." He paused and spoke more fondly. "Chuy. He's everything to me, Elizabeth. I can't let the Angel of Death take him. That's why I'm begging you, ignore that book. It's just an outdated instruction manual. I'm a real person, and I need your help." He squeezed her hand one final time. "Please."

Beth thought a moment while she adjusted her glasses again. She really was quite beautiful despite her own opinion. She had a sprinkle of freckles across her nose, bright green eyes, and dimples when she smiled. "How do I let you go?"

Oh, thank god and all the heavens it had worked! Why hadn't he remembered the concubines sooner? Eventually, they'd all sided with him. Ash had always been good with women, and these modern girls were no different. In fact, they might have been taken for Solomon themselves if they'd been alive under his rule.

It was all too easy to win Beth to his side, but Ash reminded himself to do it carefully. It could go wrong so fast. He leaned in and murmured, "Just break the circle. Cut the net. You can do it with one little finger if you like. No one will even know it was you."

"And you'll be in my debt?" she whispered.

Ash nodded somberly and resisted the urge to laugh at her attempt to bargain. "You will get something out of this, Elizabeth. I've seen your most fervent wish, and I intend to grant it immediately."

Beth chewed her cheek for a moment. Then, swift as a frightened gecko, her hand darted out and back again. She had drawn a line with her finger across the barrier of the circle. Ash rose and began to laugh maniacally as Beth backed away from him, clearly reconsidering her decision.

"I am free!" The demon king's rumbling voice shook the foundation of the house. The other girls turned their heads and gasped as the dangerous creature they thought they'd captured stepped out of his prison and into their fragile, little world. The first move Ash made was to manifest his wings, unfurling them until they nearly filled the room. Let the brats try to call him unimpressive now. "You can no longer command me. Now you'll learn how dangerous it is to play with fire."

He stepped toward Beth before continuing his show. She backed into the wall, and he lowered his voice. "Or you would have . . . except . . ."

He lifted Beth's chin with the tips of his fingers. "Except my conjuror is the most beautiful woman I've seen in a thousand years. I cannot raise a hand against anyone in her presence." He stroked Beth's cheek with the backs of his fingers and bent to kiss her. She went soft in his arms and barely even noticed when he slipped the book from her hands. "If anyone ever hurts you, my darling Elizabeth, I will send them straight to hell."

Then, his lips to her ear, he whispered, "Enjoy your new status. Your friends are already impressed." They were, indeed, openly gawking at the scene, and more than one of them had turned a shade to match Beth's. "And you *are* beautiful. I wasn't lying about that." He straightened and spoke louder. "I will return for you one day and make you my queen." He winked down at his young costar.

All three audience members gasped, and Beth blushed even deeper.

With a pinch of regret, Ash realized he would have to kill the romance of the moment for practicality's sake. "By the way, do any of you happen to have a car?"

Beth leapt to the rescue. "Take my parents' car. They won't mind. Insurance will cover it. Follow me." She was darling when she was excited—a little too impulsive, perhaps. He hated to take advantage, but what choice did he have? She led him downstairs and grabbed a keychain from a crystal bowl near the door. Then she twisted a key off the ring and handed it to him.

He took the key, feeling more grateful than he had in ages. "Thank you for your kindness, Elizabeth." Then he felt an uncontrollable urge to do better. She had risked so much to help him. "Can I offer you something more? A kiss is hardly adequate payment for freeing the demon king."

She smiled up at him and shrugged. "Maybe introduce me to your boyfriend one day. I'd like to meet him."

Boyfriend. "I will. You may have saved his life today. Goodbye, Elizabeth. When you meet me again, you may consider me a friend."

Ash sped away from that suburban house with a warm feeling and a thousand questions. How had such a young girl performed a successful, high-level conjuration without an angelic partner? Most of the solo conjurations he'd witnessed were accomplished by old, learned men who wanted to prove their own greatness. As if having another being do all your work for you proved you were anything other than incurably lazy.

He glanced down at the tome he'd taken from Elizabeth. Whatever this book was, at least she wouldn't be able to get herself into trouble with it again. There were demons out there who would have no qualms about harming a young conjuror, regardless of what her reasons were. They most certainly would not have shown mercy to a group of innocent girls who thought they were only playing a game. No one liked to be interrupted, forcibly relocated, and made demands of. Most demons would have beheaded all four girls as soon as they'd fulfilled their contracts.

But Elizabeth hadn't summoned just any demon. No, she'd summoned their one and only king. This book, whatever it was, had enormous power, and Ashmedai had every intention of examining its contents as soon as he knew Chuy was safe.

Chapter Twelve

"Stars are amazing." Bryony lay on her stomach before a glowing hearth and turned the pages of her fiancé's most recent gift to her. It was a book on astronomy. Michael had made her close her eyes, laid the heavy volume in her hands, and proudly told her when she could look. She'd scarcely thanked him before she cracked it open and buried her nose in it. After an hour of marveling over the colorful pictures, she finally began to read, and everything she read was mind-blowing. "Do you know about nebulae?"

Michael chuckled from his place on the couch. "I do."

She couldn't help telling him anyway. "It says here they're made of dead stars. Did you know stars could die? I didn't. They die and then turn into these huge, gorgeous clouds. See?" She held up her book, and he leaned in to see the picture she indicated. "New stars are formed inside the clouds. That's why they call star graveyards *nurseries.* How odd, don't you think? I love it. Why don't we call our own graveyards nurseries? We should. Don't our bodies help to make life too? It's like . . . nothing really disappears. Everything just changes shape."

Michael laid the romance he was reading face down in his lap and said, "*Endless forms most beautiful.*"

Bryony sat up. "Is that from a poem?"

"It's from a book—*On the Origin of Species*. You may have come across it in the cargo hold while you were digging around for books on gigantism."

Oh, right. That. She'd almost forgotten. Bryony felt her cheeks color as she recalled the way she'd hidden the book from him, chased it across the floor during a squall, and wound up needing to be rescued from her own stupidity.

Michael's smile was warm and broad. "Are you still embarrassed about that? You were only trying to help. I loved that you cared enough to do research about me." He slipped from the couch and joined her on the floor. Suddenly, his hand was tracing the path of her spine, reminding her body of other moments she'd almost forgotten. "I wanted you so badly that night," he murmured. "Do you have any idea how hard I fought not to pull you into my arms and kiss you after the squall? It was torture holding you at arm's length. If anyone should be embarrassed—"

"It's not you," Bryony said. "You did everything right. You always do everything right."

"Not always." He pulled her closer and kissed her throat. His skin began to warm as he tangled his fingers in her hair. "I should have told you I loved you sooner."

"I won't disagree with that." She began to unbutton his shirt and kissed each new inch of skin as it was revealed.

He cleared his throat and fought his desire, though he had to know it was a losing battle. "I read *On the Origin of Species* shortly after I measured over seven feet for the first time. The milestone depressed me, so I tried to take my mind off it by reading something new."

Bryony tugged his shirttails from his pants and spoke into his skin. "Go on."

He gulped and leaned back on his hands. "Well . . . Darwin's idea was that all life came from the same ancestor. As living things are born and die, they slowly change and branch off into species. That's why biodiversity exists. It was amazing, that book. I memorized the last sentence because it was so beautiful."

Bryony stopped fidgeting with his belt buckle and sat back. "Well? Let's have the recitation."

"In exchange for another kiss?"

She grinned. "In exchange for much more than a kiss."

His expression lit up, and he pulled her into his massive chest. As he recited the words of Charles Darwin, his resonant voice sent them vibrating all through her. "*There is grandeur in this view of life, with its several powers, having been originally breathed into a few forms or into one; and that, whilst this planet has gone cycling on according to the fixed law of gravity, from so simple a beginning endless forms most beautiful and most wonderful have been, and are being, evolved.*"

Endless forms most beautiful . . . And none of it would be possible without mortality, just like new stars would not be possible without the death of the old ones. As species changed, they molded themselves to suit the world they lived in. They found *home* wherever they were.

"If only angels could evolve," Bryony mused, thinking of how devastating it must have been for these creatures to suddenly find themselves in an unfamiliar world. "Unless . . ." She pulled back and laughed at a realization she'd only begun to have. "Unless they *are*. Michael, Michael!" She shook him as though trying to wake him. "What if the watchers triggered the evolution of angels? Do you think? Maybe angels couldn't evolve before because they weren't dying or reproducing, and they needed human partners so they could. What if the watchers weren't aberrant, really? What if they were just changing to suit the world they lived in?"

"That's a beautiful idea." Michael nuzzled her. "But if it's true, the nephilim are the mutation that failed."

"Pfft! Only if perfect reproduction is the goal."

"Survival is the goal, I believe."

"Then you're a success." She climbed back into his lap and pushed his shirt from his shoulders. "And so is everyone else descended from angels. Because you exist, their evolution succeeded." She kissed his skin again. "You are part of the diversity of life."

His skin grew feverish. "My love . . ." He slid his hands up her thighs to her hips and pulled her closer. "How on earth did you manage to make Darwin seductive?" He drew his knees in to lift her and kissed and kissed her mouth.

There was always something fascinating in the way Michael appreciated her body—something ever so slightly inhuman. He was meticulous when he undressed her, and he touched her as though he was afraid to break her. She wondered whether it had anything to do with his lineage, or whether it was just him. She'd recently learned that his appreciation for her bones came from his angelic side. But where did the gentleness come from—that trembling touch? Was it because of his size or because he knew instinctively how fragile mortal lives were? Did that instinct come from his father?

As if in answer, the house shook to its bones, and the sound of lightning striking too close made Bryony reflexively cover her own ears.

Michael gripped her tight and spoke through gritted teeth. "Damn him."

The Angel of Death had arrived, as was his habit, at a most inopportune moment. Bryony began hurriedly putting her clothes back on.

"Why can't he just warn us?" Michael said, buttoning his shirt. "Why does he always have to come at night?"

Bryony tugged on her stockings. "Maybe he's trying to avoid imposing himself on bystanders."

"He should worry more about imposing himself on me," Michael grumbled, and he rose to his full height.

Bryony leapt onto the couch so she could wrap her arms around his neck and kiss him. "I love you. Please, don't take this the wrong way, but I think . . ." She hesitated to voice her suspicions. "I think your father's just lonely."

Michael scoffed and began gently untangling Bryony's hair with his fingers. "Of course he's lonely, but that doesn't mean he has to make it our problem."

"Who else's problem could it possibly be?" she said. "We're the only family he has left." And she realized, seconds after she spoke the words, how true they were. Any other children of Samael surely did not know him. Any women he might have loved had long since turned to dust. Bryony began to wonder whether the Angel of Death had taken on his most recent crusade in order to excuse his involvement in her life. Perhaps he only wanted to sit and talk with someone who wasn't paralyzed with grief, but he didn't know how to ask for something as simple as company.

"Just promise you'll be careful." Michael's voice broke through her thoughts. "I can see the compassion you're trying to hide right now." He tapped her forehead with his index finger. "It's as obvious as a sunburn. You're so kind, and you know I love you for it. But my father is not a fallen songbird you can nurse back to health and release. He'll take your kindness and twist it. He'll use it against you. That's how he is. It's how he's always been. Bryony . . ." He squinted down at her. "Are you hearing me?"

She nodded, but it was only performative. In her head, she was already rehearsing what she would say to Samael when she saw him. Somehow, she'd convinced herself that if she could only say the right words at the right moment—if she could crack the code of the devil's heart—maybe she could save Chuy and give Michael back his father in the process.

Samael waited in Bryony's grove of plum trees. She hadn't expected to find him there, but he seemed to be enjoying the space. She watched him walk slowly from tree to tree, laying his hand on each one as though they whispered secrets to him.

He's just lonely, she reminded herself, and she fortified her mantle of morbidity to address him. "Sama, it's Bryony."

He paused and turned toward her. "I have come to discuss my progress."

Of course. But it was the last thing she wanted to hear about, so like a fool, she tried to stall. "Don't you want a cup of tea first?"

The graveyard angel stiffened. He clearly hadn't expected an invitation and seemed quite unsure what to do with it now that he had it.

Bryony decided not to leave him lost. She tried to channel Azazel's spirit of hospitality. "Of course you do—I won't let you refuse. Come in and sit down. Would you like my arm?"

Samael dropped his wings, held out his hand, and waited for Bryony to take it. She led him to her house, and he managed the porch steps as though he already visited regularly. Michael must have heard them coming and gone upstairs. She would have given anything to have her fiancé with her, but she knew it was impossible. "I'm afraid the fire is going out," she said to his father. "But I can stoke it if you give me a moment."

"Is anyone in your kitchen now?" he asked.

"Not this time."

"Then I prefer to take tea there."

"Sure." For a moment, Samael's request baffled Bryony. To her, the living room was warm and comfortable, the best place to receive guests. But the kitchen was where her friends gathered. The kitchen was where Loki failed to pick fights with Michael, where Martha and Azazel made mouthwatering meals together. The living room was for guests, but the kitchen was for family. And suddenly, she understood.

She walked with Samael to her kitchen table and offered him a chair. It was dark, and she had to turn on the lights before she could make his tea, which reminded her how much she still didn't know about him. For example, she knew he was blind, but was blindness in angels the same as blindness in humans? Were there different kinds of angelic blindness, or was he an anomaly? It didn't take long for her curiosity to get the better of her. "Do you see light?"

"No," he answered.

"Not even a little bit?"

He scowled at her. "I do not have eyes, Bryony."

Oh! That was new information. She had assumed his eyes were blind, not that he lacked them altogether. "So the voids I saw—"

"Voids?"

She flushed. "On your body, when you look like a seraph. There are so many. I thought they were your eyes, but you're saying they really are voids?"

He brought one knuckle to his mouth in thought. "*Voids.* I had not heard them described so before."

"How are they usually described?" He tilted his chin up suddenly, and she realized she'd asked an insensitive question. "Never mind, don't tell me. I'm sorry. Do you like peppermint?"

He nodded but refused to allow her to drop the subject. "How else would you describe these voids? Tell me. Satisfy my curiosity." There was his vanity making its usual appearance.

She thought about it as she put the kettle on. "Well, to me, they look kind of like outer space, I guess."

"Outer space." He smiled briefly at that, and she was pleased she'd somehow found an answer he didn't immediately despise.

She decided it was best to end the conversation on a high note and quickly changed the subject. "I've been learning to pronounce my name like you suggested."

The graveyard angel's brows rose. "Have you?"

"Yes."

A long period of silence followed. It was so agonizing, Bryony actually jumped when the kettle began to whistle. She was going to have to get used to Samael's awkward conversation style. As angels went, she'd now spoken to exactly four. Azza and Raphael were both chatty and personable. Daniel didn't speak at all, but his written vulgarity was endearing to her. Samael, on the other hand, was a hard egg to crack. He didn't carry on a conversation if he didn't have anything more to say. He was perfectly content to sit in silence, which drove Bryony to mini-fits of anxiety. She felt like she was babbling endlessly and making a fool of herself while the Angel of Death silently judged her from across her kitchen table.

Bryony poured water from the kettle into a delicate teacup, dropped a bag of peppermint tea into it, and brought it to him after it had steeped a while. "I don't suppose you need any sugar?"

He shook his head and drew his cup close before he spoke. "How does my son feel about your lessons?"

"Well . . ." She was almost certain Samael already knew the answer to that and was only torturing her by asking, but she didn't think it wise to say so. "I haven't exactly told him yet."

"Why not?" The angel lifted his cup to his lips and sipped it. His black eyes widened suddenly, and Bryony thought this might actually be the first time he'd ever tasted peppermint.

"I just worry it'll make him feel jealous. You know . . . because it's so . . ." Saying the word *intimate* to Samael felt far less natural than saying it to Azza. In fact, it was downright uncomfortable. She opted not to finish her sentence rather than suffer through the rest of it.

Samael laughed under his breath, and the sight of his smug expression made Bryony instantly less concerned about his feelings. He muttered into his tea. "My son was bound to grow jealous the moment Azazel became involved."

"That's entirely your fault, you know." She glared at him for her own sake. "If you hadn't said those terrible things to him—"

"I only told him the truth."

"You could have had some tact about it."

"You could have told him yourself, and I wouldn't have had to step in."

"You didn't *have* to do anything!" Oh dear lord, was she really arguing with the Angel of Death? *Not smart, Bryony Moss. Not smart.* But where Michael was concerned, Bryony seemed unable to censor herself. She lowered her voice. "You only said it to hurt me, not for his sake. I know that. Do what you want to me—I can handle it—but I don't want you to hurt Michael any more. You're his father, for god's sake."

Samael took another infuriating sip of tea. "I have heard that Azazel is uniquely beautiful, is he not?"

"I mean, yes." Bryony shrugged. "But so is Michael. And Azza's beautiful like a sunset is beautiful. It doesn't make me want to sleep with him." As soon as the words left her mouth, she regretted saying them. The implication she allowed to hang in the air was palpable. Samael smiled over his teacup, the question clearly lingering between them. *What makes you want to sleep with my son?* He was, at least, gentleman enough not to ask it aloud, wasn't he?

Wasn't he?

"Tell me more about what draws you to my son."

Oh, for the love of god. "Listen. If you want to know about your son, maybe you should try talking to him yourself."

"He cannot look upon me." A fair point.

"So make him use a blindfold."

"He does not enjoy my company."

"Then be nicer to him."

"He's a stubborn child."

"Because he takes after you!" She could feel the heat creep into her cheeks. It was so significant she wasn't at all sure Samael couldn't actually feel it from across the table. But she didn't want to give up now that she'd started down this road. There was a chink somewhere in the Angel of Death's armor. Bryony knew it was there, and she was more determined than ever to find it. "Fine. It was his smile I noticed first—I mean after his height. He has this dimple on the left side of his mouth, you know? Just the left. His smile is warm, and he's always kind. Always.

He seemed so sure of himself when I met him, even though everyone treated him like shit. He seemed content and happy and so above it all. I guess I just found that extremely attractive."

"He was always so." Samael set his cup on its saucer.

"How would you know?" She narrowed her eyes at him. "You never knew him."

"I did. He stole my sword, if you recall."

How could he be so complacent about this? He'd missed his son's entire life, left him homeless and alone as a child, and Bryony couldn't stand the angel's refusal to acknowledge it. She found her teeth and bit. "About the only time I've ever seen him really angry is when he's talking about you. He deserved so much better than what you gave him, Sama. He deserved to have a father."

"I am not—"

"I don't care. That's the thing. I don't care what you're not, or what you can't do, or who you can't be. He needed someone to answer his questions and guide him through life. He needed someone who had an inkling of what he was going through and why he was going through it. You just walked away. Already, Azazel has been more of a father to him than you ever were."

That was, apparently, a bridge too far. Samael, who had shown no concern over the uncomfortable direction of the conversation or Bryony's petulance, suddenly stood. He knocked his chair back, and Bryony nearly fell out of hers trying to scramble away from him.

"Azazel has *what*?" he roared.

Ah, so Azazel was the line. She should have guessed. Here, at last, was Samael's infamous jealousy. Here was the unpredictability, the dangerous calm followed by a sudden storm she could not have begun to prepare for. *Azazel is uniquely beautiful.* Was that really what this was about? Beauty? Would Samael have become this angry if she'd suggested Loki was a better father to Michael? She doubted it.

No, the wound the Angel of Death suffered had been inflicted eons ago, and then again, and again, and again. One little god telling him he was beautiful was not going to override a lifetime of evidence to the contrary. *Azazel is beautiful, and Samael is hideous*—that was the reality he lived with. Just that. No one could bear to look at him because he'd been born wrong.

The graveyard angel stood in Bryony's kitchen and quietly seethed. He was so furious she was shocked he hadn't smashed her teacup to splinters. Loki certainly would have. Regardless, she knew she was about to get a sizeable draft of Samael's temper. But when it finally came down on her, it didn't look at all like she expected it to. There was no fire in him, no violence, no tantrum. No, his temper was calm, cold, and deadly. Samael wasn't someone who argued or fought. He just stood over you and slowly, mercilessly crushed you under his heel.

The first indication Bryony had that she'd messed up well beyond anything a sincere apology would fix was that the Angel of Death stopped holding back his poison. She fell to her knees and heard a long, low moan emanate from the back of her own throat. Her mantle disintegrated under the weight of her grief. She could see no beauty in death now. It was a void, an emptiness, a perversion of life.

"I have come to discuss my progress." Samael repeated his initial greeting, effectively erasing the last twenty minutes. This time, his voice was controlled and terrifying. She could not convince herself he was the same lonely, fish-out-of-water angel she'd accepted as her future father-in-law. All his vulnerability had melted away. "My host has successfully slipped a beacon to the demon king. It is the *Sefer Raziel,* the bona fide book of the Angel of Secrets. To activate it, Ashmedai need only open it, and there is no book in existence Ashmedai can resist opening."

From her place on the floor, through a barely suppressed, keening howl, Bryony begged, "Please, Sama . . . Please, don't do this . . ."

Samael tilted his chin up. "Then assassinate the archangel Michael with your current conjuring partner, and accept that the watcher may be consumed in the process."

"I can't . . . do that." She bawled. "Please! There has to be another way."

For a moment, there was silence, and Bryony actually wondered if Samael had heard her plea. He approached her, crouched down, and cocked his head. "There is another way," he said in that saccharine, soothing voice. "But I may need Ashmedai's cooperation to accomplish it. And to ensure Ashmedai's cooperation, I must remove his reason to resist. Either way, my daughter, your captain is key." He reached out to where she knelt and found the top of her head with his hand. When he rested it there, Bryony got the distinct impression he was imitating some kind of priest. "I will bring your captain to you soon."

Samael lifted his hand and stood. Then he carefully made his way to the back door. Bryony supposed she should be grateful he still intended to spare her home. He certainly could have flattened it if he wanted to. But she would have traded her home for the lives of her friends in a heartbeat. As it stood, the only trade Samael seemed willing to make was Chuy's innocence for the life of the watcher Azazel, and Bryony could not—would not—make that kind of deal.

Chapter Thirteen

The closer Ash got to his cabin in the woods, the more his thoughts raced. He had switched his headlights off as soon as he reached the turnoff and continued on with only the stars and moon to light his path. It wouldn't pose a problem for him, and it would draw less attention from Samael's host. But what if they'd already found the cabin? And Chuy. Those girls who'd conjured him had no idea the damage they might have done.

Damage, like his captive was an object instead of a person. Ash cringed. He was already building up a wall under the assumption that he'd lost Chuy, that he'd somehow misread his own visions of death's mysterious retreat. He pulled into the drive and approached the cabin slowly. It looked to be in one piece. A lamp was still lit inside. Did Chuy forget to extinguish it before he fell asleep? Or perhaps he'd waited up all night.

Traffic had been a frustrating mess. It was the wee hours now, and Ash knew he'd been gone too long. He exited the vehicle in silence, watching and listening for angels. The last thing he wanted to do was walk into a trap. But when the sound of gunfire assaulted his ears, he lost all his resolve to be cautious. He stormed into the cabin—already growing his body to intimidating proportions—and he found it empty.

Another gunshot.

Ash barreled through the back door, following each report with an ever-growing sense of panic. None of this was right. He abandoned his human body in favor of his demonic one. He was a beast, a monster crashing through the forest with heavy claws and wings of black skin and bone. He allowed his two animal faces to join his human one. He allowed his tail to grow long and serpentine. He became the chimera, the cherub's child, and he prepared to fight an entire host of angels.

There was a fifth gunshot, and Ash began to doubt what he was up against. Angels did not use guns. Ever. They had their own weapons, which were far superior to anything the mortal world had produced. Had humans attacked? But why?

About a mile from the cabin, Ashmedai finally found him. Chuy was shirtless and shivering, drenched from a downpour that had already come and gone. He had a rifle in his hands, but he didn't seem to be shooting at anything in particular. He was alone. After a flood of relief came the questions and the uncanny feeling that something was very, very off. Ash watched a moment as Chuy struggled to reload the rifle, swaying and fumbling. And then the bottle on the ground caught his eye. Bourbon, half gone. Chuy was drunk and very close to shooting his own head off as poorly as he was handling that rifle. Ash covered the distance between them in one step, snatched the rifle from the captain's hands, and threw it into the forest. Then he lifted Chuy in one fist as though the man were nothing more than a doll.

"What is this?" he roared.

Chuy struggled and screamed.

Ash held him tighter. "Answer me! I am your keeper. What has happened here?" Chuy wore himself out fighting the demon king. It was a hopeless struggle, of course, and Ash was patient enough to wait until Chuy realized it before he repeated his question. "What has happened here?"

Chuy bowed his head and mumbled, "My coat disappeared." And then he passed out.

Clearly, a meaningful conversation about any of this would be impossible tonight. Ash brought Chuy back to the cabin and slowly shrank down to his human form. When they arrived, he carried Chuy over his shoulder and dropped him like a sack of laundry onto the bed.

"This is absurd," Ash said. "I was away for one day." He glanced around the cabin and saw several more bottles, each at different stages of gone. A small pantry had been opened, and inside were rows of liquor all lined up like a church choir. Ash groaned, disgusted by his own carelessness. He should have searched the cabin more carefully. He knew Chuy's history. This should not have come as a surprise.

As Chuy lay sprawled and shivering on the bed, Ash went about rebuilding the fire that had long since gone out. When he was finished, he closed up the cabin and began attending to Chuy himself. The man was freezing. "You're a fool," Ash murmured. "I told you I was coming back."

He towel-dried Chuy's hair and torso before turning down the sheets, a tricky maneuver to perform while the bed was occupied. Then he crawled over his captive, so focused on accomplishing his task without waking the man, he didn't even consider how close he was, how precarious his situation. But when Ash slipped an arm under Chuy's back to lift him an inch and free the last of the sheets, Chuy woke and grabbed his collar. And all Ash's blissful ignorance came tumbling down around him.

He tried to pull away, but the captain's insistence allied with his own body's rebellion and trapped him where he was. Chuy lifted himself off the mattress, and Ash pinned him down again, straddling his abdomen to ensure he stayed put. "That's enough," the demon king commanded. "Settle down and sober up."

But it wasn't enough, and Chuy refused to settle down. "Hey . . ." he slurred. "Hey, I've gotta question for ya. C'mere." Chuy crooked his finger, and Ash obeyed, lowering his head to hear whatever it was the captain had to tell him. How could he not? This was all his fault, after all. "Hey," Chuy whispered. "Why d'you spend so much energy on the living?"

Nonsense. Ash sat up and slid backward, still straddling the man's body and ready to pin him down again if necessary.

Chuy smiled a wicked smile and said, "I think I know why," in a singsong voice. "Not like you've been subtle 'bout it or anything." He laughed, and Ash felt the blood rush to his face. "Stare, stare, stare—"

Before he quite understood why he was doing it, Ash had leaned on one hand and covered Chuy's mouth with the other. "Don't."

A quick tongue darted into his palm, and Ash was startled into removing his hand. "Stare, stare," Chuy finished. "You like me. I can tell. But 's okay. I like you too." He was viper-quick as he grabbed Ash by the shirt and pulled him all the way down. "See?"

Ash did see, or rather he felt that the captain was far from lying. Now his position was even more precarious, not least because he was having trouble convincing himself it was precarious and not, in fact, extremely pleasurable. *He's the wine in the well,* Ash reminded himself as he lowered his forehead until it just touched Chuy's. *He's the wine in the well.* "Stop it, stop it, stop it," Ash begged both himself and the man tempting him.

"Why?" Chuy's hands slid around to Ash's backside and applied more pressure.

"Because you don't know what you're doing."

Chuy immediately misunderstood. "Oh, I know what I'm doin', Yer Majesty. You won' be disappointed." He laughed, and the vibration of that laugh hit Ash's stomach like a shot of whisky.

Ash groaned as Chuy's hands slid up his back and pulled his shirt along with them. "You're drunk."

"That only makes me better." Chuy paused to consider. "Or so I've been told."

Suddenly, Ash didn't have a thought to spare for his own situation. All he cared about was finding whoever had told Chuy that disgusting lie and relieving them of their head. Was it the man who'd given him that pendant? Ash hadn't seen many other men in Chuy's life. *Maybe one . . . that first experiment . . .* And now he was picturing it, and now he was hard and needy, and to add insult to injury, his skin was warming to an alarming degree. His body, it seemed, had forgotten he'd been dead for ages and meant to carry on just like it had when he was alive.

He repeated his mantra. "Do not drink the wine in—"

But Chuy didn't let him finish. While Ash's eyes were closed and his thoughts occupied with his own battle, Chuy rose up and kissed his mouth. And Ash, lord help him, kissed the captain back. He tasted of bourbon but something else too. Something familiar and calming. Something sweet like honey. Ash opened his mouth and let Chuy's tongue past his lips. He took hold of the brass bars on the headboard to steady himself, but every time he involuntarily flexed his arms, his body shifted against Chuy's. And every time his body shifted, a bolt of overwhelming pleasure shot all through him.

What was that sweet flavor anyway? Ash convinced himself he was only kissing the captain to find out. He'd stop as soon as he recognized it. He would. But his hands had wandered down to Chuy's stomach, and Chuy had already unbuttoned Ash's shirt, and god that skin felt so cool against his, and Ash was already on fire.

Help, he pleaded to no one in his head. And then aloud, "Help me."

"I'm trying," Chuy answered, and it took Ash a moment to realize he was talking about unfastening Ash's belt buckle.

Ash pulled away and muttered, "No." But there was no weight behind it. He needed this—with all his soul he needed it. He rolled onto his side, grabbed the waistband of Chuy's jeans, tugged him close, and kissed him deeper. Sweet, soft, and familiar.

Do not drink the wine in the well.

But Ash didn't care anymore. He'd give up his freedom for this man in a heartbeat. He'd give up his principles, his title, his power. He'd drink himself weak, and harmless, and stupid just to hold Chuy one more time. Then he realized, with a jolt, that he wasn't the one who was drunk—not this time. The one who was vulnerable this time was

Chuy, and Ash was the one taking advantage of it. He was behaving like King Solomon.

He pushed himself away from Chuy as though the man had spontaneously burst into flames. He knelt on the mattress and dragged his sleeve over his mouth. "Oh my god." He scrambled from the bed as Chuy watched after him, a bemused expression on his beautiful face.

"Where'ya goin'?"

"Nowhere," Ash answered. He walked backward, grabbed a chair, and sat and stared as though turning his back on the captain could get him killed. He ordered himself to stay rooted to the spot. That was close—way, way too close. Ash buttoned his shirt and re-buckled his belt. When Chuy sat up, Ash pointed a finger at him. "Stay! You stay there and sober up." He sounded like a dog trainer, even to himself, so he softened his tone. "Please. Just try to sleep. We'll talk about this in the morning."

"Ya don' want me." Chuy fell back and groaned.

"I do. Jesus Christ I do—that's the whole problem."

"I'm so stupid," Chuy said into his pillow.

"No, I am. You're drunk, and I'm stupid. This was my fault and my mistake. I . . ." Ash took a long, trembling breath. "I shouldn't have let it go that far." And he knew it was more than true as he said it. As many times as Ash had relived his obscured visions of their future together—as much as he tried to forget that Chuy was destined to break his heart—to the wayward captain of *Papillon*, the demon king was little more than a stranger. What Chuy had attempted tonight was not the start of a new relationship. It was a very specific kind of self-destruction. Only now, instead of a bottle and a rifle, Chuy had chosen to use the demon king.

"I already love you too much," Ash said, shocked it was something he was ready to admit. "Ask me to die a second time, and I'll find a way for you. But I can't give this to you. I won't be the one who breaks you."

As firm as he was on the subject, Ash knew he was only talking to himself. Chuy had already fallen asleep.

Soldiers all standing in a row.

Ash had spent the last hours before dawn clearing the hunting cabin of liquor and queueing up every bottle outside. He'd opened every drawer, every cabinet. He'd even looked under the bed. And now, as the rising sun provided a cold light in the morning mist, he stood before those glass soldiers with deadly intention. He picked up the first, a still unopened Jägermeister, and threw it against a boulder with far more force than was strictly necessary. It shattered, painted the stone with dark liquid, and filled the air with a smell that reminded Ash of a very specific brand of cough syrup.

Next, the vodka. There were two bottles of vodka, and Ash enjoyed smashing both of them. It was cathartic, and he had no intention of stopping until every last bottle was reduced to a pile of colorful shards, even the empty ones. He became so engrossed in his ritual destruction that he didn't notice Chuy's approach until the man spoke.

"You're back." The captain stood just behind Ash in his jeans and white T-shirt, his hair adorably disheveled from hours of restless sleep.

Last night came back to Ash in vivid flashes, and he took it out on another bottle. "Yes," he answered over the sound of shattering glass. "I arrived in the early hours."

Chuy bowed his head and absently scratched a spot on his thigh. "Right." He looked wan and tired, and Ash wondered if he'd been sick already. "I . . . suppose I made a fool of myself."

"No, you did not." The honest answer was easy as far as Ash was concerned. The one who'd made a fool of himself last night was him, though he was not about to admit it.

"Ah . . ." Chuy shifted from foot to foot and rubbed his bare arms with his hands. "The thing is . . . I kind of blacked out. So . . . I mean whatever happened . . . I'm sorry."

"Do not apologize," Ash growled.

"Think I probably should."

Ash whirled on him with a large bottle of tequila clutched in one hand. "No, you should not!" Chuy flinched, and Ash immediately regretted his temper. He tried to soften his voice. "All of this was my fault. I saw enough of your history to know better." He threw the tequila and savored the sound of its violent end. "I just wasn't careful."

"It shouldn't be your responsibility to keep me sober." Chuy crouched to conserve his own heat, and Ash wanted to punch himself for failing to notice the man's shivering again.

"You still need a coat." Ash deserted the bottles and approached Chuy, who stepped back. His wariness sent a pang through the demon king's heart. "May I?" Ash held out a hand, and Chuy nodded once.

As though diving deep into something he wasn't sure he could get out of, Ash took a deep breath and held it while he laid his hand on Chuy's chest. Slowly, the coat formed around Chuy's tattooed arms and narrow torso. Ash came very close to losing the coat entirely when Chuy brought a hand up and laid it over his. "Please," Chuy said. "I know something happened last night, but I don't know what. I can only guess, and my guesses keep getting worse and worse."

Ash finished the coat and slipped his hand out from under Chuy's. "It was the wine in the well."

"The wine in the what?"

Ash turned back to his orchestrated massacre, and another bottle met its end against the boulder. "I take it you don't study demonology."

"Not even a little." Chuy laughed.

It was so good to hear that laugh again. All right then. Time to share. Ash had seen too much of Chuy's history, and it would be monstrous not to make himself equally vulnerable. "When I was a new demon and still learning to manifest a body, I became dependent on routine." Another crash of glass. "Routine made manifestation easier, more predictable. It also organized my life in a way that made productivity possible. Being stretched between two worlds has a tendency to distract one from getting an education, and I was desperate for an education."

He glanced back to see Chuy clutching his coat closed. Ash threw another bottle—whisky this time—and continued his humiliating story. "I had two teachers at the time, a celestial teacher and a terrestrial one. I divided my lessons between them, learning the languages, histories, sciences, and arts of both worlds. Usually, at the end of each long day, I became thirsty. It was all psychological, of course. I'd managed to outgrow hunger after my death, but I hadn't quite eliminated thirst. So I kept a cistern."

More whisky crashed against the boulder. Ash gritted his teeth against his own trepidation. Admitting weakness was a dangerous business. But if he couldn't trust the last innocent man, who could he trust? It didn't matter anyway. He would say whatever it took to wipe the look of shame off Chuy's face. "I trusted no one in those days—for good reason—and I sealed my supply against tampering. I thought I was being smart about it. I wasn't. Solomon's men just drained my water supply from below and replaced it with wine.

"It was an obvious trap, but they knew me well. I needed to drink. I steeled myself against the craving with every proverb I knew. *Don't drink the wine*, they all assured me. *It makes you stupid and vulnerable. It makes you weak.* But there was one line in one psalm that seemed to contradict the rest. *Wine that makes glad the heart of man . . .* It was nothing, a fragment of a verse, but it was enough. I decided I deserved a little happiness."

Chuy didn't say a word, and Ash almost wished he would. An interruption would have been welcome. Anything to keep him from telling this humiliating story. "I drank the wine." Ash picked up a bottle of wine from the glass army and crushed it in his bare hands. He hated it. He hated all of it. "Unused to drink and unused to my manifested body, I intoxicated myself. I passed out. When I woke, I was in chains, bound by the Ineffable Name, which someone had foolishly taught to King Solomon. I have my suspicions as to who."

He turned back to Chuy, and his anger softened at the sight of the man he loved. "For years, I was enslaved to a mortal king. I built Solomon's temple with my own hands, and after it was finished, he decided to keep me around just in case. It was a miracle I ever escaped him. So many years of education, freedom, and training lost, all because I let down my guard once. All because I wanted a moment of happiness, one idle evening, just a sip of normal life. All because I wanted to taste the wine in the well."

When Ash finished his story, he bowed his head and waited for the admonishment he knew would come, a derisive joke perhaps, or extremely belated, useless advice. He should have known better. Chuy just stood there, held his coat closed in the chill, and patiently waited for the demon king to answer his question. Ash shook off his shame and obliged him the only way he could. "What happened last night was the wine in the well. A moment of happiness—a lifetime of consequences. I will not allow it to happen again."

For a moment, Chuy lifted his fingers to his own lips, as though the ghost of something there still haunted him. Ash felt an immediate need to mitigate with a simpler answer. "You were drunk and shooting a rifle. I took it from you and put you to bed."

"Sorry," Chuy muttered. Then he stepped in and glanced down at what was left of the row of bottles. "Mind if I join you?"

"Not at all." Ash picked up the bottle of bourbon he'd recovered from the scene. "This was what I found you with last night. I was saving it for last." He handed it to Chuy and stepped back.

Chuy glanced down at the bottle, the self-disgust and anger evident in his usually carefree expression. He held it upside down by its neck and hurled it at the stone. It hit and shattered, and Chuy laughed. "That felt good. Can I have another?"

In the end, it was Chuy who demolished the last of them. When every bottle was smashed, they headed inside. Ash stoked the fire and asked Chuy if he'd eaten.

"Didn't have much of an appetite." Chuy shrugged.

"Well, you're eating something now." Ash sat him down at the table, got him a new crossword puzzle from the stack of papers in the coat closet, and set a glass of water before him. "Drink all of it." He then retrieved a can of chicken soup from the cupboard and made a face at it. "I wish you'd let me get you something fresh."

Chuy shook his head. "How 'bout not. I didn't exactly get top marks last time you left."

Ash stared into the pot of soup as he stirred and quietly battled his own overwhelming shame. Not only had he failed to foresee a possible conjuration, but he'd failed to resist the wine in the well. Again. And this time, it wasn't his own safety he risked. It was Chuy's.

"Where did you go exactly?" Chuy asked.

"I was summoned"—Ash grimaced—"by teenagers. Four girls at a sleepover in Portland somehow managed to conjure up the demon king."

Chuy choked on his water and slapped the table. "No way!" He was in sudden hysterics, but Ash could take all manner of humiliation if it brought that smile back again. "What did they want?"

Ash shrugged. "They didn't know. I honestly don't think they expected it to work."

"I thought Samael had gotten you."

"So did I." He stirred the soup one more time and fished a bowl from the cabinets. "But the more I think on it, the less sense it would have made. Samael wouldn't bother to conjure me because it isn't really me he wants. It's you. And as you saw, I don't automatically bring you along when I'm summoned. On top of that, the Angel of Death is no conjuror." Ash ladled the soup into a bowl and served it to Chuy, but his mind was elsewhere. "What's most unsettling to me is the fact that the ensnaring circle they used has long been lost to history. It was only known to the old magicians, back when the watchers were still teaching mankind the secrets of heaven. These days, only the original conjuring angels know how to draw that circle. So I wonder, how did four young girls manage it?"

Chuy tasted his soup and frowned. He was clearly still feeling his hangover. "Maybe they had help," he said.

"That's what I'm thinking. The conjuror—this adorable thing, I'll tell you about her later—had a book she was reading from. I took it from her before I left. It's still in the passenger seat of the car she loaned me."

"So she let you go and gave you the book?" Chuy's eyes grew wide. "And a car?"

Ash nodded. "I offered her a gift, and she was happy to accept. She parted with the car and the book quite easily. Come to think of it, I meant to examine that book as soon as I got back." He stood and started for the door, but Chuy's abrupt reaction gave him pause. The captain reacted like the prey he was and froze. "I'll just be a second," Ash assured him. "I swear I won't leave you again." But he wasn't convinced his word meant anything anymore.

He practically ran to the car to retrieve the book. When he returned, he cleared half the table and laid the tome on it. It was an enormous green-and-gold volume with no title or author on the cover. Something about it was strangely familiar. Ash ran his finger along its spine and came away with a fine, white film. He sniffed it, tasted it, and muttered, "Salt."

Chuy leaned in. "That's the book?"

"Yes. Hopefully, this is the only copy. I don't want to be summoned again. It's an extraordinarily unpleasant business."

Chuy nodded and sipped another spoonful of soup as Ash opened the book.

The paper inside was stiff, coated with the same salty film. He turned page after page, examining each with the caution and care it was due. Finally, he pulled out his spectacles and put them on. And for the first time in ages, Ashmedai doubted his own eyes. "It can't be." He turned another page and leaned in to see the strokes of penmanship he'd come to know so well over the years. "But it is."

"What is it?" Clearly, Ash's amazement translated because Chuy had abandoned his soup and crossword, and now stared fixedly at the book.

Ash barely believed the answer, even as the words left his own mouth. "It's a recent incarnation of the *Sefer Raziel*—the book of the Angel of Secrets, my celestial teacher."

Chapter Fourteen

The kitchen table needed refinishing. Bryony couldn't help but notice because she was staring down at the woodgrain in an attempt to avoid eye contact with Michael. He'd taken the news that Bryony had learned to pronounce her angelic name better than she'd expected him to. In fact, he'd asked if he could learn it too. Bryony, forgetting the lesson would have to come from Azazel, had told him she didn't see why not.

That was how they came to this incredibly uncomfortable situation. Azazel sat beside Bryony and attempted to explain the affection required for angelic name sharing. He assured them that his teaching Michael Bryony's name would be no trouble at all. "I absolutely adore you, petal. I'd pinch your cheeks if you allowed it." But now Michael was about to learn the level of affection *he* would have to feel before he could repeat that name back to Azza. And that meant he was very close to learning how much Bryony had grown to love the watcher.

And if he was anything at all like his father . . .

Bryony dug her fingernails into the grooves on the underside of her table and picked away little splinters of wood. This was agonizing, and it was clear Azza planned to take his time with the lesson. On one hand, she appreciated his treating the conversation with the caution she felt it deserved. On the other hand, when the ear-splitting crack of lightning nearly drove her under the table, she did not hesitate to use it as an excuse to withdraw.

"Samael's here," she said. "I'd better go."

Michael narrowed his eyes at her, but Azza just waved her on. "We'll be fine, darling. You go ahead. We'll wait patiently for your return."

Unfortunately, Samael was not so patient.

"I have come to discuss my progress and the nature of our agreement," he said while Bryony was still making her way toward him. He waited in her little grove of plum trees, which seemed to be the ritual he now preferred. She almost regretted showing them to him. His nightly invasion of her sanctuary in order to discuss a plan she hated was beginning to try *her* patience.

"Oh, have you?" No point in hiding her irritation now. She waited for his admonishment, but as usual, Samael refused to be predictable.

"I have also come to apologize for the way I left you on my last visit."

Bryony blinked. An apology? From the Angel of Death? She must have heard wrong. "I'm sorry, what?"

"I was exhausted, and I lost control. It was not my intention." The golden color of the setting sun reflected off the graveyard angel, who stood as still as a marble statue at the center of the grove. She stared at him, desperate to figure him out, but he was beyond figuring. "First order of business," he said, holding up one finger as though he were nothing more than an under-zealous preacher. "My progress. I am happy to report that Ashmedai has opened the book as expected. My host quickly pinpointed his location and will retrieve your captain tonight."

Bryony's hopes plummeted. She wanted to scream at Ashmedai for being so gullible, but she honestly wasn't sure she wouldn't have made the same mistake.

"I imagine you're unhappy to hear this news," Samael said, and Bryony snapped back to attention. "I suspected you had a hand in warning the demon king of my pursuit. You only confirmed it when you begged me not to eliminate your captain's innocence."

All this time, Bryony believed she'd successfully hidden her move against the Angel of Death, but she'd been a fool to think she could keep anything from him. "Okay, fine. I asked that Ashmedai be warned. But I wouldn't have had to if you weren't so dead set on destroying an innocent man's . . . well, innocence. Why? Chuy means nothing to you, and he's done nothing to hurt you. Why punish him?"

"It is not a punishment." Samael stood so eerily still Bryony had to avert her eyes. He didn't look alive at all. She realized she'd grown used to Azza and Ash's well-honed manifestations. Clearly, the medium of flesh was not the Angel of Death's strong suit.

"How else could you possibly categorize it?" she asked.

"It is an amputation. Ashmedai has an unhealthy obsession, and your captain is the embodiment of it. Think of his innocence as a gangrenous limb that needs to be removed before the infection spreads."

Bryony scowled up at him. "Innocence is not an infection."

"That's arguable." Samael felt for a tree and made himself comfortable leaning against it. He looked much less intimidating in such a casual pose, and Bryony had to wonder whether he'd heard the discomfort in her voice and was attempting to assuage it. "Innocence encourages belief in dangerous lies: faith is a virtue, the world is a beautiful place, people are all good at heart, and angels are here to protect you. He has, no doubt, been disabused of that last sentiment, as has most of the world. I merely intend to disabuse him of the rest."

As terrible as Samael's view of the world was, Bryony had to admit she'd shared it most of her life. But Chuy didn't think that way, and that was one of the things she loved best about him. "What will he believe when you're through with him?"

"Only the truth."

"And what is the truth?"

The graveyard angel straightened from his calculated slouch. "That faith is a sin and gullibility a crime. The world is merciless and ugly. People are self-interested liars at their core. And there is no such thing as a good angel."

There wasn't much there Bryony would have argued with a year ago. But recently . . . Recently, she'd been proven wrong on several counts, one of which could be easily demonstrated. "Azazel is a good angel."

Samael threw his head back and laughed. It was a cruel laugh, sent like a malediction to the crisscrossing branches of Bryony's sanctuary. She hated the sound of it, beautiful though it was. Angels and their voices—she would never get used to them. "Azazel is not a good angel," Samael said, his voice still tinged with dark mirth. "He is a manipulator of men and a seducer of women."

Now it was Bryony's turn to laugh. "If that's true, then you're just as bad, Sama."

Samael narrowed his empty eyes at her. "I never claimed to be good."

"But you could be," Bryony pointed out. "That's what I think Chuy believes in. It's something I've only just begun to understand. It's not inherent goodness he sees in people but potential. He believes in anyone who gives him the slightest reason to. I actually think it was Chuy's influence that led me to listen to Azza when I first met him instead of killing him outright. Now I have a friend in him."

"We shall see." Samael frowned. "Perhaps he has only seduced you."

"That's absurd."

"It is not. You love him because he's beautiful. You would not love him if he were ugly."

Bryony rolled her eyes. "You're ridiculous, do you know that? I'm not a child anymore. I don't love anyone just because they're beautiful. Honestly, I've told you I think you're beautiful, and I certainly don't have any love for you." The graveyard angel stiffened at that. Had it hurt him? How . . . unexpected. She'd been under the impression his primary concern was for his appearance. If that were the case, he should have taken her comment as a compliment. She tried to shake the unsettling guilt she suddenly felt. "I love Azza because he's kind. He's had plenty of opportunity to abuse my trust, and he hasn't. He's completely turned himself around. As we speak, he's sitting in my kitchen, teaching Michael to pronounce—"

"What?" Samael broke in, his voice and posture tarnished with sudden rage. Bryony was certain that, if he could manifest color, his face would have turned bright red. He started down the path to her house, his strides so long she had to run to keep up. Through his teeth, he growled, "I will not allow that creature to lay a hand on my son."

"Oh, for god's sake!" She panted behind him. "Like you have any right to march in and get possessive over a son you abandoned before he was even born!"

"I did *not* abandon him." He was so adamant, Bryony almost believed him.

"Yes! You did! Letting a child steal your god damned weapon doesn't count as taking responsibility for him!" He was as far as her veranda now, and Bryony couldn't help shouting, "Stairs, Sama!" when he reached them. He paused, found the handrail, and climbed to the front door.

Predictably, Bryony's attempt to reason with the Angel of Death was getting nowhere. Once he made up his mind, nothing would convince him to rethink his conclusions. She followed him into her living room and shouted to warn the others. "Incoming! And he's really, really pissed!"

Two chairs scraped against the kitchen floor, and as soon as Samael entered the room, two bodies thudded to the ground. Bryony followed and found Michael on his knees, covering his eyes with his hands. Azza had gone fetal, whimpering softly with his forehead to the floor.

"You." Samael addressed Azazel first. "Stay away from my son." Then, to Michael, he said, "I will teach you your name. I gave it to you. I will teach you to pronounce it. How could this imbecile even begin to understand such a name? He has never given a gift in his life. He only receives them."

"That's not true," Bryony muttered, though she knew it would be useless to argue the point. Louder, she said, "You've misunderstood, Sama. It isn't his name Azazel is teaching him. It's mine."

Samael's shoulders relaxed suddenly. "Oh." He seemed to have run out of steam for a moment, and then it was back again in force. "I don't care. The boy should learn his ancestral language from his father, not some fool watcher."

"Stop it." Bryony had definitely had enough of Samael's tantrum. He was being unreasonable, and no matter how powerful a spirit he was, someone had to tell him so. "It's not fair to deny your son a teacher. You said it yourself—he can't even stand in your presence."

The graveyard angel hovered over Michael like an ill omen. At last, he said to Bryony, "You will teach him to stand in my presence. You know how." His voice had settled, but his shoulders were still at his ears.

She sighed. "I don't know if it's something a person can be taught."

"He will learn." Samael paused, thought a moment, and then nodded to himself. "He's a clever boy."

"And why should he put so much effort in when you haven't?" she said, still not satisfied that he understood what he was asking. "Why should he work so hard to learn anyone's name from you? You won't even call him by the name he chose for himself."

"Because it is the *worst* name!" Samael shouted, and Bryony thought it was the first time she'd ever heard him shout. He quickly lowered his voice again. "It is the worst name anyone could have chosen for him."

Out of the corner of her eye, Bryony saw Michael's mouth twitch. Dear god, he was smiling. This was the reason he'd chosen his name, and it had worked like a charm. Samael hated it—passionately, viscerally hated it.

Abruptly, the graveyard angel changed tack. "Second order of business," he said as though the last several minutes hadn't even happened. "Our agreement. I have considered it carefully and come to the conclusion that your end cannot be fulfilled in the way I originally demanded. It is impossible. You cannot summon the archangel"—he paused and snarled as he said the name in three distinct syllables—"Mi-cha-EL with this watcher as your partner. You've grown too fond, and your body will not allow possession if you fear it, even if your fear is for the safety of the one possessing you."

Bryony tried not to breathe a sigh of relief and failed spectacularly.

Once again, the graveyard angel assumed the pose of a preacher with one finger pointed skyward and his chin lifted. "In that vein, your body will also reject any new conjuring partners you may find. Conjuring with a partner requires possession, and possession requires trust. Due to your past experience with angels, you are unlikely to trust any you haven't come to know on a deeper level. And due to your needy heart, you are unlikely to form a close relationship without developing some affection for the creature. Thus, you will be unable to risk the safety of any of your conjuring partners."

Of all the otherworldly creatures she'd come to know—and that list included Loki—the Angel of Death was the most likely to give Bryony emotional whiplash. First, he admitted he'd been unreasonable in his expectations, which gave her some modicum of hope. Then he insulted her by calling her needy. She wanted to simultaneously hug and slap him. Instead, she cleared her throat and said, "Go on."

If he noticed her agitation, Samael did not let on. "The solution to this problem is simple. You need a conjuring partner who does not require your permission or trust to possess you."

At that, Azazel's entire body shuddered as though it were a pool of water someone had thrown a giant stone into. It did not go unnoticed by Bryony. The watcher's back and fingers arched as he fought to break free from the Angel of Death's curse. Whatever it was he wanted to say, he was risking too much to say it.

Samael's finger was still pointed skyward. It was a counterfeit gesture, and he didn't seem to know when to bring it down. The awkward pose made him seem even more alien than he already was. "Luckily," he said, "I know of an angel who can do exactly that. And as it happens, I have in my possession an item he greatly desires. No doubt, he'll be happy to oblige."

Again, Azazel's manifested flesh rippled in his futile effort to object.

Samael did not notice. "The angel's name is Raziel. If you and your current partner summon him, there will be no danger to your partner. Azazel can then step aside and let Raziel perform the more perilous task of facilitating the assassination. As Raziel is a stranger to you, his safety should not weigh heavily on your mind." The graveyard angel paused and chuckled to himself. "That angel will do anything to get his precious book out of my hands before I manage to irrevocably corrupt it."

Now Michael's distress grew to match Azza's, but Michael was able to voice his objection from behind the wall of his hands. "No," he said firmly. "She refuses. Find another way."

Samael cocked his head. "Son, I understand you've become engaged to this woman, but you must know, that doesn't mean you may make decisions on her behalf. She will tell me if she refuses."

Good fatherly advice, Bryony thought, but she doubted it was entirely sincere. She had the distinct impression that, were Michael to come down on his father's side, Samael would encourage as much authoritarianism as was required to make Bryony comply. As it was, she felt rather ambivalent about the proposition. Though the idea of being possessed without permission rubbed her wrong, the idea of disengaging Azza from such a dangerous mission tempted her. Whoever this Raziel was, perhaps he and Bryony could cooperate as two strangers with a similar goal instead of two people who loved each other.

"She refuses," Michael repeated. "Accept it."

"Who is Raziel?" Bryony finally asked. The name sounded vaguely familiar.

Both Michael and his father answered.

Samael said, "The Angel of Secrets," which sounded harmless enough.

But Michael said, "One of the ophanim," which sent Bryony into an icy state of shock.

An ophan who can possess without permission. The thought nauseated her. She'd had very few childhood experiences with angels—most of her knowledge of them had come to her second hand—but the one she would never, ever forget was watching an ophan consume an entire town in seconds. The creature had been as bright as the sun itself, and it had an indescribable shape that made her head hurt to think about. Wheels within wheels. Eyes within eyes. And that mouth—that monstrous, gaping maw that closed over everything and everyone at once.

Now Bryony understood why Azza and Michael had fought so hard to object. They knew how she felt about the ophanim. She opened and closed her mouth a number of times before she managed to make a sound. "I . . . I can't." She harnessed Michael's defiance. "I refuse."

Samael didn't seem at all troubled. "It doesn't matter whether you refuse—that's the entire point. Raziel will come and do as I ask. And if you don't want him to possess you a second time, you will kill your target on the first."

"Father," Michael said, his hands still hovering before his eyes. "I can't allow her to be taken by an ophan."

"Why not?" Samael seemed genuinely confused. "The ophanim are the purest among us. Not one of them has fallen. You don't have to worry about an ophan seducing your betrothed the way you do with this one." He gestured in Azza's general direction. "They are blameless."

"They're unmerciful monsters and you know it." Michael managed to pull his hands an inch from his face.

Samael shrugged. "They only enforce the law as it is handed down to them. It's in their nature to do so. When their leader is dead, they will no longer enforce his law. It's perfect, the more I think on it. The archangel will never suspect an unimportant god and an ophan of being assassins." He laughed. "The look on his face will be priceless. I will be sad to miss it."

A sharp breath escaped Michael's lips as he struggled to argue with his father. It was a dark echo of all the times Bryony had stood in this very kitchen, hands on her hips, in childish defiance of her own parents. "Father, Bryony was traumatized by an ophan as a child. Few angels understand trauma the way you do. Please. You can't do this to her."

Azza's fingernails scraped across the floor as he echoed, "Please." It seemed all he was able to say.

The smile faded from the graveyard angel's face. It was replaced by that cold anger Bryony had come to know so well. In Michael, it saddened her. In his father, it absolutely terrified her. "You will do as I ask," Samael said. Though he was furious, his voice never lost its soothing tone. "If you refuse, you will discover that your captain has more than just his innocence to lose."

That threat was the very last straw for Bryony. Until now, she'd been forgiving of Samael's insistence and impatience, understanding on some level the way he felt about the archangel. But this was beyond unacceptable.

"How dare you!" she snapped, which by the look on Samael's face, was not the reaction he expected. "Chuy has nothing to do with this, but you're willing to destroy him over some stupid, ancient feud? It's disgusting. You're disgusting! Why do you hate the archangel so much anyway? Even I'm not willing to risk innocent lives to get to him, and as far as I'm concerned, he killed my entire family. So he defeated you once. Besides your pride, what's he ever taken from you? Who have *you* lost because of him? Help me to understand because I've tried, and I . . . I just can't justify any of this."

The stillness Samael exuded spoke louder than any words or expression could. Bryony had forced him to consider his past, and apparently, he didn't like it at all. She fought the urge to back away as he turned toward her and moved closer. When there were only inches between them, he said, "It is not what he took, but what he gave that makes him worthy of my hatred."

The graveyard angel's arm shot out so quickly Bryony didn't even see it happen. Before she knew it, his enormous hand was at the base of her skull, clinging and squeezing and tilting her face up to his. From somewhere behind her, Michael shouted, "Let go! Don't touch her!"

Samael behaved as though he couldn't even hear his son. "You will never understand how I feel because you are not an angel. But I can bring you close." He bowed over her and brought his face so near that Bryony had the momentary and ridiculous fear the Angel of Death might kiss her. But no, she knew what this was. And the way he held her—so close she could feel the warmth of his manifested skin, his lips parted just enough to breathe into her—let her know she did not mistake him. His hand steadied the back of her head, and his powerful fingers tangled in her hair.

As soon as she received what Samael sent to her, Bryony wanted to give it back. It was the most hideous feeling she'd ever had in her life. It was a once-beautiful creature with a bloated stomach and pecked out eyes; a headless, muddy songbird; the unmistakable, saccharine smell of decaying flesh; the breakdown and chaos of mortality. It was a disgusting perversion of life. She gagged and swallowed her own bile.

Slowly, Samael relaxed his grip on the back of Bryony's head. When he finally released her, she fell to the floor with the others. "That is my name," he said, "chosen for me by the archangel Michael. A name, to us, is not simply what we're called. It is our entire identity. How do you feel about mine?"

Bryony wept for him. She bowed low and crossed her arms over her face to hide her tears. The terrible emptiness that name left behind, the devastation, the hopelessness—she knew it all well. Every momentous decision she'd made in her life was to avoid ever having to feel it again. She'd become a god to avoid having to feel it again. And for Samael, that feeling was who he was. He could not choose to escape it. He could never, ever hope to forget it.

By the time she found the strength to look up again, the Angel of Death had gone, and Michael's arms were already closing around her. "I'm so sorry," he whispered. "I couldn't stop him."

Bryony wanted to comfort him, but she had no comfort to give. All the life had been sucked out of her, and she was so, so tired. No wonder Samael had been shocked when she'd called him beautiful—no wonder if that name was the essence of who he believed himself to be, if that name was how his peers really saw him. She barely noticed when Michael lifted her into his arms and moved her to the living-room couch. He sat down with her, let her rest her head in his lap, and began gently stroking her hair.

Minutes later, Azza joined them and built a fire. He used his bare hands and said very little. Finally, he sat in his usual chair beside the hearth and steepled his fingers. "We will not summon Raziel," he said, his voice tinged with bitterness. "I can't believe he would even suggest such a thing. Forced possession is despicable." Samael seemed to have forgotten that Azazel was a watcher—by definition, a rebellious angel—and unlikely to take orders from anyone.

"Thank you, Azza," Michael said. The weight behind his gratitude could not be mistaken.

The angel acknowledged his thanks before leaning closer to Bryony. "Darling, would you like me to play for you?" What he really meant to ask was whether Bryony required a sip of worship. Every time he played her father's piano, Azazel sent a little prayer her way. Bryony experienced it like a gentle daze, a sweet scent on the wind, a lazy afternoon. She nodded in answer, and Azza stood. But before he walked away, he crouched beside her and took her hand. "Will you be all right?" he asked. Bryony nodded again, and Azza shook his head. "I'm glad. Although I must say, little orb-weaver, you've been much too ambitious this time."

Bryony narrowed her eyes at him, unsure quite what he was getting at.

He just smiled. "The quarry you've caught is perhaps too big for your web. It will certainly wreak havoc in its fight to free itself."

"What are you talking about?" Michael asked on Bryony's behalf. She was grateful because, just now, she was not in the mood to interpret Azza's metaphors. "Do you mean my father?"

"Samael. Yes." Azza stood and straightened his tunic. "I would not have expected it, honestly, but there you see my ability to predict the future is not so good as Ashmedai's."

Michael's lap was warm and comfortable, and Bryony might have fallen asleep right there if Azza's words hadn't troubled her. She knit her brow. "How have I caught Samael in my web? If anything, he's caught me in his."

"Oh, I don't think so," Azza said. "That seraph's as entangled as I was the day you first forgave me. Though, there's no telling how long he'll stay caught. He has a talent for disentangling himself, that one." He shrugged. "But for however long it lasts, little orb-weaver, Samael loves you."

Michael and Bryony reacted in unison. "What?"

Bryony sat up and groaned when she realized Azazel had to be joking. "Yes, ha-ha, Azza. Very funny."

Azazel frowned. "I may not be an expert in affairs of the heart, you know—especially not *his* heart—but some things are universal, darling. As unpleasant as it must have been for you, Samael has made his introduction. To you. Do you understand?"

She did, and she fell back into Michael's lap with an exhausted groan. She could not deal with this right now.

Michael resumed stroking her hair. "*I* don't understand. Explain it to me."

"Ah, sorry, petal. Of course, I was getting to it, if I'd only been allowed to complete our lesson. Well, we'll consider Samael our in-class demonstration. In order to make an introduction the way your father did . . . Well, how shall I put this exactly? An exchange of names, for us, is not as simple as it is for you. What we share is our most secret identity. It isn't given out to just anyone. That kind of introduction does not—*cannot*—happen without a great deal of affection behind it. Do you see?"

"But he hates me right now," Bryony protested, rubbing the back of her head where Samael's fingers had bruised her.

"Have you never been angry with someone you loved, especially family?" Azza tucked a lock of deep-purple hair behind his ear and mused, "It's possible he already thinks of you as a daughter. It's been a long time since he's spoken to anyone who wasn't prone and weeping. You must have reeled him in with your delightful personality. Darling, don't make that face at me. I'm not flattering you. Just be careful. Consider this warning—Samael once loved the archangel Michael, deeply, which was how the archangel was able to name him in the first place. You've seen how that turned out. Break the Angel of Death's heart at your peril, and don't expect him to forget it. Ever. Best not to win his heart in the first place."

Michael's hand tightened over Bryony's shoulder. "So you're saying she should distance herself from him."

"As much as possible, yes. Do not allow his affection to deepen."

"I agree." Michael nodded.

But Bryony couldn't help asking, "Isn't that what everyone else has already done to him, though?" It wasn't that she was keen to form a deep and abiding relationship with the Angel of Death—especially not one as unhealthy as this was turning out to be—but hadn't everyone already tried avoidance? How was keeping Samael at a distance supposed to help Chuy? She muttered, "He clearly doesn't respond well to being ostracized."

Azazel patted her cheek as though she were a naïve child. "He's made his own bed, darling."

"Oh, I think he had some help there. That name . . ." She gagged at the mere thought of it and immediately put it out of her mind. "No, it doesn't matter. My focus right now is keeping you and Chuy safe however I can. It's my fault Samael is involved in your lives. I'll take the heat from him if this goes south."

"Not alone, you won't," Azza said. When Michael nodded his agreement, Bryony had to bury her face in his belly so they wouldn't see the sentimental tears she failed to keep from gathering in her eyes.

Chapter Fifteen

As a rule, Ash tended to avoid spending time around people who drank. The very idea of allowing oneself to become so weak made him relive his own painful history. He didn't, therefore, have a lot of experience in treating hangovers. Food and water—that's all he knew. So he raided the pantry and put together the best dinner he could manage with canned goods alone.

Chuy slouched at the table and squinted at an old newspaper. Ash set a plate of sautéed water chestnuts, another bowl of soup, and a glass of cold water in front of him. "Eat. Drink." He overcompensated with a harsh, commanding tone to hide the tenderness he felt.

"You don't have to do all this for me," Chuy said without tearing his eyes from the paper. "I can make my own food."

"Nonsense. You need to recuperate." Ash sat opposite him and resumed his examination of the *Sefer Raziel*. He'd been reading it most of the day. Seeing the book after all these years brought back so many memories. The last he'd heard, the angels had stolen it and thrown it into the deep. Again. The sea really was their favorite place to hide things from each other. So predictable. He wondered if Raziel even knew the book had resurfaced, let alone that it had somehow gotten into the hands of schoolgirls.

"Can I borrow your glasses?" Chuy broke into his thoughts. The man held the newspaper almost to his nose now. "Mine are still on *Papillon*, and I wanna read these captions. This paper's from before the massacre."

There were very few human traits Ashmedai found more attractive than intellectual curiosity. He saw an image of the captain wearing square-rimmed glasses, reading books on the deck of his ship, and the image quickly weakened his resolve. He knew better than to relinquish his spectacles to anyone. He could almost hear Raziel's distinctive whisper warning him. *They are an extension of your own eyes, Ashmedai. Keep them close.* Still he reached into his pocket and handed them to Chuy with less than a breath of hesitation. The sight of the captain in spectacles would be worth the risk.

This kind of carelessness was exactly why the demon king avoided serious relationships. He knew that, as soon as he fell in love, he'd become soft and stupid, an easy target for anyone looking to overthrow or enslave him. He stared unabashedly as Chuy turned the golden spectacles over in his hands. How were such calloused fingers so incredibly gentle? Ash was desperate to examine them more closely. Oh, who was he kidding? He was desperate to be examined *by* them.

He abruptly cleared his throat. "You can try the spectacles, but they may not work the way you need them to."

"How do you mean?"

"They aren't regular magnifiers. They were developed by my celestial teacher to help me interpret the world as I saw it."

"Ya don't say." Chuy set the spectacles beside his paper and rested his chin on his fist. "How do they work?"

And just like that, Ash understood why the watchers had given all their forbidden knowledge to the women they fell for. How could they not? Whatever Chuy wanted to know, Ash was going to tell him. "When I look at a person—really look at them—their entire lives appear to happen all at once. It becomes difficult to discern anything beyond birth and death—birth being darkness, and death being light.

Everything in between is indistinct. The spectacles help me to focus. With them, I can more clearly see those events that change a person. The more ritualistic the event, the easier it is for me to interpret, but anything momentous enough will stand out."

Chuy held the golden frames at arm's length and squinted at them. "Well, now I definitely have to try 'em."

"Do." Ash smiled from across the table. "I'm dying to know how they work for someone who doesn't see time the way I do."

"You mean you've never loaned these to anyone else?"

So much for pretending this wasn't one of the most significant moments in Ash's life. "You are the first."

"Guess I'm your guinea pig." Chuy shrugged and slipped the spectacles over his nose. His faith really was a thing of beauty. He was willing to test something that had never been tested simply because Ashmedai allowed it. Already, Chuy knew the demon king would never allow harm to come to him. Maybe he'd always known. Maybe Chuy had his own version of expanded vision. Could innocence really come of seeing more instead of less?

As soon as the spectacles were in place, Chuy stood and said, "Oh my god." Ash watched, curious beyond measure, as Chuy made his way around the cabin and marveled at everything like he'd just opened his eyes for the first time. "This is incredible!"

"What do you see?" Ash asked.

"I can't . . . I can't really explain it. It's like light maybe. I don't know. Things look different. I gotta go outside! Can I take these outside?"

Ash nodded and rose to follow him. "Take them anywhere you like. You look incredible in them." *Damn it.* That was too much. *Keep it platonic, Ash, you fool. Chuy doesn't know you from Adam. To him, you're a monster who recently abducted him—not a lover of any kind.*

Except for last night.

Ash pushed the distracting memory from his mind as he joined the captain outside. The evening had a biting chill to it. He could see the ghost of Chuy's breath lingering in the air. The stars had just begun to come out.

"Oh my god!" Chuy repeated. "The sky! It's so bright. What's that color? Never seen anything like it."

So that was the answer. "The spectacles seem to have broadened the visible light spectrum for you. You'll see wavelengths that didn't exist to you before."

"No shit." Chuy spun around and pointed. "You look all glowy too."

"Infrared."

"And the stars! They're . . . They're . . . I mean wow!"

Ash chuckled. "Probably ultraviolet."

"I can hardly make out the sky cause the stars are so bright. Michael would go crazy if he could see this."

"I bet he would," Ash muttered. Michael was obscenely lucky to have known Chuy as long as he had, and Ash would bet his own spectacles the nephil didn't even realize how fortunate he was. It was useless to think on it, though. Ash closed his eyes, clenched his teeth, and tried to swallow his jealousy.

Had he been less distracted by his own struggle, he might have noticed that Chuy had gone silent and was slowly backing toward him. As it was, the thump of the captain's back against his chest came as a shock. He assumed it was an accident and quickly moved away, but Chuy collided with him again and whispered, "Ash. What's that?" He pointed into the forest. "In that clearing over there. There's two of 'em. They look like amber, but they move like they're alive. I can't still be drunk, can I?"

Chuy's brief description was all Ash needed to identify the creatures. His whole body went cold as he answered, "Hashmallim." It wasn't possible. It was too soon. But when he followed Chuy's arm to the clearing in question, he saw them. Without thinking, he laid a hand on Chuy's shoulder and squeezed. He didn't have time to worry about discretion. "Samael's host has found us. I'll try to fight them off, but . . . Get ready to run."

Without turning around, Chuy removed the spectacles and handed them back to Ash. "I can't see them anymore," he whispered.

"They haven't manifested physical bodies yet. They'll have to in order to carry you." All Ash wanted to do was wrap his arms around the captain and take him somewhere safe, but he knew it was useless. "Go inside. I'll handle this."

"That's two against one," Chuy said.

"I'll handle this," Ash repeated, and he began to grow. Like a plant unfurling new leaves, Ashmedai unfurled his demonic form. He took on as much matter as he could to supplement his monstrous body and spread his terrible wings. "Go!" His own voice echoed like distant thunder, and Chuy ran into the cabin.

The hashmallim chose that moment to manifest, and before Ashmedai could decide whether to strike or run, they were on him. They were hard as gemstones when they hit, but the second Ash hit them back, they became malleable and sticky. He had to expend significant energy to pull himself free of them. Hashmallim were not usually in the warrior class. They were essentially workhorses, so Ash doubted they'd been sent here to fight. More likely, they'd been sent to track him. Had Chuy not spotted them when he did, they would have quietly carried him away when Ash's back was turned.

Ash swiped at the translucent, four-legged beasts, but they didn't seem overly troubled by him. They struck hard and sent him flying. He hit a tree and slid to the ground. In seconds, he was back on his feet again, and he rushed them. Each time they caught him in their sticky flesh, he had to fight to pull free again. It was like battling living tree sap. Ash's physical body wouldn't last at the rate he was expending energy, but he couldn't stop to think of a plan either. He backed away to get a running start at his opponents, and that was when he heard a gunshot.

One hashmal's leg shattered like candy. Ash spun around to see Chuy standing yards away, a lever-action rifle nestled against his shoulder, his eye at the sights. He fired again, and the other hashmal lost its head.

They would rebuild quickly, of course, but it gave Ash time to think. He was suddenly grateful he hadn't rid the cabin of all its weapons.

Chuy was an excellent shot. He fired and levered his weapon like it was second nature to him. Each pump of the rifle was a heartbeat during which the demon king could strike, and he did with full force. Whenever Ash had to fight to free himself from the gummy body of an opponent, Chuy would set his sights on the other hashmal. No angel could be killed without a death sword, but they could be exhausted. The hashmallim needed mass to carry Chuy, and mass took energy to maintain. If Chuy forced them to expend enough energy that they became unable to manifest . . .

But hashmallim were not stupid. They quickly caught on to the strategy and responded in kind. While Chuy reloaded his weapon, both amber monsters attacked Ash at once. Each one took hold of him and pulled, thrashing their heads like dogs. When his wings were torn from his body, Ashmedai screamed, and Chuy echoed his cry. There was a noticeable difference in tenor, though. Ash's scream was born of pain, and Chuy's was pure rage.

The shots came more quickly now, and Ash saw the hashmallim knocked back repeatedly. They couldn't reform as fast as the rifle dismantled them. For now, Chuy's weapon seemed to be doing the trick, but Ash knew it had a limited supply of ammunition. Exhausted, he began to retreat. There was no sense in losing his other limbs too. Demons could not reform as quickly as angels could. He backed up until he stood behind his defender.

"Are you all right?" Chuy asked, still firing his weapon.

"No," Ash answered honestly. "If this keeps up, I won't be able to manifest much longer. I can't even replace the wings I lost. Exhaust your ammunition. Then tell me to run. They'll follow, but if I save my energy and you expend theirs, we may be able to outrun them."

Chuy nodded and continued to fire his weapon. It felt wrong, hiding behind a mortal man. But against Samael's host, not even the demon king stood a chance in hell. This plan was the best shot they had, and Ash would be damned if he wasn't going to take it.

The heartbeat of the lever and trigger continued.

Click-click. Boom!

Click-click. Boom!

Click-click. Boom!

Each hashmal broke apart again and again. It would take some time for them to recover at least. Chuy spent his last few rounds shattering their heads, and then he dropped the gun. "Run," he said.

Ashmedai lifted the captain in one hand and bolted into the forest.

Chapter Sixteen

Lightning struck again well past midnight. Bryony was in bed with Michael, who had quickly drifted off with his arms around her. She, on the other hand, hadn't slept at all. How could she? Every passing minute had her imagining something worse and asking new, more horrible questions. What was Samael doing to Chuy right now? Would the angel bring him to her before or after breaking him? And how . . . How was he going to break such a sweet, gentle heart? Well, she was about to find out, wasn't she?

Oh god. She whimpered.

When she tried to roll out of bed, Michael's powerful arms held her in place. She shoved at his hands clasped over her stomach, but he only gripped her tighter.

"I know you're awake," she muttered. "You have to let me go."

Michael nuzzled into her hair and squeezed her. "Every time you go to him, I'm afraid it's the last time I'll ever see you."

If only he knew how badly she wanted to stay safe in his arms, warm in their bed. "But Chuy . . ." she said, and her voice caught before she could finish her sentence. "He might have Chuy. I have to go."

Michael groaned and sat up against the headboard. "I wish dealing with my father was anyone's job but yours. I wish I could do it myself."

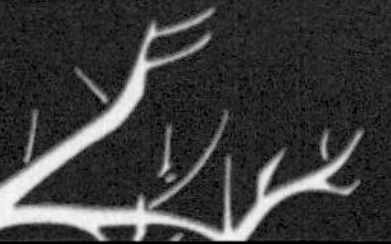

"I summoned him. He's my responsibility." She scooted out of bed and began bundling up against the cold. Warm pants, an undershirt, her hoodie, and a scarf. When she was dressed, she leaned across the bed to kiss his cheek, but he leapt up and took her in his arms instead.

Every time she walked away from Michael, it got harder and harder to do. She could feel his worry for her, and there was no way she could convince him that hers wasn't the life at stake—at least, not yet. She felt her way downstairs in the dark and pulled on her tall boots at the front door.

Samael stood several yards from her veranda, waiting on the path, still as a statue. He wore his wings, which told her he had no intention of coming inside, and for some wonderful or terrible reason, he did not have Chuy with him.

"Sama," she said.

His greeting was icy. "I have come to discuss my progress."

As tempting as it was, Bryony decided not to return his coolness with disdain. He was used to disdain, she reminded herself. It wouldn't change anything. "Where is Chuy? And why weren't you waiting in the grove this time?"

"I did not think you would appreciate my invading your sanctuary now that you know what I am."

Bryony rolled her eyes despite the uselessness of the gesture. "I've hardly known you long enough to make a judgment in that respect, and I'm certainly not going to take the archangel Michael's word for it."

The corners of Samael's mouth turned ever so slightly down at the mention of his hated rival. "You should," was all he said. Then he tilted his chin up and began his report. "You will be pleased to learn that your captain has escaped again. He repeatedly fired a weapon at my hashmallim, which damaged them significantly, before he and Ashmedai fled."

Bryony failed to hide her relief. "Yes, Chuy!" She pumped a triumphant fist for her friend.

"Perfectly innocent hashmallim." The graveyard angel glowered at her. "You will be less pleased to learn that the demon king lost his wings in the fight. He is exhausted and cannot manifest new limbs. For that reason, he had to escape on foot and is likely to leave a trail. My host will track him down, and this time, when they find him, I will go to collect your captain myself."

Bryony caught her breath at that. All her pride and relief deflated like a downed helium balloon. Of course Chuy hadn't won. He would never win against Samael because Samael would never give up the chase. "You *will* be gentle," she said to her terrifying future father-in-law.

"I don't know what you mean."

"Sama!" She wanted to hit him or fall to her knees and grovel, but he was so formal, she couldn't bring herself to do either. Talking to him was more like talking to a lawyer than a king. He did not mince words, but neither did he demand or expect deference. "I'm asking you to be gentle with him. And swear you won't destroy his innocence until I've apologized to him first." Every minute she could buy was precious.

"Why would you apologize?" Samael asked. "It is not your doing."

"But it's my fault. I'm the one who showed him to the demon king, and I'm the one who summoned and made a deal with you. I'm the one who brought you both into his life."

"I did try to warn you." The graveyard angel's voice was close to a whisper. "You do not want me in your life—neither does my son. I am not gentle."

"You will be this time." She ignored his halfhearted attempt to sabotage his relationship with his son. It was so typical of him. He would always work against his own best interest, given the chance. "You'll be gentle with Chuy because you're acting on my behalf. I don't care who you think you are." She preempted his usual excuse. "You're going to act like someone else if you have to. You're going to reach down deep and find that angel who fell in love with the woman in the garden. Surely you were gentle with her. Surely you're capable of *some* tenderness." Her stomach was in knots. This was her last chance, and she couldn't keep her voice from betraying her anxiety. "You . . . You have no idea what he means to me."

In a gesture so slight it would have gone unnoticed had Bryony not been avoiding his eyes by staring down, the graveyard angel reached out and then quickly retracted his hand again. It looked almost like he wanted to comfort her. But that was impossible, wasn't it? Could Azazel have been right when he'd insisted Samael loved her? She'd doubted the watcher at the time, but now she second guessed herself. Azza had also said, *Do not allow his affection to deepen.* But what other weapon did she have?

She took a deep breath, reached out, and caught the graveyard angel's hand in hers. It was far from the first time she'd held his hand, but before, she'd only been guiding him through unfamiliar environments. Now she wanted to guide him through something much more perilous—an unfamiliar idea. "You don't have to be who the archangel Michael thinks you are. You know that, right?" She stepped closer, hoping he could feel her nearness and know she was neither afraid nor disgusted by him. "Sama?"

The graveyard angel's back grew even more rigid than it already was. His hand twitched. "I know what you're doing," he said. "It will not work."

"And what am I doing?"

"You're trying to heal the devil with kindness." He tilted his face down to her. He was overwhelming, as always, and humiliatingly accurate. "You will hold your nose and pretend affection in the hopes that all I need is a little love. This is not the first time it's been attempted. As you see, nothing changes. I am what I am. It is best to give up now."

Bryony gritted her teeth against the instinct to do just as he said. A last chance was a last chance. "This time is different," she said in her most unshakeable voice. "This time it's family, and you don't give up on family."

He blinked down at her, and she did her best not to look away. She appreciated the fact that he bothered to blink at all, considering his eyes were nothing more than an aesthetic choice. "Do you believe," he said in that unnervingly soothing tone, "that family can be chosen?"

Where was he going with this? She decided to answer honestly. "Yes."

"Then you must also believe that family can be rejected." When she didn't respond, he reached out his other hand and touched the tips of his fingers to the underside of her chin. "Reject me, Bryony Moss. Please, before it's too late. Reject me before I destroy your faith in the power of love."

She harnessed her own stubbornness. "No."

He looked truly surprised by her answer. "You will suffer."

"I already have."

Had anyone passed by in that moment, Bryony was certain they would have thought they were looking at a sculpture, a propaganda piece called "The Angels Are Our Friends" or something equally deranged. After what felt like the most terrifying five-minute staring contest she had ever been involved in, the hand in hers began to tremble.

"My daughter," Samael said, and she shivered at the sound of his voice. "You have exhausted me."

For a moment, she was unsure what he meant. Then she remembered. "The poison?"

"Yes."

With his answer came the first wave of grief. Bryony's knees buckled, and she caught hold of both his hands to keep from falling. "I'm sorry," she said.

"You are not. All the same, I accept your apology."

She let go of him, doubled over, and held herself, rocking back and forth to fight the scream gathering at the back of her throat.

"I will leave you now," he said, and she hated that she felt relieved. "The next time you see me, I will have your captain." With that, Samael's marble body began to grow, and Bryony's grief finally clawed its way past her lips. The angel shook his head and sighed. "Turn away, you obstinate thing. The poison is cumulative."

"I know." She blinked back tears and watched as his body lengthened and stretched into a twelve-winged, serpentine monster. He really was beautiful. She hadn't lied about that. He was a brilliant, awe-inspiring creature. He was bewildering and dizzying. She fell onto her hands and sobbed but kept her eyes trained on him. "Turning away from death doesn't change anything."

"It will change you if you look too long," said the seraph.

"It already has!" she shouted up at him as his body stretched to the heavens and began to dissolve. "I've been taking your poison my entire life!"

And then he was gone.

CHAPTER SEVENTEEN

Ashmedai remembered running. He remembered crashing through the forest like a bull, clinging to his precious cargo like it would kill him to let go. He knew if he could only run fast enough, he would make it to his labyrinth—that maze of underground lava tubes only he knew how to navigate. He could not avoid leaving a trail, but the caves would be a stronghold he could defend. There, he would not be surrounded. He would not be surprised or ambushed. Even the hashmallim would struggle to sniff him out. All it would buy him was time, but time was what he needed most. He was exhausted, and he needed to rest.

When he reached the underground river at the heart of his labyrinth, he finally allowed his grip on Chuy to relax. He didn't wait to rebuild his human body. He wanted . . . He *needed* to be a man again. His chimeric form made him feel like a monster.

So the demon king stood ankle deep at the edge of his private river and screamed with the effort it took to rebuild his impeccable, human body. He was a perfectionist when it came to his own flesh. Every organ had to be functional, every ligament just as it was when he was alive. He started at the top and worked his way down. He included every hair follicle—despite having a shaved head—every sweat gland, and all the viscera he would never need. The transformation took every ounce of strength the demon king had, and it didn't take long for him to overextend himself and lose consciousness.

He woke once with his face in the water. Had he been a living man, he would have drowned. As it was, he just reshaped his hips and thighs and passed out again. He woke the second time to the feeling of being dragged from behind. Someone's arms were under his shoulders and locked around his chest. Ash hurriedly finished manifesting his suit and lost consciousness again.

When he opened his eyes for the third and final time, Ashmedai found he'd been propped against someone else's body. Someone's chest rose and fell behind him. Sinewy arms remained locked around him, and his legs were nestled between someone else's legs.

Chuy.

Ash had been pulled unconscious from the river by the man he was supposed to protect. He felt useless and weak. He spent several seconds berating himself for his own stupid pride before he found himself in its clutches again. As he stared down the length of his own body, it became embarrassingly clear he'd passed out before managing to manifest shoes.

He leapt up and backed away from Chuy, hoping the captain was somehow asleep. But no. Chuy's eyes were wide open. He'd been sitting there—god only knew how long—staring down the length of Ash's body, right at those demonic feet. Ash crouched in a pathetic attempt to cover his shame. He desperately tried to manifest shoes again and again, but he was exhausted. So he crossed his arms over a pair of feet that belonged on no living creature, let alone a man. They had powerful, black talons that dug into the rock beneath them. They were heavily scaled and matched the russet color of the rest of his skin. Three toes forward, one toe back. Ash knew his feet by heart, and he despised them.

Chuy stared at him, unblinking, and Ash felt as vulnerable as a child. He was ashamed, and the more he tried to hide his feet, the more humiliated he became. It was too late to pretend he didn't care now—far, far too late. He could only watch in horror as Chuy pushed himself to standing and said, "Guess we solved the mystery of why you wear shoes to bed."

The outraged cry that escaped Ash's mouth must have been a shock because Chuy immediately began to curtail the damage he'd done. "It's really not a big deal, you know. You shouldn't be so worried about it. We all have something weird, right? I mean I have this thing . . ." He quickly removed one of his own shoes. "See?" He pulled something out from inside it. "One of my legs is longer than the other, and I have to wear this stupid lift. Can't see what good it does, though, because my knees still hurt at the end of every day. Maybe it's not tall enough." He turned it over in his hands, examining the thing as though it were the first time he'd ever seen it.

Ash stood and stepped closer to see the lift before he quite realized what he was doing. Damn exhaustion, damn curiosity, and damn Chuy's confounded ability to put him at ease. Chuy grinned, cocked his head, and looked back down at Ash's feet. Instinctively, Ash darted toward him and took him by the chin to keep his eyes up. He wanted to say something by way of explanation, but he couldn't. What was there to even say? There was no excuse for his behavior. All he could do was hold his fingers under the captain's chin and actively hate himself as he repeatedly failed to manifest shoes.

With his back against the rock wall, Chuy had nowhere to go and no reason to struggle, so he didn't. What he also would not do to save his own life, apparently, was stop talking. "There's nothing wrong with ya is all I'm saying." Ash wanted to cover the man's mouth, but he remembered where that led the last time he'd tried it. Then Chuy broadened his enchanting smile and said, "Honestly, I think your feet look kind of—"

"Shut up." Ash hated to snap at the man he loved, but he couldn't help it. His struggle was quickly evolving from one of humiliation to one of overwhelming desire. He was too close, but he wanted to be closer. He leaned his forehead against Chuy's, brought himself nose to nose with the captain, and swallowed hard. "Just shut up," he whispered. "Please." His heart thundered, and his every limb pulsed with the rhythm of it. Heat crept up his neck to his cheeks. The situation was quickly spiraling out of control . . . like it had that night.

And now he was remembering what it was like to join Chuy in bed. His stomach knotted into a quivering ball of nerves and longing. His breath came shallow. Then he felt a touch—soft, barely there, a tentative hand at his waist—and he was undone. "God damn it," he muttered, and he closed the last half-inch between them to kiss the captain's intractable mouth.

And the captain kissed him back.

This kiss was one Ash knew all too well. He'd seen it like an echo across time, and it was magnificent. Without the lazy carelessness of intoxication, Chuy's kiss had an almost desperate urgency to it. He drew in Ash's lower lip and bit gently. Ash leaned in, and his fingers found that inky hair he'd been yearning to wade through since he first laid eyes on it. As he moved from Chuy's mouth to that elegant neck, Ash drew his tongue along the tattooed flames that marked it. He pushed his hands under Chuy's shirt and felt the coolness of the captain's skin. Ash's temperature had to be over a hundred degrees by now. He was a walking fever, but he couldn't bring himself to care. All his most beautiful fantasies were coming true.

Chuy stole a moment to catch his breath. "Well, I was gonna be low-key and say I thought your feet looked kind of cool." He began unbuttoning Ash's vest. "But now I may as well be honest and tell you they're irresistible."

"Just stop." Ash groaned and kissed Chuy's mouth again to shut him up. He never wanted to hear about his feet again. He pushed Chuy's shirt up over his head, crouched down, and began tracing more of those intricate tattoos with his tongue. God how he'd dreamed of this. Or had he remembered it? He couldn't tell, and it didn't matter. He kissed every inch of Chuy's delicious torso with an open mouth and just a touch of suction. He worked his way down and tucked his tongue between Chuy's skin and waistband, teasing until the captain's breath came quicker. Then he began to unbutton Chuy's jeans with his teeth, his hands thoroughly occupied elsewhere.

Chuy leaned back against the wall, panting. "You don't waste time, do you?"

"I don't play games."

"What if I like games?" Chuy said, and Ash was back on his feet at once.

"Then play me, Captain Jesús of *Papillon*. I am your instrument. Do whatever you wish with me." The brief desire to worship rose in Ash, but he easily tamped it down again. He was no young, inexperienced demon. He knew how to harness the man in him to counteract the cherub.

"This is what you really meant when you said I'd break your heart, isn't it?" Chuy toyed with Ash's collar. "I thought you were just talkin' poetry, but you knew we'd end up . . . like this."

Ash nodded and let his hands trail back up Chuy's chest, admiring the feel of his ribcage. There wasn't much to the captain. Perhaps some would suggest he was too thin, but to Ash, he was perfect. He would never, ever be anything other than perfect. "Since the day I first saw you, I've longed for you. I tried to fight it—god knows I did—but you . . ." His voice petered out as Chuy finished unbuttoning his shirt and ran his calloused hands over Ash's exposed flesh. Ash resisted the urge to rush things. "You're so beautiful. Do you know that? You're the most beautiful man I've ever seen."

"You saw my future *and* my past?" Chuy asked, his voice a near whisper.

Again, Ash nodded, still ashamed to have invaded the man's privacy the way he did.

"And you still want me?"

"Want you?" Ash let Chuy probe his body. It felt so right to finally be touched by the man whose absence he'd felt for as long as he could remember. "If this is want, then I've never wanted anything before now. I need you." He quickly added, "I know you can't return it.

You don't know me the way I know you. But I . . ." He hesitated. He was admitting too much too soon. Still he couldn't stop himself from speaking the truth. "I love you. I have always . . . *will* always love you. You've already won."

Chuy's eyes grew wide. "What's that mean exactly?"

"It means I surrender." Ash bowed his head. "I'm yours, Captain. I can refuse you nothing. I can neither betray nor abandon you as long as you live. The demon king is at your disposal. If you ask it of me, I will give it to you. Forbidden secrets, the key to heaven, my own life. For you, the answer will always be *yes*."

A brief smile flitted across Chuy's face before he feigned seriousness again. "You mean I don't have to beat you at checkers to get my questions answered? I can just ask, and you have to tell me what I want to know?"

"I should have known you wouldn't play fair." Ash brought his mouth to Chuy's ear and kissed it gently.

"Then there's something I want to know right now."

"Be careful, Chuy." Ash continued to kiss his skin as he warned, "Some knowledge is forbidden for good reason."

"What really happened the night I blacked out?"

Ash froze, his mouth lingering on Chuy's bare shoulder. "Of all things . . ." he muttered.

"It's been bothering me. It bothers me even more because you don't wanna tell me."

Ash wrapped his arms around Chuy and held him tight. Just now, nothing frightened him more than what might happen if he answered honestly. He knew Chuy was bound to break his heart. What he didn't know was when and why. What if the time was now, and the reason was this? What if all those kisses he'd seen, layered one upon the other, really were just an echo of this moment, and there were to be no more? Ever. Ash shuddered and stalled. "You were drunk and reckless and firing a rifle. I took it from you and carried you to bed."

"And?"

Ash tightened his hold as though any moment the captain might slip through his arms and fade into darkness. "And you didn't know what you were doing."

"All the same, I'd like to know now."

Ash closed his eyes. "You pulled me down and kissed me, and I . . . I let it go too far."

"How far did it go?"

"You had my belt off before I came to my senses. It didn't go further than that."

"Oh." There was relief in Chuy's voice, and Ash silently thanked every person in his life who'd ever helped to teach him self-control. Then Chuy said, "Sorry I did that to you."

Ash couldn't believe what he was hearing. He leaned back to look directly into Chuy's eyes and repeated, "You didn't know what you were doing."

But Chuy shook his head. "Just because I can't remember doesn't mean I didn't make the wrong choice. And I did know a little," he admitted with a smile. "I knew you liked me. It's not like you were subtle about it."

"So you said." Ash cupped Chuy's cheek and resisted the urge to kiss him again. "But the wrong choice made was mine."

"Possible we both made wrong choices, isn't it?"

Ash wanted to protest, but he knew it was useless. Chuy needed absolution, and whatever Chuy needed from Ash, Chuy was going to get. "I forgive you, Captain. Will you forgive me in return?"

"Course." Chuy tugged him closer and breathed a sigh of relief. "Glad that's out of the way. You know, I was imagining much worse. Kinda wish I could remember it now that I know what it was—first kiss and all."

"It doesn't count."

"Tell me it was good at least."

The memory of that kiss flashed through Ash's mind. God it was beautiful. His answer couldn't come close to doing it justice. "You tasted like honey."

Chuy grinned. "Let's do it right this time, so I can remember too." He pushed Ash's shirt and vest off his shoulders, and Ash allowed them both to dissolve.

This time, when they came together, they were deliberate and gentle. Ash turned them so neither one was backed against the wall. He pulled Chuy in by his waistband, intentionally echoing that first night. But when he kissed the captain this time, he didn't even try to stop himself. Only once did he pause to whisper, "You still taste like honey."

Each new kiss brought the first into brighter focus. As Ash's fever intensified, the coolness of the captain's skin became less of a luxury and more of a necessity. He needed Chuy's touch like he once needed water—like he needed the wine in the well. He moaned hungrily and drew up against his partner's body like it was the only thing keeping him alive.

The demon king was drowning in desire, but he never wanted the moment to end. The only thing that brought him back to the surface was the cross pendant, still hanging like a curse around Chuy's neck. Every once in a while, it pricked Ash's skin. The pain was nothing, but the jealousy it inspired infuriated him. Ash grabbed it to move it out of the way, and Chuy caught his wrist. They met each other's eyes. Although Ash fought to hide his own weakness, he would have bet his entire fortune on his failure.

"You said you could never betray or abandon me," Chuy reminded him. Ash opened his hand and let Chuy take the pendant back. "You said that because you saw what he did, didn't you?"

"I said it because it was true."

Yes, the man who'd fashioned the cross had not been careful with its recipient's heart. The fact that Chuy continued to love the bastard and grieve his death made Ash want to scream. Chuy gazed down at the gold cross in his hand. He gulped and blinked too much, and Ash knew he was fighting back tears. Why had Ash even touched that damned pendant? He could be kissing Chuy right now. Instead, he'd let jealousy creep in and put a stop to true bliss.

Before Ash could find the words to apologize, Chuy bowed his head and slipped the chain over it. A gold chain combing through the captain's black hair had been one of the more haunting images Ash had seen through his spectacles. At the time, he hadn't been able to interpret it, but now . . . This was momentous. This was the first time Chuy had intentionally removed that pendant since the day he'd received it.

"You keep it." Chuy handed the cross to Ash, who closed his fist around it in a state of utter shock. "Let it remind you that you're loved."

It wasn't often the demon king found himself lost for words, but he'd be damned if he could think of a single thing to say in response. He imagined he looked quite the fool, gaping like a fish on a line, but he didn't have to imagine it long. A sudden, thunderous quake shook the cavern. Stones rained from the ceiling, and Ash leapt to protect Chuy from the worst of them.

They were both already on the ground by the time the Angel of Death, flanked and guided by his hashmallim, entered the space. The demon king kept his back to the ceiling with the captain sheltered beneath him. As soon as he saw Samael, he sank lower and covered Chuy's eyes with one hand. "Don't move," he ordered, a pathetic tremor already creeping into his voice.

In contrast, Samael's voice was sure and calm. "There you are," he said, and Ash had to swallow a whimper before it escaped his throat. "You've given me quite the thrilling hunt, Your Majesty. After what you did to my poor hashmallim, I thought I'd better come for you myself."

The hashmallim stood like giant, amber sentinels on either side of the stone seraph. Their manifested forms were like liquid—ever shifting, ever changing—with pulsing electrical storms at their cores. Samael approached slowly, and Ash used what little strength he had left to manifest his enormous, cherubic claws and bury them in the rock. Then he clamped down with his already taloned feet and prepared to resist what he knew was coming.

The wait was maddening. The Angel of Death never had to rush, and so he rarely did. He preferred to pick his way across the terrain, getting to know it stone by stone. The closer he drew, the more violently the body under Ash's trembled. "I won't let him touch you," Ash whispered to Chuy. "Be still."

"It would be easiest if you surrendered the captain to me now," Samael said. "Although, being privy to at least a little of your . . . conversation, I'm fairly certain you will not."

Ash dug his talons deeper into the rock as the Angel of Death reached out to him. Cool hands began to probe his shoulders, and it was a disgusting perversion of the touch Chuy had given him only moments ago. Samael followed the demon king's arms down and found them anchored to the cavern floor. "Let go now, Ashmedai," he said. "Time to stop playing with your toys."

Ash came dangerously close to just doing as he was told. The voice of death incarnate was more than a little compelling. Somehow, he managed to growl, "Fuck you, Samael. You don't always get what you want."

"No," Samael agreed. "Not always. But this time, I do." And with one hand, the stone seraph crushed the bones in Ashmedai's arm. Ash howled, and Chuy writhed under him. Samael casually patted the demon king's head. "Go ahead, Your Majesty. Dissolve your flesh, and the pain will disappear."

"No!" Ash screamed at him.

Samael easily found Ash's other arm and crushed the bones in that one too. "Let go, you stubborn thing."

"No!"

"Dissolve your flesh or I will bind you to it and bury it."

That threat struck at the heart of Ashmedai. He'd been bound and buried before, and he felt faint at the mere thought of it. His first escape had been so much happenstance. He was certain he would never be so lucky again. And the darkness—just recalling those millennia of darkness and isolation was almost more than he could bear. Then Chuy's body shuddered under him, and Ash found the strength to say, "No."

Samael sighed and began to probe the base of Ash's neck, muttering, "You always were such a stickler for accuracy, feet notwithstanding." He chuckled, and Ash wanted to take a swipe at him, but the poison emanating from the seraph was more than enough to prevent him. "Where is it?" Samael continued to probe until he found what he was looking for. "Ah, there it is."

Suddenly, Ashmedai was struck by such a blow that his entire world went white with pain. Searing, screaming, oppressive pain. He collapsed onto Chuy and found it impossible to push himself up again. He could no longer move his own body. He couldn't feel anything below his neck—not a limb, not his torso, not even the pain in his broken arms.

Now Samael easily pried the demon king's claws from the ground. Ash was a rag doll, a limp body with a head attached. He was powerless to do anything more than watch as the Angel of Death turned his body over to find Chuy sheltering there like an insect under a log.

"Why?" Ash wheezed.

"I am under contract," the angel answered.

"But . . . you don't . . . honor your contracts."

"I am honoring this one." And for some unholy reason, the Angel of Death actually smiled. "It comes from family."

Family? One name came immediately to mind. "Bryony." Ash scowled. The woman had crossed him for the last time.

"Yes. My daughter." Samael lifted Chuy, who appeared to have passed out, into his marble arms. "She insisted I be gentle with the captain. Can you imagine? But I've decided to honor her request. I felt it best not to take any chances with you. You might have made it necessary for me to fight, and I think we both know the many, many ways that could have gone wrong. Ah, look at me—inconveniencing myself for one sentimental, little god. I am eager to see what the archangel Michael makes of her . . . right before she kills him." He laughed, and Ash came very close to asking how he managed to twirl his mustache without any facial hair. But Samael and his hashmallim rose up and crashed through the ceiling before the demon king could get another word out.

Furious tears gathered in the corners of Ash's eyes as the cavern collapsed around him. Sand and pebbles filtered down through the boulders with a soft shush, sealing the light away. All Ash could do was wonder how long he'd be buried this time and whether he actually deserved it. He'd failed his only mission—to keep Chuy safe from both Samael and himself. He'd drunk from the wine in the well again, and he should have known better. Now he was weak, caught, bound, and buried. Why did he never learn?

Even in the blackness, Ashmedai could see the little, gold cross still half clasped in his useless hand. At least he had this one comfort. At least he could glance at the pendant over the next thousand years and relive his brief reprieve from loneliness.

If only he could have warned himself that the entirety of his relationship with the captain would take place in the space of a few days, that all his visions of intimacy amounted to one perfect hour at the heart of a labyrinth. If only he could have seen past the blinding light of death in Chuy's future. Then Ash might have known this entire ordeal ended with him bound and buried again. Perhaps he could have avoided the relationship and the binding altogether. But would he have avoided it, given the chance? Would he sacrifice his time with Chuy to spare himself this fate? He finally let himself weep when he realized the answer.

For a week with Chuy, Ashmedai would spend a thousand years bound in darkness. Again and again, he would make that trade, given the choice. He blinked through his tears at the cross in his hand. *Let it remind you that you're loved.*

"Yes," Ash said to no one in particular. "I remember."

Chapter Eighteen

Early in the morning, the Angel of Death appeared on Bryony's veranda with a limp, unconscious man in his arms. Bryony had only just drifted off to sleep in the chair beside her hearth. Her anxiety was better than black coffee at keeping her up through the night. Though Michael had refused to go to bed without her, he'd quickly fallen asleep on the couch and was now rested, reclined, and comfortably reading. How he managed to stay relatively calm in the face of all this chaos was beyond her. She heard thunder, stumbled to her front door, and flung it open but forgot to prepare her mantle in her haste. She was on her knees in seconds, clinging for dear life to the doorknob.

"I have come to deliver your captain," Samael said, and he walked straight past her into the living room. He deposited Chuy unceremoniously on the floor behind the couch and waited. Bryony was briefly reminded of a retriever dropping a dead duck before its handler and wagging its tail expectantly.

With some effort, she applied her mantle and stood to survey the damage. Chuy did not look well. "Why is he half naked and unconscious?" she said. "What did you do to him?"

"Nothing." Samael looked a little perturbed by Bryony's lack of unquestioning gratitude. "I retrieved him gently, as you requested. I was forced to bind the demon king to do so, however, and I imagine your captain will not be happy about that. Which brings me to his state of undress." The angel squared his shoulders and assumed his usual proud stance. "You will be pleased to learn it no longer makes sense to destroy this man's innocence. Ashmedai will never lose interest in him regardless. They had already coupled by the time I found them."

Bryony took a moment to register what she was hearing. "Wait. Coupled?"

"It means the demon king has fallen in love, and this one has returned his feelings in some fashion."

"Yes, I know what it means. It's just . . ." She couldn't wrap her head around it. All this time, she'd imagined Chuy being held against his will, miserable and alone.

Michael grunted from his place on the couch. He appeared to have dropped his book over his eyes, shoved a throw pillow over that, and held the entire makeshift blindfold with both arms. He was, therefore, not groveling on the floor for once, and he took the opportunity to participate in the conversation. "But Ashmedai prefers the company of women," he said, as though reciting from a book he'd once read. His deep, muffled voice made Bryony adore him all the more.

Samael's mouth twitched in a half-smile she was certain had everything to do with the obstinacy of his son, and nothing to do with the rest of the situation. "For *company*, Ashmedai prefers women. For sins of the flesh, he has always tended toward men." Bryony snorted like an unruly schoolgirl at his use of *sins of the flesh*. The graveyard angel just cocked his head. "I thought this was common knowledge."

"No, it is not common knowledge!" Michael shouted from under his book. "There's no such thing as common knowledge anymore. None of us knows anything about any of you, and no one bothers to tell us anything."

Bryony knelt down and gently palmed Chuy's face. He didn't respond. "Except Azza," she corrected absentmindedly. "Azza tells us things."

Had she wanted to get a rise out of the Angel of Death, she could not have chosen a better topic. His hands balled into fists, and his jaw clenched at the name. "Azazel is next to be bound," he muttered.

Bryony was on her feet in an instant. "Try it and see what happens!"

Apparently, no matter what she said or asked for, Samael would find a way to twist it into something terrible. Poor Ashmedai. She recalled the studious demon in the well-tailored suit and polished shoes. She'd walked with him to various shops and restaurants in her hometown, having tricked him into a bargain she had no intention of honoring. They'd occasionally made conversation along the way. He hadn't seemed a bad sort. Now he was bound, and she didn't quite know how to feel about it. She was still bitter that he'd abducted Michael—he really did need to get a handle on his abduction habit—but if Azza and Loki's experiences were anything to go on, being bound was a kind of hell she wouldn't wish on her worst enemy.

The mere thought of Azazel bound in darkness again sent Bryony into a fit of rage. She narrowed her eyes and spoke through her teeth. "Sama, if you lay a finger on Azazel, I'll find a way to ruin everything for you. Do you hear me? I'll warn the archangel Michael that you mean to kill him. I'll tell him everything, and I'll help him to hunt! you! down!" She prodded Samael in the chest for each of her last three words—a punctuation to prove she meant it, to prove she wasn't afraid of him.

The Angel of Death frowned down at her. "That would make you a bad daughter."

"Oh my god!" She started shoving him. "No. I can't deal with this right now. Out! Get out, father of the year! Back out of my house and leave!"

He did, but not before saying, "I will return tomorrow with Raziel's book. You and your partner will use it to conjure him."

"My partner will do no such thing!" she shouted after him.

"He will, I expect," was the graveyard angel's only response before Bryony slammed the door in his face.

She breathed deep to calm her temper and turned back to her living room. She didn't expect to see Chuy wide awake and sitting on her living room floor, but he was. His eyes were puffy and dark-rimmed. He looked like a gentle breeze would knock him over, but he was alive.

"Chuy!" She rushed in to hug him, and he reflexively hugged her back, a blank expression on his face. "I was so worried. I'm so, so sorry. I didn't mean for any of this to happen. I'd take it all back if I could. I swear it."

Michael sat up and looked over the back of the couch. He knit his brow and said, "Chuy, where's your pendant?"

There was a beat of silence from the typically easygoing captain, and then he lost his composure completely. Bryony had never seen anything like it. He screamed, first at nothing and then at the door where Samael had stood moments before. He let loose a string of furious Spanish that Bryony was certain remained better untranslated. His eyes wept, but the rest of him shook with rage.

Michael rounded the couch and crouched down. "What happened?"

Chuy shrieked, "Que se regrese al infierno el diablo!" Then he sucked in a ragged breath and slammed his fists into the floor. "That devil broke his neck!"

Bryony sat in stunned disbelief. "What?"

His burst of furious energy spent, Chuy finally slumped and wept. Bryony had never seen anyone so angry and miserable, and she wanted to kill the person . . . the angel who had done this to her friend. "He was only trying to protect me," Chuy said from behind shaking hands. "For that, the devil broke his neck and buried him."

"His neck?" Michael asked.

Chuy looked up at him. "And his arms. I heard it, the fucking crunch. I heard it and there was nothing I could do."

"Damn." Michael rose and shook his head. "This is why you don't involve my father, Bryony. This is why you never, ever involve my father. He can't change. If anyone could have changed him, it would have been you. I know it. But he is what he is, and that's all he'll ever be." He marched upstairs, and Bryony swallowed a pathetic whimper.

Of course she'd ruined everything. She always destroyed whatever she touched. She should have stayed in her lonely house with her pet crow and never involved herself in anyone else's lives. Perhaps that's why she'd taken to Samael in the beginning. He was so utterly broken there was no way she could possibly bring him lower. But somehow, by some miracle, she'd managed to do just that, and the shockwaves from his implosion affected everyone around him.

Bryony didn't realize she was crying until she felt Chuy's arms around her shoulders. He was comforting her as though he wasn't the true victim here, as though she deserved any kind of comfort. "I'm so sorry," she murmured. "We'll get him back. Somehow, we'll get him back."

Michael returned with a blanket, and Bryony breathed a sigh of relief. For a moment, she actually thought he'd left because he hated her, but she should have known better. This was Michael, after all. He draped the blanket around Chuy's shoulders and helped him to the couch. "When is Azazel due to arrive?" he asked.

"Teatime," Bryony said. "Probably eleven."

"Can he do anything about this?"

She lifted her open palms in a desperate half-shrug. "I hope. It's Azazel. Loki seems to think he's a powerful magician."

As the hours crawled by, Chuy grew more and more distressed. Michael tried to keep him occupied to no avail. Occasionally, mercifully, Chuy dozed out of pure exhaustion. He was asleep on the couch when Azazel finally arrived.

Bryony met the watcher at her back door with a grateful hug.

"What is it, darling?" He squeezed her. "You're shaking like a leaf."

"Can you break a binding?" she asked.

"What?"

She buried her face in his chest and tried to hold herself together. "Ashmedai has been bound."

Azazel caught his breath. "Oh, no. Again? He can't go through that again."

"I know!" She tugged at the intricate, pastel tunic he wore. "That's why we have to get him out as soon as possible. Please tell me you can."

The angel stroked the back of her head in a way that was somehow both comforting and insistent. "Do you know what kind of binding it was?"

She shook her head and looked up at him. "Samael did it. That's all I know. And Chuy said his neck was broken."

At that, Azza's grip tightened, and deep in his chest, Bryony could have sworn she heard a growl. Was he angry? Azazel was rarely angry, but if the way he spoke about Ashmedai was any indication, the two had been close in the past. When he'd taken control of his temper, the angel asked, "How do you know his neck was broken? Do you mean to tell me there was a witness?"

"Yes. He's in my living room."

Azazel pushed past her so quickly, she barely had time to notice how gloriously pink and gray his hair was. She followed him to her living room and watched him extend a hand to Chuy. "You must be the witness," he said.

Chuy stood at once, shed his blanket, and took the angel's hand. "Captain Jesús of *Papillon*." Bryony had never heard him introduce himself so formally.

"Excellent." Azza squeezed his hand and bowed slightly. "I was a captain as well, once upon a time. Azazel at your service."

"You're Azazel!" Chuy dropped his formality completely. "I remember seeing you on *Dragonfly*, right after . . ." *Right after Bryony summoned the Angel of Death.* That's what he'd been about to say, but he couldn't. The moment was too painful a memory now. Bryony lowered her eyes as Chuy found his voice again. "They said you might be able to break a binding. Can you?"

"Sit, Captain Jesús." Azza gestured to the couch and sat himself down beside the hearth. His eyes darted to the front door, and Bryony immediately went to open it for him. He never even needed to ask anymore. His claustrophobia had been one of the first things Bryony had discovered about him. It was the moment she realized that angels could be vulnerable, that they were a little like people that way. It was the moment her world began to change.

Chuy sat at the edge of the couch, his every muscle tensed.

"Tell me everything," Azza said.

"There was this quake, and Ash . . ." Chuy's voice faltered when he said the demon king's name. "Ashmedai shielded me with his body. Had a hold of the ground, you know?" He formed one hand into a claw, and Azza seemed to understand. "And he wouldn't let go, so the devil broke his arms. Then he said, 'Dissolve your body or I'll bind you to it and bury you,' or something like that, but Ash refused, so the devil broke his neck. And the sound was so awful." Anger crept back into Chuy's expression, and Bryony braced for another string of Spanish obscenities. But the captain calmed himself again. "Then the devil buried him in the caves."

Michael, who sat beside Chuy and listened quietly, suddenly perked up. "Caves? Was there a river by any chance?"

"Yeah." Chuy nodded vigorously. "You know it?"

Michael groaned. "Overly well. Ashmedai had me chained to the wall there."

Chuy opened his mouth and then closed it again, lost for words. "Sorry," he muttered.

"Why are you sorry?" Michael said. "You had nothing to do with it."

Chuy shrugged and pulled the blanket back around his shoulders. The open door created quite a draft. Thankfully, Azazel noticed and had already begun to build a fire. But halfway through stacking the logs, he stopped. He straightened from his crouch and turned back to Chuy, a quizzical expression on his objectively beautiful face. "One moment, if you please. Are you trying to tell me that His Majesty"—with a sweeping, sarcastic bow, Azza let everyone know exactly what he thought of Ash's title—"King Ashmedai chose to be broken and bound over temporary dissolution? For you?"

Chuy just nodded.

The watcher's mouth fell open. "Well, well. I would have lost that bet and been glad to do so. Our little Ash resisted for so long." He tsked.

"What do you mean?" Chuy asked.

"He loves you, obviously. Do you feel the same?" Azza was beside himself with excitement.

"I . . ." Chuy seemed more than a little confused by the sudden lightening of the mood. Had he known Azazel longer, he might have expected it. "I guess so."

"Then congratulations." Azza offered his hand. As soon as Chuy took it, the angel leaned in and kissed both his cheeks. "And let me be the first to welcome you to the family."

Seeing Chuy flinch away from Azazel's affection almost made the moment worth the stress that got them there. Bryony knew she'd treasure the sight of it for the rest of her life, as well as the brief conversation that followed.

"What do you mean *family*?" Chuy asked. He really shouldn't have.

"Well!" Azza grinned madly. "Ashmedai is my compatriot's son. Although I'll never really know who sired him, thanks to his mother's well-deserved popularity. Ah, she was a whisper of silk, that one—how I miss her. Anyway, I watched our Ash grow from a wee petal into the scrupulous demon he is today. He was such a somber child, as I recall, that same thoughtful frown always painted across his little face. Let's just say he wasn't winning any hearts at that age." Azza pressed a finger to his lips and lost himself for a moment. Then he shook off the memories and smiled. "I doubted he would find much to love in his life. And then came you. That's why I say welcome to the family."

Chuy groaned. "Well, I won't call you tío."

Azza laughed and resumed building the fire. "I don't expect you to, darling. But do me a favor and explain your situation to Daniel one day. I believe you'll find he instantly adores you as well. All the watchers would, were we free of our bonds. Anyone who makes our children happy is a miracle to us. Anyone who eases their suffering, even a little, is a gift."

"But I haven't eased his suffering. I just made him weak . . ." Chuy trailed off, and a heartbreaking grimace replaced the baffled look on his face. "I'm the wine in the well. Oh my god, that's what he meant."

"The wine in the well?" Azza sank back into his chair, a healthy fire now crackling away in the hearth. "Is he still harping on about that?"

"I made him weak and stupid." Chuy buried his face in his hands, and Bryony wished Michael would either hurry up and hug him or get out of the way so she could.

"You made him happy," Azza corrected. "Do you know what the wine in the well represents to Ashmedai? It's his belief that he deserves a little joy in his life. If you are indeed the wine in the well to him, then you've made him believe himself worthy of happiness. There's nothing weak or stupid about that." He winked. "Michael darling, would you be good enough to brew two cups of tea?" As soon as Michael left, Azza took his place on the couch. He was so much better with people than Bryony was. She would never lose her appreciation for that. "May I embrace you, Captain?"

Numbly, Chuy nodded, and Azza's arms were around him in a heartbeat. Chuy's eyes darted to Bryony, who winced and mouthed a silent apology. It was all for show, though. She knew from personal experience how comforting Azazel's embrace could be, and she wasn't at all surprised to see Chuy relax in the angel's arms.

"I'll bring Ashmedai out of the darkness," Azza said. "No need to worry. If it helps, try to remember he's not entirely human. I won't pretend he isn't suffering now, but he's not as fragile as you think he is. He'll come out the other side of this in one piece. He's done so before." He chuckled a little. "But this time, if he tries to commission me to bind Samael in retaliation, I think I'll have to decline."

Bryony wished she could do more to reassure Chuy, but the situation was in Azazel's hands now. All any of them could do was have faith in the watcher. "Azza can save him," she said with a nod. "I know he can."

Azazel stood and stretched. "I absolutely can. I will need your help, though, little orb-weaver. I assume you're up for it."

She knew at once what he meant—possession. "Yes."

"Good. I'll require tea, salt, and an area large enough to build a circle."

Bryony immediately began pushing the furniture back to make more space. Chuy quickly caught on and helped her.

Azazel paced the room, measuring with his own footsteps as he mused. "I'm almost certain Samael bound Ash to the injury itself. It's his favorite binding, if I recall. He has a talent for injury." He made a disgusted face. "The easy part will be getting Ash here. We'll have to conjure him, of course, but he won't be able to shed his broken flesh. It'll reform around him like shackles. You need to be ready to see that. Once he's here, we'll deal with his injuries." He turned to Chuy. "I assume the neck is the binding blow?"

Chuy nodded. "Yeah, I think probably."

Michael returned with two steaming mugs. "You didn't say what kind you wanted, so I decided on green."

"It honestly doesn't matter." Azza gestured to the couch that was now pushed back against a wall. "I need both of you to sit." Chuy and Michael obeyed without question. "Now, each of you hold a mug of tea. Keep it in your hands, and don't spill a drop of it. That's all I want you to do. Understand? Guard the tea, and don't move from that spot."

"I see." Michael handed a mug to Chuy, who took it and held it with two hands. "You want us out of the way."

"Out of the way and present, darlings. Keep your eyes open and your hands to yourselves." He took Bryony by the arm and walked her to the kitchen. As soon as they were alone, he dropped his smile. "This is not going to be pleasant."

She stared up at him. He looked wrong for the occasion, all Easter and springtime. But there was something comforting in the fact that Azazel would always look wrong for any occasion requiring solemnity. She reached up and tucked the gray ends of his hair behind one of his ears. "I'm ready," she said, gathering her love for him, her trust.

"Excellent." He took both her hands in his. "Then let's begin."

CHAPTER NINETEEN

As the hours wore on and the dust settled between the stones, Ashmedai's vision grew dim. His own efforts to breathe sounded like dying to him, so he just stopped. What was the point anyway? No one was here to see his pantomime of life. He was alone, utterly, and nothing mattered anymore. He lay on his side and strained to see the gold pendant that was still half-clasped in his outstretched hand, but even that had faded from view. If only he could feel it. If only he could grip the cross and let it prick the palm of his hand.

Let it remind you that you're loved.

Oppressive darkness drowned everything out. Ash willed the pendant to give off some kind of light. He prayed for a miracle knowing it would be to no avail. Who would hear the prayers of the demon king anyway? What god would grant such a ridiculous request from a useless abomination?

But then, the strangest thing happened. Some god did. Ashmedai's prayer was answered, and Chuy's cross flickered with a mysterious, warm light. Maybe the shape of it was indistinct, but Ash could see something other than darkness, something golden and beautiful. It didn't matter that he was bound and buried, paralyzed, and probably going mad. He could see the glint of that pendant, and he remembered that he was loved. He was loved. He blinked back tears as the light grew brighter and began to give off warmth. It shifted and danced in his eyes.

It flickered.

It crackled.

And Ash's heart sank when he realized that what he'd assumed to be the cross giving off its own holy light, was nothing more than hallucinated flames—hellfire. He could see his hand now, and the cross was no longer in it. Despair washed over him. He couldn't even keep one little token, not even the representation of a happiness he'd once had and lost. Tears ran over the bridge of his nose and down one temple. He didn't bother to fight them. What dignity did he have left to lose? Who was going to see his pathetic display here? No one.

But a movement of shadows in the corner of his eye caught his attention. And he heard voices—subdued, concerned voices—all around him. This had to be some kind of delirium. That was the only reasonable explanation. Then he saw a face tilt sideways to mirror his and examine him. Something about it was familiar. As Ash's vision refocused, he noticed pink-and-gray hair, amber eyes, and a perfectly symmetrical bone structure.

Ash sucked in a raspy breath. "Azza." He ground out the name. "Why are . . . you here? Who else is . . . in this dream?"

"You aren't dreaming, Ash darling. You're in Bryony's living room."

Ash scowled as best he could under the circumstances. "That . . . woman."

"Yes, she's here too. And I'm certain she'll be more than happy to forgive your rudeness, considering. Later, you can thank her for making your conjuration possible."

A conjuration. Of course. That explained everything. Why hadn't he even considered the possibility? He hadn't expected Azazel would care enough to try.

"Why?" Ash rasped at the watcher.

"Because I couldn't have done it without her, obviously." Azazel answered the wrong question. "Now, let's have a look at what that foul beast did to you."

"No." Ash glared up at him. "Why . . . would you . . . bother?"

"Why wouldn't I?" Azazel knelt beside him. "I like you, Ashmedai, as much as we may butt heads. I'd tell you you're entirely too cynical, but I'm sure you already know that. It's a good thing you found a boyfriend to balance out your bitterness."

Ash gaped at his savior and fought to feel his own body, to move a limb, to do anything other than lie there like a helpless fool. He sucked in another shuddering breath. "Chuy . . ." Why couldn't he just turn his head, damn it? He needed to see the rest of the room.

"Chuy's here." A woman's voice mercifully answered the question Ash hesitated to ask. He assumed it was Bryony.

He squeezed his eyes shut and fought off a new barrage of tears. Now people were watching him. Now he had dignity to lose. "Alive?"

"Yes." Bryony sounded surprised at the question.

A sharp pain hit as Azza began to probe Ash's neck, and it took all his concentration just to tamp down the scream building in his lungs. Somehow, he managed to reduce his reaction to a whimper.

Behind him, Azza gasped. "Goodness! That heartless creature really did a number on you, didn't he? Poor petal."

Ash cringed. "Don't . . . call me that. I'm not . . . a child. Where . . . is Chuy?"

The watcher ignored his question and stood. "Well, this will be a trick, no doubt about it. Now listen, Ash darling. I'm certain you're in unbearable pain right now, and it's about to get a thousand times worse. Samael bound you to your injury, which means you'll have to stitch it back together yourself. I can help speed the process along, but this is going to take some time and a fairly invasive surgery."

All Ash could do was groan. Azazel really was the most insufferable angel he'd ever met. Of all people, it was Bryony who spoke on Ashmedai's behalf. "Can't we let him see Chuy just once, Azza? So he can trust his own eyes instead of our word? I know I'd need to see Michael if it were me."

Azza sighed, clearly perturbed by any delay in his process. "That's up to the captain, I suppose. Captain, do you think you can stand to see your sweetheart in this state? I will warn you he looks rather dead, and I won't have you passing out in front of him."

"I can handle it." Oh, that voice! Chuy was alive. Ash could hardly believe it.

"Then hand your tea to your tea partner, and come see the patient." Azazel's nonsense could hardly bother Ash now. Chuy was safe, and nothing else mattered.

He heard the captain catch his breath and swallow hard, and then he saw those feet, those knees, that face as Chuy crouched down before him. How Ash ached to hold him. "You are . . . still you?"

"Course I am, Ash."

"I thought . . . you were gone. I thought . . . he would break you."

"He didn't, but this might. You look awful." Chuy shook his head, and all Ash wanted to do was tangle his fingers in that gorgeous, black hair.

"You look . . . beautiful." Ash no longer cared about his own pride or what he'd once considered dignity. He refused to waste another breath pretending indifference. "I love you . . . Chuy." The name was honey on his tongue, and Ash was reminded of the captain's kiss. If he could just get through this, he would be able to taste that kiss again. "I'm ready," he said to Azazel.

"Good." Azza clapped his hands and adopted a commanding air that Ash hadn't seen in him since before the flood. "Captain, go back to the couch and guard your tea. If you need to leave the room at any time, I suggest you do so. This is not going to be easy for you to hear."

The half-smile that alighted on Chuy's face and was gone again, quick as a butterfly, set Ash's heart on fire. "I can handle it," Chuy repeated, and Ash knew he wasn't lying. Captain Jesús of *Papillon* had seen things, awful things that marked him deeper than anyone else in the room would ever know. "I'll be right here, okay?" Chuy said. "I'm not going anywhere. Also . . ." He paused, and that fleeting smile crossed his face again. "Also, I think I love you too. For real. So you have to get through this. You have to. I can't—"

"I know," Ash cut in.

The captain had already lost one love to the violence of the angels, and he couldn't bear to lose another. No matter how much Ash hated Chuy's most recent partner, the pain Chuy had suffered from the loss of him was real and far too much for a young man to have borne in such a short lifetime. If Ash's spectacles were good for anything, it was this. Chuy would never have to recount those painful memories because Ash had already seen them. They were shared memories now. Ash didn't need to hear the details nor did he want to. Right now, all he wanted to hear were the words, *I think I love you too*, again and again, until the end of time.

Chapter Twenty

When Azazel sent Michael to the sewing room for a utility knife, a needle, and some thread, Bryony realized why the watcher had advised Chuy to leave the room if he needed to. This wasn't going to be a metaphorical surgery. It was going to be literal surgery—literal surgery without anesthetic.

"Guard your tea with your life," Azza said to Chuy. "That's your job. That's what I need you to do. Understand?" Then he turned to Bryony. "Darling, do you menstruate?"

Bryony blinked. "Excuse me?"

"Sorry. Is that an inappropriate question?"

At her feet, Ashmedai wheezed out an answer. "Yes."

Bryony was grateful to him for answering on her behalf despite the pain it obviously caused him. She shrugged and agreed. "I mean it is a bit weird."

"Ah." Azza pushed a hand through his hair. "I'm merely trying to ascertain how comfortable you are with blood."

Again, Ash wheezed, "It's not . . . the same . . . you dolt." And again, Bryony had to be grateful.

"I doubt it'll make much difference in the wash," Azza said. "Anyway, I'll need you to brace the patient, and you won't necessarily be out of the flood zone."

This was getting ridiculous. Bryony sighed and answered, "Okay, fine. Yes, you are correct, Azza. Occasionally, I've had to clean blood out of fabric. I'm quite comfortable doing it, if that's what you want to know. Although I think it's strange that, of all the concerns you might have right now, your greatest appears to be for my wardrobe." She scowled at him and then shook her head. "Honestly, I don't know why it surprises me. This is *you* we're talking about."

From his place on the floor, Ashmedai actually laughed. It was a weak and breathy version of the laugh Bryony remembered, but it was something. Azazel winked at her and smiled. Then he resumed giving orders. "Kneel at his head, darling, if you would. We're going to turn him onto his stomach, and I want his face between your legs."

Ash and Bryony had the same response. "What?"

Azazel waved away their concerns. "His head is what he can move, and I need it braced. I'd ask Michael to brace him, but I really think someone who used to be a healing god is less likely to be squeamish. The captain is out of the question. I need an uninvolved assistant."

He had a point. Bryony knelt tentatively beside the head of Ashmedai—the demon king, the villain who'd abducted Michael and chained him to a cavern wall. It never ceased to amaze her the way the universe turned one hundred and eighty degrees every time she thought she knew exactly where she stood. This was for Chuy, she reminded herself. So she made a pocket in her skirt between her knees. Though it was certainly impossible to suffocate a demon, she supposed he would not enjoy being smothered, all the same.

"I'm going to turn him and lift him an inch or two into your lap," Azza said. "Support his head, please. Ah, Michael, bring me the knife and join your tea partner on the couch. It'll be your job to get the captain out of here if you think he needs some distance."

While Azza was busy giving orders, Bryony bent down to let Ashmedai see her face. "Sorry about this," she said. "I'll try to be gentle." He was half naked and broken with tears in his eyes, though he did not let them fall. Bryony had never seen him look so vulnerable. To her, he'd always seemed stoic—not even the death sword intimidated him. She hated to see him laid so low. He made a much better foe than a victim.

Azazel carefully drew the demon king's arm out from under his body and took hold of his shoulders. "Bryony." He nodded to his assistant. "Follow my lead." She did, and in seconds, she'd helped lift Ashmedai's head into her lap. "Brace him now," Azza said. "Hard. He's stronger than he looks. Treat him like a tiger."

Bryony pinched Ashmedai's head between her knees and impulsively patted the back of it with her hand.

His muffled voice protested, "I'm not . . . a dog."

"Sorry," she muttered. He was right, of course. The demon king was far from a docile, domesticated creature. His claws were massive, and they looked so sharp Bryony was sure he could easily disembowel her in one quick movement. His scaled feet had enormous talons that had no business fitting into any pair of shoes, let alone the elegant dress shoes he usually wore.

Without ceremony or warning, Azza straddled Ashmedai's torso and drew the utility knife down the back of his neck. Ash screamed, and every muscle in Bryony's body tensed. She'd never been good at ignoring the sounds of a suffering creature, no matter what kind of creature it was. Blood ran down the demon king's neck and soaked into Bryony's skirt, though it was his scream that truly undid her. She felt dizzy, and it took a great deal of effort to steady herself again. But she managed it. For Chuy.

Azza squinted into the wound he had made. "I'll need this held open while I work. Bryony?"

Bryony swallowed her fear and leaned over Ash's body. His spine was nothing like what she'd seen in anatomy books. Those perfect models of bone and tissue had not prepared her for the reality—the messy, wet reality. She clenched her teeth, touched her fingers to either side of the wound, and pulled it open. Ash screamed again.

"Sorry, sorry, sorry, sorry," she said, though she knew it wouldn't do any good.

"Perfect. Keep it just like that." Azza leaned closer to the wound. "Oh, petal, you've been crushed, haven't you? You always build far too faithful a replica of your living self—aside from those spectacular feet, obviously." Ashmedai growled into Bryony's lap, but Azza didn't seem to notice. "I'm going to piece you back together now, Ash darling, and I'll need you to dig deep and find that last store of energy. Use it to hold each fragment in place. Once you're whole again, you can work on healing the fractures. Understand?"

Ash whimpered in the affirmative, and Azazel began his work. His dexterous fingers were in the wound, and every time he moved them, Ashmedai cried out. Then Azazel would stop and say, "Hold." And Ash, presumably, would obey. "Good," Azza would say. "Next piece."

It went on like that for a good hour before Azza gave Bryony another order. "He's tiring, darling. Would you lend him some of your energy?"

Bryony glanced up at him. "What, me? How?"

"Talk to him."

Now that she'd been put on the spot, Bryony had no idea what to say. She chewed her lip and bent close to the demon king. "Um . . . Well . . . Hello again, Ashmedai." *What big talons you have, Grandma!* She shuddered and told herself to breathe. And then she noticed something interesting. "Wait, are you wearing cologne? You smell amazing." She leaned down and sampled the scent. "What is that?"

Azza answered for the demon king. "It's probably manifested. Ash has always been a fussy boy. He won't tolerate slovenliness, will you Ash?"

Ash grunted.

Bryony resisted the urge to pat his head again. "Is that a cherub thing?"

"No, it's an Ash thing." Azza laughed. "Isn't it, petal?" He pinched another bone fragment into place. "Hold."

"Surely you modeled your scent after something," Bryony said. Was this really how one lent one's energy? "Let's see if I can guess." She leaned closer and sniffed him. "Citrus, I think. Right?"

From between her knees the demon king groaned, "Mandarin."

She inhaled again. "And some kind of spice. It has to be. Nutmeg?"

Ash screamed as Azazel fished around for another fragment. It really was the worst surgery she could have imagined to be her first. Then Azza said, "Hold," and the demon king quieted.

After a minute, Ash mumbled, "Cardamom and clove."

Bryony guessed several more scents, and Ashmedai corrected her. He did love to correct her, she noticed. She decided to continue in that vein. "And I'm going to guess you prefer . . . classical music."

"Baroque," he grunted.

"Opera?"

"Yesssss." The answer turned into a pained hiss.

"Hold," Azza said.

Bryony unconsciously touched the back of the demon king's head, and this time, he did not protest. She asked him about poetry and didn't recognize any of the poets he thought every student should know. They were not English, and she was not well traveled. She argued the merits of Poe and Whitman, although she felt wholly ignorant on the subject. It didn't matter. The objective was to lend him energy.

At some point, she said, "Your speech is getting smoother, Ash. Have you noticed?"

"No," he grumbled. As long as he couldn't strike, his temper made him almost adorable. He was like a tiger, after all, only now he was caged and injured, and Bryony was resisting the urge to pet him. *Demon king*, she reminded herself. *Demon. King.*

By the time Azazel was ready to sew Ashmedai back up, Bryony had gotten quite comfortable with the surgery. Keeping the demon king's mind busy was keeping her mind busy, and she had to wonder if that hadn't been Azza's plan all along. His talent for dealing with people really was admirable.

"There. All closed up." Azza wiped his hands on some towels Michael had brought him. "I'm going to suggest our patient move as little as possible. We should do our best to make him comfortable where he is. Shall we roll him onto his back?" They managed it slowly and carefully, and Bryony found a pillow for the demon king's head. Then Azza went about cleaning the mess—the blood and salt—while Michael moved the couch back into place. Ashmedai was laid out where the coffee table usually sat, so it stayed pushed against a far wall.

The first thing Chuy did when he was finally relieved of his tea duties was drape the blanket he'd been using over Ashmedai's feet. Then he sat on the sofa and stared down at the supine demon. The love in his expression was evident. Bryony wouldn't have needed anyone to point it out to her had she not already known. *Chuy and the demon king.* She shook her head. Rose was absolutely going to kill her for this.

Ashmedai was barely conscious. Azza explained that the demon's energy was being siphoned into healing the wound he was bound to. Azza himself was fresh, clean, and perfectly cheery. No one would have guessed he'd just performed an impromptu, bloody surgery in the middle of Bryony's living room floor. He rubbed his hands together, satisfied with his own good work. "Once his spine is healed, he can dissolve his body and rebuild it with unbroken arms. It should only take a month or so, and he'll be good as new."

"No," Ash murmured.

Azazel looked down at him, surprised. "Why not?"

"It's too long."

"Too long for what?"

But Bryony understood. It was too long to be physically separated from Chuy, too long to be unable to protect him, too long to miss his touch. Michael would have felt the same. They were both nephilim, she realized, and nephilim couldn't love in halves—Michael had taught her that. When the demon king fell for Chuy, he would have immediately fallen hard. From day one, his love would have bordered on obsession, on unhealthy attachment and neediness. She wondered if Chuy was aware and whether he would feel as comfortable with the relationship if he knew.

By the time Bryony finally stripped from her bloody dress and put it in cold water to soak, it was evening. She threw on a pair of sweatpants and a sweatshirt, tied her hair back, and tiptoed over to kiss Michael, who had gone to bed early feeling sick to his stomach. "I never want to see anything like that ever again," he mumbled into his pillow.

"So you're not a pacifist just because you believe in peace." She laughed. "You really are squeamish. Speaking of which, I assume you're skipping dinner?"

He groaned and rolled over.

"That's what I thought." She went downstairs to make pancakes for herself and Chuy. She had no intention of asking the captain if he even wanted dinner. He was going to eat whether he liked it or not.

Azza had gone to set a perimeter around the house. "If Samael crosses it, we'll know. It will sound like a disturbed hornets' nest." When Bryony told him it was unnecessary, he smiled down at her and shook his head. "He chooses to announce himself, darling. He doesn't have to if he doesn't want to. I wouldn't put it past him to favor the element of surprise from now on." And that was that.

Bryony spread jam on Chuy's pancakes, just the way she knew he liked them. She'd served him breakfast a number of times aboard *Dragonfly* when he was supposed to be recovering from a broken rib. Now he was recovering from something deeper, and she was determined to make sure he took care of himself.

She marched his dinner to the living room couch, where he still sat sentinel. "Eat," she said, handing him his plate. "It's breakfast for dinner tonight. I'm exhausted. Also, drink something." She handed him a glass of orange juice. "I haven't seen you take a sip of anything all day."

She sat down beside him and set her own plate on her lap. At their feet, the demon king lay unconscious. Bryony could still feel his head between her knees and hear his agonizing screams. She tried to shake the memories off.

When they finished dinner, she took their plates back to the kitchen, turned out the lights, and sat beside her friend. The crackling of the fire in the hearth sounded like home, like family. She couldn't help leaning her head on Chuy's shoulder. She'd done nothing but fear for his life and his innocence for days, and now she needed to know he was safe. He put an arm around her shoulder and drew her close.

"I have a spare bed," she said after a while. "I'll make it up for you tonight."

"No, thanks." Chuy drew his feet onto the couch and hugged his knees. "I'll just sleep here, if it's okay."

"Of course it's okay. Take the entire house if you want. Stay as long as you need." She paused. "Both of you." It was an offer she hadn't intended to make, but the moment she made it, she knew it was right. Demon king or not, Ashmedai was important to Chuy, and Chuy was important to Bryony, more important than she let herself admit really. "I suppose you and I have something big in common now, huh?" she mused aloud.

"Yeah," he said.

She leaned into him again. Tonight, she'd seen Ashmedai with new eyes. She'd seen him afraid and felt his whole body quake from the pain of his injuries. She'd seen him love someone other than himself. He seemed more human to her now, despite his claws and talons. But once he was healed and strong again, wouldn't he just go back to his old, patronizing self? She recalled him cold and aloof, not warm and affectionate. What was it Chuy saw in him anyway?

"I can't seem to wrap my head around you and him," she admitted. "You're polar opposites. I mean, Chuy . . . The demon king? Really? I swear I'll fight for you no matter what. But honestly, why him? Help me understand because all I know about him is that he's really into abduction and can't resist a wager."

Chuy sighed and rested his chin on one knee. "I dunno. He tries to be cruel and heartless, but he's just so bad at it. It was weird. He took me, and I just . . . got the feeling he wasn't gonna hurt me. He was sort of . . . hospitable, you know? He gave me food, let me shower, and once, he pitched a fit because I didn't tell him my ankle was bruised from the cuff he'd put around it." He laughed. "You should've seen him. He was so mad. And he spent one whole night just reading the Bible. Can you believe that?"

Bryony frowned, trying and failing to picture it. "Not really."

"It's true. He loves to read. And he's crazy good at crosswords. You can't do 'em with him because he already knows all the answers." When he talked about Ash, Chuy's demeanor immediately brightened. His voice raised in pitch, and he grew excited despite his exhaustion. It took Bryony a moment to figure out why, but once she saw it, she couldn't unsee it. Chuy was proud of Ashmedai. He admired the demon king, and he was proud to be loved by someone like that. Somehow, Ashmedai's love made Chuy aware of his own value.

"He liked me from the start," Chuy was saying. "I could tell. He tried so hard to pretend he didn't. I mean who'd have thought a demon could be shy? But then I . . ." He hesitated, and his expression darkened. "I got drunk one night."

Bryony felt a pang of shame because the last time Chuy had broken his sobriety, she'd been responsible for it. She supposed she was indirectly responsible for it this time too. She took his hand and squeezed.

He cleared his throat and went on. "I guess . . . Ash got conjured, and I got scared. It was the only time I felt afraid, and it was because he was gone. S'pose I didn't want to feel that way anymore, so I had a drink . . . or ten. I blacked out. God it's so embarrassing."

"Sorry." She almost regretted asking.

"Don't be." Chuy tilted his head back and watched the shadows from the fire dance on the ceiling. "I came on to him that night. That's what I found out later. I'm such an idiot."

"No, you're not," Bryony said, though she knew he was unlikely to take her word for it.

"Do you know what he did the next morning? He apologized. *Him*. To me. He apologized like it was his fault or something. Can you believe it?"

Yes, Bryony thought. *Because it's you. Because you bring that out in people, the very best parts of them.* She just shrugged and said, "I guess he loved you."

"Yeah." He drew his knees in tighter to his chest and crossed his ankles, still watching the shadows on the ceiling. The firelight made his tattoos look almost alive, and Bryony couldn't help admiring them. She tried to remember what each of them meant to him. He'd told her once before. She still wondered what the flames on his neck meant—that inked fire that crawled up his throat and licked at his chin—but she didn't ask. Had he wanted her to know, he would have already told her.

He smiled to himself. "Been a while since I dated, but . . . I don't think I ever felt this way before. That's what everyone says, isn't it?" He pushed a hand through his hair. "Seeing someone hurt him like that was . . . I can't think of anything worse. Thought I might be kind of into him before that, but when that devil broke him, I knew. I can't imagine the world without him anymore. Just isn't possible, you know?"

"I do." A world without Michael wasn't possible anymore either, not to her. She didn't even want to imagine it.

"Bryony?" Chuy turned his head, and she saw the question in his eyes before he even asked it. "Is he safe here? Can you really stand up to the Angel of Death? I heard you chew him out when he brought me." He smiled a mischievous smile. "Wasn't really as passed out as I seemed. I could hardly believe it, though. You actually kicked the devil out."

Bryony grinned at him. "And I'll do it again." She decided not to mention the fact that she was only able to sway Samael because he seemed to have grown fond of her in an incredibly twisted way. Who knew how long that would last? Chuy didn't need to worry about it tonight. None of them did. If Azza's alarm went off, Bryony would go meet the Angel of Death alone. He was never, ever going to touch Chuy or anyone she loved again—not if she could help it.

In the dimming light of the fire, Chuy stood and stretched, and Bryony noticed a little of what Ash probably saw in him. He was subtly attractive. No one would notice just passing him on the street, but there was a movement to him, an easiness that had to be irresistible to people like Bryony and Ash—people who couldn't stop worrying for fear relaxation might just kill them.

"I gotta pee," Chuy said, and he started for the stairs.

Bryony called after him. "While you're up there, there's more blankets and a couple pillows in the linen closet. Grab some for yourself, and we'll make up a bed for you on the couch. Oh, and there's a spare toothbrush in the medicine cabinet if you want to brush your teeth."

"Thanks." He smiled and left.

And Bryony suddenly found herself looking down into the wide-open eyes of Ashmedai. "I suppose you heard all that," she murmured.

Ash didn't answer.

"So now you know how much he loves you, and if you ever hurt him—"

"I won't," Ash said. "I can't. You, of all people, should know that."

"Good." Bryony lay flat on her stomach across the couch, hugged a throw pillow under her chin, and stared down at the demon on her living room floor.

They were silent some moments before Ash spoke again. "Ms. Moss?"

"Oh, I think anyone who's had their head between my legs can go ahead and call me Bryony."

He laughed quietly through his nose. "Yes. Bryony, I find myself in the uncomfortable position of needing to ask your forgiveness. I didn't know how much you'd suffer when I took my little brother from you. Now, I think I do. You bore it well." He stared at the ceiling, and Bryony thought she saw an extra shimmer to his eyes. "When that beast took him . . . I've never known such helplessness. I hated Samael, and I don't hate anyone—not like that. Maybe you don't know that about me, but it's true. I don't hate anyone because I know I'll win in the end. There's always another round. But this time . . ." Tears tracked from the corners of his eyes to his ears, and Bryony watched his throat work as he tried to swallow his pain. "You have every right to hate me."

She hugged her pillow tighter. "I hated you a little. But if Chuy loves you, then I think I should reevaluate. He'd never love a monster."

"He did once." Ash blinked back more tears. "But it wasn't me. What I don't understand was how that bastard couldn't see the value of what he had. It's impossible, isn't it? You see it, don't you? It isn't just me and my unusual eyes. It's obvious."

Bryony nodded into her pillow. She was stunned, honestly. She could never have predicted the direction this conversation would take. Ashmedai was not the person she'd originally taken him for. When he let his underbelly show—when he was opened up and his heart exposed—he was more like Michael than she would have ever guessed. Then again, Chuy had a talent for finding the buried good in people and dragging it to the surface.

She decided to tell the truth. "When I first met Chuy, I was trying to con him, but he trusted me and treated me like a friend. He was so sincere. I felt filthy every time I lied to him. He gave me the benefit of the doubt over and over again. I didn't deserve it, but I wanted to. Whoever Chuy thought I was, I wanted to be that person. Maybe that's what innocence really does. Don't you think? Maybe its value isn't just in the person who has it, but in the way they change everyone around them."

Ash closed his eyes, and his breathing became so measured Bryony thought perhaps he'd really fallen asleep this time. Then he murmured, "I never thought of it that way before," and fell silent again.

Chuy returned with a stack of blankets and pillows that barely fit under his chin. She helped him make up a bed on the couch and hugged him one last time before she made her way to her own bed. When she crawled under the sheets beside Michael, he turned to her and pulled her into his broad chest.

"Michael," she whispered.

"Hmm?" he mumbled, a little more than half asleep.

"Did I ever tell you that you're everything?" He grunted in the negative. It always had been a feat and a half to wake him, so Bryony willed her words into his dreams. "Well, you are, Michael. You're everything."

Chapter Twenty-One

Demons don't sleep as a rule, but Ashmedai had focused so much of his consciousness and energy on healing the injury to which he was bound, he'd become completely unaware of his surroundings. The process reminded him of extreme meditation. Suffice it to say, sometime between midnight and dawn, long after the fire had faded, Ash finally began to feel his arms. He came to consciousness screaming. The pain was unbearable, and the darkness fooled him into believing he was still buried. His rescue had been a dream. He was bound and blinded by dust and exhaustion. He was alone and Chuy was dead.

A voice called his name, but he knew that was a dream too. The shadows, the furniture, and the light touch of a hand on his shoulder were nothing more than delusion. He'd had similar delusions a hundred years into his first binding. Apparently, they were starting early this time. He thought, *Let me die, let me die, let me die.* But he was already dead. There would be no rest for the demon king. Never, never again.

And then someone turned on a light.

Ash blinked up at a dusty, cobweb-covered chandelier he was almost certain he would not have imagined in his worst nightmares. Oh no, this was real. He fell silent and began mentally criticizing the housekeeper to avoid dealing with his humiliation. *Who let it get to this state? How hard can it be to break out a feather duster every once in a while?*

A woman's voice groggily said, "What's going on?" Ash recognized it as Bryony—the owner of the offending light fixture.

By the grace of god, the voice that answered her belonged to Chuy. "Don't know. He just started screaming."

The woman spoke again. "Ashmedai. Are you awake?"

And Chuy. "Ash?"

Despite excruciating pain, Ash's eyes somehow focused on the figure hovering over him. It was Chuy, kneeling on the floor beside him. It must have been his hand Ash had felt on his shoulder. Ash took a moment to breathe through his pain. "My . . . arms."

"Samael broke them," Chuy reminded him. "Can you feel them now?"

Ash cringed. "Yes."

In his periphery, he saw Bryony leave the room and return with two bags of frozen vegetables. "Sometimes cold can dull the pain a little," she said. She peeled back the blankets that covered Ash's arms, and he looked away, not wanting to see his chimeric flesh. It didn't seem to bother Bryony, though. She examined his broken arms and replaced the sheet, carefully positioning the frozen vegetables over his injuries. "Is that better?"

"No," Ash answered. He couldn't help scowling. He still wanted to hate her, though she'd done more to help him than anyone else in her position would. If someone had asked him what it was he disliked about the woman, Ash honestly couldn't have told them. Her involvement with Samael was hardly excuse enough. Heaven knew no one could manage an interaction with that monster without unintended tragedy. Perhaps Ash disliked her because he understood her. She reminded him of a kinder version of himself, a version he hadn't seen since he lost Sarah.

"Can you move your feet?" Chuy asked.

"Don't uncover them," Ash growled.

Chuy looked offended. "Course I won't. Still don't know why you're not proud to show 'em off, though."

Ash groaned.

Bryony hummed a moment in thought. "It's a good sign that you can feel your arms, isn't it? Soon you'll be able to start healing them." She yawned and stretched. "Well, if you don't need anything else, I'll head back to bed."

When her hand went to the light switch, Ash panicked. "No!" he shouted, and she froze. What was wrong with him? He could see in the dark, couldn't he? More clearly than most people saw in the light of day when he wasn't writhing in unbearable pain. But he didn't want to come to consciousness and doubt his rescue again. He couldn't stand to feel that kind of hopelessness. He didn't even want to be reminded of it. "I'm not . . . I can't stand the dark right now. It feels . . ." He searched for a description a human would understand. "It feels like I'm suffocating."

She knit her brow, and then her eyes grew wide. "Oh, like Azza and the doors. Hold on, I think I have something that'll help."

Chuy cocked his head, and Ash felt the need to defend himself. "I'm not afraid of the dark."

"Why not?" Chuy asked. It was not at all the response Ash expected. Then again, this was Chuy, and if the conversation were a game of checkers, he would have already won.

"Because I can see in it," Ash answered despite his bafflement.

Chuy shrugged. "I think things you can see are scarier than things you can't." He bent closer, and his sleep-mussed hair tickled the skin on Ash's face. "Hey, Ash?" he whispered. But whatever he was going to say would have to wait.

Bryony returned holding a spherical device, which she set on a coffee table against the far wall. She plugged the device in, and suddenly, the ceiling was filled with little pinpricks of light—a counterfeit night sky.

"Now it'll feel more like you're out in the open. My brother and I used it when we were little." She stared up at the simulated stars, and the briefest look of sorrow crossed her face. "I haven't seen it in years. I'm glad it still works." She shook off her melancholy and forced a smile. "I'll stoke the fire too. That should give you enough light until morning."

Ash tried to glare at her, but he still couldn't move. Calling her over just to give her a disapproving look seemed less than reasonable. "I'm not a child," he said.

"Neither am I." Bryony piled more wood on the glowing embers and prodded the fire back to life with a poker. "There are still things that scare me, though—things that make me relive old traumas—like ophanim." She shivered at the word. "I saw one eat a neighboring town when I was a kid, and I've had nightmares about them ever since."

"The ophanim are horrifying," Ash agreed. "Their form defies the mathematical laws of this world—that's why. It's difficult to look at them for long without losing your mind."

"Oh, I think it's probably just because they eat entire towns in one bite." She straightened, finally satisfied with the state of the fire. For a moment, her face screwed up in thought, and she chewed her lower lip before braving a question. "I still wonder, what happens to a person when an angel eats them? Do they just die? What if the person getting eaten is immortal?"

Ash admired her curiosity. She deserved a better answer than he could give. "Unfortunately, the only people who could tell us for sure are the ones who've been eaten, and no one ever sees or hears from them again. The standing theory is complete dissolution. In short, whatever creature is devoured simply ceases to exist as an individual. They become part of the angel. It's much the same as what happens when humans eat food."

"You mean they're digested?"

"Sorry. I know that won't do much to help you overcome your fear."

She crossed her arms and hunched her shoulders. "Do you think it hurts?"

"I don't imagine it feels good," Ash answered. Her expression fell, and he immediately wanted to take his answer back. "The truth is no one knows. It's possible complete dissolution is a simple *un-becoming*. It might not feel like anything at all."

"Well, hopefully none of us finds out any time soon." Bryony tried to laugh, but a dark look in her eyes told Ash something more was haunting her. She waved a dismissive hand. "It doesn't matter anyway. Come to think of it, I've never seen a cherub eat anyone. That's probably why nothing about the way you look really bothers me, even though you're part angel. So . . . you know, maybe don't worry about your feet so much."

Ash glowered at her. Somehow, the woman had pinpointed his insecurity and chosen placation. Well, two could play at that game. "Then I should tell you there's also nothing about the way you look that bothers me, even though you're a washed-up healing god."

Bryony perked up at that. "Aww, thanks, Ash!" She blew him a kiss, and he both hated and loved her for it. "Good night. And good night, Chuy. We both think you're beautiful just the way you are." Then she turned out the light and trotted up the stairs.

Ashmedai stared at a ceiling of false stars and was silently more grateful than he could have expressed if he'd tried.

The next time Ash came to consciousness, the fire had burned to cinders and morning light filtered into the room. There were bags of thawed vegetables on his arms and an empty couch beside him. He heard distant voices, a coffee maker, dishes clanking. He spent a good five minutes reassuring himself it was not a delusion before Chuy appeared and brought reality back into sharp focus.

The captain sat at Ash's head and leaned over him, upside down. Water dripped from the ends of his hair onto Ash's face like the first heavy raindrops before a storm. He must have had a shower, and he still wasn't wearing a shirt. "Good morning," he said. "We're still safe." He tilted his head and smiled. "You know, you really do have the prettiest mouth I've ever seen. Even from this angle."

"Keep talking like that, and you'll find out what I can do with it." Ash couldn't help himself. Only yesterday, he'd been certain all his visions of their future together were a mirage, the distorted echo of a single night. He was painfully aware that the man he loved was mortal and their time together short. He didn't want to waste another minute. "Kiss me."

"Aren't ya kind of fragile right now?"

"Please. I thought I'd never see you again."

Chuy grinned and leaned in close. He drew Ash's lower lip into his mouth in a half kiss, and Ash lifted an arm to slip his talons between the wet strands of Chuy's hair. The pain was nothing. "Wait, you can move?" Chuy started to pull back, but Ash tugged him down again and lifted his own head to close the space between them. Heat still rolled off the captain's skin from his very recent shower, and the perfumed scent of shaving cream was sweet in the air.

Ash memorized every sensation before he allowed himself to fall back onto his pillow, only a little ashamed he'd been so needy. "I'm sorry my hands are still wrong."

"Quiet," Chuy said. "You're insulting my taste in men."

Ash chuckled and closed his eyes for a moment. As soon as the darkness behind his eyelids hit, he was back in the caves, hearing the sound of his own bones break, feeling the boulders fall around him, watching the sand sift down to seal him in. His eyes snapped open again, and his entire body shuddered.

If Chuy noticed, he didn't let on. "Hey, can I get you something? I mean is there anything you need?"

"You," Ash said. "The answer will always be *you.*"

Chuy took his sentimentality in stride. "Can you sit up on your own?"

"I don't think so."

"Then I'll bring my breakfast out here." He stood and left. Ash wanted to beg him to stay but stopped himself. His neediness was getting out of hand. He'd have to rein it in if he wanted to build a relationship that was in any way sustainable. Perhaps his little brother could give him some pointers, if Ash could ever swallow enough of his pride to ask. Son of Samael or not, the nephil had actually achieved resonance with his partner and yet somehow did not turn into a quivering mass of useless jello whenever Bryony was in the room.

If there was one person Ash most assuredly would *not* go to for advice, it was the damned watcher, who was currently gliding across the room to greet him. "How are you healing, petal?"

Petal. Ash hated the endearment, but it was Azza's habit with nephilim. Ash only protested once in a while. It never did any good, and it never would. Azazel had watched him grow up. Being one of the few nephilim who did not know his father, Ash had been raised by all the watchers, which meant very little in the end. The watchers were not known for their parenting skills. But Azza had visited Ash's mother often, and he was always patient when her child demanded attention. Ash's failure to hide his soft spot for the colorful ish was inevitable.

Still . . . *petal.* Ash rolled his eyes and answered, "I'm healing." Then he let gratitude get the better of his pride. "Thank you, Azza, for what you did. I'll be in your debt for the rest of my existence."

"Nonsense." Azza crouched down to examine his patient. "Not every interaction is a transaction, you know."

Ash suddenly felt very young. "I know that. Obviously, I know that."

To add insult to injury, Azazel stroked the demon king's cheek with a tenderness rarely found in angels. Then he bent down to kiss Ash's forehead and murmur, "I always wished you'd been my son. You were a good boy, Ashmedai. You still are."

Ash froze. The moment had caught him completely off guard. He knew Azazel was fond of him, but he'd always thought of that fondness as a common personality trait among the ishim. They were good with people. They were always warm and polite. Now Ash was forced to contend with the possibility that, from the beginning, his relationship with Azazel might have gone much deeper than he suspected.

Mercifully, Chuy emerged with a plate and interrupted the moment. "Azza, do you think he can sit up yet?"

Azazel thought a moment. "Can you feel your legs, Ash darling?"

"Barely," Ash answered.

"Barely is something. Your neck is probably strong enough. Let's get you off the floor." Azazel lifted Ash easily and set him on the couch. Then he draped the blanket over Ash's lap, and Ash tucked his feet behind it. He couldn't seem to get over his shame where his feet were concerned, despite everyone having already seen them.

When Azazel finally left, Chuy sat beside Ash and offered him a bite of omelet. Ash declined. "You sure?" Chuy said. "Azza made it."

Did he indeed? "Well, if Azza made it . . ."

Chuy handed him a forkful, and Ash took it gratefully. He didn't need to eat, but he would never refuse a meal prepared by Azazel. It was nostalgia on a plate. "Let me know if you want more," Chuy said. "It's really good, right? Never met an angel who cooked. They usually just swoop in and murder your family."

Ash chuckled at the captain's dark humor. "Azazel has always been the exception that proved the rules. He used to cook for my mother and me when he visited."

"You knew him when you were alive?"

"I knew most of the watchers. They were my mother's clients. They all took this ridiculous vow that they'd fall from grace the same way their chief captain did, but they hadn't counted on the difficulty of finding wives in a world that distrusted them. Many initially used my mother's services to honor their vow. They came back because she was good at her job." He glanced at Chuy to gauge his reaction. "My mother was a prostitute."

To Ash's ultimate delight, Chuy didn't even blink. "You must've met Daniel then. Always been curious about whether he used to talk."

"Daniel was one of the few who never visited, though I do remember hearing his voice at some point. Azazel, on the other hand, was a regular, and my mother was always happy to have him. He would cook and clean and help mind me in addition to paying generously for her services." Ash stared down at his lap and let himself recall old times. Thinking back, he really ought to have been more patient with Azazel over the years. Anyone who made his mother smile . . . "The watchers' chief captain was also a regular. *Shemjaza*, they called him, because he shared a name with Azza."

"Really?" Chuy spoke through a mouthful of eggs. Only in such a beautiful man could terrible manners be so damnably charming.

"Really. They each used a different honorific to set themselves apart. Shemjaza went with *Shem*, and Azazel kept the more traditional *El*. It was like knowing two Elizabeths and calling one of them Beth and the other Eliza." He smiled at the memory of the girl who'd conjured him. "The Azzas shared a name, but they couldn't have been more different. Whenever Shemjaza visited, my mother became agitated hours beforehand. She scrubbed and cleaned, and she was often short with me. Shemjaza wasn't cruel, but he was strict. He would look down at me and say, 'Behave,' whenever I got in the way. That was all he ever needed to say. I was terrified of him. I hid whenever he came over." Ash frowned. If only he could see Shemjaza now. He would show that brutish cherub he wasn't afraid anymore. "Azazel, on the other hand . . . Well, you've met him. I practically hung off his shawl every time he visited. He didn't mind at all."

"Can't picture you as a kid," Chuy said.

"I looked the same but smaller."

Chuy laughed, and the sound was like being rescued all over again. "So, what was your mother's name?"

"Naamah. I lost my mind the day she died. The world was worse for the loss of her, but it never really deserved her. The stories they tell about her now are disgusting." Ash didn't realize a shadow had come upon him until Chuy slipped a hand in his and dispelled it.

"I love hearing about your past," Chuy said.

"I love telling you."

"I love *you*."

I love you. Not, *I think I love you.* Just, *I love you.* Ash tried not to read too much into it. Chuy lifted Ash's monstrous, taloned hand to his lips. And it was in that moment—in that perfect, hopeful moment—that the alarm finally sounded.

Suddenly, the once-empty living room was full of people. Bryony and Azza emerged from the kitchen. Michael marched heavily down the stairs. Ash wished they would all just leave so he could have his panic attack in private. He gripped Chuy's hand far too tightly. The alarm was useless, like a fire alarm when the fire is impossible to escape. It was an alarm to announce you had already lost.

Ash looked to Bryony, angry that she hadn't found a safer hiding place, angry at himself for trusting her when he knew damn well he shouldn't. He searched for words, any words to say to her, and found his own store of language depleted. Then, before his eyes, that fragile woman began to change. A shadow fell over her, but instead of burying her, it adorned her. She wore it like a crown. She walked like she was Queen of the Shadow Realm.

She squared her shoulders and turned to Ash. "Don't be afraid. He will not come into this house." And somehow, Ash couldn't help but believe her.

Chapter Twenty-Two

Azazel had not done his alarm justice when he'd described it as a disturbed hornets' nest. It was more like a nest of giant, prehistoric wasps descending on a creature the size of a dandelion seed. Bryony's teeth clattered at the sound, and she could have sworn her bones were being ground into sand. Oddly, it was more the alarm itself that frightened her than what it represented. Any fear she had of Samael was clouded with indignation.

Before she walked out to meet her infuriating future father-in-law, Bryony took a moment to survey his victims. Ashmedai's wrecked body twitched in what she recognized as a strong instinct to run combined with a complete inability to do so. Chuy clung to him as though he could somehow both protect the demon king and shelter behind him. Both of them knew they didn't stand a chance. They had already fought and lost this battle.

Michael stood at the bottom of the stairs and balled his hands into fists. "I don't like this."

"I know," she said, but there was nothing for it. So she closed her eyes, fortified her mantel, and marched to her little grove of plum trees to wait. When Samael emerged from the forest, she called to him. He wore his wings and carried a large, antique volume in one hand. He looked like someone's marble representation of judgment day, which Bryony

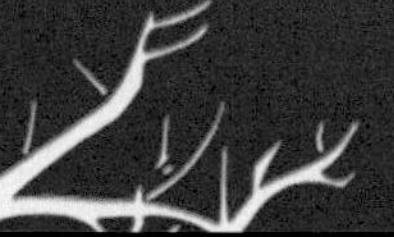

felt was appropriate imagery, considering. When he finally reached her, he stopped and waited.

The silence was unbearable, so Bryony broke it. "How could you, Sama?"

"I don't know what you mean." He was obstinate, always.

"You broke his neck."

The corners of his broad mouth turned down, and he spread his arms in a regal shrug. "Did you not demand I retrieve your captain gently? Did I not deliver him to you whole and untouched? I even spared his innocence. Why are you not pleased?"

"Because you broke someone's neck in the process. You paralyzed and buried a person who didn't come close to deserving it."

Samael blinked his empty eyes. "It was necessary in order to retrieve your captain gently." Now his voice had a pinch of impatience to it. "I have only done what *you* asked of me. I even honored the stipulations you added after the fact, though it was hardly required. What more do you want from me?"

"A little kindness maybe!" she shouted and immediately suppressed her temper. She would never get anywhere with him by yelling. *You catch more flies with honey*, she reminded herself. "You knew Chuy loved him—you were the one who told me so. You took stock of the situation, and you chose cruelty. How could you? Why couldn't you just acknowledge things had changed and improvise a kinder solution?"

Physically, Samael remained unchanged, but Bryony felt a brief wave of grief that let her know she was getting to him. It didn't take long for his expression to match his mood. "I am *not* kind," he snapped. Anger looked wrong on a graveyard angel. They were supposed to be weeping and praying, not exploding at their headstrong daughters. "I have warned you of my nature, and still you persist in your attempts to change what I am. Learn this before you deal with angels further. You cannot make of us anything more or less than what we are. Be grateful I had not my weapon, or I would have killed him instead."

"Damn it, Sama." Frustrated tears sprang into her eyes, but she blinked them back again. "I'm trying so hard not to hate you, but you're making it *so fucking difficult*." She was stunned when he flinched at her last three words.

Then Samael regained his composure and spoke in his most soothing, patronizing voice. "I warned you, my daughter. I told you to reject me. I bring nothing but suffering to the world."

"That's not true." She rubbed her eyes with the end of her sleeve. "You brought Michael . . . You brought your son to the world, and he's kind, and gentle, and good."

"Those traits he inherited from his mother, and she is dead. Had I stayed with her, she would have died sooner." Without a hint of warning, the graveyard angel's hand shot out and grabbed hold of Bryony's collar. He pushed her hard into the trunk of a tree and held her there.

Oh, this was definitely the end for Bryony. She was dead—no doubt about it. She should have hugged Michael before she left him. She should have properly thanked Ashmedai. She had dabbled in things she should never have dabbled in, and now she was going to pay the price. Hadn't her mother warned her when she was little? *Stay away from magics, Bryony. Never pray to angels.* Her whole body began to quake.

"Reject me," the angel snarled.

Foolishly, Bryony stood her ground and whispered, "No."

"Reject me." He brought his face an inch from hers.

Louder, she said, "No."

"Let me go, Bryony Moss, while you still can. Kill the archangel, and rid yourself of our contract. Never conjure or speak to me again. Listen! I am putrescence. I am death. I am rot and loss and grief. Wed my son if you must. Be happy and content with the life you have left. But *reject* me."

"I can't." Was she actually crying over this? She didn't want to believe it. She wanted to blame the poison, but she would have been fooling herself.

Samael wrung her collar in his fist. "Why?"

Her own answer shocked her. "Because I don't want to lose another father!" He released her, and she fell to the ground, weak from a grief that had nothing to do with his presence. "Please," she begged and doubled over. Her forehead rested on his bare feet. Her tears fell on his marble skin. She didn't know what she wanted from him anymore. She didn't know anything except that the loss of her first father had been the end of everything.

It was the end of hot summer nights filled with piano and song, the familiar scent of pipe tobacco wafting in through the front door. It was the end of home as she knew it. Her father's voice, his embrace, the way he made her feel safe no matter where they were. The day her mother died, she lost him for the first time. He became a stranger, angry and drunk. But his voice and scent were still familiar, albeit a little changed, and he would sometimes wake from his stupor long enough to hug her and tell her he loved her. And then, one night, while he was feverish on the couch in a fit of delirium, she lost him again. Even the stranger he'd become was gone. Dead. Forever.

Slowly, the Angel of Death slipped his feet out from under Bryony and backed away. She didn't know what she expected to see when she finally looked up again, but the distress in his expression was far from it. He gripped the book he carried with both hands. "You are the strangest child I have ever met," he said. "Fine. You have moved me. I offer you one last gift. May you accept it and learn to rein in your greediness. Do not ask me for more."

She didn't answer him. She could make no such promise. If there was one thing Bryony knew about herself, it was that she would always, always ask for more.

He continued to back away slowly. "I will allow you to keep the watcher Azazel. I will neither bind him nor force him to participate in any conjuration. May he offer paternal comfort to you in my stead. I have told you there is another way to find Raziel. It is less efficient, but it does not require conjuration. I will implement it now. This is my gift to you. Expect no other. You will still honor your part of our contract. I shall return with the Angel of Secrets. Goodbye."

He was gone before Bryony looked up again.

Shakily, she pushed herself to standing and steadied herself against the trunk of the tree she'd been thrust into. What was she even doing? Was she really trying to give Michael a gift by returning his father to him? Sometimes, people were better off without their parents in their lives—a lot of times, actually—and Michael's case was textbook. But whenever the opportunity to sever her relationship with Samael arose, some selfish part of her fought it. It had taken her too long to finally realize why, and the reason was laughable. In what twisted universe could an angel fill the gaping hole her own father had left in her heart? The Angel of Death, no less—as though death could ever be anything other than emptiness. Samael was right. She was being unreasonable and so, so stupid.

She trudged back to her house, humbled and lost. Well, at least she'd gotten something out of the encounter. At least it wasn't a total loss. She pushed open her front door and stumbled into her living room.

Michael immediately rushed to steady her. "What did he do to you?" he said.

But Bryony's eyes were on Azazel—her one win—Samael's parting gift. "Sama has agreed that you will not be part of the contract. He says he won't bind you or force you to conjure anyone."

Azazel's jaw dropped. He had traded his pastels for a suit of midnight blue with silver accents. His hair was the color of burnt umber, and he wore copper jewelry around his neck and wrists that jangled every time he moved. Today, his attire was unusually masculine, but no less decorative for that. Bryony kept her eyes trained on him because, even if she lost everything else, at least she'd gained this. His safety was worth it. Azazel was more than worth it.

After several seconds of silence, Ash voiced what everyone else had likely been thinking. "You negotiated? With the Angel of Death. How?"

"Not successfully." She bowed her head into Michael's stomach and he pressed a hand between her shoulders. "He won't release me from the contract." *And he won't let me know him better*, she thought. But why did she want to know the Angel of Death so badly? Perhaps that was what baffled Samael in the end. She'd lived in death's shadow for so long. Her family, her friends and their families, those congregants she didn't heal in time—death was all around her. Did she really think knowing it better would make it easier to bear?

Yes. Somehow, yes, she did.

Michael's embrace was warm and tender, and she let herself shelter there a while. He sat on the stairs, pulled her head into his shoulder, and caressed the back of her neck with one hand. "You did so well," he whispered. "You're amazing."

From across the room, she heard Azza say, "Bryony? Darling." When she didn't acknowledge him, he sent a wave of worship so powerful it could hardly be called a sip. Bryony drank it in and decided not to call him out on it. She needed it, and so did he it seemed.

Between Michael's comfort and Azza's nourishment, the wound Samael had opened in Bryony slowly began to heal. When she'd recovered some strength, she turned to see Ash and Chuy sitting side by side on her couch, their hands intertwined. Her mind stuttered at the sight of them. Something was off. Something was unexpected. When she realized what it was, she wanted to slap herself. "Oh, Ash! You're sitting up on your own, and I never even offered you coffee. I'm such a terrible hostess. How did you sleep? Wait. Do you sleep? You're my first demonic guest."

Ash deadpanned, "You need to dust your chandelier."

Bryony covered her mouth with one hand and laughed. The demon king was beginning to sound like his old self. "I apologize for the chandelier, but I won't evict the spiders. They're good house guests." She paused. "So are you. I wanted to say thank you . . . for protecting Chuy. I know you did it for your own reasons, but I'm grateful all the same. And I'll repay you someday."

Ash waved her offer away. "Not every interaction is a transaction."

The grin that spread across Azza's face could have lit up the entire room. "That's my boy." He swooped in behind the couch to wrap his arms around both Chuy and the demon king. Ash bore it with as much dignity as anyone could. "I claim you as my son, Ashmedai." Azza kissed the demon king's cheek. "There's no taking it back now."

Michael squeezed Bryony's shoulders a little too tightly, and she immediately understood why. He still hurt for the family he lacked, the family he'd never known. His was a childhood full of empty beach houses, stale food, and worn paperbacks. He was haunted by the sounds of crashing waves and shore birds and little else. She desperately wanted to give him the kind of family he needed, but it wasn't hers to give.

Then, as though she'd spoken her thoughts aloud, Azza crossed the room and reached up to press a palm to Michael's cheek. "And you, petal. I claim you, too, if you'll have me. You both make me so proud. Your fathers have no idea the treasures they tossed aside. Well, their loss is my immeasurable gain."

Something passed between Michael and Ashmedai when they met each other's eyes from across the room. Neither of them quite knew what to do with Azza's offer. It seemed they both wore independence like armor, and the removal of it made them squirm. Ash scoffed to hide his tremor. "This would be the weirdest family anyone's ever had."

"But it *is* a family," Bryony said. Something broken in her heart had begun to knit itself back together at the very idea. "It is, isn't it?"

From his place on the couch, Chuy grinned at her. "Yeah. It is."

Chapter Twenty-Three

By evening, Ash had mostly restored his spine, his arms, and human hands. He chose to expend the necessary energy to manifest the rest of his three-piece suit, dignity being more than a luxury to him, and he could walk short distances with help. He honestly couldn't have said whether his lingering weakness was due to the energy loss from healing or a psychological response to trauma. It didn't really matter in the end. The result was the same. Injury was injury, and Ashmedai was useless.

He decided to walk outside and work on regaining some strength. To his delight, Chuy jumped to join him. "Could use some fresh air," the captain said.

The night was crisp, and a few flakes of snow drifted like feathers from a blanket of gray clouds. On their way out, Bryony had given Chuy a long, black coat and wool scarf that had belonged to her father, and she'd insisted he keep both of them. Ash couldn't stop himself from repeatedly glancing at the man walking alongside him. "The, um . . ." He cleared his throat and tried to sound nonchalant. "The coat suits you."

"Thanks." Chuy grinned. "Good thing Bryony thought of it. It's freezing out here."

Without thinking, Ash offered his arm. "Stay close to me then." He nearly chided himself for recklessness, and then he remembered he didn't have to hide how he felt anymore. They were an item—a real, honest-to-god item. They'd kissed and confessed everything to each other. His skin warmed at the memory of that blissful hour in the caves.

When Ash began to feel his injuries, Chuy became his support without comment. Despite his wiry frame, the captain had more than his fair share of strength. Sailors usually did. All that hoisting and clinging to rigging like spiders in a windstorm. Ash leaned on his partner perhaps a little too much, but he never felt unstable on Chuy's arm.

"I want to see your ship one day," Ash said offhandedly.

"Really? Think we're gonna get out of this alive, do ya?"

Ash nodded. "Absolutely. And when we do, I want to see your ship."

"It's probably someone else's ship by now. No way the commodore would let it go so long without a captain." How Chuy could be so calm about so much upheaval in his life was a mystery to Ash, who responded to every minor shift in the prevailing winds as analytically as a meteorologist.

"I should not have taken you," Ash finally admitted. He bowed his head, ashamed and humbled, though even he knew the humility wouldn't last.

"What else were you gonna do with 'the world's last innocent man?'" Chuy's sarcasm was evident.

Ash could hardly blame him. "You're worth so much more than that. I knew it the moment I really saw you. I . . . only used your innocence as an excuse." He gritted his teeth and repeated, "I should not have taken you."

Chuy shrugged. "I was in a rut. Change is probably good for me. Also, there's you. Pretty sure you're worth all of it put together."

Now the heat crept past Ash's collar and into his cheeks. His cherubic mind tortured him with one resounding refrain—*marry me*. He punched it back down, but it was his nature to be absurdly devoted, to crave after promises and contracts, and he knew he couldn't resist his nature for long.

"Okay . . ." Chuy mercifully broke the silence. "Guess it's time to ask the scary question."

"And what's that?"

Chuy hesitated, and his breath drifted out before him like mist. Ash waited, appreciating the pleasant crunch of the ground as they walked. Finally, Chuy got his nerve up. "What are we exactly?"

Were they already so in synch? "Well . . . I can only answer for myself. I love you, and I would like to continue seeing you, if you'll allow it."

"Exclusively?"

"It would have to be." Ash didn't even need to think about it. There was only one possible answer for him, dangerous though it was. As many men as he'd sampled over his many years of existence, he knew better than to fall for any of them. It would have been idiotic to even hint at a lasting relationship. It was more than foolish now. *So I'm a fool*, he thought, and he annihilated every possible evasion. "I'm not entirely human. I'm not even sure my human half continued to exist after I died. What definitely continued is half of a creature that feasts on its own devotion. I cannot love another while you're alive, even if you choose to let me go. It's that simple. You're as good as god to me." He paused and corrected his course. "What I mean to say is I'm already yours. Whether or not you would like to be mine is entirely up to you."

Chuy kicked at the frosted blades of grass. "Just, you know, I've been burned before."

"I know."

"So if there's a chance you might get bored with me . . ."

"What?" Ash stopped in his tracks. "I just told you that's impossible."

"Yeah, but you still might wanna rethink the exclusivity. I don't mean emotionally. Just . . . I might not be quite as . . . as good as you're used to."

Ash narrowed his eyes at the specter of Chuy's ex rearing its ugly head again. He knew exactly what this was about, but having the kind of vision he did, he'd learned early on it was best to let people tell their own stories.

Still Chuy wasn't about to let Ash off the hook so easily. "You know," he said. "I mean you do, right? Already know?"

Ash breathed deep and resumed the walk. "Tell me anyway. If you don't, I may guess incorrectly, and that will be awkward." As it stood, he wanted to go back in time and throttle the man who'd convinced Chuy he was an inadequate lover. It was a disgusting lie, but Ash wisely held his tongue.

"It's gonna be awkward anyhow," Chuy mumbled. He knit his brow in a way that made Ash want to grab and kiss him until all his worries melted away. "Okay. Gotta get it out of the way eventually." He took a deep breath. "So I don't really go out with a lot of people. And the people I have gone out with tend to assume I'm maybe more . . . adventurous than I am because . . ." He gestured to the tattoos under his chin. "I don't know. Guess they get the impression I'm up for anything. Uh . . . I don't . . . I'm not. So you might wanna rethink exclusivity is all I'm saying, if there's certain things you need. Because I don't get drunk anymore, I'm maybe less exciting than you thought I was."

Ash wanted to scream. He'd known it was coming, this lie Chuy believed, but he wasn't ready to confront it with the kind of composure he felt it deserved. "It isn't true," he said under his breath.

"What?"

"In the cabin, you said something to me. I told you that you were drunk, and you said, 'That only makes me better.'"

"Oh." Chuy shoved his hands into his coat pockets and shrank into himself.

"It isn't true, what he told you." Ash clenched his teeth and clung more tightly to Chuy's arm as he hissed, "Don't make me say his name."

"Won't."

"Thank you." Ash continued—one foot in front of the other, figuratively and literally. "People like him . . . They want someone they can push around. It turns them on when they get you to do things you don't want to do. It wouldn't have mattered what you did or did not want to do with him. He would have pushed past your boundaries regardless, not because he needed something more from you, but because he wanted you to submit."

Chuy's voice was quiet. "How do you know that?"

"I've met many like him over the years. By now, they're easy to recognize."

"Oh, yeah. I forgot you've been around a lot longer than me."

"Don't think about it. It means nothing." At the corner of the house they made a wide turn and headed toward the forest. Dusk was dwindling and the cloud cover eliminated any moonlight that might have lit their path. Ash curled his fingers around Chuy's forearm and began to take the lead. "Forgive me, but when I looked, I thought I saw four lovers in your past. Am I missing any?"

Chuy shook his head. "No, but this is so weird."

"I know. Stay with me now. I promise I'm going somewhere with this. Four lovers. One was new. One was safe. Two were bullies. The bullies were attracted to your innocence. Maybe they told you they were misled by your tattoos. They weren't. They sniffed you out like a sweet perfume. *He* knew you'd do anything for him, not because you're a fool, but because you're a generous lover and you trusted him. He knew he could wear you down, and that's exactly what he wanted from you. He threatened you with infidelity, didn't he?"

Chuy nodded. He looked mortified, and Ash hated that he was screwing this up. He'd wanted to comfort the man.

"The point is, it wouldn't have mattered what you did. It wasn't your fault. He desired your subjugation. If you'd told him you didn't like to chew gum, he would have convinced you it was the only way he could get off. I'm . . . sorry if it hurts to know that."

"It's true though, isn't it?" Chuy squeezed his arm. "Better to know the truth than believe a lie."

"I thought you'd feel that way."

An old, abandoned van was parked across the lawn at the edge of the property. Ash stopped walking and leaned against the side of it. "I need to rest," he said. Chuy joined him and crossed his ankles in a casual pose, although the conversation was far from casual. "I didn't mean to open old wounds," Ash muttered.

"It's okay."

The snow fell more steadily now. It was just beginning to stick to the ground. Ash took Chuy by the arm and gently tugged him closer. "I only wanted you to understand what I mean when I tell you I'll never do that to you. You're all I'll ever need. I love *you*. No one else can give me what you do because no one else is you. Does . . . Does that make sense?"

Chuy shrugged.

Ash sighed and tried to put it another way. "When I was buried, my only thoughts were of you. I knew I could get by on just the memory of you—just the knowledge that I met someone like you in this agonizing afterlife of mine. You're such a beautiful person. Your mere existence is enough. Forget everything you've ever learned about love. This is something else entirely. I could have lived a thousand years in that prison with only the pendant to remind me, and . . . and . . ." And it was gone. He'd lost the only object Chuy had ever entrusted to him. He ground his teeth. Why was everything so hard to say? "Listen . . . The pendant didn't come with me in the conjuration. It's still buried. I'm sorry."

Chuy leaned away and stared at him like he'd never seen a stranger creature in his life. "Okay, why do you think I'd care about that?"

"It was important to you, wasn't it?"

Chuy opened his mouth to respond and quickly snapped it shut again. "Nah, you know what? I'm not as good with words as you are." He straightened from his slouch, pivoted into Ash, and kissed him hard. Ash lifted himself off the van, but Chuy pushed him back into it. The captain's long fingers curled around Ash's hips and squeezed. For the first time since that night in the cabin, Chuy was aggressive, and Ash was weak for him.

When Chuy pulled away, Ash let his head fall back against the van with a loud thump. "My god, why would you ever think I'd need more than that?"

A sharp laugh escaped the captain's flushed lips. "You can't be serious. So, even if this is all you ever get from me, you're not gonna mess around?"

Ash shook his head. "Never." It was more than a promise. It was a fact.

"Okay." Chuy smiled like he still couldn't believe it. "Okay, I think I get it. So we're official?"

Ash reached out and took his hand. "Yes." *Official.* The conversation was making his breath come quicker. He cupped the captain's cheek and pulled him close again. He kissed behind Chuy's ear and down his long throat. He murmured, "Honey," as he untied the scarf and proceeded to kiss every inch of skin it had covered.

"That my new nickname?"

"If you like," Ash said. "You have me craving it. I'll never taste honey again without thinking of you." He reached out to push a lock of hair from Chuy's eyes, and he let his fingers trail down along Chuy's jaw as his thumb drew a line across that wicked mouth. The captain's smile faded. "What's wrong?" Ash whispered.

"No one touches me like that."

"For the rest of your life, someone will." Ash leaned in and let his lips brush the captain's ear as he added, "If you like."

"Yeah, I like." Chuy shivered.

"Do you want to go back inside?"

"Don't make me."

There was, of course, an obvious and pleasant solution to the cold. Ash quickly unbuttoned his jacket. Then he fingered the top button of Chuy's long coat. "May I?"

Chuy arched an eyebrow. "Course, but . . . I mean right here? You sure?"

"No, honey." The man was too precious for words. "I'm only keeping you warm." He took the captain's hand and pressed it to his own stomach.

Chuy's eyes grew wide when he felt the unnatural warmth of Ash's body. "That's crazy."

"It's to be expected. The heat is a barometer for my desire. It's the angelic version of getting hard." Ash laughed. "You can imagine how troublesome it was during adolescence, but it's useful for cold weather." Though the buttons on Chuy's coat were large, Ash still struggled with them. His fingers were not as nimble as they'd been before Samael broke him.

When Chuy finally stepped into Ash's arms, his shivering stopped at once. "Wow," he whispered.

"Now we can stay a little longer."

"Only as long as I turn you on, right?"

Forever, you will. Ash warmed another degree as Chuy's long fingers worked their way under his shirt to his burning, bare skin. The captain pushed the heel of one hand into the soft flesh just inside Ash's hipbone, and the world stopped spinning. He was so close, and Ash ached for him. *Hard* would have been an understatement. Ash brought his mouth to Chuy's ear. "Do what you like. My body belongs to you. Every time I build it, from now on, it will be for you."

Chuy tipped his forehead onto Ash's shoulder and groaned. "I promised myself I wasn't gonna get serious so quickly again."

"Then don't," Ash said, and he meant it. "Take your time. I'll wait for you. You know that, don't you? I'll be here when you're ready. I will always be here."

Chuy's hands trembled, and Ash could feel that fragile, human heart pounding away in his chest. Then the captain sucked in a sharp breath, said, "Ah, what the hell," and threw himself at the demon king.

Chapter Twenty-Four

A collision—that's what it felt like. Despite the fact that they were already pressed together, despite the fact that they'd already spoken of love and grieved the loss of one another, this was a ground-shaking, world-shattering collision. Chuy pinned Ash to the van and thrust into him. He was every bit as ready and needy as Ash, and to be wanted like that, by this man, was everything. Ash fumbled for the door behind him and slid it open, thanking heaven it was neither locked nor rusted shut. The vehicle had two front seats and an empty cargo space. Ash slid backward into the van. Chuy followed and closed the door behind him.

Who could have known such an easygoing man would have so much fire stored up behind those hazel eyes? He was not at all the languid, mellow lover he'd been when he was drunk. Because this time, Ash realized, Chuy wasn't offering himself up as some kind of consolation prize. This time, he wasn't playing Russian roulette with a demon instead of a gun. This time, he was taking what he wanted, and Ash had every intention of giving it to him.

Somewhere between each kiss and every caress, Ash found a moment to slide Chuy's coat off his shoulders and pull his shirt over his head. He watched those beautiful lines of ink move through the darkness, smooth and fluid like sharks in the deep. It drove him mad, the way

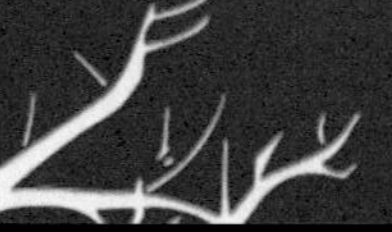

Chuy moved, the way his body undulated from shoulder to hip. Ash's own flesh bruised against the unforgiving surface of the van's floor, but he didn't care. Each time the captain's cool skin came into contact with his, it was like a sip of something he needed to survive, something he'd thirsted for all the years he'd been alive and beyond.

When Chuy moved from kissing Ash's mouth to his bared chest and stomach, Ash seized the opportunity to ask, "What do you like? Tell me what you want." Though his flesh thrilled at the downward path of Chuy's tongue, he didn't want to receive the gift being offered. Not yet. No lover had ever given Chuy what he craved. No lover had been as generous with him as he always was with them. Ash had seen that much, and he wanted to be the first. He needed to be the first. "Tell me. Please."

Chuy paused and looked up, an expression of pure puzzlement on his flushed face. Ash was horrified when he realized why. *He doesn't know the answer. Dear god, he doesn't even know what he wants.* Chuy had fallen too easily into his pattern of giving, thinking only of how to satisfy his partner. Ash drew in a long, trembling breath, and begged, "Please, tell me what you want." *Please, don't make me into an echo of him.*

"I . . ." Chuy shifted back up to meet Ash face to face. He looked more than lost. "Well . . ." He still didn't know what to say. He struggled to speak, to want, to be anything other than a fucking machine, and Ash hated it.

"I love you," Ash reminded him. "There's nothing you can say that will convince me otherwise. Tell me what pleases you. I want to please you."

Silence. Chuy curled his fingers into Ash's chest, and Ash's heart broke for him. Why was this so uncomfortable for him? Why was the simple act of asking for love so difficult?

Ash offered his hand to Chuy. "If you can't say it, then show me."

The demon king had looked deep into so many lives. He knew which men would want him and which wouldn't. He knew who liked it rough and who liked it gentle. He knew his vision made him a magnificent lover. Often, it felt like cheating on an important exam. But when he'd looked into Chuy's past, all he'd seen were the desires of others. This was a test for which Ash had been given all the wrong answers. It was the strangest thing to have finally found the man to whom he wanted to give the world, and to have no idea where to even start. It was so unnerving, in fact, that he actually breathed a sigh of relief when Chuy finally took his hand.

To start, Chuy was shy, tentative. He placed Ash's hand over his heart and drew it down past his ribcage and around to his back in a sweet, almost chaste caress. Ash stared into his eyes and memorized the path his own fingers took under Chuy's guidance. Then the captain grew bolder, and he moved Ash's hand over his hips and navel, down to the buttons on his jeans. Ash unbuttoned him but went no further until Chuy took his hand again and demonstrated exactly what he wanted.

This was the point. This was the reason Ash hesitated at all. When Chuy closed his eyes, Ash knew he'd managed to open a new door for the captain. For the first time in his life, Chuy would experience a real partnership in which the pleasure he took mattered every bit as much as the pleasure he gave. He moaned quietly and pushed into Ash's hand, begging for more pressure, and Ash happily complied. Still he could tell Chuy was holding back.

"Let go," Ash whispered. "What are you afraid of? Just let go."

Chuy opened his eyes and frowned. "Can't," he said. "Sorry."

"All right." Ash stopped, and Chuy's expression fell. Perhaps the captain's fears of inadequacy were coming into play, but Ash wasn't giving up on him. Instead, he removed the rest of his own clothes, including his shoes. He would make himself just as vulnerable if that's what it took. When he was truly naked, he lay back and let Chuy's eyes travel up and down his body. He didn't even try to hide his feet—the way his skin transitioned into scales below his knees, the way his toes branched out like something alien and wrong. "Go ahead and touch them," he said when he caught Chuy staring. "I give you permission. They make you happy, don't they? So touch them."

"Nah, you don't want that." Chuy looked wary but secretly pleased.

"I do."

Ash watched as his new lover crawled toward the front of the van to examine his feet. It was all he could do not to sit up and tuck them under his legs in a panic. The first touch made him flinch, but he soon grew accustomed. His newfound courage nearly came to a screeching halt, though, when Chuy bent down and began to kiss one toe, then his ankle, and on to his shin. Ash's body warmed a little each time those cool lips came into contact with his skin. The van felt like a sauna from the heat he gave off.

"I think you've got the most amazing body," Chuy said. "You've gotta know it's beautiful."

"I don't think so," Ash answered truthfully. While he knew his human body had been a thing to behold while he was alive—he'd had perfect skin, sculpted muscle, and delicate features—after death, he'd always believed his feet completely ruined the effect. "I'm not whole, am I? I'm half of one thing and half of another."

"Mm . . ." Chuy's mouth was at his thighs now. "You're all of *you*." He made his way up, mumbled, "A whole lotta you," and laughed.

That laugh was music to Ashmedai's ears. He would endure all manner of humiliation just to hear that laugh again. So the key was for Chuy to feel needed. That was why he gave and gave and never took. Once he had a role to play—once he had someone to put at ease—his confidence soared. He became a true captain. He took command, and anyone under him would be grateful for his leadership.

Ash was under him now and feeling exponentially grateful. Chuy had stripped off the rest of his own clothes and brought their bodies into perfect alignment. He moved his hand between them and caressed them both at once. He took control and showed Ash how to touch him until Ash could handle the job without instruction. They were locked together like they shared the world's last breath of air between them.

Their frenzy built anew, and this time, neither one of them tried to stop it.

As the pace Chuy set slowly accelerated, Ash managed to match it beat for beat. Soon they moved in unison, and Ash couldn't have said who drove who anymore. It hardly mattered. Every flex of his muscles, every roll of his hips possessed him a little more until, finally, he lost his mind, his composure, and his dignity and moaned into Chuy's mouth. For once, his perfectionism seemed to have paid off. He'd manifested an almost perfectly human body, and it functioned exactly as it had in life.

Exactly, until . . . His breath caught. His heart stuttered as though someone had reached into his chest and flipped a switch. He was suddenly taking someone else's breaths, moving with someone else's rhythm. And the harmonizing music of someone else's pleasure escalated, emphasized, and amplified his own. When he realized what was happening, he gasped. "Oh my god."

Chuy stopped, and his mouth fell open. The ghosts of Ash's batlike wings were curled around the inside walls of the van, blocking the windows. The space around them glowed with a warm, coppery light that emanated from the apparition of Ash's cherubic body.

"What's happening?" Chuy asked.

Nothing. Everything. "Don't stop," Ash begged. "It's resonance—don't stop. I've never . . . It's my first . . ." He forgot he was talking when Chuy resumed. Heaven had nothing on this ridiculous, rusty van because here he was welcome. His demonic body had materialized over his human one like a hellish, three-dimensional transparency, but still he was welcome. He was wanted. And with resonance, Ash could feel that want for himself along with all the pleasure and pain his partner felt. It engulfed him and magnified in him. There was no greater intimacy than this. His heart beat in time with Chuy's. His breath came in time with Chuy's. His pleasure mounted with Chuy's, and god he was getting close.

"Ash . . ." Chuy murmured, but Ash didn't need the warning.

"I know." He gripped his partner's body tighter and crushed himself against the only man he had ever loved. "I have you. Don't stop." That seemed to be Ash's refrain tonight. *Don't stop*—not just the sex, but the whole heartbreaking ride—the relationship, the mess of a life they were about to live together. *I have you.* It was all that really mattered. Ash experienced their shared climax as one pulsing heartbeat. Matched. Beautiful. Stereophonic ecstasy. He let his own cry die in Chuy's mouth and fell back as Chuy collapsed on top of him, breathing like he'd just run a marathon.

When the light faded, so did the specter of the half-formed cherub. Had anyone told Ash to get up, he couldn't have complied, no matter who had given the command or what the consequences were for defying it. He kept his arms wrapped around his partner, clinging like he was afraid to let go. Chuy tried to push off him, but Ash only held him tighter.

"Sorry," Chuy whispered.

What? "What?" Ash echoed his own thoughts. Since when had he become a demon of so few words? For the first time in his life, he suspected his brain wasn't working right.

"How do you want me to finish you off?" Chuy asked. "I didn't mean to come so fast."

He hadn't noticed? How hadn't he noticed? "It wasn't just you."

Chuy cocked his head in disbelief.

Ash grinned and kissed his partner between each word. "You . . . are . . . amazing. I've never had anything like that, Captain. Never in my life. Never, you beautiful man."

Chuy snorted. "Okay, but seriously . . ."

"I'm not lying. I couldn't fake that if I wanted to. Do you know what that was?" Chuy shook his head, and Ash finally loosened his hold so the poor man could sit up. "It was resonance." Ash picked up his own shirt and gently mopped at Chuy's stomach and then his own. "You lied when you told me you weren't exciting, didn't you? You didn't want me to know you were a fucking professional." He opened the door a crack, tossed the soiled shirt outside, and let it dissolve. He would manifest another later.

"Sure." Chuy rolled his eyes. "Don't try to stroke my ego, Your Majesty. I know I'm nothing special."

"Don't you dare." Ash propped himself against the back doors of the van to pull on his pants and refasten his belt. "You have no idea what you've just given me. My kind knows better than to expect resonance with a lover. We hope for it, dream of it, and then we accept whatever inferior connection we manage to make instead. For us, resonance is the holy grail of intimacy."

Chuy pulled his own clothes back on in silent disbelief. Then he sat beside Ash and muttered, "Holy grail. What's that even mean?"

"It means you're the best I've ever had." Ash put his arms around Chuy, and the coolness of his body soothed like a balm. Heat still radiated from Ash's own skin, and it would probably be some time before it dissipated. "I don't care what your other partners told you. They know nothing. You brought my world down around me. I . . . I barely have words to express this." He pinched the bridge of his nose. If he could only make Chuy understand the magnitude of what they'd just experienced. But he couldn't because no human being in this day and age had even heard of it. "Listen. We felt the same thing. That's what resonance does. It . . . links you with your partner. So if you want to know how it was for me, just ask yourself, how was it for you?"

Chuy chuckled and sank into a deep slouch. "Really, really, really good."

"Exactly."

"Well . . ." With a satisfied smile, Chuy linked his fingers behind his head and stretched his long body out on the floor. "I *am* good."

"And I'm grateful." Ash leaned over and kissed the upturned corner of his mouth. "If you don't mind, I want to stay here a while longer, just until the warmth fades."

"Sounds good." Chuy scooted closer. "Maybe, while we're alone, you could tell me more about your life. Maybe something you couldn't tell me in front of other people. You know lots about me, but I don't feel like I know much about you."

Ash curled his arm around Chuy and pulled him in. It was a fair request. He supposed he owed Chuy the revelation of a few secrets, considering. "What do you want to know?"

Chuy shrugged. "Something embarrassing? Definitely something embarrassing."

Ash chuckled. "Well, I was quite a bit taller than Michael when I died. Although that was more inconvenient than embarrassing. Hmm, let me think." He tucked one foot under his leg and absent-mindedly combed his fingers through the back of Chuy's hair. "I was an unpopular child, and teenager, and adult. I was obsessed with academics and never bothered to practice basic human interaction. Most of my peers thought I was prudish. It didn't help that I wasn't interested in girls."

"Did you always go for men?"

Ash nodded.

"I didn't." Chuy bit a thumbnail as he considered. "It went boy, girl, girl, boy." He laughed. "Sounds like I couldn't make up my mind, doesn't it?"

"No." Ash didn't hesitate. "I've met others like you. You're an open person, capable of seeing deeper than most, and you don't need a pair of spectacles to do it. When you fall in love, it's because you've seen through the bullshit, the masks and expectations. You see through costumes and performances, way down to the core of a person."

Chuy thought a moment and scoffed. "How'd I end up with someone like *him*, then?"

"Because seeing isn't everything. Interpretation is key."

"Ah. So I interpreted him badly?"

"In a way." Ash wrapped a lock of Chuy's hair around one finger and considered how best to phrase what he wanted to say. "You saw the real him, but you missed the corruption, the tarnish. You always miss the corruption. That's the nature of innocence. If I'm honest, you've missed the corruption in me as well." Chuy stiffened, and Ash had to wonder if he wasn't making a huge mistake in admitting this much.

"So," Chuy said, "what's the corruption I missed in you?"

"You mean aside from the obvious?" Ash pointed to himself. "I'm the king of demons, honey—the sovereign of angelic refuse and human sin, the watchers' firstborn abomination."

"Nah." Chuy shook his head. "There's no crime in being born. Mamá used to say, 'You can't help how you came in, but you can sure as hell do something about the way you go out.' Speaking of which, how'd you die anyway?"

He'd asked the question so casually that Ash didn't register it straight away. It took him a second to hear the words and parse their meaning, and when he did, his shoulders drooped. He groaned and admitted, "I killed myself."

Chuy pulled back and knit his brow. "Why'd you do that?"

And Ash had a moment of real panic and shame. His death was almost as humiliating as his feet, and he hated talking about it. But he owed Chuy an explanation, didn't he? He owed Chuy the truth about who he was and what had corrupted him. "There was famine, and I was starving. Most of the other nephilim had killed each other over food. I didn't want to live like that, so I poisoned myself. Well, first I tried to drown myself, but that was a miserable failure." He laughed without a hint of mirth. "I suppose that qualifies as something embarrassing. I should have just waited for the flood."

In the dark, Chuy put a hand on either side of Ash's face and leaned in to kiss the tip of his nose. The moment was so unexpected, Ash actually forgot what they'd been talking about. Then Chuy said, "Must've been lonely, dying like that," and it all came flooding back.

It was the lack of judgment that hit Ash hardest. He blinked away tears that threatened to expose how deeply Chuy's words had touched him. The truth was his death had been terrible, desperate, and yes, incredibly lonely. He'd carried poison up a mountain, hidden in a cave, and swallowed it. All the throes of death—the sweats, the stomach cramps, the disembodied echoes of his own primal screams—still haunted him. Even now, he struggled to tamp down the memories of that day and the years of emptiness that followed.

"It's time to go," Ash muttered when he realized how long he'd been sitting in silence. The warmth had faded, and his partner had begun to shiver again. Ash found Chuy's coat in the dark and draped it over his shoulders. Then he found his own vest and jacket. He tried to manifest another shirt to go under them, but he was more exhausted than he'd anticipated.

"Try this." Chuy wrapped the wool scarf around Ash's neck and tucked the ends of it inside his jacket. "There. Now no one can tell you've got no shirt." He grinned, and Ash grabbed and kissed him one last time before they had to return to the house.

The entire walk back, Ash fought his urge to propose. He craved a promise, a lifelong commitment. He craved it more than he cared to admit. Anything less than Chuy's entire lifespan would feel like a split second in time. To Ash, the end was already nigh, and he was desperate to cling to every second he had left.

Not one of the three occupants of Bryony's unkempt farmhouse even looked up when Chuy and Ash returned. They all read contentedly by the fire. Azazel reclined in a chair and studied a book of sheet music. Michael sat at one end of the couch with . . . Was that a horror novel? Dear god. And Bryony lay with her head in his lap, absolutely mesmerized by a large, illustrated, astronomy book.

"You won't be allowed to keep it," Ash said to her.

She looked up. "Huh?"

"That book. The angels will destroy it if they find it."

"Then we won't let them find it." Bryony winked badly, and Ash came very close to feeling real affection for her. "Sit, you two. You look frozen half to death."

She made room for Ash and Chuy on her couch. It was tight, but they managed it with Bryony in the lap of the giant and Chuy in the middle, perfectly content to be squeezed on all sides. In the narrow space between them, Chuy took Ash's hand and interlaced their fingers.

"How was your walk?" Michael asked. "Are you back to normal?"

"Not quite, little brother." Ash made a point of using the familial term to remind himself he was not alone in the room. Beside him sat another nephil—another creature who was not whole. Although Michael's knees were at a sharp angle and his back slouched, he looked comfortable here. Ash was happy for him, and a little jealous perhaps. Michael was still alive, and his days still felt like days instead of minutes. Ash tried to smile as he added, "I am pleased with my progress, though." The briefest memory of resonance flashed through his mind, and he blushed like a teenager. He was glad for his dark complexion, but as usual, it wasn't enough to hide his feelings from Azza.

The angel glanced up, his drama detector clearly in fine working order. "Ooh!" He closed his book of music. "Something happened between you two, didn't it? Tell me everything. I *love* love stories. Share share share, or I'll drag it out of you."

Ash growled, "You insufferable ish. Keep out of it."

"But your new papa wants to know." Azza pouted. "Will we have an addition to our little family? And will he be this positively gorgeous man holding your hand like he means to never let it go?"

Instinctively, Ash tried to pull his hand away, but Chuy only gripped it tighter. "Well," Chuy said, "we're only getting started, but I'll probably say yes when he asks. He'd make a good husband, don't you think?"

"Yes!" Azza clapped his hands. "I've always said so, haven't I, Ash? 'Ashmedai will make someone a marvelous husband one day,' I said."

"You've said nothing of the kind," Ash grumbled. He hated when Azza teased him like this. It made him feel young again, and if anything irritated the demon king more than slovenliness, it was being made to feel young.

Azazel waved Ash's protest aside. "Well, maybe not to you, but I told your mother all the time."

"It's a wonder she put up with you," Ash said, though his vitriol failed to completely obscure his affection.

"She adored me, and you know it."

Ash wanted to protest, but he couldn't. It was true, his mother had been unreasonably fond of Azazel. When she was candid, she even admitted to worrying about her level of attachment. It was unprofessional, she said, and if the watcher ever fell in love with her and became jealous, there would be trouble. She would refuse to quit her job—she was adamant about that. But Azza never did grow overly attached. Instead, he found himself an unremarkable woman, fell head over heels after a lengthy courtship, and had several rather monstrous daughters.

Chuy laughed. "Pretty sure Ash adored you, too, if the way he talks about you is anything to go on." The betrayal was almost too much to bear.

Azazel leaned back in his chair with a smug smile. "He was such a needy child, our little Ash—always clinging and begging for attention—especially when he woke from his nightmares, which was quite often I'm afraid." The angel's smile broadened as Ash glared across the room at him. "But, you know, I couldn't get enough of the wee petal."

Warmth, home, family. Ash never thought any of those words would apply to him again. They were as good as greeting-card sentiments. But here he sat before a glowing hearth, beside a brother of a kind, being good-naturedly teased by the angel he secretly wished was his father. And he held the hand of the man he loved—a man who truly, unabashedly loved him back. Wasn't that just something? Wasn't it just *everything*? For the first time since his death, Ashmedai began to believe, beyond all reason, that he might actually find a moment of peace in his long, torturous existence.

That belief melted away at the sound of Azazel's alarm.

<h1 style="text-align:center">Chapter Twenty-Five</h1>

Someone had kicked the proverbial hornet's nest, and Bryony knew she wasn't wrong in assuming it had probably been her. Her entire house buzzed and thrummed with the sound of Azazel's alarm. She squeezed her eyes shut and tried to compose herself. Had anyone asked, she would have told them it was impossible for the Angel of Death to get any more erratic. It wasn't impossible. And in demonstration of the fact, the angel in question burst into her house without so much as a knock or warning.

He'd never come in unannounced before. Bryony was livid. He stood taller than usual, his wings abandoned, his expression severe. Right now, not only was he furious, but he took great pains to express it. Bryony stood and stumbled. She caught herself on the back of her couch and fought to form her protective mantle. She wanted to get Samael out as quickly as she could, especially having seen the way two of her guests reacted to him.

Michael and Azazel had both doubled over, and she heard them muffle their grief as they always did. But Chuy and Ash froze. She couldn't even be sure Ashmedai continued to breathe by the way he looked right now. Both their complexions grew wan and sickly, and the tears that streamed down their faces did so unhidden and unresisted. Bryony looked at them meaningfully and held a finger to her lips.

Samael was blind. If they didn't make a sound, he wouldn't know they were here. Ash quickly caught on and took Chuy into his arms, pressing a hand tightly to the captain's mouth.

Bryony clenched her teeth and stood her ground between the Angel of Death and her new family, to which she'd grown inordinately fond in a surprisingly short time. Even Ash, who had clearly despised her, now seemed more like a haughty older brother than an enemy. Death had taken her first family, and she'd be damned if she was going to let it take her second. She rounded on Samael, ready to ridicule him right out the door if she had to. "I don't recall inviting you inside," she snapped.

Samael said nothing in response. Instead, he held out one arm and dropped something from his hand. It dangled on the end of a long, gold chain, and Bryony recognized it at once. Chuy's pendant.

"Where did you get that?" she asked.

"I went to retrieve the demon king." He scowled down at her. "For you. The Angel of Secrets is his teacher. He could easily locate Raziel without conjuration. I intended to set him to the task after unbinding him. Imagine my surprise when I found his burial site empty, except for this." His eyes narrowed as though he'd been betrayed in the worst possible way, as though Bryony owed him any loyalty at all. "I know you are responsible for this."

"Give me that." Bryony reached for the pendant, but Samael snatched it back.

"No." He pocketed it, and Bryony was suddenly distracted by the fact that he even had pockets in that marble-looking robe. Of course, he had created the garment, so why wouldn't he have added pockets?

She felt like a fool and tried to scoff. "I don't know how you think I could disappear a paralyzed demon king when I didn't even know where he was."

"Oh, I don't think you were capable of doing so on your own," Samael said, and for a moment, Bryony was actually offended. "But you have friends in low places, don't you, disloyal child? One in particular. I know he is here. He is always here." He glowered at no one in particular. "And he owes me an explanation."

Azza shifted but said nothing.

"Azazel doesn't owe you anything." Bryony used the most assertive voice she could manage under the circumstances. It was useless to deny the truth. Better to fight truth with more truth. "He's not made a contract with you—I have. I've agreed to kill the archangel Michael, but I haven't agreed to when I'll do it. There's no deadline here."

"There is, indeed, a *deadline.*" Samael chuckled quietly. A fleeting, sad smile barely animated his marble face and was gone again. "Entropy will inevitably come for you, my daughter. Anything that can happen will, given enough time. One day, even you will die. I want to see the end of the archangel before that day comes. You're a rare creature who has dared to make this contract with me. I am not guaranteed another."

Bryony gaped at him. Was he really trying to claim his impatience was due to the extremely unlikely possibility that she would die in the near future? Infuriating! And, if she was totally honest with herself, she was more than a little hurt. She thought she'd made some headway in her relationship with her future father-in-law, but apparently, when he thought of her death, his only consideration was for whether or not she had fulfilled her end of their contract. "You really are heartless, aren't you?" she said.

"I tried to warn you."

"And selfish," she added.

"Yes."

"And unbelievably impatient."

"I am."

It was difficult to insult someone who just agreed with everything you hurled at them. Bryony wrung her skirt as she deliberated. What other avenue did she have? She could only think of one. "I'm done." She proffered her wrist, which was still banded with Samael's weapon, and took a note from Ash's playbook. "Take back your sword. You've involved other parties, so the contract is void."

To her complete and utter horror, the Angel of Death showed his teeth. It was not a smile. "The contract is void when I say it is void." He called out, "Ashmedai! I know you're here!" His voice shook Bryony's house to its foundation. "I will hunt your lover down if you continue to resist me! My hashmallim know his scent! I *will* devour him and soon! Your lives will be haunted by my presence, by the daily threat of my advancing hand! Do as I ask, and I'll leave you both alone for the rest of his natural life!" He chuckled and lowered his voice. "Now who will you protect, demon king—this woman or the man you love? Let's find out."

That was the end of any hope Bryony had that she might successfully defy the Angel of Death. Now Chuy's life was on the line, and if Ash didn't cave to this pressure, she most certainly would. In one fell swoop, Samael had unearthed both their weaknesses.

Bryony knew what was coming seconds before Ashmedai's fingers curled over the back of her couch. He still held one hand tightly over Chuy's mouth. It glistened from all the tears Chuy shed in the presence of Samael's poison. The demon king's eyes were down, his normally proud countenance twisted with grief and whatever paralyzing fear he still experienced from the abuse he had suffered. Still he was somehow more dignified than anyone else in the room, including the Angel of Death. He clenched his jaw and drew a deep breath through his nose before answering. "Stop shouting. I'm right here. Tell me what you want from me."

Samael lifted his chin and looked overly pleased with himself. "Ah, there you are." He turned in Ash's general direction. "I need you to fetch your celestial teacher. All I ask of him is a single conjuration. He'll summon the archangel Michael with my daughter. He need not know why—it would only complicate matters. Just tell him his reward will be the return of his book, and warn him to prepare for a hostile possession." The graveyard angel heaved an irritated sigh. "Honestly, I do not understand the reluctance from either of you. Get this over with, and I will be out of your lives forever. That is what you desire, is it not?"

Ash's eyes darted to Bryony and back again. "Forced possession is wrong," he said. There was no hesitation in his answer. He sounded as though he were reciting an undisputed fact.

The graveyard angel shifted where he stood, clearly itching to leave. He was becoming uncomfortable, and Bryony was glad to see it. Maybe next time he would think twice before entering her home uninvited. "Your celestial teacher does not agree," he said. "Do you not trust his judgement in this matter?"

"I do not." Ash's voice wavered less and less as he spoke. "And neither should you. The ophanim don't understand the concepts of bodily autonomy and lasting trauma, nor can they be expected to. They haven't walked among mankind the way you and I have. Why do you think I kept a terrestrial teacher? To learn the things Raziel could not teach me." The demon king's eyes fell on Bryony again, but this time, he didn't look away. "As I understand it, this woman has had a lifelong fear of the ophanim. How can you demand she take one into her body?"

He remembered. Bryony could have wept for gratitude.

"She won't involve her usual partner," Samael said with an infuriating shrug. "She's refusing to fulfill her end of our contract."

"So you'll force her?" Ashmedai's hackles were every bit as raised as the graveyard angel's, and for the first time, Bryony began to see the king in him. Not even a threat from the Angel of Death could steal his principles away. "It's wrong—you know it is."

"It is not wrong!" Once again, Samael's voice rattled Bryony's house, and she actually began to fear for its integrity. "I won't allow that archangel another day of existence. I won't allow him another day of peace. He has abused the monster he himself created, and it's time he felt the sting of it."

Bryony bowed her head and muttered, "You're not a monster just because an archangel tells you so."

"What difference does it make?" Samael whirled on her, and she shrank from him. "You humans . . . It's so easy for you to just choose another identity, isn't it? It does not work that way in our world. Once an archangel names you, you wear that name to your end. Try to fight it, and you'll be quickly reminded of your place. I am what they say I am. It doesn't matter what I believe. I cannot *be* anything else!" His face lost all expression, and Bryony knew it was over.

She bowed her head and said, "Ash, go and get Raziel. Please."

Ashmedai silently questioned her with his eyes. Aloud, he said, "Listen. The ophanim don't understand gentleness or mercy. This won't be like it is with Azza. Raziel will not wait for your permission. It'll feel as though you've been split in two, and then you'll lose time until he decides to let you go. He could take your entire life on a whim, and I won't be able to stop him. Do you understand? He's a force, not a person. He's an ophan."

"I know." She fought the tears that threatened to well in her eyes. They were frightened tears, childish tears, and they wouldn't do anyone any good right now.

From his knees, Michael begged, "Please, my love, don't do this."

The sound of his crestfallen voice almost broke her. But then she glanced at Chuy, who struggled to free himself from Ashmedai's protective embrace, and she couldn't imagine taking any other course. "I've made up my mind." She squared her shoulders and dug deep for her last store of courage. "If there's a chance for all of us to survive this, I have to take it. I won't sacrifice one of you to correct my own mistake"—she turned and glared hard at Samael, hoping he could hear the disappointment in her voice—"my own stupid belief that no one is completely heartless."

"Bryony . . ." Ash began.

"It won't be a forced possession," she assured him, but even she could hear her courage waver. "I'll allow it, so it won't be forced. You're family now, you and Chuy. I choose to believe it, and in our world, what you believe actually does make a difference." She hoped Samael understood her admonition. "Azza made us family. I fight for my family. I wouldn't know who I was if I didn't."

The look on Ashmedai's face made her throat burn and her eyes well up. She had never seen him so conflicted. She tried to remember the monster who'd abducted Michael, threatened her, and taken on the entire crew of *Dragonfly* alone. He didn't seem like the same creature now. Suddenly, the demon king clenched his jaw in a new, unwavering determination. "I will bring Raziel to you," he said.

Samael smiled. "Thank you, Your Majesty. That is all I ask."

Chapter Twenty-Six

The night was freezing, and Bryony waited in her grove of plum trees with the Angel of Death. There was cloud cover and darkness and the romance of falling snow, but nothing about this situation was remotely romantic. Bryony wrapped her arms around herself, and tried to disguise the chattering of her teeth by occasionally stomping snow off her boots.

The graveyard angel had resumed his wings, though his expression was still far from serene. He wasn't pressing his palms together in prayer for the souls of the dead. He wasn't looking to the heavens as rain ran down his face in a subtle mimicry of tears. No, he glowered down at Bryony with his arms crossed and one foot tapping in a theatrical show of irritation. At last, he spoke. "Are you cold, or are you frightened?"

"As if you care." Bryony held her own forehead and groaned. "Fine. I'm both, if you must know, although I'd have thought the cold was obvious. It's the middle of the night, and it's snowing."

"I did not notice." There wasn't a touch of sarcasm in his voice.

She blew her bangs out of her eyes and continued to shiver. "Of course you didn't."

Samael sighed like an overwrought father on a long road trip with an unruly child. He crooked one index finger and held the knuckle to his lips in a posture of deep concentration. Before long, Bryony began to feel warmer, as though someone had enclosed the grove and plugged in a space heater. "Better?" he asked.

If Bryony had learned one thing about herself over the years, it was that she could take massive amounts of abuse in stride, as long as she knew to expect it. But the most innocuous show of unanticipated kindness would trigger a landslide in her. Apparently, she hated surprises more than she hated cruelty. She clenched her fists and fantasized about punching her future father-in-law repeatedly. "You . . . You're . . . You're so totally bizarre! Why are you doing this to me? What kind of absurd, angelic torture is this? You're going to offer my body to an ophan in a minute. I'll probably be eaten after I'm possessed, but suddenly you're worried I might be cold? How can you be like this—all ruthless one minute and kind the next? Is it your aim to confuse me? Because you're doing a fantastic job of it." She offered him deeply unenthusiastic applause. "Congratulations."

"It was not my intention to be kind," he said matter-of-factly.

"How silly of me to assume." She rolled her eyes.

"I was simply distracted by the sound of your shivering."

"Of course," she said. "We wouldn't want you to get distracted. I'll try to keep that in mind next time I'm standing out in the cold waiting to be forcibly possessed by a monster that's haunted my nightmares since I was a child."

Samael felt for the trunk of a plum tree and leaned back against it. "You are being overdramatic. Raziel is hardly a monster."

"Then why would he force a possession?"

"Because he wants his book back, and to him, you're a barely sentient entity, so there is no harm done. His only qualm may be in the summoning of the archangel, but I'm certain he wants his weapon more than he worries for that beast."

"His weapon?" Was the ophan really unarmed? For a moment, hope began to distract Bryony from her outrage. Then she reminded herself that any creature with a mouth like that didn't need a weapon.

Samael casually reached into his robe and pulled out a large, green-and-gold book. The thing was enormous. There was absolutely no way he'd been able to smuggle it around like that unseen. Some chicanery was afoot. "This is Raziel's sword," he said, offering the book to Bryony, who took it without really considering whether she wanted to.

It was heavy in her hands, and it was coated in a white film that came off on her fingertips. She quickly handed it back and wiped her hands on her skirt. "It's filthy," she grumbled.

"It is salt." He tucked the book away, and it seemed to vanish once again into his robe. "The *Sefer Raziel* is the most powerful and dangerous weapon in existence. For that reason, other angels frequently steal it and throw it into the sea. The archangel Michael and I are the only two who can retrieve it, though I highly doubt the archangel Michael will be doing Raziel any favors . . . especially if he's dead." He chuckled, and the sound of it chilled Bryony to her bones.

She advised herself not to ask any more questions, but she couldn't help it. Curiosity trumped fear, apparently. "How is some salty book a more dangerous weapon than yours?"

"Knowledge is power, my daughter." He patted his belly as though he'd just consumed the volume for dinner and was now digesting it. "It is a cliché, is it not? My weapon can only end a life—Raziel's can take control of it. Inside the book are recipes to conjure and contain any angel or demon in our combined worlds. The Angel of Secrets' weapon always takes the shape of the written word, and it is always devastating for whichever poor souls find themselves on the wrong end of it. Time and again I have said, the stories confuse the essence of the Angel of Secrets. He is not *hidden knowledge*—he is *knowledge withheld.* He is the soul of oppression. That is why he won't need permission to possess you."

Bryony chewed her nail more and more ferociously as she listened. Finally, she couldn't help muttering, "I hate you for this, you know."

"I know." Samael sounded as though he actually regretted the unfortunate consequence. He paused, and Bryony saw his fingers curl at some thought that troubled him. "It will be over quickly."

"That's exactly what I used to say to crew right before I did something that really, really hurt." She frowned. "So does it . . . hurt?"

The angel shrugged. "I have never been possessed, forcibly or otherwise."

"Of course you haven't." She wanted to cry. She wanted to sink to her knees and wallow in her misery like a lost child. But the ground shifted, and the world began to buzz, and Bryony knew the ophan was coming for her. Azazel's alarm sounded for any intruding angel, it seemed. Just now, she would rather not have seen it coming.

She trembled. Samael stood tall, tilted his head back, and sniffed the air. Could he really sniff out an ophan? Then it hit her—the high—and she knew what it was Samael could smell. Azza had begun bombarding her with worship. Her fear was drowned in it. Her muscles could not help but relax. *Bless him. Bless him.*

"I'll leave you now," Samael said. "Raziel must do his work without the imposition of my presence. Remind me to thank Azazel for the provided anesthetic when this is over."

"How do you know I'll even exist when this is over?" Bryony said, more to herself than to him.

Samael responded anyway. "Trust me, you will."

"Trust you?" She laughed an empty laugh and held herself tighter. "That's impossible."

"Then have faith your loved ones will fight for you."

"I can't believe I ever thought you'd be one of them."

The graveyard angel stiffened, and Bryony felt a wave of grief intermingle with the worship Azza sent. It was the strangest feeling, blissful misery. She could barely focus her eyes, but the fixed, emotionless expression Samael wore as he stretched and vanished was unmistakable. She'd overwhelmed him one last time. It was over for her—she had no doubt about that—but she was proud she'd managed to bite before she was butchered.

The arrival of the ophan hit Bryony like a night terror. Her half-conscious mind registered the monster as a wavering, spinning light. Its eyes were everywhere, blinking in no particular pattern. The longer she looked, the dizzier those wheels within wheels within wheels made her. Her mind fought unsuccessfully to comprehend the thing descending upon her. Too late, she realized she'd begun to run from it. Her legs carried her outside her sanctuary, and her own scream filled her ears.

And then the creature opened its mouth.

The void was even more maddening than the shape the monster took. A breath and a half later, Bryony realized what was happening to her. Raziel had no intention of possessing her. He meant to consume her, which she honestly should have guessed. What else did ophanim do? There was no point in running. No matter how far she got, the ophan could just cover the expanse with its ever-widening mouth. So she dropped to her knees and let go.

For the briefest moment, before the unfathomable thing's mouth closed over her body, Bryony had the petty thought that, at least, the Angel of Death wasn't going to get what he wanted. Raziel would eat her along with the death sword, and then what? Nothing, probably. She hoped it infuriated Samael. She hoped he screamed and stomped and was swallowed up like Rumpelstiltskin when his plan unraveled at the seams. This was about as close as she was ever going to get to siding with an ophan.

Yes, Raziel! Don't give that bastard what he wants, she thought. It was at this point she realized she'd been eaten by an angel and was still having thoughts at all, absurd though they may be. She hadn't ceased to exist as a sentient being. She quickly checked her limbs to see that they were all there. She hadn't even been injured. She was floating in a cloud of light, being born aloft by something that crackled like electricity.

Surely this wasn't what it was like to be consumed by an angel. Surely the experience wasn't this benign. She sincerely doubted Azza's worship could cut through the horror of being digested and make it feel so . . . soft.

Suddenly, there was earth under her feet, a forest around her, and powerful arms holding her back tight against a masculine chest. A hand clamped over her mouth, and she had the terrible realization that Raziel had only moved her and probably still intended to possess her. She began to tremble again, until Raziel tipped her head back and forced her to look into his face. And it wasn't Raziel.

It was Loki.

She broke at the sight of him. She shuddered and wept tears of relief and clung to the Jötunn's muscular arms.

Have faith your loved ones will fight for you. Samael had no idea how right he'd been when he'd spoken those condescending words. If she was honest, Bryony hadn't realized how right he'd been either. It wasn't bitterness that had caused her to doubt. She'd just known none of her new allies could take on an ophan, especially not a high-ranking one who was working alongside the Angel of Death. It would have been foolhardy for any of them to even try. What she hadn't taken into account was who her new allies were. Loki, for example, didn't play by anyone's rules and never had. Wasn't foolhardiness what he was famous for?

The Jötunn's mouth was at her ear, confirming every new conclusion she might have come to had she been given a moment to think. "I don't know how you did it, you mad woman, but you actually won the demon king. I hardly believed it when he came to me begging for help—and at such an ungodly hour too." He chuckled. "Now buckle up. You're going for a ride."

He took his hand from her mouth and locked both arms around her waist, lifting her until her feet just left the ground. Then, all at once, the world receded at an impossible pace. Loki surged backward through the atmosphere like a rocket. Trees and hills and valleys all flew by in a blur. Bryony watched whole mountains grow small and disappear from her horizon in seconds. She lost her breath and her orientation. She wanted to ask where they were going, but the wind flew by so quickly she couldn't draw in air enough to say anything at all.

When her feet touched down again, they sank into soft, powdery sand. Loki let her go and rubbed his hands together like he'd just completed a satisfying chore. Bryony took a moment to get her bearings.

They were in a desert. Dunes rose up around them, each one wind-textured with thousands of little ripples. They looked almost like enormous, ocean waves—only less erratic, less chaotic, less Samael. The silhouette of mountains loomed in the distance, stark against a star-filled sky. Bryony wanted to ask where they were, but first thing had to be first. She threw her arms around her friend and squeezed him tight. "I love you, Shakespeare," she said into his chest.

Her old crow squeezed her back and, so quick she thought she might have imagined it, kissed the top of her head. After she released him, he grinned proudly and said, "I thought, if that snake is so comfortable with the sea, we should probably head for its opposite."

She glanced again at the desert around them. "Where are we?"

"Death Valley." He cackled. "Ironic, isn't it?"

Despite everything, Bryony actually smiled. "Admit it. You chose this place mostly for the irony."

"Obviously." He sat down and patted the sand, inviting her to join him. "And now we wait for the cavalry to arrive."

"The cavalry?"

"Your other allies, Bryony. You're wearing Samael's weapon. As soon as he realizes I'm not Raziel, he's going to come for both of us. We have a little time, though, and Ashmedai has gone to retrieve your angel, who should be here in"—Loki checked an invisible wrist watch—"no time at all."

So it wasn't over. She should have known. The Angel of Death did not give up easily. But Azazel was on his way, so at least her inevitable defeat would be beautiful. She chuckled miserably, plunked down beside Loki, and dug her heels and hands into the sand. It was cool under the surface and fine between her fingers. "So now we just wait for Samael to get wise?"

"Essentially." He shrugged. "There's not a lot more we can do. I'm hoping Azazel has something up his sleeve. He's no slouch, so we have that. My compliments on your choice of pet angel, by the way. I can't imagine many others who'd be willing to take on death itself."

"He's brave." She smiled and kicked her companion gently. "Like you."

Loki snorted. "Not a quality I'm known for."

"It's how I'll always think of you." Offhandedly, she added, "Well, that and your apparent need to scare the living daylights out of me regularly. Why'd you have to actually eat me, huh? Come to think of it, why'd you have to become an ophan at all? Sama was already gone by the time you got there."

"Ashmedai told me I needed to be a believable enough angel to trip Azazel's alarm. And Samael wasn't so far off he couldn't hear you scream. I needed you to behave like you would if you'd seen the real Raziel. Let's be honest—acting is not your forte."

She pouted. "I could've done it." She should have been happier than she was, hopeful even. But her heart grew heavy when she thought about how much her friends were risking for her. "I don't want anyone to die for this. I mean, it's just a delay, isn't it? Azza can't fight Samael. None of you can. It doesn't matter how many of you there are—you'll all bow before him."

"Sure, we probably will." Loki leaned back on his palms and stared up at the stars. "But *you* won't, and that's the crux of it." He turned to her and winked, and she drove herself crazy trying to figure out what the hell he was talking about.

CHAPTER TWENTY-SEVEN

Forced possession was beyond wrong. Ash would not have allowed it had the victim been someone he hated, let alone a woman who had just rescued him from his own grave. She'd immediately adopted him as a kind of brother too—despite her usually cynical nature—just because Azazel suggested it. She made her weakness for family obvious and easy to exploit. She made herself into a perfect target for the Angel of Death. Ash shook his head at the thought. He might have given the woman a pointer or two on how to deal with difficult angels had he known what was coming. The first piece of advice he'd have given her was to never, ever make contracts with those who did not honor them.

As far as the Jötnar were concerned, Bryony seemed to have done rather well for herself. It was a simple matter to find Loki and get him on the same page. He was unreasonably fond of a local café, Ash recalled, and could usually be found loitering around it. So, as soon as Ash was sent to retrieve his celestial teacher, he made his way to Martha's instead. He marched to the tiny cabin hidden behind the café and hammered on the restaurateur's front door with abandon. Though he was a studious demon, Ashmedai had never been timid.

Loki flung the door open, grabbed Ash by the lapels, and dragged him away from the front porch. "You ass," the Jötunn hissed. "If you've woken Martha . . . Do you have any idea how hard she works? Do you?" His eyes flashed.

"The woman is not your infant." Ash shook himself free. "Be reasonable." He straightened his lapels with some concern that he was still hiding his bare chest behind little more than a large, wool scarf. "Listen, I need your help. Bryony needs your help."

Loki arched one ginger brow. "Tell her whatever pickle she's in is not my fault this time, so I've no obligation to fix it. Especially if it involves her new best friend. The poisonous snake is her problem, not mine. She summoned him. She invited him in. She served him tea."

"Are you kidding?" For a second, Ash was actually lost for words. He'd heard Loki could be occasionally childish on his best days and an infuriating coward on his worst, but Ash had been certain most of it was hyperbole. No ancient creature could be that immature, could they? Ash sighed and massaged his brow. "You know what? Never mind. How are you at imitating ophanim?"

All at once, Loki's muscles tensed, and the cocky smile left his face. "Why?"

"Because Samael is demanding that the Angel of Secrets forcibly possess Bryony to summon the archangel Michael. And the Angel of Secrets is an ophan."

"No!" It was as though someone had flipped a switch in the Jötunn. His cheeks flushed and his eyes widened in horrified outrage. "He can't do that! I will murder his face first!"

Ash chuckled. "I hoped you'd say that."

Loki was not amused. "Do you have any idea how that poor girl feels about ophanim? And after everything we've put her through."

We? Ash frowned. He supposed he deserved that. "She's given me some indication, which is why I came to you. I think you may be able to buy the rest of us some time."

"Who is *the rest of us?*"

"Azazel and I."

Loki was beside himself. "And what do you think the two of you can do about any of this? We'll all fall flat on our faces. I've seen Azazel crash in that snake's presence with my own eyes, and Azazel scares the shit out of me. Not even *you* scare the shit out of me—do you get what I'm saying? Samael is a horror show."

But Ash wasn't close to giving up. "Forced possession is wrong," he growled. "I won't stand by and watch it happen. Samael may outrank us in raw power, but we have something he doesn't."

Loki threw his hands up. "And what's that?"

Ash shook his head, surprised the Jötunn hadn't already guessed the answer. "Bryony, of course."

Sometime before midnight, Ash took it upon himself to raid a local gun shop. He stole two rifles with plenty of ammunition and walked back to Bryony's house at a brisk pace. With some regret, he saved the energy he normally would have spent hovering an inch above the ground. There were more important things than perfect shoes right now, albeit very few.

Back at the house, Chuy, Azza, and Michael had gathered in the living room. They knelt around the coffee table with cups of tea and sheets of paper upon which they appeared to be strategizing.

"What's all this?" Ash said abruptly. They all turned to him at once, and he was reminded of a three headed creature with one brain. "Put this nonsense away. There's only one way to handle this." He swept the papers to the floor, dropped the rifles on the table, and tossed the ammunition beside them. "The Jötunn has hidden Bryony and bought us some time, but it won't be much."

Michael's jaw dropped. He looked like he was ten seconds from losing his composure right there on the living room floor. He must have been barely holding himself together until now. He choked on his words. "Loki . . . has her?"

Ash nodded. "Didn't I just say as much? The Jötunn has hidden her. But she carries Samael's weapon, and as soon as he realizes he's been had, he's going to pitch a fit like none of us has ever seen in our lifetimes. Azza, she's under your protection, isn't she?"

Azazel nodded.

"Then locate her. Use your mark. You and I are going to be there when that bastard finds her."

"Yes." Azza stood. "And do what, Ash darling? Tell me you have a plan. You always have a plan."

Ashmedai sighed. "I do. It's not foolproof, but it's a chance. You'll be taking the greatest risk, but she's your god, isn't she? You'll risk something to save her."

"You know I will," Azza muttered. It did not escape Ash's notice the way Michael cringed at the affection in the angel's voice. Samael's son had predictably misinterpreted, but Ash didn't have time to babysit him now.

Chuy stood and gestured to the rifles. "I assume one of these is for me."

"Correct." Ash handed him a rifle and a box of ammunition. "It's similar to the one you handled at the cabin. I was . . . quite impressed." He smiled, inadvertently stepped closer, and then lowered his voice. "If any hashmallim come for you, shoot them like you did before. Exhaust them. Then run." Ash picked up the second rifle and handed it to Michael, who just blinked at it.

"I've never handled a gun before," he said.

"Really?" Ash very much doubted it. "After all that time in the Black Armada?"

Michael shrugged. "The commodore forbade firearms, and . . . I'm a pacifist."

"A *what*?" Ash glared up at his little brother. "Never mind. I don't care and neither do the hashmallim." He shoved the rifle into Michael's hands. "Take lessons from Chuy. Fire it indiscriminately if you have to. Just do it. You *will* do whatever it takes to protect my beloved while I am doing what it takes to protect yours. Do you understand?"

Michael nodded.

"Good."

"Why can't we come with you?" Chuy asked, already loading his weapon. "Wouldn't staying together make more sense?"

"Not in this case." Ash gritted his teeth. It was going to kill him to leave Chuy's side. "Neither of you can do much in Samael's presence. You'll only be liabilities."

Michael looked doubtful. "You and Azazel can't do much more than we can."

"Incorrect." Ash was pacing, eager and terrified. "We'll have Bryony. Her body has built up a resistance to Samael's poison. The poison is all he has, so if we find a way around it—"

"Of course!" Azazel gasped. Then he laughed triumphantly and threw his arms around the demon king. "You brilliant boy. I knew you'd come up with something."

Michael held his rifle like it was a child he'd been told to protect. "Will someone please tell me what the plan is?"

"With pleasure, petal." Azazel's hopeful tone brought some comfort to Ash. He had no idea whether his plan stood a chance, but if Azza thought there was something to it, then maybe it did. "I'm going to possess our girl and use her semi-immunity to cast against Samael."

Chuy finished loading his weapon. "Can you really do that?"

Ash answered, "If anyone can, it's Azza. We have to try anyway. We can't just stand by and let this happen. I won't allow it."

The expression that blossomed on Chuy's face was one of unmistakable pride. He carefully laid his rifle back on the table, reeled Ash in by the scarf, and kissed him. Ash savored that kiss like it was the last one he'd ever be given. Eventually, in a background world, Michael cleared his throat. Ash broke away from Chuy and glared at his little brother, who dared to linger after even Azazel had taken the hint and left.

"I'll just . . . see if I can help Azza in the kitchen," Michael said.

"You do that." Ash followed him with a hard stare as the giant ducked through the kitchen door.

When they were alone, Chuy let out a low chuckle. "It's only Michael. He's the least judgmental person I know."

"Judgment can go to hell, and my little brother can go to the kitchen." Ash was finding it difficult to care about anything other than the man in his arms. "If we don't all make it through this—"

"We will," Chuy said.

"You can't know that for sure."

"But *you* can. You've seen it, right?" That smile. That ridiculous optimism. Ash closed his eyes and breathed in, savoring Chuy's scent. The future was too bright, and that wasn't a good thing. Both Samael and his son were blinding, indistinguishable from actual death, and obscuring Ash's view. But he didn't want to remind Chuy of that fact. *Let him fight with hope in his heart.*

"You're right," Ash said. "We'll make it through this, and when we do . . ." He stopped himself because he was about to say something intolerably stupid. He groaned and tamped the cherub back down. Once again, the beast wanted to propose, or at least talk very seriously about cohabitation. It was an insatiable part of him, always craving after people who stayed, relationships that lasted, promises and commitments. Contracts. In short, Ash needed to devote himself to the man he loved in every possible way, but he reminded himself to do it subtly, slowly, like a normal person would.

Apparently, subtlety was no longer among his strong suits, nor was predicting the behavior of normal people, because Chuy pulled Ash close and said, "When we do, we'll marry. That's what you wanted to say, right? Well, even if it wasn't . . ." The captain gave him another irresistibly aggressive kiss, and Ash could no more argue than he could resist a wager. There was a very real possibility he'd developed another dangerous addiction.

"I do love you," Ash said when Chuy allowed him to catch his breath. "But I don't want to overwhelm you. I'm trying to keep a manageable pace. For your sake."

"Fuck a manageable pace." Chuy squeezed his upper arm with a familial intimacy that gave the cherubic part of Ash something more to blush about. "When you know, you know. And I know."

Ash felt as though he'd just failed to bluff while holding a royal flush. But this wasn't a game, and Chuy wasn't an opponent. He was a partner. He was . . . "Can I call you my fiancé?" So much for subtlety.

"Course you can." Chuy lifted Ash's knuckles to his lips and frowned when he noticed the way the demon king's hands trembled.

Ash noticed too. In explanation, he quietly repeated the prophecy he'd once announced to a ship full of pirates. "You will break my heart."

"Hey." Chuy squeezed his hand. "Hey, I'm not gonna leave you, okay? I swear. Don't get spooked and go all nephil on me right at the beginning. At least give us a few good years first." He laughed.

"It's the beginning and the end to me all at once," Ash admitted. "I can see the edges of us, and it terrifies me. My nature is unforgiving that way." He knit his brow and began to bounce his heel. "How do you already know so much about nephilim anyway?"

Chuy shrugged. "Michael's real chatty when you get to know him."

Michael. Ash didn't know whether to slap or hug his little brother for oversharing. "I feel like a fool."

"Why?"

The question was sincere, so Ash answered it sincerely. "I learned about angelic phobias at an early age. I saw more than one watcher fall in love with my mother and fall apart shortly after. I thought them all weak. When I saw that Samael's son was as lost as the watchers, I laughed at him. Now I know better. I'm just as weak as the rest of them."

"You think it's weakness, falling in love?" Chuy looked dismayed, and Ash couldn't understand why.

"Isn't it?" Ash cupped the captain's face and stroked his cheek with one thumb. "The thought of losing you makes me crazy. Life without you is both inevitable and unthinkable. When I dwell on it too long, I start to shake. If that isn't weakness, then what is?"

It was a rhetorical question, but Chuy answered in earnest. "Well, I think weakness is when you're so scared to need anyone, you just avoid love altogether. Strength is when you let yourself love someone so much, you'd do anything to protect 'em. That's the tougher position to be in, isn't it? That takes courage." He wrapped an arm around Ash's waist and leaned in until they were nose to nose. "So, I say you're the strong one. You're the brave one. Samael is weak."

Ash's heel stopped bouncing, and he muttered, "I don't deserve you," just as Michael walked in.

"The circle is ready," Michael announced.

"But I'm not," Ash said. One last kiss. One last taste. One last moment of being so lost in someone else, he couldn't begin to consider the hopelessness of what he was about to attempt. He mirrored Chuy's body and pulled him close. He curled his fingers into that inky hair and let Chuy deepen the kiss until it was downright inappropriate. Michael sighed impatiently in the background, but Ash didn't care. "I will love you for the rest of your life," Ash murmured into Chuy's ear. "I will fight to protect you and every principle you value. What is precious to you is now precious to me." He began to recite, "*Wherever you go, I will go, and wherever you stay, I will stay. Your people will be my people, and your gods will be my gods.*" It was the most powerful promise he could have pulled from scripture.

"You're some kinda perfect boyfriend, aren't you?" Chuy laughed under his breath.

"Fiancé," Ash corrected. Then he closed his eyes and kissed Chuy's forehead. *The hashmallim won't even come for him,* he told himself, and he made himself believe it. Surely, the enraged Angel of Death would lock onto his own weapon and threaten its wielder directly, now that he knew threatening Chuy wasn't going to get him what he wanted.

Still it was nearly impossible to leave Chuy. Ash had to do it in little steps. *I'm only across the room from him. I'm only in the kitchen. I'm only standing in one of Azza's gateway circles. He's still right next door.* When Azazel stepped into the circle alongside him, Ash realized he'd never been so glad for a father figure. The angel took his hand and squeezed.

Ash expected Azza to put his mind at ease, but it was Michael, in the end, who managed to curb his anxiety. "I won't let anything touch him," the giant said. His voice was deep and powerful, and in his eyes was a ferocity Ash hadn't seen before. "I swear it. If he's taken, it'll be because I'm dead, and as you know, I have every reason in the world to survive."

"I know." Ash clenched his fists and reminded himself why he was doing this, why he was risking everything for the sake of one woman. Right was right, and wrong was wrong. If the demon king didn't have his principles, he didn't have anything at all. Samael's son was the same. He didn't have his lineage to fall back on when he thought of the kind of person he wanted to be. All he had were his choices. "We're coming out of this together or not at all."

Michael smiled and stepped back as the circle began to energize and burn. "Thank you," he said while the world slid away. They really were the strangest kind of family, but whoever threatened one of them was going to have to contend with them all.

Chapter Twenty-Eight

At some point, Loki tired of vigilance and stretched out in the sand with his fingers interlaced behind his head. Bryony joined him, and they chatted about old times and constellations. Those constellations he knew were different from the ones she did, and the stories behind them were fascinating. He had always been a magnificent storyteller. It was one of the things Bryony most appreciated about him. He could make the most mundane tale fascinating with his inflection, pregnant pauses, and what she was sure were details improvised in the moment.

It was easy to lose herself in his world—so easy she almost forgot why they were there. Then the sky lit up like it had gone from midnight to noon in five seconds flat, and Bryony's entire body jolted. *Samael.*

She scrambled to her feet, and Loki stood with her. "Calm down," he said. "It's only your angel and the demon king."

He was right. Bryony squinted into the distance and saw two figures approach. They were giants, far bigger than Michael would ever grow to be. One had batlike wings and the other had a fire at its breast. It was easier for them to take their angelic forms, Bryony recalled. They were saving themselves for a fight—for her fight. "Azza," she murmured. "Ash."

"Told you." Loki lifted her into his arms and grew until he could match them stride for stride. It took him only a few steps to reach them. Distance was nothing to these creatures, and Bryony reminded herself that Samael was one of them. The Angel of Death would not take long to arrive once he realized the truth.

As soon as the four of them were face to face—or in Ash's case, face to face to face to face—Azazel took charge. "Take our vessel to the mountain and shelter there," he commanded. "Prepare her, Loki, if you will. I need her calm and confident. Ash will carve our transference into stone. You know the mark, don't you, Ash darling? It's one of the first Raziel would have taught. Basic arithmetic, yes?"

Ash nodded.

"Good. When I'm finished here, I'll come to collect her."

Once Azza's instructions were thoroughly disseminated, Loki and Ash carried their living cargo toward a mountainous silhouette. Bryony closed her eyes and clung to Loki. She allowed herself to feel fear, weakness, and self-pity. She knew, in a few minutes, she would no longer be able to have any of those feelings. There would be no room for trembling or hesitation, no time for tears or worry. These were short-lived luxuries.

She didn't open her eyes again until Loki set her down. The three of them stood between the mountainside and a colossal boulder upon which Ash immediately began to carve a perfect circle. He used his talons, and the rock fell away like sandstone. The demon king's strength was subtle but astonishing. Bryony watched a while before she found voice enough to ask, "What are we doing?"

Without taking his eyes off his project, Ash answered, "I'll siphon the rest of my energy to Azza while Loki shields me from Samael's light." His voice was a low, harsh growl. This last push would clearly be all the demon had left to give.

Loki shrank enough to lay a hand on Bryony's shoulder. "You're the only one who can stand before the Angel of Death, Bryony. All we can do is send energy to the one possessing your body and hope your immunity translates to him."

"I'm going to be possessed?"

"Yes," Ash said, still carving. "If you permit him, Azza will use your body to fight Samael. In you, he should be able to stand. Samael hasn't battled anyone unaffected by his poison since the archangel Michael overthrew him. Hopefully, he'll be shocked enough to make some mistakes. His arrogance is in our favor." Ash finished carving his circle and tested it by pressing his taloned hand to its center. It flashed like gold reflecting fire, and he nodded, apparently pleased with his own work. "Remember, our goal is to exhaust him. Don't get discouraged when Azza doesn't go on the offensive right away. If Samael is weakened enough, Azza may be able to bind him to the desert."

"Bind him . . . to the desert?" Something in Bryony rebelled at the idea. Azza had told her that kind of binding stole one's identity entirely. Samael would no longer be the Angel of Death. He would, instead, become Death Valley itself. She kept picturing the graveyard angel inspecting her piano, sipping tea before her fire, introducing himself to Martha. No one deserved to be bound the way Azza was, not even Samael. But if this was the only way to keep an ophan from taking her body . . . "I wish he wouldn't make us do this to him."

"It's Samael," Ash said, as though that were answer enough. He shrank back to human form, and Bryony wanted to tell him it wasn't necessary. Surely, it took energy to change shape like that, and she'd gotten over her fear of cherubim for the most part. But she also knew Ash would find a way to take offense, so she said nothing. For an ancient demon, he really was a sensitive soul. He continued, "The Angel of Death is the most relentless creature in our worlds. He doesn't let things go once he's made up his mind. And after what he did to me, I'll be happy to see him bound."

Bryony had almost forgotten the way Samael had brutalized Ashmedai. She felt partly responsible and bowed her head. "He shouldn't have done that. I don't know what he was thinking."

"He wasn't thinking, Bryony—he was hunting." Ash's tone was low and dark. "And he'll be hunting again soon. For you. He won't see you as you. You'll be prey. Do you understand?"

She nodded. A blinding, flickering light illuminated the sky and sent long shadows from the boulder to the mountain behind it. Loki covered Bryony's eyes with one hand and pulled her back into his chest.

Ash scoffed. "It's only Azza."

"Still not good for the retinas," Loki said.

The half-cherub sighed, and Bryony felt his hand come to rest atop her head for a fraction of a second before it was gone again. "Humans are so fragile," he said.

"Yet we're useless against the Angel of Death without this one."

It took Bryony a moment to realize it was *Loki* arguing for her strength—the very same creature who'd chosen her as his mark because she was too tenderhearted. She wanted to beg him to stop. He was wrong this time. She had no super power, no hidden strength. In fact, the only reason she could stand in Samael's presence was because she'd failed to overcome her own grief. Either she found the beauty in death or buckled under its weight. Black gowns and graveyard promenades were a fashion choice, not a strength. Her immunity was as fake as her godhood, just some magical misdirection. One of these days, Sama would realize as much and rip her mantle away.

With eyes wide open and a heart well guarded, Bryony watched the approach of the angel everyone kept calling *hers.* Azazel was beautiful—no one in their right mind would argue otherwise—even in his angelic form. His frozen body refracted light like a prism, so the fire at his breast painted little rainbows over the sand. He made Death Valley look like a butterfly garden. He caught her up in his arms without giving her a moment for goodbyes. He was in earnest, and Bryony knew why. Samael was on his way.

When the glacial angel set her down again, the heels of her shoes clinked upon something like crystal. All around her was a giant, circular platform with more circles etched into it. The entire piece was so intricate it looked like it had been inlaid with diamonds. "What's this?" she asked.

"Glass. I've drawn our circles and made them to last." Azza gestured to his own creation. "Do you like it? The glass took substantial energy to create, but it would have taken even more to redraw the circles every time a gust of wind blew through."

"It's beautiful."

"Of course it is, darling—that's who I am." Azza shrank down and took human form. His smile was infectious, though Bryony knew he only wore it for her sake. He pointed to the etched circle on the far left. "This one is for sound. While we use it, the desert will be filled with the most raucous noise known to man." Then he introduced the next. "This one is for fluidity. It will shift and change the sand around us until the desert itself swallows the Angel of Death. It won't be permanent, but it'll cause him great difficulty of movement. Because he cannot see, confusing his senses of touch and hearing will benefit us."

Bryony frowned. "That seems unfair."

"Know your opponent's weaknesses." Azza shrugged. "Samael would not hesitate to use yours against you. Don't handle him gently, little orb-weaver, though you know I love that about you. It's time to find your venom and bite."

Azazel was right. Bryony had given Sama so many chances. He'd told her he was cruel from the beginning, and she hadn't believed him. Well, now she did. It just hurt so much to give up on him, but she would not bow down and surrender her body to him or any other angel she didn't trust. That was the line she drew. If she was going to face the archangel Michael, she would do it her way, in her own time.

She pointed to a third circle. "I suppose that one's to block his sense of smell."

"Now you're onto it." Azza smiled proudly. "That one will build a pillar of wind around its target. It lasts longer than the others, so we'll activate it first. He'll find it impossible to catch the scent of the worship I'll be sending you. Don't argue, darling." He cut in when she opened her mouth to protest. "I will be sending it. I've been easy on your body in the past because I could, but we aren't just summoning a monster this time. We're riding into battle against him, and I'll require every ounce of your strength. You'll want the salve. Trust me."

She snorted. "I suppose I'm the horse in this scenario? Okay, so what's the fourth circle then? Some kind of sixth sense or something?"

Azza's smile vanished. "No. That one is for shockwaves. We're going to shatter his body and force him to rebuild it again and again. The goal is to drain his energy to almost nothing. Hopefully, by the time he reaches the fifth circle—you didn't even notice it, did you, darling—he will be exhausted enough for me to bind."

Bryony looked around at the surrounding platform. It was a perfect circle, about the size of a large pond. Whatever markings Azza had etched into it were so small, she couldn't even see them. "So . . . we're going to lure him here?"

"And net him." Azza nodded. He already knew how she would feel about it. She could tell by the concerned look in his eyes. "You're such a soft little god. Let me take the reins now. I can be cruel when I need to. Close your eyes to it. Take no responsibility. When you wake again, it will be done."

She wanted to protest, but she couldn't. She *was* soft. It was a weakness Loki had pegged early on, and it surely hadn't escaped Sama's notice. She felt like a fool for opening up to him the way she had, for thinking a creature like that could ever replace her own warmhearted father—that slow-talking man who played piano and watched the stars with a smoking pipe in his hand. Sometimes, love wasn't enough, and acceptance wasn't enough, and family wasn't enough. In the end, Samael couldn't let go of his hatred. It trumped everything else in his world.

"Okay." She took a deep breath to settle her nerves. "I think I'm ready. But I won't let you do this alone. I won't close my eyes to it."

"How did I know you'd say that?" Azza leaned in and kissed her forehead. "I love you, darling. You know that, don't you? I won't let him hurt you." Then he pulled her in tight to his chest. "Let me in now."

She did, and she was amazed at how effortless possession had become. Azazel slipped past her borders with an ease that spoke of familiarity and practice. Bryony felt like they'd unknowingly trained for this moment for months. She felt his ice in her extremities and his fire in her chest, flickering in the hearth of her ribcage.

Bryony opened her eyes.

One pulse of energy emanated from the mountain. It was the single beat of a giant kettledrum that shook and invigorated her. From within, Azza explained, *That would be our first dose of Ash's energy. Delicious, isn't it?*

She laughed. *Don't be weird, Azza.*

Nothing weird about appreciating a generous gift, darling. With Bryony's hand, Azza gave Ash a distant thumbs-up. Then they waited—together in one body, legs at shoulder width, arms open and ready.

As soon as Bryony saw that familiar light bloom in the distance, Azza fired his first shot. He didn't even wait for Samael to completely manifest. He slammed Bryony's palm into the third circle and sent a cyclone to cloak the approaching seraph. Then he moved her body to the first circle and struck it with a fist. A sound like a massive foghorn filled the air. The entire desert vibrated with it, and she saw the shape of the seraph in the distance shrink down. At first, she thought he'd been weakened by the forces Azza sent to him. Then she realized he had only become the graveyard angel and continued on his way.

Bryony was already discouraged, but with Azza at the helm, she moved faster than she could even think. She ran to the second circle, stomped on it, and the desert swallowed Samael completely. For a moment, she felt triumphant, but the graveyard angel quickly resurfaced and advanced. Again, Azazel slammed Bryony's fist into the first circle and sent a wave of that deafening sound into the desert, but the sound was weaker this time. Azza was weaker.

Then there was a kettledrum beat of energy from Ash. Immediately after, Azza sent a wave of worship, a melody to accompany the drum.

Finally, Bryony stood over the fourth circle. The angel possessing her brought her hands together, fingertip to fingertip, and she felt the world tighten like a rubber band between her palms. When her fingers finally separated, the air around them snapped, and in the distance, the graveyard angel shattered and collapsed. *Yes!* she thought, and she was certain she felt Azza smile with her mouth.

Bryony's body moved as though she were playing a giant musical instrument. Her possessor's patterns quickly became familiar to her. He relied heavily on sound, occasionally renewed the wind, and let the desert swallow his opponent once every couple of turns. For every few feet the Angel of Death advanced, Azazel slammed him with a shockwave that shattered his body. But each time he was shattered, the graveyard angel reformed and advanced, and advanced, and advanced.

Another beat of energy. Another wave of worship.

Samael was getting closer. Bryony could see him clearly now, the outline of his marble wings, the frantic whipping of his robe in the pillar of wind around him.

She began to panic. *Azza!*

I know, darling. I know.

Azazel didn't reassure her because he couldn't. The closer Samael drew, the more Bryony began to doubt her possessor's plan. It became harder and harder to watch her future father-in-law crumble to pieces. His expression grew more furious each time he reformed. Eventually, she could see his hands, rigid and ready to strike, and she felt an echo of her own father's drunken rage.

Azazel struck again with the shockwave. This time, when the graveyard angel reformed, he was close enough that Bryony could actually see the misery behind his rage, and her infuriatingly tender heart broke for him. This was Michael's father. She'd wanted so badly to heal him, and now she was trying to bind him to a desert. She'd failed to give her fiancé the one wedding gift that would even come close to how much he deserved.

Don't blame yourself, darling. Bryony didn't realize she'd been thinking at Azza until he responded. *Samael was broken long ago. No one can reach him. You can't be expected to succeed where even the archangel Raphael failed.*

Bryony stole one of her hands back to quickly rub the sand from her eyes. *Raphael tried?*

Yes. Many times, little god. Many times. Azza sent another blast of sound as the Angel of Death rose up from the desert like a resurrected vampire. He was close now. Very close. Had he smiled, Bryony thought she might have been able to see his individual teeth. And then she realized . . . Samael wasn't manifesting as a seraph. He was a man. Didn't that take more energy? Why wouldn't he conserve it if he was being drained? There was only one possible answer—he wasn't.

Samael had risen up so many times. He had crumbled and rebuilt and continued to advance in his more costly form. *He wants us to know.* She sent the thought to Azza. *He's telling us we haven't even tired him.*

Azza moved Bryony's body to the fourth circle and knelt in its center. *We'll stay here. The circles that confound his senses aren't having the effect I'd hoped for. His weapon is too much of a beacon. He's locating you easily.*

Again and again, the watcher Azazel shattered the graveyard angel. Before Samael could begin to reform, Azza brought Bryony's hands together to build another wave. The process was agonizing. Samael could only ever take one step before his body was shattered. But one step moved him forward, and while it was a sluggish pace, still he advanced.

It's useless, darling, Azza thought. *The beacon is too strong. Is there any chance you can take his weapon off?*

No, she answered. *It's sheathed. He told me I could only draw it in the presence of an archangel.*

There was a beat during which Samael managed three steps before Azza shattered him. At first, Bryony thought Azazel was finally giving up, but then the watcher sent her a thought. *Power or rank?*

What?

For the archangel, does the sword acknowledge power or rank?

What do you mean?

Four more steps.

Samael was an archangel. He's lost his rank, but his power remains. Try to draw his weapon, darling. Now!

Chapter Twenty-Nine

Just as Azza said the word *now*, Samael crossed the boundary into the outer circle. His foot found the glass the same way he'd found the steps of Bryony's veranda. She felt sick to her stomach, but she gathered her intention. She would defend herself and the people she loved against the Angel of Death, and she would do it with his own weapon. Before she quite realized what had happened, the circlet around her wrist grew like a spring shoot into a formidable reaper's scythe. She gripped the staff and stood her ground.

Bryony . . . Azza's disapproving tone was obvious despite his not having an actual voice.

I'm sorry! I can't control the shape of it. It has a mind of its own.

Samael didn't speak a word as he approached. He was clearly done with conversation—done with deals, bargains, and contracts. Bryony tried to match his drive, but she hesitated.

Swing, Azza commanded, and her arms did his bidding whether she was ready for it or not. She held the scythe with two hands and swung. Samael dodged it, but the expression on his face shifted from confidence to trepidation. He backed up as Azza swung the scythe over the glass again. This time, Bryony successfully flexed one muscle on her own terms and missed her target intentionally.

Darling, Azza chided again.

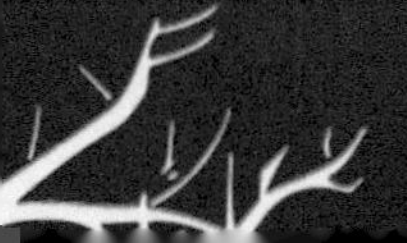

I can't kill him!

You'll have to try. Azazel swiped at the graveyard angel's legs like they were a crop he meant to harvest. But Samael leapt back and out of the way every single time. He read his weapon as accurately as he would if he could actually see it.

Why can't I move fast enough? Bryony thought.

Her possessor answered, *Because Ash is drained and so am I. We won't be able to bind him, little orb-weaver. I'm so sorry. The last chance we have is in your hands.*

Samael backed off the glass circle onto the sand, and Bryony followed. He was retreating, which put her on the offense. She grunted as she swung the scythe again. "Why are you doing this to me?" she asked the graveyard angel, an edge of resentment slipping into her voice. It was time to use the only other weapon she had—the only weapon that had ever worked for her. "This won't convince me to kill the archangel sooner. All you're doing is hurting both our chances to see him dead."

When Samael finally opened his mouth, his voice rang out like thunder. "You violated our agreement!" Neither his tongue nor his lips moved as he spoke, though he wasn't remotely exhausted. He was only trying to frighten her. Each time she swung the scythe, she felt Azza put more force behind it. Every step she took was accelerated exponentially. The watcher was going to wear himself to nothing for her. She pushed across the desert, darting forward with random bursts of angelic energy, pursuing the Angel of Death to the mountains. He retreated like a mirage, matching her step for step.

"I didn't violate anything!" She brought the weapon over her head and swung straight down. "You're being unreasonable!" She gritted her teeth and tried to remind herself of the angel who needed an excuse to visit, who tasted peppermint for the first time in her kitchen, who was so easy to overwhelm and manipulate. He had a heart. She knew he did. He was only Michael's father. "You're too impatient," she concluded, and she backed him into the side of the mountain.

Bryony Moss had the Angel of Death pinned against a rock wall, and the Angel of Death did not try to run from her. Was he finally exhausted? She reached down deep and tried to question Azza, but he could not be found. He was done, burned out like a spent candle. She banished the watcher from her body to give him rest. She heard him scatter across the sand around her, but she couldn't look away from her target. When she swung the weapon again, it chipped the rock beside his head. Samael flinched but recovered so quickly Bryony thought perhaps she had imagined it.

"You are unfaithful," the graveyard angel growled. She wanted to tease him for his word choice, but now was hardly the time. *Unfaithful,* like she'd cheated on a romantic partner. He was so isolated he may as well have been bound with Azazel and Ashmedai.

"I'm not *unfaithful.* I just choose to do my part without harming anyone other than my target."

"Raziel would harm no one."

She glared at her adversary, matching his temper as best she could. "And without letting an ophan take my body."

"The ish has taken you." He reached for his weapon, but Bryony jerked it back before he could touch it.

She pushed the dull edge of the scythe under his chin to threaten him. "Azza had my permission because I trusted him to let me go again. I don't trust Raziel."

"Raziel is blameless." God but he was stubborn.

"That has nothing to do with it!" She pushed the scythe harder into his throat. She was angry, furious that he'd betrayed her like this. He'd made her think she could have a father again and then pulled that hope out from under her like it meant nothing. "I hate you. I *hate* you!" She fought back against overwhelming frustration and saw the head of the scythe tremble in her weakening grip.

Samael reached for his weapon again but caught himself and lowered his hand. This time, she knew he could have taken it. Surely he felt her shaking through the blade at his throat. But he behaved as though she'd already beaten him.

"Why aren't you fighting me?" she said

He closed his empty eyes and waited.

"Sama! Why aren't you fighting me?" Did he want to die? She cocked her head and squinted at him, taking in his resignation—his surrender—and she suddenly understood why she'd even managed to pin him. He wanted to lose. He wanted to die like this, by her hand, out here in the lonely desert. "I won't kill you." It was a vow when she said it, and she got the impression he understood that.

He swallowed against the blade at his throat. "Why?"

"Because you're still family, damn it." She paused and considered the truth behind her outburst. He was Michael's father, whether she liked him or not, and despite everything, she couldn't stand to give up on him. This . . . This wasn't who he was. She refused to believe it.

"Annihilate me," he muttered.

"Sama . . ."

"Save yourself. Send me to my grave."

She drew the scythe back and swung it again, but she only buried its tip in the rock. "No. We're not doing suicide by daughter-in-law today."

He spoke through his teeth as though afraid some onlooker might read his lips. "I cannot turn the weapon on myself."

Then it hit her—the sudden understanding of everything she knew about this creature, his cruelty, and the infuriating way he treated his son . . . or whoever happened to hold his weapon. "You wanted your own son to kill you, didn't you? That's why you let him keep your sword. That's why you treated him like shit. You hoped he would hunt you down when he grew up. For god's sake, why? Why would you do that to him?"

"This has become tiresome." In a flash, Samael's marble hand was at her throat. "Never forget that I gave you a chance, my daughter. Never forget that I offered you freedom, and you rejected it."

She reached out for the handle of the scythe, but she couldn't extract it from the rock.

Samael's voice grew thunderous again. "You had the opportunity to destroy two monsters, and you wasted it. You could have cut the head off the snake that killed your people, but you refused. And now you've thrown away your only chance to rid the world of the spirit of putrescence. You're selfish and stubborn and wrong. They should hang you from the stars as an example of how not to be a god. How dare you let us go on living when you had the means and the opportunity to end us both. How *dare* you!"

"I will kill the archangel Michael," she choked out.

"You will not. You have demonstrated as much tonight. If you haven't the courage to kill death itself, you haven't the courage to kill anyone."

"You don't know what courage is." She gasped when he squeezed her throat tighter. This was still Michael's father, wasn't it? This was still the angel who had spared her plum grove and mocked her conjuration. *In fair and comely form . . .* "Strangle me or let me go," she said. "Make up your mind."

He let her go. Because Samael was not a monster, no matter how many times he insisted he was. He'd only been told a lie and believed it. He'd been told the same lie over and over again by everyone who knew him. By now, it would have become impossible for anyone to doubt the truth of it, let alone a creature as isolated as he was.

And when your own name reflects the lie you've been told . . .

Like the jolt of electricity that brought Frankenstein's monster to life, the answer struck her, and Bryony stood dumbfounded. It was so obvious. It was so ridiculously clear. Death wasn't just rot. It wasn't a perversion of life—it was the source. She recalled the nebulae, the clouds of stardust that were nothing less than the remains of dead stars giving birth to new ones. She recalled *On the Origin of Species*. Death was life in motion—shifting, changing, evolving.

The longer Bryony stared at the graveyard angel, the more she appreciated what he really was. In her eyes, with her new understanding, he became something fascinating. He became change, possibility, the diversity of life.

"I'm sorry you were given such an ugly name," she said, and she meant it. She had no desire to manipulate him now, no instinct for self-preservation. There was only the truth, and the injustice of the lie he'd been told. "It wasn't fair at all. You should have been named by someone who knew you, not an archangel. How can someone who's never been mortal ever really know you? You were born among strangers, but . . . I know you. I met you many years ago in my own house. It was so hard to be close to you then, and it always will be, but you're the reason I exist at all. You're the reason any of this exists." She gestured to the desert around them. "You're the reason life is precious and every day counts. Every second. Every breath. Do you understand?" She took hold of his upper arms, bracing him. "I *know* you."

Bryony swallowed her fear and closed the space between them. She stood on her toes and pulled the graveyard angel down to meet her. "Sorry for this," she muttered. "It doesn't mean anything. It's just the only way I know how."

He didn't feel like marble when she kissed him—he felt like life. She closed her eyes to visualize the beauty of the nebulae, the complexity of a dragonfly's wing, her flowering plum trees, and bioluminescence. *Endless forms most beautiful.* She kneaded it all into a feeling of awe and wonder, into the realization of how enormous the universe really was, how unfathomable its scope. And she made that feeling into a name.

Then she breathed the name into him.

The graveyard angel froze. His own breath stopped. His muscles turned to stone. She pulled back for a moment, lingering as close as she could without touching him. She wanted him to feel her there, overwhelmed though he was. She wanted him to know she wasn't afraid or disgusted. "You're so beautiful. Believe me, please. The angels only hate you because they're afraid of change, and that's the essence of who you are. I know you like they never will, and as your daughter, I've decided to give you a better name. Throw the old one away. It's a lie, Sama. Just throw it away."

The sound that followed, born deep in the graveyard angel's throat, was anything but human. Still Bryony recognized it. It started out guttural and slowly evolved into a wild, unbridled howl. Soon the entire desert echoed with Samael's primal scream, while the graveyard angel itself grew silent and hollow. Cracks, like the shadowy legs of enormous spiders, spread across the statue's face, and the marble robe that once moved with such fluidity began to chip and discolor.

Samael's abandoned body looked more like a deteriorated grave marker than ever. The angel himself was somewhere else—whether in the wind, the mountains, or howling beneath the sands, Bryony couldn't have said. It didn't matter. She could still hear him, and the sound he made was all she needed to understand exactly what was happening. More than once, she'd heard that sound born in her own throat. It was nothing short of pure, unbearable grief.

The Angel of Death had taken a massive dose of his own poison.

Chapter Thirty

Ashmedai woke to a sound that reminded him of flood and famine. He'd heard watchers make the sound when their wives died unexpectedly, when their children succumbed to starvation or violence. He heard it once from his own throat the day his mother breathed her last. It was beyond grief. By the way the sound shook the earth now, it undoubtedly came from the mouth of an angel. Was it Azazel? Where was Bryony?

He leapt to his feet before considering whether it was the wise thing to do. He was disoriented and dizzy. He held his aching head in his hands and groaned as that haunting sound began to die. It felt like the second worst hangover he'd ever had. He clambered to the edges of the darkness only to find it was made up of unnaturally large, black feathers. As his eyes adjusted, he saw a beak planted into the ground like a tentpole, with the long neck of the bird rising to the dome above. It was surreal, almost as though he'd begun dreaming again in his post-living state. He nursed his headache as more of his circumstances came back to him. "Where the hell am I?"

The lanky bird answered. "Death Valley, demon king. You've exhausted your energy in a fight against the Angel of Death."

Ashmedai blinked in the darkness. "Loki?"

"Welcome back, Your Majesty." Slowly, the umbrella of feathers folded away, and the long neck of the bird rose up. Ash vaguely remembered that Loki had shifted into a giant black heron before the fight. "I shielded you from the light while you fed your partner," the Jötunn explained. "At some point, you just keeled over and wouldn't wake up. We never even had the chance to discuss payment."

"Payment?"

"You owe me now, demon." Loki laughed. "Don't you remember? We made a contract. You owe me a year of your labor, building me whatever I desire, and I desire at least seven vacation houses in the seven most beautiful corners of the earth. I want extremes, you understand." He held out his primary feathers as though he were counting off locations on his fingers. "Antarctica, Mount Everest, the Mariana Trench . . ." He looked around as though noticing their location for the first time. "Also here. I'll think of the rest later, but one of them will be behind a waterfall."

Ash rubbed his eyes and tried to focus. Tricksters really were the worst. Well, one good lie deserved another. "Of course I remember. And you promised me full access to your wife, if I recall. Well, a contract is a contract." He held out his hand as though to shake, and the bird shrank back into a ginger-bearded man. He was, regretfully, not wearing a stitch of clothing. Less regretfully, his physique was nothing short of perfect.

"Good game." Loki grabbed Ash's hand and shook it. "You win."

Ash cleared his throat and resisted the urge to critique Loki's shameless lack of costume. "Why is it suddenly so quiet? Is it over? Did we win or lose?"

"Don't know." Loki squinted into the desert. "I'm not currently a useless, blubbering mess, so . . . the snake must be gone, one way or another. I'm going down there." Before Ash could say a word in response, Loki's body had shifted into that of an average-sized crow that spiraled downward in graceless flight.

When Ash rounded the boulder and looked down, he saw Bryony and breathed an enormous sigh of relief. She stood alone at the mountain's base with a large scythe lodged into the rock beside her. Loki quickly joined her, became a man again, and lifted her into his arms without even bothering to shift into pants. Some people had no sense of decency. Ash shook his head. He was certain Michael would have something to say about this.

It took significant energy to stay in his human form as he climbed down the steep side of the mountain. He had little to no energy to work with, but his appearance meant everything to him, so he opted to pay the toll. "Is it done?" he asked when he'd come close enough to be heard without shouting. "Did Azza really bind that devil?"

Loki set Bryony back on her feet, and she made a concerted effort to avert her eyes from his nakedness. Ash had to give some credit where it was due. Society had not completely degenerated into a Hieronymus Bosch painting . . . yet. "We couldn't bind him," she answered. "We couldn't even drain him enough to try."

Ash sensed Azazel's exhausted presence and knew she was telling the truth. "Then where is Samael?"

"I don't know," she said. "His body crumbled, and he just left it." She gestured to a pile of what looked like shattered marble on the ground at her feet.

Ash's hope quickly faded to nothing. "You know he doesn't give up. Ever. He'll be back, and he'll make every one of us pay for this." Though Ash never doubted he'd done the right thing—forced possession, like forced marriage and slavery, would always be something he'd fight to abolish—the cost, this time, was going to be monumental. Vengeance was most definitely *not* the Lord's, he thought bitterly. Vengeance was and always had been Samael's and Samael's alone. "All four of us are effectively immortal." Ash curled his taloned feet into the sand, ashamed he still didn't have the energy to manifest shoes. "He's going to make us pay forever. No one we love will ever be safe again."

Ash choked at the thought of what Samael would do to Chuy. But Bryony only shrugged and kicked the rubble at her feet as though it hadn't been the chosen form of death incarnate only minutes before. "Oh, I don't know," she mused. "I kind of think he might react differently this time."

"Impossible." Ash began to pace. "What did you do to drive him off?"

Bryony gripped the scythe with both hands and attempted to free it from the stone unsuccessfully. "I didn't drive him off." She grunted with the effort. "I just gave him a new name."

"A new . . ." Ash had reached out to help the woman and then frozen completely. "A new *what?*"

She braced herself against the wall with one foot and tugged at the staff again. "A new name in his language. He didn't like the one he had." She said it like people went around renaming angels every day.

"But how?"

"I don't know—I just did." Bryony tugged at the staff one more time. When it finally came dislodged, it threw her off balance. Loki stepped back to avoid the blade and let her fall on her behind. Ash glared at the Jötunn, who cleared his throat and casually backed away further, pretending to notice the stars and desert for the first time. If he'd had pockets, he definitely would have shoved his hands into them and whistled. Cowardice was incurable, apparently. Ash sighed, offered Bryony a hand, and helped her to her feet.

She dusted the sand from her skirts and continued her explanation. "I thought of the perfect name for him, so I just gave it to him. It suits him much better than the old one." She made a disgusted face, and Ash had to agree. Though he'd never been formally introduced—a formal introduction from Samael was nigh on unheard of—as he understood it, the Angel of Death's angelic name was so repulsive, even the archangel who gave it to him avoided using it.

"What did you name him?" he asked, more than curious now.

"Uh . . ." She picked at the staff of the scythe. "I don't know how to describe it exactly. Have you read Darwin?"

Ash nodded, a little offended she needed to ask.

"Well, it's like that but with nebulae, and bioluminescence, and *endless forms—*"

"*Endless forms most beautiful and most wonderful*," Ash finished for her. He knew the concept. He knew the work. He knew the power behind that famous last sentence. The first time he read it, he'd shivered at the magnitude of the work and the meaning behind those final words. He couldn't imagine what the Angel of Death would have made of such a name. No wonder Samael had retreated. No wonder he'd lost the fight. "You made him into something beautiful."

Bryony shook her head. "It's what he always was. We're just too close to see it. Life can't evolve without death, can it? It's so much bigger than we are. Up close, death is a horror, but in the grander scheme of things . . ."

"In the grander scheme, it makes everything possible." Ash couldn't help it any longer. He was pulsing with excitement. He pulled Bryony into his arms, and she dropped her scythe. She was so small, such a little thing, but she'd bested the Angel of Death, the Angel of Poison, the Wrath of God—and she'd done it with a name. "You . . . You amazing woman! No one in heaven or on earth ever thought to give that creature a new name. No angel could imagine an ounce of beauty in him—no angel wanted to." He held her at arm's length and examined her. "How did you know that would neutralize him? It's mad. What gave you the idea?"

She shrugged. "Sama did. I just listened to him. He talks about it all the time. He thinks he's ugly, and he hates it. It's not like he's hiding the fact." She scrunched up her face in thought. "No one ever really listens to him, do they?"

"They can't. They're too busy drowning in his poison. My god . . ." Ash laughed aloud, relief putting a serious dent in his self-control. "See, this is what I kept telling Solomon. 'Give your women some authority,' I said. 'They think differently. You'll see the implementation of strategies you never could have imagined on your own.' But no, no. He wouldn't hear of it. Told me to stick to construction and stay out of politics." Ash rubbed the top of his head vigorously. "I thought I was smart, but you're a damned genius."

With the kind of complexion she had, Bryony's face lit up like a stoplight. She was clearly not the sort of person who could take a compliment without some mitigation. "Well . . ." She cleared her throat. "I mean I couldn't have done any of it without you and Azza. Where is Azza, by the way?"

"He's still here. Do you want to see him?" Ash regretted his offer almost as soon as he voiced it. Did he really want to start trusting humans again? It had brought nothing but pain in the past. But this one had seen him at his lowest, helped to save his life, and fought alongside him in a hopeless battle she actually managed to win. *Misery really does acquaint a man with strange bedfellows*, he thought. "Try these." He pulled his spectacles from his vest pocket and handed them to her.

She held them away from her body and made a face at them. Ash hadn't realized how accustomed he'd become to being trusted without question. Compared to Chuy, Bryony was shockingly cynical.

"They won't burn you," Ash reassured her. "They just broaden your scope."

"Will I . . . see the future?"

"No." He shrugged. "At least, Chuy didn't."

"Oh." She brought them to her eyes and peeked through the lenses without really wearing them. Ash suddenly had no idea why he hadn't given his spectacles to mortals before now. It was delightful to watch them. Bryony's mouth hung open as the true nature of the desert around them was revealed to her. She reached out her hands as if to touch something that wasn't really there and quickly drew back again. "I think I see him," she said at last.

"He'll be vaguely human-shaped and unapologetically garish. He's the brightest and most colorful of the ishim."

"Yeah, I definitely see him." She grinned and turned back to Ash. "I see you too. Is that a tail?"

Quick as a striking eel, Ash snatched his spectacles back. "That'll be quite enough of that."

Bryony laughed. "I keep learning new things about you, Ashmedai. I never thought I'd meet a demon who was even shyer than I am."

He dismissed her amusement. "We should get back to the house—make sure Samael's hashmallim haven't carried off our fiancés."

"Fiancé?" Bryony cocked her head at him. "Are you that serious already?"

"I was that serious the moment I first took his hand. Surely you know that." He stared down at her and narrowed his eyes. "Surely you know Michael was that serious about you from day one. Nephilim are incapable of anything else. That's why it's advisable to practice caution when you attempt to seduce one. You will most definitely get more than you bargained for—some desperate, lonely stray following you for the rest of your life. Speaking of which . . ." He glanced around and realized. "Your Jötunn has gone."

She wrinkled her nose. "He's probably gone back to Martha's."

"And left you all alone with me." Ash frowned as her eyes widened. Now she realized. Now she was afraid. That Jötunn really was unreliable. He sighed. "I'll take you home. But you may wish to close your eyes." She did, and he let his body shift to its cherubic form. It was a relief, really, like releasing a long-held breath. He lifted Bryony into his arms, gripped her scythe with his taloned feet, and flew.

High in the air, with the wind disheveling her hair, Bryony opened her eyes. "It's okay as long as I don't look down, right?"

Oh, for crying out loud. Ash gripped her tighter. Now she was going to have a mid-flight panic and squirm in his arms. But she didn't, and Ash began to realize that it wasn't his appearance she was afraid of—it was falling. He was the one protecting her from her fears. *Like Sarah.*

He tried not to think of the young woman—the child, really—he'd failed all those years ago. He tried not to recall watching her play along the path he habitually walked, building up the courage to speak to her, and finally, after years of friendship, revealing his demonic form. It had been her first wish of those he'd promised to grant. She didn't scream or run like he expected. She'd just called him her guardian and made her second wish—that she never be forced to marry. Ash had vowed to protect her, but he'd lost in the end. The score was seven to one, but all that mattered was the *one*.

"I think they'll be all right," Bryony said, snapping him from his unpleasant revery. "Michael's a lot stronger than he pretends to be. He won't let anything happen to Chuy."

Ash rolled his eyes. "My little brother cannot even handle a gun."

"Because he doesn't need one," she pointed out, incorrectly.

"No, because he hates his heritage. His pacifism is more tantrum than principle. You do know that, don't you? If anyone fights off the hashmallim, between the two of them, I'd bet on the captain."

Bryony chuckled under her breath. "Oh, you would, would you?"

Damn it. He did not just make that mistake again. "What I mean to say is Chuy can shoot. You should have seen him take aim at those monsters the first time they came for us. He fought them off more efficiently than I did. There's no doubt in my mind he's protecting my little brother as we speak."

"No doubt," she muttered. "You sound pretty confident. You did say you'd bet on it. So what are the stakes?"

He growled. "I will never forgive Azza for opening his mouth about my weaknesses."

"I think it's cute." She wrapped both her arms around one of his significantly larger ones in an awkward, midair hug. "Okay. Winner gets to marry first."

"That's . . ." He flushed and nearly dropped her when his skin warmed at the thought of marriage. Had she felt it? She probably had. He pushed the idea out of his head. "Those are terrible stakes."

"Then you think of better ones."

He couldn't, but only because he couldn't think of anything right now. If he tried, his mind would wander to the promises he wanted to make and those he longed to receive in return. "You wicked little thing," he murmured. "I accept."

Chapter Thirty-One

Bryony heard Azazel's alarm before she touched down on her front walk. It meant an angel had invaded her home, but she didn't have time to panic. The demon king beat her to it. He dropped her a few feet from the ground and ran for the open front door at a superhuman pace. He reached it before he'd fully reduced his size. Bryony was sure he'd catch his wings on the doorframe, but at the last second, he drew them into himself and they were gone. She followed, her limbs tingling with adrenaline. Michael was safe. Chuy was safe. They had to be. Samael wouldn't come for them now, would he?

She berated herself all the way up her front walk and onto her veranda. Why did she think she could change the Angel of Death? How arrogant to believe she'd actually won. All she'd done was ensure his outrage, his violent retaliation. When she finally rushed into her own living room, the relief was so extreme she felt in danger of passing out.

It was only Daniel. He was sitting on her couch, taking abuse from Ash with his usual stoicism. As soon as he saw Bryony, he stood and handed her a piece of paper from his notebook. It read as follows:

Michael and Chuy have boarded Dragonfly and are under the protection of the Black Armada. They'll wait for you there. No hashmallim will track them over the sea.

PS—I relate, under protest, the following messages: Michael says he loves you and can't wait to hold you in his arms again. (That one is for Bryony, obviously.) Ashmedai, Chuy insists you calm down. He says he's fine and worrying won't do any good. (Seems he already knows you well, although I disagree with his conclusion. Worrying is a defense against the unknown and has saved numerous mortals in unpredictable conditions.)

PPS—Your alarm will not stop sounding, and I resent being forced to wait in this fucking cacophony.

Bryony finished reading and immediately handed the message to Ash, who collapsed onto the sofa in a heap of audible relief. Apparently, if Azazel wasn't around to disable his alarm, it would continue to sound until the intruding angel left the perimeter.

"Thank you, Daniel," Bryony said to the massive cherub.

Daniel nodded.

Ash sat up. "I have to go. You know I have to go, right?"

"I know," she said. The temptation to demand he take her with him bordered on unbearable, but Bryony knew better than to leave her post. "Can you find the armada?"

Daniel gestured to himself and mouthed the words *follow me* to Ash.

"Go on," she insisted. "Tell Michael I'm safe at home."

Ash groaned and pinched the bridge of his nose. "But I can't just leave you alone—not while Samael is still out there."

She smiled at him. "Oh, I think Azza should be here shortly. Anyway, it'll be nice to have the house to myself for a bit." It was a lie, but it was for the greater good. Neither Ash nor Azza could do much of anything if Samael came for Bryony, and she had no doubt he would, eventually. Whether he was angry, pleased, or some other unfathomable emotion, she couldn't predict. But if he was angry, she would rather face him alone. With the Angel of Death, she seemed to do better one on one.

If Ash was onto her lie, he didn't protest. She hadn't expected him to anyway. He needed an excuse to rush to Chuy's side, and Bryony was happy to give it to him. The demon king stood, embraced her, and murmured, "I believe I'll enjoy having a sister. Thank you . . . for everything. I'll be right back. Don't do anything stupid." He let her go and lifted her chin with one finger. "Your new brother is watching." His sharp, hooded eyes bored into her, and Bryony suddenly felt very small and vulnerable. There was immense power behind those eyes. Like Azazel, Ashmedai was no warrior. His strength lay elsewhere, but it was nothing to trifle with.

On his way out the door, the only warrior angel Bryony had ever met took her hand. She hadn't really appreciated the massive size of Daniel's hands until now. They were almost as big as Michael's. He squeezed and bowed and ducked out the door.

Then the alarm went quiet, and Bryony was alone.

It took her all of thirty seconds to regret her bravado in sending Ash on his way. Alone was a decidedly unpleasant state to be in after all she'd suffered. Alone meant she had time to think and worry whether she'd made the right choices. If Azza were here, he would tell her to have a cup of tea. But her kitchen was too quiet, and she didn't want to confirm its emptiness with her own eyes. Seeing the empty chair beside her lifeless hearth and knowing no one was about to fill it was hard enough. She thought of going upstairs and lying down to rest, but the mere idea of her cold, lonely bed made her hands tremble.

Yesterday, her house had been full of life, and now it was silent. The stark contrast reminded her too much of the way she'd felt after losing her family. It had all happened so fast. Was it possible her recent life had been little more than a fever dream? She might have imagined it after all—angels, demons, and talking crows. It seemed like something she would have dreamed up in the throes of a terminal illness.

Alone in the dark, she began to doubt both her good fortune and her sanity. The feeling was so unnerving she was actually relieved when Azazel's alarm startled her out of it. She ran to the door, only a little surprised to see a familiar figure walking toward her winter-bare sanctuary. It was Samael, still in the form of a graveyard angel, doggedly unchanged, and she loved him for it. She threw on a heavy coat, grabbed the death scythe, and went to meet him. It was easy to get partway there, but the last half of the journey had her heart beating like a second alarm in her chest. She'd been so worried about whether he was real, she'd forgotten to worry about whether he was furious.

When Bryony stepped under those branches made heavy with snow, she suddenly found herself cocooned in warmth and silence. Samael had made her little grove a comfortable temperature and smothered the sound of Azza's alarm. She hoped this meant he wasn't planning to kill her right away. She cleared her throat, leaned the scythe against a tree trunk, and shoved her hands into her coat pockets. "You're right," she said to him. "It's a really annoying sound." She didn't bother announcing herself because she knew he could sense his weapon, and now she knew just how accurate that sense was.

They stood in silence for some time. Bryony made a deal with herself that she would not push for conversation. If he had something to say to her, he could just say it without the precursory chitchat. Several times, he seemed about to begin, but he faded back into contemplation before a single syllable left his mouth. When he finally did speak, he dug his heels in. "You will still fulfill your end," he said. He was so incredibly stubborn. "However, I will concede that you have not specified a time or place, and I will try to wait."

Bryony bit back a smile. "I can agree to that."

"I will come to check on your progress from time to time."

It sounded like a threat, the way he said it, but Bryony refused to see it that way. "You could also come to visit and not even mention our contract."

"I don't think so."

"Sama . . ." She tried to scold him, but he beat her to it.

"I have done nothing but antagonize you from the beginning. You have no reason to desire my company other than misplaced pity."

"It's not pity," she mumbled.

He went on mercilessly. "What I have done is unforgivable and irrevocable. You must not attempt to right this, my daughter. We will continue our partnership because we have a common goal, but I have done nothing to earn your friendship." He was downcast and humble. It was so utterly unlike him, Bryony almost wanted to take everything back.

"You still don't get it," she said. "You can't earn my friendship because we're not ever going to be friends." She paused and saw his expression fall before she finished her thought. "We're family."

His eyes grew wide, and Bryony was proud to have shocked him. She hoped it was a good surprise rather than an unpleasant one. It had been clear from the start he had something particular on his mind but was reluctant to actually say it. Maybe this would give him the courage to say what he came to say. He frowned down at her. "I do not know how to be family."

She fidgeted with the staff of the scythe. "Well, I think the occasional visit is a good place to start. Maybe introduce Michael and I to some of your . . . host." That was a suggestion she immediately regretted and hoped he hadn't really heard. She'd been thinking of his friends and realized the closest thing he probably had to friends was his army of angels. Being introduced to an army of angels was not a prospect Bryony enjoyed thinking about.

To her horror, Samael perked up at the suggestion. "Have you ever met a hashmal?"

"Um . . ." She gulped. "No?"

"I have many." He was downright giddy. "They are relatively unaffected by my poison and excellent trackers. They are far superior to any other species of angel."

Oh, how quickly the course of a conversation could change. "Are they?"

He nodded, his relief palpable. Whatever it was he was waiting to say, he now had an excuse to put it off longer. "I believe you would like them."

"What makes you say that?"

"They're uncomplicated, like animals. You are fond of animals." He paused, snatched his enthusiasm back, and stuffed it down somewhere deep. Subdued, he added, "If I have guessed correctly."

"You guessed correctly. I'm fond of all kinds of animals. What animal are they most like?"

He thought a moment, pressing a finger to his chin. "Canines, perhaps."

"Dogs?" Suddenly, she didn't care what he'd come to say. All she wanted to do was talk about hashmallim for the rest of the morning. "I love dogs! Well, you *have* to bring them now. No choice in the matter." She reached out and took his hand to shake it. "See? It's an agreement. A contract. You will introduce me to your puppies."

He chuckled under his breath. "They are not puppies."

"All dogs are puppies." She tried to take her hand back, but Samael would not let go. He gripped her fingers, turning her palm as though he were examining it for imperfections, his brow furrowed in deep contemplation. The tip of his thumb pressed into her flesh until it almost hurt.

He muttered, "I don't understand why you refuse to reject me." Ah, there it was—the cusp of the idea that had caught in his throat and prompted an awkward conversation about hashmallim. He quickly veered away from it again. "Life is not as varied in our world because we do not evolve, but we have some differences among us. For example, unlike ophanim, hashmallim do not speak and are easy to train. I could teach you someday, if you wished it."

He was stalling again. This time, she decided not to play his game. "Sama, what is it you really came here to say?"

He turned her hand over again. "I should go."

"Just say it," she pressed. Impatience colored her voice far more than she intended it to. He tensed, and she felt he was on the verge of backing out. So she flooded him. "Just say it, whatever it is. It's fine. It's okay to talk to me. I'm your daughter, aren't I? Nothing's going to change that. You can just say it already."

In an unexpected surge of determination, Samael pulled her close and held her head between his hands. She knew what was coming seconds before it did. He bowed and met her mouth with his. His lips barely brushed hers as he breathed his new name into her. It was even more beautiful than she remembered. Her awe renewed, her wonder kindled, she couldn't help a smile. *Endless forms most beautiful.*

"You are smiling," he said, and she realized he'd felt the expression with his own mouth. He pulled away and let his hands fall to his sides. "Have I mispronounced it?"

"No, it was perfect. I just . . ." She blushed. "You like it. I'm so glad. I didn't know if you would."

"You lied when you gave it to me." No visit from Samael would be complete without emotional whiplash.

Bryony blinked. "I'm sorry . . . What?"

"You said it didn't mean anything." He stepped closer, and she did her best not to back away.

"Oh, that was just because . . . You know, I'm still new to the whole introduction thing, so I have to actually—"

"It meant everything."

"Oh." More whiplash. Slowly, the Angel of Death began to drop to one knee, and Bryony panicked. "No, no! Please don't. I know it seems like I'm wanting for congregants, but that's only because I'm trying to wean off. I mean I appreciate it and everything. It's just not something I need from you." How much more could she possibly offend him? Apparently, she was determined to find out. "Not because it's you or anything. I'm sure worship from you is lovely. I've had it from your son, and that was like a five-course meal with an entire bottle of red, so no doubt yours is—"

Mercifully, he interrupted her. "Worship?" He had frozen halfway to his knee and now wore a baffled expression like he was being bombarded with nonsense, which if Bryony was honest, wasn't entirely inaccurate. "I was only going to offer my gratitude."

There could be no doubt she was beyond red in the cheeks now. She'd made a fool of herself, and she knew it. "Sorry. That was . . . That was a stupid assumption."

He knit his brow and continued despite her rude interruption, lowering himself onto one knee and speaking more formally. "My daughter, I am in your debt. I have never received so lavish a gift as the one you gave me this night. I wish to reciprocate. I am not an angel of great means, but I am an angel of great power. Speak your deepest desire to me, and if it is within my power, I will bring it to fruition. I will track down and annihilate your enemies. My entire host will be at your disposal—"

"Including the puppies?" She tried to laugh at what she felt was a ridiculous situation.

He did not. "Including the hashmallim, yes."

Bryony picked at the sleeves of her coat. The conversation was making her more and more uncomfortable. She didn't want submission any more than she wanted worship. But it would have been a lie to insist she wanted nothing from him. "Okay, there is something I want." He bowed a little deeper, and she grimaced at the gesture. "When I first got to know you—after the conjuration, you know, for tea—I was excited about the idea that . . ." She twisted her skirt in her hands. "That maybe I could have a father again. I love Azza. I really do. But if I'm his god, how can he be like a father to me? You, on the other hand . . . Oh, please stand up. I hate this."

He stood and waited.

She cleared her throat and forced herself to stop fidgeting. "I'm going to marry your son, so you're my father by default. But . . . I'd hoped . . . maybe it could be more than *default*, you know?"

"Your deepest desire is for the Angel of Death to be a true father to you?"

"Yes." She blushed and chewed her lower lip. This was awkward to say the least. It seemed equally unsettling for him.

Samael confirmed her suspicion with a frown. "It is not in my nature to be a father to anyone." She was about to back down and apologize for such an unreasonable request when he pressed a finger to his lips thoughtfully and said, "You would have to teach me."

She wanted to cry out for joy, but she stifled it. There may have been a muffled, triumphant whimper. She tried to channel her mother's ability to switch off her feelings and pretend someone else's instead. "It wouldn't be difficult, I think. I'm already raised, so the tricky bit's done. You could just visit from time to time, maybe teach me how to train a hashmal, like you said. The hardest part would probably be emotional support."

He cocked his head at her. "Emotional support?"

"Uh . . ." She cringed, but there was no way out of the conversation now. She'd started it, and it was up to her to follow it through. "Like a hug if I'm sad, or company if I'm lonely. Just being present is enough, really. You could give me advice sometimes, or tell me I'm being unreasonable when no one else will. You could even side with me sometimes when Michael and I have a fight."

The graveyard angel laughed, and Bryony clung to the sound as hope. Then his smile faded, and he was heartbreakingly downcast. "None of this is especially wise, my daughter. Do you wish to end up like the boy's mother? The poison is cumulative."

"Oh, bullshit." She said it before she even realized it was on the tip of her tongue. It was insensitive, perhaps, but of all the lies Samael believed, this was one of the most insidious. "I don't feel any weaker after hours in your presence. Be honest. Do you really know what happened to Michael's mother? You assume her death was either your fault or his, but what if it was just a coincidence? I'm no doctor, but I read about several motor neuron diseases that result in exactly the symptoms she had. You said she believed she was dying. What if she was right? Maybe she was already sick when you met her. Maybe, rather than paralyzing her, you gave her a gift that meant she didn't have to go through it alone—she didn't have to die without having her dream come true."

At that, Samael's mouth fell open, and he stopped breathing completely. There was a moment—fleeting, shocking—in which Bryony felt a wave of something come her way. It was a tsunami of light and life, worship unlike any she had known before. But at the last second, it was snatched back. Apparently, much like his son, Samael had impeccable restraint. He swallowed hard and grumbled, "For a god who does not wish to be worshiped, you are certainly signaling otherwise. Your gifts are too generous and demand something in return."

"No, they don't."

"Yes, they do." He was adamant. "Take some of them back."

"I won't."

He glared at her. "Stubborn child."

"That's a very fatherly thing to say." She grinned, and his mouth twitched briefly. "But, Sama, you have to believe me. I felt your poison long before I ever met you. I don't think it's unique to you. It's . . . It's just grief."

"You believe my presence brings sorrow?"

"Not sorrow. Grief. I think they're different animals. But, yes, your presence brings grief. It doesn't cause permanent paralysis or anything. I think it just hits angels harder because they don't experience it often."

"I see." He took a deep breath like he was gearing up for something difficult. Then he opened his arms and waited. When she hesitated, he quickly explained himself. "If my presence brings you grief, I must offer emotional support. Such was your deepest desire, was it not? You also wished for me to tell you when you were being unreasonable." He paused. "You are being unreasonable now, and this situation is absurd. But come." He curled his fingers to beckon her. "I offer comfort for the grief I myself have brought upon you."

Bryony had no idea how to refuse him, so she stepped into the waiting arms of the Angel of Death and let them enfold her. He was nothing like her own father—he never would be—and that was okay. He was here, and that was enough. She felt his chest rise and fall and heard a heartbeat buried behind his robe. All this, she knew, he manifested for her sake, so she would have someone real to hug. Grateful, she slipped her arms under his and wrapped them around his ribcage. She settled so easily into that embrace it almost frightened her.

Never in her life had she wanted the love of an angel this much. Never had she wanted the acceptance of a father this much. Why? What was death to her? A lifelong companion, an old familiar face, that too quiet house in the back of her mind. She shuddered as she considered it, and he squeezed her tighter. He held her far longer than normal social graces would allow, but it didn't matter. No matter how much he had to give, she wanted more.

After several minutes, he bowed over her and whispered, "Is it working?"

"Yes, now shut up." Tears pricked at the corners of her eyes. She never wanted him to let go. She needed the embrace to reach back further, beyond her young adulthood, beyond her teen years, beyond even her father's death—back to before he started drinking, when he was someone she would go to with her problems, someone she admired. Her father had been the soft one in the family. Her mother was the disciplinarian, and her father was the one she ran to afterwards for comfort. How she missed that presence in her life. She needed it now more than ever. "Please, don't ask me to reject you again," she said at last. "I can't."

"Bryony." He called her by her name, and it still felt strange. "You have to let go."

"Just a few more seconds."

He trembled. "I am becoming exhausted."

"Sorry." She let him go, ashamed she'd forgotten how difficult it was for him to hold the poison back.

"There is nothing to be sorry for." The way he said it wasn't placation—it was a simple fact. He kept a hand on her shoulder as he stepped around her and picked up his weapon. In his custody, it became the scimitar, that fang-like sword Bryony recognized as Michael's. But it wasn't Michael's, was it? It wasn't hers either. It belonged to the Angel of Death, and the Angel of Death was finally taking it back. Then he sheathed it, and as he did, it took on another familiar shape. "Right or left?" he asked.

"Sorry?"

"Which wrist do you prefer?" Of course. He still expected her to fulfill her end of their agreement, and so she would still need to carry his weapon. She offered her right wrist. But as Samael clasped the metal band into place, he said something that made her think she had misjudged him enormously. "This will make it easier for me to find you, will it not?" The ring was complete, and Samael stepped back, apparently satisfied. "Goodbye, my daughter."

He left her stunned in the freezing cold, cradling her right wrist as though it had been injured. She wandered back to her house, unsure quite how to define what had just happened. What had she done? What kind of surrogate family had she acquired in her sad desperation? A rejected trickster, the original scapegoat, the demon king, and the devil himself. What would her parents say if they knew? What would her brother say? Well, that was a question easily answered. Her little brother would say, *That's so cool!* and ask for all the details. She should strive to be more like her brother.

As she trudged back to her house, she was haunted by a silence that meant Samael had left the perimeter. She should have been relieved by his absence, but she wasn't. Her home was empty again. It was the quiet that tore at her in the end. She wandered through her living room and into her kitchen, ready to collapse. But the beautiful dream she'd been doubting waited for her there. Azza stood in the frame of the kitchen's back door. As soon as she saw him, she threw her arms around him and finally lost her composure into his black-and-gold smoking jacket.

"My goodness, darling, but what have you been up to? I just got in." He held her at arm's length and examined her. "Ah, I see. *He* was already here." He touched the band around her wrist. "And he left you with a little gift. I do wish he'd take the time to envision a more elegant design, although this one is a step up from the last."

"Isn't it the same?" She lifted her wrist to examine the band herself. Though its shape was unchanged, the image in the charm no longer showed the archangel Michael defeating the devil. Now it bore the image of a plum blossom, and Bryony knew exactly what it meant. *Sanctuary.*

Chapter Thirty-Two

Ash alighted alongside Daniel on the quarterdeck of *Dragonfly*, feeling every bit the intruder he was. He quickly manifested his human flesh, even more ashamed of his demonic form now that he stood beside the perfect specimen of a cherub. Understandably, no one came near either of them. A bearded man, who looked remarkably like Loki, was coiling line while a woman Ash recognized as the commodore stood at the helm. The man took one look at Ash and left. The commodore secured the wheel and sidled up next to Daniel, who embraced and kissed her tenderly. They were playful, like a couple who'd been together a long time. Ash envied their ease with each other.

Once Daniel had gone, Ash was left with the distinct feeling of strategic abandonment. He was alone with the commodore, who somehow managed to intimidate him despite his own title. Authority practically oozed from her pores. She reminded him of Shemjaza, now that he took a moment to consider it.

She held out her hand and hastily introduced herself. "Raeni."

"Ashmedai." He took her hand and amended his introduction. "Ash."

"Good." She leaned back against the bulwarks. "I despise formalities. You have passed my first test."

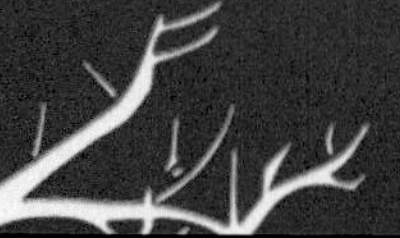

She was baiting him, but he didn't care. Only one thing mattered. "Where is he?"

Raeni folded her arms and crossed her ankles. "Safe and sound and fast asleep, demon. Let him rest a while longer. You and I need to have a little talk." She gestured for Ash to join her against the bulwarks. "By the way, Daniel has told me a great deal about you. Break out your spectacles at your peril."

Ash tried to smile at her. "I remain nearsighted at your request."

"Second test." She drew an invisible check mark in the air. "Passed. Are you ready for the third?"

Ash gathered his patience and nodded.

"My navigator disapproved of my relationship with Daniel at first. Did he tell you that? He changed his mind when our medic seduced him, but I know he still despises what he is. I hope that's not a problem you share."

While the interrogation was exasperating, Ash knew he had only one opportunity to get it right, and for some unfathomable reason, he cared. He cleared his throat and stood a little taller. "I don't believe there's anything inherently wrong with what I am. I reject the generally accepted view that the watchers committed a crime against nature. They arrived in this world and chose to live peacefully among its inhabitants rather than conquer them. They integrated, traded goods and information, and participated in their communities. It was the other angels who made it ugly. We nephilim never asked to be born, yet we were punished for it. We were told we were naturally violent and insatiable, and we believed it. I won't excuse the crimes of my kindred, but they were never the abominations they believed themselves to be. Still I won't lie to you." He bowed his head. "Hating oneself is a difficult habit to break once it's learned. I have, perhaps, overcorrected as a result. I choose to be this." He gestured to his well-dressed, human body. "And I avoid my demonic form whenever I can."

"Why?" The commodore uncrossed her arms and leaned closer.

It wasn't the question Ash had expected, so it took him a moment to find the answer. "Because it's incomplete."

"Nonsense," Raeni said without doubt or hesitation. She spoke as though the truth were obvious and Ash was just too dense to see it.

Ash glanced down at his feet, which he had finally managed to cover with shoes. "I'm not completely human, nor am I completely cherub. So what am I?"

Raeni shrugged. "A demon. Just like all the other demons. You are king of them, in fact, and you look exactly the way you're supposed to look." The commodore leaned back on her hands, and out of the corner of his eye, Ash saw her dig her fingernails into the rail. "I do have some experience with self-hatred, though you may not believe it to look at me." She laughed heartily, and Ash had to smile. "I hated my body when I was young. I was built wrong—that's how it felt. When I first joined the armada, I presented myself as a man. My father's ideals still had a vice grip on me. As I began to feel safer here, I corrected my presentation. Now, it's no secret who I am.

"Here, you're either for the armada or against it, and that's all that matters. If you fight alongside the crew, you're family, and you'd better be proud of it. So I became proud. And I became Raeni. And I became the commodore. Even after all that, I did not accept myself as whole and perfect until Daniel did. Sometimes we need others to teach us what we should already know about ourselves, yes?" Raeni turned to Ash and pursed her lips a moment before she spoke again. "Now that you've passed my third test—the right answer was honesty, demon—I'll deliver a message to you. From Rose."

"Rose?"

"The one with the frying pan."

"Ah." How could Ash forget her? She'd been a menace to the backs of his calves.

Raeni folded her arms and gave Ash the kind of withering look he'd only ever received from his mother. "As I'm sure you already know, Chuy was the only baby the Black Armada allowed ourselves. He was our exception, our little pleasure. The entire fleet brought him up. We are all his family. And if you ever harm him or allow harm to come to him, you will rue the day. That's what Rose wanted me to tell you." She chuckled. "Those were her exact words, in fact—*rue the day.*"

Ash imagined the woman with the frying pan flying at him in a rage and tried not to laugh. "Tell her I understand."

"Don't underestimate her, demon. She's my second in command for a reason." Raeni winked. "Now, you and I both know you couldn't betray that boy if you wanted to. As I said, that message was from Rose, not me. She's still not familiar with your ways, and she's not keen to learn."

Raeni pushed off the rail and turned to face Ash in a movement so smooth it may as well have been a dance. "This next message is mine. Chuy told me you defied the Angel of Death and allowed your body to be broken and bound in your effort to protect him. Here's what I understand that he doesn't. That fight was futile, and you knew it. You were never going to win against that monster. You gave everything you had just so our captain wouldn't die without knowing how hard he'd been fought for."

Once more, Raeni reached out her hand, and once more, Ash took it. She needn't have bothered. Her sincerity was crystal clear as she said, "In all my years working with this fleet, I have yet to see that kind of courage and loyalty. You have my well-earned respect, Your Majesty. From this day forward, the Black Armada will ally with you. When you have freed your subjects, we will uphold your sovereignty."

"I . . ." Ash hardly knew what to say. That the commodore of the Black Armada believed him capable of freeing and leading his people struck him deep. While Azazel had always made Ash feel young, Raeni made him feel every year of his exceptional age. "Thank you."

"Now go." She inclined her head toward the stairway. "Our boy's been anxious to see you all night. We had a hell of a time convincing him to get some sleep."

"Where is he?"

"In the captain's quarters, right below us. And Michael is on watch for another hour. Just so you know." She grinned.

Ash rushed to the captain's quarters as though someone had fired a starting pistol. When he reached the door, he pushed it open and crept in. Even in the dark, he saw the state of the room. A disorganized work table was its crowning ornament. There was a desk to one side, a long bench under a row of heavily curtained windows at the back, and several closed lockers. Everything had been built of the same dark wood with carved images and beautiful brass details.

As stunning as the cabin was, only one feature drew him closer—a quiet alcove with a gently breathing figure tucked into it. Ash moved to the edge of the mattress and manifested a golden light. It hovered before him like an abnormally large firefly. He never really needed the light for himself, but he didn't regret asking Raziel to teach him the trick. Now he manifested it so his own face would be illuminated as he leaned in and brushed the captain's hair from his forehead. Tattoos peeked out from under Chuy's hairline and continued back onto his scalp. Even through his spectacles, Ash hadn't deciphered why Chuy had once shaved and tattooed his head. He wondered if the thing had been done in grief or celebration as he trailed his fingers over those perfect cheekbones and cupped the captain's face in his hand.

"Despierta, mi cielo," he murmured.

Chuy's eyes flew open. His arms were around Ash's neck before Ash even realized he was awake. "You're alive!" Chuy cried, and he pulled Ash down with him.

Ash chuckled. "I'm not alive."

"You're alive in all the ways that matter." Chuy drew him close. "I was so worried. Let's never do that again."

It was all Ash could do to keep from squeezing Chuy half to death. "I worried for you too," he admitted. "If Daniel hadn't been there to tell me where you'd gone, I don't know what I would have done."

Chuy dragged the backs of his nails gently across Ash's cheek. Then he draped his long fingers over Ash's spine where Samael had broken him. Ash shivered as Chuy pulled him closer to kiss him. The rest of Ash's body seemed to crawl into the bunk of its own accord. Rather than resist, he crushed the captain to himself and kissed and kissed and kissed him back.

Each breath Chuy drew between kisses was deep and long, and Ashmedai savored the sound of it. For now, his captain was alive. Yes, death would inevitably come for him. Someday, Ash would reach the border of Chuy's existence, but not today. From now until the end, that would be Ash's refrain. *Someday, but not today. Thank god, not today.*

"I can't stand not feeling your skin," Chuy said. His deft fingers quickly undid the buttons on Ash's vest. The light, now hovering above them both, illuminated his face in a gentle, golden hue. He looked like a god, Ash thought. He looked absolutely gorgeous. Then Chuy slipped his hands under Ash's shirt.

The fever nearly drove Ashmedai to thoughtless abandon, but no kind of thoughtlessness ever took the demon king without a fight. Against his own physical instinct and a rising tide of desire, Ash began to analyze the nature of the relationship. "Chuy." He reluctantly interrupted his passionate partner. "We have to talk."

"Later," Chuy murmured. He brought his tongue to the notch between Ash's collarbones and sent an overwhelming wave of heat all through the demon's body.

"Wait, damn it." Ash pushed Chuy back, and the look of hurt on the captain's face doused Ash's fever. He immediately tried to reverse the damage. "I love you. I love you more than I've ever loved anyone. I can hardly stand to stop kissing you, but I need you to listen for a second. I may be alive in all the ways that matter, but there are some ways in which I'm not. I think you should know about them before you commit to me."

"Too late, isn't it?" Chuy looked troubled. "I already committed."

That was so good to hear Ash almost abandoned his plan to say the rest. But love wasn't love unless it was true. "You can't commit to something you don't understand. Listen. My body . . . It isn't like yours. I built it. It takes energy to maintain. Occasionally, I have to rest. That means I'll disappear, literally, sometimes for months at a time. I won't be able to touch you, speak to you, or love you this way."

Chuy arched an eyebrow and cracked a wry smile. "You forget I was raised in the armada. Every relationship I've ever had has been long distance."

But there was more. "And I can't promise there will never be another conjuration. I was lucky last time. My conjuror was just a girl who meant no harm and was kind enough to let me go. Next time, I might not be so lucky. Next time, I could be forced to sign a contract promising my own labor—"

"Then I'll find you and sneak away with you on your breaks."

Ash laughed. Chuy was making this too easy. "And if I'm made to perform atrocities?"

Chuy drew a finger over Ash's lips. "I'll gather angels to fight you until you're useless to the guy who conjured you. Easy. Maybe Loki will even do it."

"Loki?" Ash laughed. "That's overly optimistic."

"My whole thing is being overly optimistic. Knew that going in, didn't ya?"

"I suppose I did." It was one of the reasons Ash had fallen for the captain in the first place—trust, acceptance, and his sincere, beautiful belief that deep inside everyone was a good person fighting to get out.

Chuy pushed himself onto his elbows and frowned. "I did have one worry, though." He was serious. The smile fled Ash's face, and his little, hovering light flickered in the dark. "I'm gonna get old," Chuy said. "But you won't, will you? Could you be happy with an old man? Maybe you'd prefer someone without an expiration date."

"Is that all?" The relief was almost too much. "Anyone without an expiration date wouldn't be you, and I don't want anyone other than you. As for growing old, I've already done it—I know exactly what it looks like and how it feels in this body—and I have every intention of doing it again with you."

"Can you . . . do that?" Chuy's eyes went wide, and Ash beamed, more than a little proud to have impressed him.

"I can. You won't grow old alone. I swear it."

"So . . ." Chuy toyed with the loose buttons on Ash's shirt. "So we really are gonna get married then? Like really? It wasn't just a feel-good moment before battle?"

Ash sat up, stunned. "Of course we are. I'd marry you right now if . . ." He caught himself and coughed. He'd almost forgotten. He'd made a wager, and to dishonor a wager was so far against his nature, he wasn't even sure he was physically capable. "That is . . . Please tell me you shot a few hashmallim. Tell me you protected Michael and not the other way around."

"Didn't even see any hashmallim." Chuy's half-smile was irresistible. "It was Michael's idea to head to *Dragonfly*. He thought the sea might disguise our scent. He was right. We didn't even have to use the rifles. I definitely owe him one."

"No!" Ash punched a pillow. "Of all the times to see reason and stay out of the fight. You inconsistent . . . crazy . . . I'll always lose when it comes to you, won't I? Checkers and any wager I ever make. I can't predict you."

"You made a wager? 'Bout me?"

Ash groaned and let his body drop onto the mattress. "That's something else you should probably know. I have a bit of a gambling problem."

Chuy's eyebrows shot up. "Really?"

"Really. And I can already tell you it's worse than you think." Ash kneaded his forehead. "Thanks to Azazel, that woman . . ." He paused and amended himself. "Bryony knows I can't refuse a wager. She bet me that Michael would be the protector between you, and I told her she was wrong. She hadn't seen you shoot. She said whoever won the bet would get to marry first."

Ash's floating light dimmed when Chuy fell back laughing. How could he possibly find this amusing? Perhaps he didn't realize just how unthinkable it would be for the demon king to dishonor a wager.

Chuy's laugh trailed off, and his expression grew serious. "Guess we'll have to get Michael married off quick because I'm not waiting. Me and you are gonna be forever." He grinned when he most certainly felt the heat rolling off Ash's skin. "Contracts are important to ya, right? So sign mine, Your Majesty."

Ash groaned. "You know better than to talk to me like that." Already, Chuy knew his weaknesses far too well, but if Ash was going to give the keys to his psyche to anyone . . . *forever.* All it took was *forever.* That one word drove him until he could barely control himself any longer. He couldn't get Chuy's clothes off fast enough. He couldn't get his own off fast enough. Every inch of Chuy's skin needed to be tasted. Every tattoo needed to be traced, every joint caressed, every moment savored. It was stupid to be this careless without a lock on the door, but all Ash could think about was how short Chuy's life would be, how little time he had to show the captain just how passionately he was loved.

Despite the depth of his desire, the second Ash removed his shoes, all his urgency gave way to shame. His taloned feet unfolded and drew his attention from everything else. They were evidence of his own failure, his inhumanity, and worse, his laziness.

"I like 'em," Chuy announced. "Nobody looks like you. I feel like I won the lottery."

Ash's cheeks burned, and he whispered, "How do you manage to make me feel even more naked than I already am?"

"Natural talent?" Chuy offered.

"Speaking of which." Ash swung one leg over both of Chuy's and stared down at him. The man was delicious—there was no arguing that. "I have a gift too," he said. He bent down and touched his lips to Chuy's. The kiss started gently but grew more ferocious as the captain's body reacted. Ash traced Chuy's long neck and kissed his way over a shoulder and down that decorated chest. He explored Chuy's stomach with his mouth and pressed his fingertips into the soft flesh at Chuy's waist. But when he came close to his objective, he hesitated. The gift he wanted to give waited on the tip of his tongue.

From the day Ash had first brought Chuy to the hotel with him, he'd wanted this. He wanted to take everything he'd ever learned from hundreds of meaningless partners and give it to someone he really loved. But Chuy was too easily swayed, and though Ash knew they would grow so close over the years that words would become unnecessary, they hadn't gotten to that point yet. "Am I permitted?" Ash asked, and he waited.

Chuy propped himself back up on his elbows. "Are you kidding?"

"No," Ash answered. "Every time I touch you, I want it to be a miracle. Never let me lose my way. Guide me. I am at your command."

Chuy laughed. "That's a fancy way of asking permission to give me head." He laid a hand on the back of Ash's skull, and Ash shuddered at the touch.

"Permit me," Ash whispered, insecurity creeping into his voice. No man, not one, ever regretted the demon king's attentions. He approached his partners with confidence, always. He saw the whole of each of them, and with the help of his spectacles, he knew the role he would play in their lives. Usually, it was small, ineffectual. But Chuy was different. Though Ash had seen him from border to border, he hadn't been able to discern his own role. He was a shadow in the light, an entangled thread of darkness. Where his influence began and where it ended was impossible to make out.

Chuy's calloused fingers came around to lift Ash's chin. Their eyes met, and Chuy smiled. "Can't believe you care so much," he said. "You make me feel important."

"You *are* important," Ash insisted. "You're the most important man in the world."

"Said the king to the pirate." Chuy's half-smile broke Ash's heart.

"Said the demon to the purest soul who ever lived."

Chuy frowned at that. "Is innocence really so important to you?"

Ash shook his head, and for the first time in his life, he doubted his own values. "Just . . . What if I break you? What if I'm the one who destroys your innocence?"

"If you break me, you break me." Chuy curled his fingers under Ash's chin, and that touch, that barely-there caress was almost more than Ash could bear. "Long as you don't think less of me for it."

"Never," Ash whispered, and he meant it. "You'll be my everything, no matter how you change. I'll change with you. I'll despise innocence if it abandons you. I'll abhor faith and cherish its opposite if that's who you become."

Chuy dropped his hand to Ash's shoulder and squeezed. "Then you have my permission." His smile dropped, and in all seriousness, he added, "For everything. Permission granted, Ashmedai."

Something about hearing his full name on those lips, in that voice, tore into Ash. He could barely bring himself to breathe. He resumed kissing Chuy's hips, moving slowly inward, teasing the captain. He was so feverish that the touch of his tongue had to border on discomfort, but Chuy didn't tell him to stop. On the contrary, he let his head fall back and audibly appreciated everything Ash was doing to him . . . for him.

Ash tested every maneuver he'd ever mastered, one after the other after the other. He made a note of how far each touch drove his partner. He mapped that pleasure and memorized it. Then he narrowed his techniques to those that made Chuy writhe the most, those that drew the captain's voice from him.

At some point, aptitude gave way to instinct, and Ash's body tuned itself to his partner's in every possible way. His cherubic form was superimposed over his human one—light over shadow, beast over man. His batlike wings filled the alcove and folded themselves in far too many places, but none of it mattered. Ash was lost in a paradise of his own making. He felt everything. His fingers curled around those perfect hips, holding his partner down when the pleasure grew too great to resist movement, when drive and need gave way to carelessness, a muffled cry, and the unmistakable shudder of climax.

When it was over, it was over for both of them. In the end, resonance made reciprocation impractical, to say the least. Ash looked up to see that Chuy had pulled the pillow from under his head and held it over his own face to smother his cries. A shiver of satisfaction went up Ash's spine. He'd seen the mark of this night lingering in Chuy's life. He hadn't known what it meant before, but now it was perfectly clear. This was a first. No one had given so exquisite a gift to Captain Jesús of *Papillon*—never in his life—without expecting something in return. He'd been manipulated, coerced, threatened, and forgotten. He'd been made to feel like any pleasure given to him was a chore for which he would always owe.

Ash kissed his way up Chuy's torso and gently removed the pillow from his face. Chuy's cheeks were cherry red, his lips full and slightly parted, and Ash wanted him all over again. "Honey, you're even more beautiful when you're satisfied," Ash said, stroking Chuy's hair. "Now go to sleep, and dream of me."

Chuy opened his mouth to speak but couldn't seem to find the words, and that was the greatest compliment he could have given. Ash lay down beside him and rested his head on that skinny, inked chest. From now on, Ashmedai—eldest son of the watchers, lord of the ancient nephilim, and king of all demons—would dedicate his life to the only man in the world who mattered. *The king is dead*, Ash thought with a chuckle. *Long live the king.*

As Chuy slept beside him, Ash slipped in and out of meditation, and he allowed himself fantasies far sweeter than any dreams he'd had while he was alive. The steady sound of Chuy's heartbeat lulled him so much that when the cabin door opened, he shot up and hit his head on the alcove. "Ouch!" He hissed and rubbed his skull as the intruder came into view.

Michael walked across the cabin like there was nothing remotely shocking about the situation. He held up a hand in greeting. "Hello,

Ash. God I forgot how much I hate that watch." And he threw himself onto his bunk with an exhausted groan.

Ash gently reminded himself that he was the only one who could see in the dark. His body was fully human again and no longer glowed with angelic light. The disheveled state of Chuy's bunk and the naked state of both its occupants was far from obvious. As far as Michael knew, they'd just been having a heart-to-heart in the dark. Although Michael was no fool.

Regardless, nothing untoward had occurred. They were all adults. So why did Ash feel like a teenager, caught doing something . . . *someone* he knew he shouldn't? He fell back, relieved that his instinctive shame was ridiculous. What would his mother say? She would tell him to relax, of course. *You're too uptight, Ash. Let go a little. Life can be good sometimes if you let it.*

Chuy stirred, awoken by Michael's careless entrance, though he didn't seem to mind the extra body in the room. He'd already told Ash he wasn't shy, and now, Ash could see the evidence of it for himself. "Hey, Michael?" Chuy said. Michael responded with a grunt, but Chuy pushed on despite his bunkmate's obvious exhaustion. "Hey, Michael, I hope you're ready to get married in a couple weeks."

Michael shot up. "Excuse me?"

"You're getting married, I said." Chuy was calm and matter-of-fact. "Unfortunately, my man here lost a bet, so we've gotta wait for you. What do you think? Two weeks? Three? You've got Azazel's help, don't you? So that should be more than enough time. I'm sure Bryony will agree. She came up with the stakes. No way she expects us to wait longer than a few weeks."

Michael fell back onto his pillows and chuckled to himself. "Well," he said. "You talk her into it, and I'll be there."

Chapter Thirty-Three

The wedding went off without a hitch, whatever that meant. At least, that was what Bryony planned to tell anyone who asked. Although she couldn't imagine anyone who wasn't already there would bother asking. Half the armada and a good third of the town were in attendance, which made Bryony all the more hesitant to attend the ceremony herself, despite being the actual bride. Anyway, it was more Azza's wedding than hers and Michael's, which was the main reason it was so objectively beautiful.

The ceremony took place in Bryony's yard, and the reception was held in her old healing tent. Azazel had decorated the interior with an array of fine, Moroccan furniture and colorful, glass lanterns. Both the ceremony and reception were supernaturally heated to a comfortable temperature, despite the fact that it was snowing outside. The entire affair practically screamed Azza's angelic name. If there was ever a way to convince Bryony to take center stage again after quitting her job as a healing god, offering her the chance to see a wedding thrown by the watcher Azazel was it.

Her gown was black with deep-blue iridescence descending like tentacles into the skirt. She'd never seen anything so lovely in her life, and she felt very much that a more attractive woman ought to be wearing it. Maybe someone taller. But Azazel had insisted it suited her

perfectly, and he was the expert after all. His only real disappointment was the death sword Bryony wore around her right wrist. It did not complement her gown, nor did it complement the makeup he'd insisted on applying despite the black veil she wore.

Late in the evening, an ornate clock in one corner of the tent sounded, and everyone present followed the instructions they'd received in their invitations. They took the thick, black blindfolds carefully arranged beside their folded napkins and helped each other put them on. Some trembled at the knowledge of what was to come, but those who'd wanted to leave before this portion of the evening already had, and those who stayed were either curious or stubborn.

Ash and Chuy, who sat at a close table and held each other's hands tightly, were of the stubborn variety. When Bryony had asked if they'd be able to handle the attendance of their tormenter, Chuy had looked to Ash, who'd taken the majority of Samael's abuse. Ash's answer had been simple. "Bryony, I'm the demon king. Don't coddle me." Now he looked less sure, but he stayed planted in his seat just as Bryony knew he would.

With her guests properly blindfolded, she made her way outside to greet her mercurial father-in-law. He waited in his usual form, flanked by two creatures she could only have described as enormous, quadrupedal gemstones. They were the color of amber, and they walked with their heads held low like big cats on the prowl. Lions, she thought, but without ears or a tail. Instead, they had what looked like noses, mouths so big they practically split the creatures' heads in two, and eyes upon eyes upon eyes, all glowing red like the embers of a dying fire. At the heart of them, bright lights flickered like ship's flares and branched out like crude circulatory systems.

Bryony froze in her tracks, but Samael was already aware of her presence. His weapon made sure of that. He answered her question before she even had a chance to ask it. "These are my hashmallim. They obey my orders. Do not fear them."

Bryony wondered whether these were the same hashmallim Chuy had shot, but she didn't dare ask. Why remind everyone of such unpleasantness? She cleared her throat. They were like canines, Sama had told her, so she tried to think of them as very large, very intimidating dogs. "Are they friendly?"

"They are if I tell them to be." He was stiff and formal.

She shifted uncomfortably. "Should I . . . let them smell me or something?"

"Unnecessary. They have already gathered all they need to know about you."

"Oh." As much as she wanted to stay outside and chat with the Angel of Death about his horrifying hashmallim, an even more horrifying crowd waited inside, and Bryony felt guilty making them sit blindfolded any longer than they had to. "Let's go in then. Um . . . follow me, I guess." She wasn't sure whether she was meant to direct instructions to Sama or the creatures guiding him, but she figured it didn't matter in the end.

As soon as Samael stepped inside the tent, a good tenth of the people present fell out of their chairs. She had warned them, but apparently curiosity had gotten the better of them. Martha, Chuy, Ash, Loki, and Azza were among those who did not try to see the Angel of Death. Those who'd already experienced his poison had no desire to experience it again.

Michael waited, stiff as a soldier in his own blindfold, looking less than eager to speak to his father on his wedding day. Bryony chewed her lip a moment before she could muster the courage to speak. "Michael is in front of you now," she said to Samael. "He's blindfolded, so he won't fall. You can talk to him."

Samael dipped his head in greeting. "I have come to offer my congratulations and offer you each a wedding gift."

The moment reminded Bryony of a film she'd once seen as a child. *Sleeping Beauty*, it was called. She remembered it quite well and felt a little rush of pride that she'd been smart enough to invite the evil fairy instead of snubbing him. For this, she could be fairly confident his gifts would not be malicious—at least, not intentionally. "Thank you," she said, loud enough that everyone could hear.

"Thank you," Michael echoed coldly.

Samael frowned, clearly displeased with his son's attitude. "First, to my daughter, I give this." He reached over and clutched at the scruff of the darker hashmal's neck. Then he lifted it, and it immediately began to shrink. When the beast was roughly the size of a large puppy, he thrust it at Bryony.

Bryony flinched and took a step back. *Really?* "I . . . don't . . ."

"Take it," Samael said, his arm extended like a yardstick with the well-behaved creature dangling off the end. "It's yours."

What could she do? She was being gifted an angel, and the thought horrified her. But no matter how poorly chosen the gift, if it was the Angel of Death who offered it, she knew she'd better accept. Bryony gripped the creature under its front limbs and held it at arm's length, letting its back limbs dangle. It felt like a warm stone wriggling in her hands.

"It is already tamed," Samael assured her, as though that was remotely the first question she would have asked. "But it will require more training and time to adjust to its new handler. You will do well, I think." He paused and pressed a finger to his lips, as though the question of Bryony's suitability as a handler had only just occurred to him. Then he nodded to himself. "Yes, you will do well. Remember, hashmallim respond to praise and affection. Do not attempt to punish them. If you do, they will withdraw. Bond well, and they will obey reliably." He waited for Bryony to speak, but when she couldn't find words quickly enough, he plowed on. "You will know a hashmal is happy when its skin is soft. A tough exterior signals fear. A sticky exterior signals aggression. They are relatively easy to read." He paused again. "Are you unhappy with the gift?"

Bryony was quick to answer. "Oh, no! I mean not at all. I'm just . . . I'm a little overwhelmed with the responsibility, you know?"

"You will not need to care for the creature, my daughter. It is perfectly capable of caring for itself. Your only goal should be in bonding and training."

"Does it . . . have a name?" She still held the thing at arm's length.

"Not a human one. I thought you would enjoy naming it." Samael sighed. He seemed well aware of Bryony's discomfort, and his own frustration reflected the fact. "Here." He approached and reached for the creature. Bryony thought perhaps he meant to take it back. Instead, he pushed it further into her arms and up against her chest. "It's frightened. Can you not feel it? You must comfort it."

"I . . . I'm not sure . . ."

Impatient as ever, the Angel of Death stepped in. "Like this." He came far too close for his demonstration, but Bryony didn't dare recoil. His hand quickly found his weapon at her wrist and followed it to the hashmal in her arms.

Bryony alone was witness to the tenderness that followed, and she was certain no one would believe her had she described it to them. Samael began by resting a palm against the creature's head. Then he followed what would have been its spine, if it had one, slowly reducing pressure until the only contact he made was with the tip of his middle finger. He repeated the motion three or four times until the hashmal began to soften. Soon, its flickering light slowed, and its body began to slump in Bryony's arms. Then Samael stepped back. "Now, you try. This is your first lesson. I will teach you more in the future."

It felt as though they were the only three life forms in the tent—Bryony, the Angel of Death, and the poor, terrified hashmal. She focused all her attention on stroking the creature the same way Samael had—first with the palm of her hand, and then gently trailing the tip of her finger along its back. And the hashmal softened even more. "It feels like silk," she finally whispered.

"Yes," Samael said. "You are establishing trust. Soon it will crave your approval, and you will be able to train it." His head was inclined toward the hashmal, and the hint of sadness and affection in his voice made

Bryony suddenly realize how much it meant that he was giving this creature to her. His hashmallim were not just workhorses to him. He loved them, each of them, individually. He was entrusting something precious to her, a living soul he cherished.

"Thank you, Sama. This is . . . the most thoughtful gift I've ever received. I promise to take good care of it."

"Good." He nodded and backed away. "Then it will train well. I will come from time to time to check your progress." So this was to be his new excuse to visit. Strange how he needed one. He could never just drop by the way others did. Abruptly, he lifted his chin and announced, "It smells good in this tent."

"Oh!" Bryony switched gears and followed his conversational lead. "That would be Azza's doing. He insisted on scenting the entire reception like orange blossoms. It smells like my shampoo, I guess. I told him it was a bit much."

Samael frowned at the mention of Azazel, but his words did not match his expression. "It was kind of him to consider me," he said, and Bryony realized he was right. The scent was never meant for her. Azazel knew Samael would not see the work he'd put into the decor, but he made sure his rival would find something to be impressed with. That watcher thought of everything.

A beat of silence followed in which Bryony had no idea what to say while Samael waited expectantly. He was one step short of planting his hands on his hips and tapping his foot at her. Finally, he scowled and took the initiative. "As I am still blind . . ." he began sourly, and Bryony felt her face turn red, realizing with a horrified shudder that she'd missed his hint completely. "I request a description of my son at least."

Just as expected, she'd offended him again, and this time, she'd done it in front of an audience. "Sorry," she muttered. "I was just overwhelmed . . . um . . . by your gift." Satisfied with her save, she turned to Michael. "Well, he's standing next to me wearing a fine suit that he made himself. It fits him perfectly, of course. It's black with a sort of blue iridescence on the vest and tie to match my dress. His hair is combed back, and he looks . . . well really beautiful, honestly. And now he's smiling a little. And blushing."

"Bryony," Michael warned.

She was suddenly indignant on Samael's behalf, realizing Michael had yet to say much of anything to his father. "What? He has a right to know, doesn't he? He's here as a guest, and if you're not going to talk to him, I'll just have to describe how you feel."

The tables of guests had begun to chatter amongst themselves. The spectacle of the Angel of Death was no longer novel, and those who'd made the mistake of indulging their curiosity had learned their lesson.

"I'll tell him how I feel." Michael glowered at his father as best he could from behind his blindfold. "I feel we're not accepting a pet as a gift."

Bryony and Samael both responded at the same time.

Samael said, "A hashmal is not a pet."

And Bryony said, "Oh, yes we are, husband. It's my gift, and I get to decide whether I accept it." The word *husband* softened Michael at once. He was so easy to manipulate, Bryony almost felt guilty doing so, but her instincts won out in the end. She pushed the little hashmal into Michael's stomach, and the poor creature turned to stone again. "Here. You have to pet it gently so it knows you're not a threat."

"I *am* a threat," Michael growled, but no one was buying his act.

"Please," she pleaded. "It's not so bad once you get used to it. It's kind of cute actually. Just feel its little feet." Never in a million years would she have predicted how badly she suddenly wanted to keep the amber beast with an oversized mouth and far too many eyes. "Just hold it for a bit, Michael. You'll see."

"Yes, Michael, just hold it." That voice was Samael's, and as soon as they heard it, both Michael and Bryony gaped at him. Michael scrambled to secure the hashmal that Bryony had let go of in her shock.

The only thing the Venom of God had ever promised his abandoned son was that he would never call him by his chosen name. But now he'd used it as easily as one might use an endearment with family.

Bryony tried not to make a big deal of it, but it was a big deal. It was monumental.

On Michael, the effect was like a bucket of cold water, dousing his temper. The nearly eight-foot-tall nephil immediately stopped arguing and did exactly as he was told. The second he began to stroke Bryony's new pet, it took to him. It seemed to like him even more than it liked Bryony, which made sense, all things considered. Michael better resembled its former handler. "It likes you," Bryony said. "Look how much it likes you. Can't we keep it? I mean *I'm* going to keep it regardless, but can't we keep it together?"

Michael groaned. "Fine." It sounded like a resignation, but Bryony could tell he was warming to the little creature in his arms. His heart was every bit as soft as hers in the end. The hashmal rested its head in the crook of Michael's elbow, and he was utterly defeated. "I guess it is kind of cute." He smiled, and the ghost of his dimple made a brief appearance. "Thank you, father."

Samael was all politeness and cordiality. "Ah, but that gift is not for you, my son. I have a separate gift for you."

"We are not taking in two hashmallim," Michael said, as though his foot were firmly down when Bryony knew damn well it wasn't.

"Of course not," the graveyard angel replied, and Michael frowned. Samael stretched out his hand and waited for his son to take it. "Do you wish to receive my gift or not?" Bryony realized neither of them could see the other and helped guide Michael to his father.

Once he'd taken hold of Michael's hand, the Angel of Death followed the length of his arm to his shoulder, and slowly began to grow. It did not take Samael long to surpass his son in height. At first, his growth seemed a simple matter of pride, but when he was satisfied with his new stature, Samael revealed his true motivation. He slipped his hand around to the back of Michael's head and drew the giant in until his forehead rested on his father's shoulder. Michael tensed but did not withdraw.

"Now, I will tell you a secret," Samael said under his breath. "Because you stole my weapon, I always knew where to find you. I visited many times when you were a boy, though I never again manifested in your presence." He curled his fingers into Michael's hair, and the look of regret on his face moved Bryony more than she would have expected. "You were such a clever boy. I remember that. You solved every puzzle you found in those empty houses, and you read every book." He chuckled quietly. "Some more than once. But you were lonely, and on occasion, I heard you cry for your mother. I am sorry I did not show myself to you then. You suffered alone because I believed my presence would only make matters worse. I believed the greatest gift I could give you was my absence. I was wrong."

"Yes," Michael hissed. "You were wrong." His face was obscured by his father's shoulder, and he still held the hashmal in his arms. But Bryony saw his broad shoulders begin to quake and knew he was close to breaking.

"I am sorry to have missed so much of your life." Samael pressed a palm to the back of Michael's head and slowly drew it down his neck, pulling away a little at a time until only the tip of his middle finger traced a line between Michael's shoulder blades. Bryony swallowed hard at the sight of it. Though the gesture itself was peculiar, its meaning could not have been clearer. Samael was trying to comfort his son the only way he knew how—the same way he comforted his hashmallim. The Angel of Death was trying to be a father.

"My wedding gift to you is this." The graveyard angel lifted his hand to his son's head again and began another long, slow journey down his back. "Though I cannot change the past, I will be present for the rest of your life and also after—especially after. I know what you will become, and I will guide you through it. As soon as you rediscover sentience, I will teach you to manifest a physical body. I will teach you to reject a summons and break a contract. No one will ever enslave you. I swear, even the demon king will envy your transition. You are not my son for nothing."

With that, Samael stood back and let his hand fall to his side. Michael kept his head bowed and clung to the little hashmal as though it were a long lost security blanket balled up in his arms. Tears soaked through his blindfold and dripped from his chin onto the creature. Bryony had seen him broken before, but never like this. No, this was total collapse. All Michael's armor was falling away.

Mercilessly, Samael went on. "I am proud of you, my son. I always was. Despite the terrible name you gave yourself, you were a good boy. Now, you have become a good man, you have married a good woman, and you have a good hashmal to look after." He smiled and pointed toward the creature, his aim only a little off. "That one is my best tracker. Command it to find me any time you wish, and it will lead me back to you. I'll teach your wife to train it for the task. I believe she is good with animals."

The Angel of Death had no way of knowing how much he had shaken his son, so Bryony took him by the wrist and squeezed. "Sama," she whispered. "You can stop now. He's crying."

Samael stiffened at the information. "Why?"

Michael's arms tightened around the little creature he held. "Excuse me. There's something . . . I have to check." And he marched out of the tent, tearing his blindfold away and taking the hashmal with him.

"I think he's just overwhelmed," Bryony admitted on her husband's behalf. "It's a lot to take in all at once."

Samael frowned down at her. "I did not intend to overwhelm him."

She shrugged. "It couldn't be helped. He didn't know you cared. I think he only hated you because loving you would have been unbearable. You just took that hatred away from him." The graveyard angel looked truly baffled, so Bryony added, "It was a good gift, Sama. It was perfect, really. He's going to love it once he gets over the shock."

"Well . . ." Samael drew a deep breath. "It is time I take my leave. You should go and offer him comfort. My son does not like to be alone. If he says he does, he's lying." His hands curled into fists at his sides. "I know that much about him at least."

Bryony followed Samael out of the tent, hastily announcing to her guests that they could remove their blindfolds.

Outside, snow was thick on the ground and the world was eerily quiet. The graveyard angel looked too appropriate for the winter scene. His complexion matched it too perfectly. Had he frozen in place, Bryony might have guessed someone had buried a loved one in her yard. Only the hashmal beside him gave his true nature away. It glowed bright against the dark, snowy backdrop, like a fire burning in amber. Occasionally, its body rippled like liquid, and she wondered whether it missed its companion.

In a moment of pure spontaneity, Bryony decided to take a risk. She called out, "Father!" to the quickly retreating angel. He stopped and turned, and just having someone answer to that name again made her heart leap. "I . . . wanted to say goodbye," she improvised.

Without a word, he opened his arms and waited. She picked up her skirts, ran to him, and squeezed him tighter than she would have been comfortable squeezing any mortal creature. He didn't seem to mind. "Congratulations," he murmured as she buried her face in his robe. Then he added, "Take good care of my son."

Chapter Thirty-Four

Bryony found Michael kneeling on the floor of their bedroom with his body doubled over and his face in his hands. He was silent at first, but when she heard him sob, she crouched beside him and gently laid her hand on the back of his head.

At her touch, he revealed a blotchy, tear-stained face. Then he groaned and let his head drop back into his enormous hands. "Why?" he said from behind his fingers. "Why am I feeling this now? I went my entire life without needing him, and now suddenly I do? He just . . . waltzes in and changes everything. Years of building independence and convincing myself I was better off without him. He takes aim one time, and it's over. I fell apart at my own wedding. In front of guests."

"If it helps, they were all blindfolded," she said, slowly combing her fingers through his hair. "And no one was paying attention to us by the end." But she knew it was futile. It wasn't humiliation Michael worried about. He was used to being the center of unwanted attention. No, what worried him was feeling anything but hatred for his father. His hatred for his father had gotten him through an entire life of isolation. Now that crutch had been kicked out from under him. Suddenly, Michael's heart was exposed and vulnerable to someone who could destroy it without even trying. "I don't think he expected your reaction," she murmured. "He's not great at timing things appropriately." She chuckled, thinking of all the inconvenient times the Angel of Death had shown up unannounced.

Michael was not amused. "I feel like a pathetic child."

She got up, brought him tissues, and knelt beside him again. "Don't hate me for saying this, but now that I've met your father, I can see how you two are alike."

He straightened and gave her perhaps the most scathing look she'd ever received from him.

"Just a little," she assured him. "I mean his old name . . . I wish you could have felt it. It was the most repulsive feeling. It was nauseating. I think his single-minded hatred for the archangel who gave it to him has been all that's kept him going for a long time. Honestly, I don't blame him. I don't blame you either. What he did to you was unforgivable. And I don't blame myself for hating the angels who killed my family, or Azza and Ash for hating Raphael the way they did. When someone takes everything from you, what else can you do? But hatred eats away at you, doesn't it? At some point, you have to let it go . . . before it becomes who you are." She frowned, doubting her own words. "Don't you?"

He shook his head. "I don't know if I can."

"That's all right." She made herself more comfortable on the floor, crossing her legs and smoothing her skirts. "You know, after I gave Sama his new name, he let out this keening howl, and I couldn't understand why. What was he grieving for? All he'd lost was a truly awful name. But I think I know now. I think he was grieving the loss of his hatred, because it had become his whole world, his only reason for going on. The thing is . . ." She chewed her lip and picked at her dress, wondering how much she should reveal. "I think he hoped you'd kill him one day. He never admitted it when I brought it up, but he didn't deny it either."

Michael's features slackened into an expression that was nothing short of pure shock. "You think that's why he let me take his weapon?"

Bryony shrugged. "Yeah, I kind of do."

He frowned but sat a little taller, his grief giving way to a hung-over awareness. To Bryony, he was even more beautiful when he gave up hiding his weaknesses. He was an imperfect man with faults and earthquakes in his heart, and she could not imagine herself loving him any more than she did right now.

"What did you tell our guests?" he asked.

"I told them I wanted to spend some time alone with you, and that they were welcome to stay as long as they wanted."

His cheeks went from blotchy to beet red. "You know what they'll think that means, don't you?"

"Obviously." Bryony winked at him. The hashmal chose that moment to creep out from under the bed and make its way cautiously toward them. It nuzzled Bryony first, but quickly bounded over to Michael and wedged itself between his long legs. "He really does seem to like you," she said.

"Oh, it's a *he* now, is it?" Michael rubbed his eyes and stared down at the creature.

"I don't know. I mean Azza says angels don't have sexual distinctions. So I guess I just picked a name and decided to adopt the pronoun too."

"What's the name?" Michael's tears had dried, and he focused all his attention on playing with the many-eyed ball of amber rolling around on the floor in front of him. He really was like his father in a lot of ways. The hashmal took to him at once, and Bryony had to wonder whether Samael had meant for the creature to be a gift to Michael, too, but knew he would be too proud to accept it. *My son does not like to be alone.*

"Well, I thought I'd call him Poe." Bryony grinned. "I named my crow Shakespeare. It seemed right to stick with the theme. What do you think?"

"It suits him." Michael smiled as the creature tripped over its own feet running in circles around him. "I don't think he's used to being so small. He's cute if you can get past all the eyes and teeth."

"I wish I could show him off," Bryony said. "Maybe we can train him to manifest as a dog in public."

Michael reached out and scratched the hashmal's head with the tips of his fingers. Poe let out a satisfied sound like a very distant roll of thunder. "I'm still angry with my father," Michael admitted. "But I guess he's trying to do better. Just . . . who gets the bride a pet as a wedding gift?"

"I told him I like puppies," she said. "He gets very excited about his hashmallim. I think they've been his only companions for a long time. He probably thinks it's a crime I've never known one." She chuckled. "The closest thing I've ever had to a pet turned out to be Loki."

Just as Bryony began to suspect Michael had found a new obsession in the little creature, his eyes locked back onto her. "That really is a gorgeous gown." He stopped stroking the hashmal and took a moment to appraise her costume. "Azazel definitely knows what he's doing. It's a shame I ruined his reception."

Bryony scoffed. "You did no such thing."

"I did, though. We didn't even get to have our first dance." The dejected look on his face was more than Bryony could bear. If anything, it had been Samael who'd ruined the reception, or Bryony who'd ruined it by inviting him, not Michael. In truth, the wedding itself was more for Michael than her, and it was a shame he felt any guilt about spoiling his own party.

She quickly stood and held out her hand. "Get up."

He cocked his head at her, and one corner of his mouth turned up momentarily. "Why?"

"Because we're having our first dance right here. And it's going to be way better than the one we would have had in front of an audience."

He took her hand and rose to his feet. Each time Michael stood, Bryony was reminded of his impressive stature. This was not going to be an easy dance, to say the least. She wished Azza had given her a few pointers beforehand, and kicked herself for not asking for them as Michael placed his free hand between her shoulder blades.

The dance began awkwardly. Bryony was inexperienced to begin with, and their difference in height did not make matters better. She found herself staring at his stomach, but he didn't let it bother him. He spun her as though he'd practiced for this, and she began to wonder whether he might have snuck out while she was busy and gotten a lesson or two. She wouldn't have put it past him. This day meant everything to him, and it was beginning to mean everything to her too.

At some point, Michael broke into a quiet hum, and the dance grew a little easier. By the time he began to sing in earnest, Bryony moved like it was second nature, like she'd also snuck out and taken secret lessons. The song he sang wasn't English. Bryony didn't recognize the language, but it sounded very much like an old folk song. It had a playful rhythm and somber notes. She wondered where he might have learned it, but she didn't want to spoil the moment with questions. So she listened. And his voice . . .

More often than not, Bryony forgot that Michael was descended from the seraphim, and perhaps that was because he did his best to hide it. He wasn't hiding it now. His voice was more exquisite than anything she'd ever heard, more beautiful even than Azza's. It knocked her back like a tidal wave. It overwhelmed her mind like a torrential downpour. She could not have described her state as anything less than a trance, though she felt perfectly comfortable, wonderfully safe. And she knew where to step, when to turn. Her body moved with his song, as though they were two parts of the same machine.

And suddenly, there was sweet smoke. There was brilliant white fire, and the shadows it created played on the walls. The wings of a serpentine angel stretched to the ceiling above, and Bryony did not close her eyes to them. She stared at the seraph, the rise and the expanse of him, the undulation of his ever-moving body. Tears formed in the corners of her eyes, but still she did not look away. He was no monster, not even close, now that she saw him fearlessly.

While Michael's eyes were closed and she was thoroughly mesmerized, Bryony gave in to the temptation to take her hand from his arm and reach through the light. She touched the tips of her fingers to the seraph's skin. It felt like impermeable liquid and looked like mother-of-pearl. "Oh my god," she whispered. "You're so soft."

He opened his eyes and saw the light. His human face went even whiter than it usually was. "What did I do? How is this happening? We aren't . . . I mean we didn't . . ." He paused and caught his breath. "How are you moving right now?"

She slid her hand along one of the coils superimposed over his human body. "I don't know. Maybe I've just gotten used to it." Maybe so much time spent in Samael's presence hadn't paralyzed her as he'd thought it would. Maybe it had immunized her instead. She'd just found a joint between the seraph's body and one of its six wings when it began to fade. "Keep dancing. I want to look at you a little longer."

He hesitated but closed his eyes and began to sing and sway again. The song rose in volume now that it emanated from both his mouths. Bryony's entire body tingled with the sound of it as she let cool white flames crawl up her arm and caress her skin. Her fingertips prickled whenever she touched the seraph, like gentle sparks of static electricity. The creature he was, the dragon with a thousand star-like eyes, wings of white fire, and skin like pearlescent liquid . . . "You're the most beautiful thing I've ever seen in my life," she murmured. "I never want to wear a blindfold again."

She concentrated on the man beneath the coils and reached for his arm to continue the dance. This time, her hand dipped past that mother-of-pearl skin and found his solid, human flesh. Curious, she pulled her arm back again and focused her attention on the seraph. Again, she could touch it. It reminded her of playing with cornstarch and water as a child. If you pushed through the mixture slowly, it was easy to dip beneath the surface, but if you struck it, the surface was unyielding. In this case, the difference was in where her attention was focused.

The seraph trembled when she touched it, and Michael drew in a sharp breath.

"How does it feel?" she asked him.

He paused his song to answer. "Like a slipstream—like something invisible brushing past. It feels amazing."

With complete and careless abandon, she leaned in and touched her lips to his seraphic body. He caught his breath, and the skin she'd kissed began to warm. His fingers closed around her upper arms, and he drew her closer—through the winged serpent, the demon, the beast. As soon as their human bodies met, the seraph coiled around her and pulled her in tight.

The world outside seemed to dissolve and go silent. She felt the same calm she'd experienced before drowning, after her body stopped fighting, just before her mind let go. That peace, that tranquil place had promised her nothing could harm her as long as she stayed. *You belong here*, it had said, *in my arms, in the earth, in the wind and sea.*

"I love you," Michael whispered, and he felt so much like home Bryony could no longer imagine another—not her house, not Martha's Café, not *Dragonfly*, not even her plum-blossom sanctuary.

Just Michael.

Always Michael.

Forever.

Acknowledgements

Many of those I have to thank were there for the first two books in this series. From my wonderful beta readers and cover artist to the book vloggers who helped spread the word. Your constant encouragement meant the world to me.

For this third book, I'd also like to thank those who have no idea how they've helped or even that I exist at all. Under the surface, much of this series was inspired by my journey out of darkness, out of my own "demon-haunted world." So, to those science communicators who renewed in me a sense of awe and wonder about the universe, *thank you* for continuing to teach those of us who didn't have the luxury of a science education as children. There's a moment in *Godhunter* when Bryony learns, for the first time, that the sun is a star. How she felt in that moment was how I felt when I learned about the cosmic microwave background radiation, when I first understood the theory of evolution without the political noise and disinformation that too often goes along with it, when it all started to click into place. The work you're doing is so important. It changed the trajectory of my life and helped inspire these books as well as the healing that went along with them.

Lastly, to Caitlyn Doughty and The Order of the Good Death: You don't know me, and you'll probably never see this, but after the rug was pulled out from under me, I was forced to re-examine mortality from a new perspective. I desperately needed a death-educator, someone who didn't dismiss the topic as "morbid" or "depressing." For me, learning to see death as a milestone rather than a taboo was so meaningful. It beautifully complemented my journey toward understanding the role death plays in creating and shaping life. From the bottom of my still-beating heart, thank you.

A Tyranny of Angels

Book 1: Godhunter

Book 2: Speak of the Devil

Book 3: The Evolution of Angels

https://www.isobellynn.com